THE *Romantic* PACT

USA TODAY BESTSELLING AUTHOR
MEGHAN QUINN

Published by Hot-Lanta Publishing, LLC

Cover Design By: RBA Designs

www.authormeghanquinn.com

Prologue

See those three boys over there?

Yeah, the kings of football?

The ones with their heads in their hands, nursing their second beers of the night and trying to figure out what the hell happened to their season?

They choked.

That's right. These All-Americans became the biggest upset in college football and a complete embarrassment to their town.

Can it really be that bad?

Yes.

Former national champions, Braxton College was annihilated this year.

No, not just annihilated, but completely and utterly destroyed.

Three games.

That's it.

They won three games all season.

Interceptions. Dropped balls. Missed blocks. Fumbles. You name it, they did it.

First, there's Crew Smith, the protective one. Once an

NFL hopeful, he now holds the record for the most interceptions thrown in a season by a quarterback.

Next, is Hollis Hudson, the mysterious tight end who keeps everything locked down. He couldn't run a route this year to save his life.

And to round out the trifecta of crap, there's River Tate, the popular frat boy. He's supposed to be a superstar wide receiver but dropped more passes than he caught this season.

Guys wanted to be them.

Girls wanted their hearts.

But at this point, no one would want to touch them with a ten-foot pole.

The truth is, they've screwed up their NFL aspirations.

Maybe their entire lives.

There are three stories to be told . . .

This is Crew's.

Chapter One

CREW

"God, look at you. You're positively glowing," Hutton, my best friend from high school, says when I open the door. He pulls me into a hug and then slides his hand down my back to my ass where he gives it a good squeeze. "Yes, my man. Squats have been good to you."

"Could you not?" I say, pushing at his chest as he laughs and walks into my childhood home.

"Dude, why the mood? You always like it when I caress your ass. It's been months since we've last seen each other. I half expected you to greet me bent over."

I shut the door and walk toward the open-concept living room where the sliding glass doors are open to allow in the sound of the ocean lapping against the cliffs beneath the house. December in Long Beach, California, lends itself to nice weather.

"Did you not see how my season went? Or were you too

distracted by all the wins you were racking up over at Brentwood?"

"Ooo, you're salty," Hutton says, taking a seat on the couch.

"And you're in an annoyingly good mood. That girl finally giving you the time of day?"

"No need to discuss my love life when you're clearly in a state of peril." He turns toward me and props his chin up on his hand while batting his eyelashes. "I'm listening."

"You think you're helping, but in reality, you're just pissing me off."

Sighing, Hutton hops off the couch and makes his way to the kitchen, where I hear him dig around in the fridge. "You realize I have one day to hang out with you and that I have to report back to Brentwood after Christmas morning, right?" The fridge door shuts and then a cabinet door opens. "Can we not spend our precious moments together fighting?"

I rub my forehead and sink into the couch farther. "Sorry, man."

Rounding the couch with a cookie tray, he sets it on the coffee table in front of me. Two sodas—one orange for him, one Sprite for me—a block of cheese, Wheat Thins, an apple, and, of course . . . Funyuns. A Smith/McMann household would not be complete without Funyuns.

Hutton reaches for the bag first and pops it open. "I accept your apology. Now, let's immerse ourselves in the fake oniony flavor of these crunchy cornmeal delights." He puts one in his mouth, crunches down, and moans. "Every time I see a bag of these in your house, it makes me want to make out with your mom."

"What the fuck, man?"

He shrugs. "Facts."

"They're in the house all the time."

"Then that should inform you about what's going on in

my head during every visit." He pops another ring in his mouth and smiles.

"I hate you."

"Hey, what did I say about fighting?" He points his finger at me.

Sighing, I pick up the Sprite and crack it open while Hutton starts to cut strips of cheese and an apple into thin slices. It's weird, but whenever he's at my house, he likes to have cheese with Wheat Thins and to top it off, a thin slice of apple. Knowing he was coming over, my mom made sure to have everything in stock. It's a weird combination, but it works.

Popping my soda open, I take a quick sip and then lean against the cushion of the couch. "I'm sorry, man. It's been a rough fucking year."

Growing serious, Hutton says, "I get that, man. You guys were really close."

And that's why he's one of my best friends, along with Hollis and River. Because they know.

Yeah, the season sucked. It was embarrassing, actually, and hugely detrimental to my chances at a professional football career.

But that's not what's on my mind.

It's my grandpa.

Or Pops, as we called him.

Bernie McMann, the patriarch of the family, the only guy I've ever known to swear by using presidents' names, and my pal, my guy . . . passed away this summer.

And it was fucking devastating.

Crushing.

I couldn't focus in the classroom. I have some of the worst grades I've ever received, and my football season, well, by now you should know how that turned out.

He was sick, something my parents didn't tell me, something Pops didn't want me to know. Said he wanted me to treat him the same way I always have.

Unfortunately, I didn't spend time with him this past summer. To be honest, I didn't visit him the past three summers, and only saw him during the holidays. I decided to stay home and train instead.

Biggest fucking regret of my life.

"I should have visited him over the summer like I used to."

"Dude, you didn't know he was going to pass away."

"Doesn't matter, life is too short." I twist the can of soda in my hand with regret. "I thought he'd be around forever."

"I don't know what to say." Hutton makes a cheese, cracker, and apple combination for me and hands it over. I take it and shove it in my mouth. "Not to make you feel any worse than you do, but do you think your season went the way it did because you weren't mentally there?"

"Yup."

"Oh, so you're aware?"

"Quite aware." I dust my fingers off and take a swig of my Sprite. "My mental game was completely shot. I was physically there on the field, but mentally, I was with Pops."

"Glad you're starting to admit that," says my dad, who walks into the living room wearing a pair of jeans and a flannel shirt. He takes the lumberjack look way too seriously. Doesn't quite fit in with the vibe here in California, but he owns it.

"Mr. Smith, good to see you," Hutton says, standing and giving my dad a solid handshake. Dad pulls him into a hug.

"When are you going to start calling me Porter?"

"Never," Hutton says. "Pretty sure my parents would murder me."

Dad chuckles. "I wouldn't say a damn thing."

"Yes, but it's a slippery slope, and before you know it, we'd see each other in the grocery store and I would call you Porter in front of my mom, and you know the kind of wallop I'd get across the back of the head."

"Ahh, Mrs. Marshall is one to fear," my dad says with a wink. Just then my mom appears in the same doorway Dad came from. Her hair is ruffled and her lipstick is smeared across her face.

Jesus Christ.

"Did I miss anything?"

"Uh, Marley." My dad touches the side of his mouth, and her eyes go wide.

"Excuse me for a second."

I groan and say, "While I was in the house? Come on."

Dad takes a seat in one of the blue chairs next to the couch and picks up a piece of cheese. "Your parents have healthy appetites for each other. Be grateful."

"He's right," Hutton says, leaning over.

I push him away. "I'm wallowing, I would prefer not to know that my parents are horndogs in the next room while I'm trying to figure out what the hell I'm going to do with my life."

Just then, Dad's laptop, which is on an end table, starts ringing with a Skype call. He accepts and immediately I hear Uncle Paul's voice.

"Where's my snookum boy? I want to see how brawny he's gotten."

Dad turns the computer toward me, and I'm graced with the sight of Uncle Paul's shoulder-length salt-and-pepper hair and massive bush of a beard that tickles the top of his nipples. Best friends since they were young, Dad and Uncle Paul have been in each other's lives forever, which is hard to believe because Uncle Paul—Mom's brother—is eccentric, to say the least. Married with five girls, he treats me as his very own boy.

Hand clasping his chest, he shakes his head and says, "God, you're handsome. You take after me. See that bone structure, Porter? That's McMann bone structure."

"Keep telling yourself that," Dad says with a knowing smile. There's no denying it. I'm a carbon copy of my father.

"Is that Paul?" Mom says, walking in, looking much more put together.

"It is. Just admiring my godson."

Mom claps her hands and says, "Now that we're all here, we can begin."

"Begin what?" I ask, sitting up.

Dad sets the computer on a chair, as if Uncle Paul is actually occupying space in the room, and all eyes fall on me.

Mom takes a seat next to me on the couch, forcing me to scoot over to the middle, and in her motherly voice, she says, "Sweetie, we want to talk to you."

I look around the room and note that Uncle Paul is already dabbing at his eyes with a tissue. "Uh, what the hell is going on? Is this some sort of intervention?"

"We don't need to put a label on it," Mom says. "But, yes. Yes, it is."

I glance over at Hutton, who has a cheese and cracker heading toward to his mouth. He pauses and says, "It's an intervention, dude, and I'm living for it."

"I promised myself I wouldn't cry, but here I am, a blubbering mess," Uncle Paul says. "I love you, Crew. You're my boy." He holds his fist out and honestly . . . how do I even react?

"We're worried about you, Crew," Dad says. "You haven't been the same since Pops passed. You have all the reason to mourn, but we're not sure if that's what you're doing."

"Didn't know there was a proper way to mourn," I say, folding my arms over my chest.

"There isn't." Mom places her hand on my leg. "Everyone mourns in their own way, but we, as the people who care most about you, need to make sure that you're doing it in a constructive way."

"Your mom is right, dude," Hutton says. "You're letting

yourself slip into a dark place and, frankly, it's scaring the shit out of me."

"Is this about my season? Because trust me, I don't need you three harping on me about it. I know I was a shitshow out there and that my chances of actually making it professionally are slim to none now. I don't need the reminder."

"We don't care about football right now," Dad says. "We're worried about you."

In a soft voice, Mom says, "We're worried you haven't found closure yet with Pops."

"Have you?" I ask, a little surprised. "He was your dad, Mom. But, then again, you guys knew he was sick, so you had time to prepare. I didn't."

"He didn't want you to know," Mom says gently.

"And why the fuck not?" I shout. "If I knew he was sick, I would have spent this past summer with him. I would have soaked up every last moment, but he took that from me. *You* took that from me."

Mom's eyes well up and I can feel the tension start to build as everyone goes silent. Minus Hutton, they all knew. And not one of them said a damn thing to me.

Finally, Dad says, "He left you something."

"Porter"—Mom shakes her head—"not the time."

"What did he leave me?" I ask.

As if I'm not in the room, Dad says to Mom, "There's too much anger here, Marley. The only way he will understand is if we tell him."

"Tell me what?"

"I think you should tell him," Uncle Paul says.

"I don't think he can handle it," Mom counters.

"Handle what?" I ask, growing even more agitated.

Everyone pauses.

The room goes silent.

Mom and Dad stare at each other.

Uncle Paul clutches his hands at his chest.

The crunch of a cracker breaks the silence followed by a mumbled "sorry" from Hutton.

"Someone better tell me what the hell is going on."

"You're going to Germany," Hutton says.

Everyone flashes their eyes in his direction. Dad says his name sternly under his breath, and my best friend cowers with a shrug.

"Sorry, but someone had to say something. I have one day with my best friend." Hutton taps his wrist. "We have to move this along; we have mindless video games to play."

Blinking, I turn back to my parents and ask, "I'm going to Germany? The country?"

Sighing, Mom glances at Dad and then back to me. "Pops left special instructions for your dad and me to send you on a trip he went on many years ago. Before Paul and I were born. It's a trip we've all been on and a trip Pops now wants you to go on. This is your final break before everything turns into extreme chaos—that's if you decide to go to the combine and try to make it professionally. Either way, the trip is booked."

"Wait." I sit taller. "You're going to just . . . send me off to Germany?"

"Yeah. Cool, right, bro?" Hutton says, hitting my shoulder. "Man, what I wouldn't give to go to Germany during Christmas."

Ignoring him, I ask, "Are you going with me?"

Mom and Dad shake their heads. "No, but you won't be alone. You, uh, will meet up with your travel companion when you get there."

"Travel companion?" I ask, my brows shooting up. "Who is it?"

"We're not at liberty to say," Dad says.

As I try to comprehend everything, I scoot to the edge of the couch, knees pressed to the coffee table.

"Hey, what's happening? I can't see Crew," Uncle Paul protests.

I ignore him too. "Let me get this straight. Before Pops passed away, he put together a trip to Germany for me and had you two book it, and I'll be joined by some mystery person on this trip?"

"Bingo bango," Hutton says, patting me on the back. "Not all brawn, this one. He's got the brains too."

"Why did you invite him?" I ask my parents.

"Trying to figure that out right now," Dad says, rubbing his hand across his forehead.

"Comedic relief?" Hutton asks with a smart-ass smile.

"Hey, I thought that's what I'm here for?" Uncle Paul says.

"How have you lightened the mood?" Hutton asks. "You've just been a blubbering mess."

"Can you blame me? Look at him." Uncle Paul chokes up. "He's become a beautiful, handsome man."

"Jesus," I mutter, as I stand and then pace the living room. "What's this trip supposed to prove? How is this supposed to help in any way?"

"He wants you to get lost, experience life, and find yourself on this trip because it's where he found himself. It was important to him, and even though he couldn't go on the trip with you, he will be there in spirit."

"Think of it as a chance to reconnect with him. To have those few stolen moments you didn't get."

"How could I possibly steal moments with him? He's gone," I say. God, this whole thing is irritating.

Mom turns to Dad and says quietly, "It's not the time, Porter. He's not in a good place, and I don't want to send him across the world like this."

"He's a man, Marley. You have to let go at some point."

"If anything, dude, just get drunk in Germany."

Dad shoots Hutton a look. "Not helping."

"Yeah, I can see how that might not have been the best comment." Motioning to me, Hutton says, "Strike that last suggestion from the record."

"You know what? I need some fresh air." Snagging my phone from the coffee table, I stuff it in the pocket of my shorts, slip on my sandals, and head out the back door.

Mom chases after me.

"Crew," she calls again, her voice breaking.

From the steps that lead down to the beach, I stop and look back at her.

"Just know, I love you so much, and whatever you decide, we'll be here for you." And then she reaches for my hand and places a folded piece of paper in it. "From Pops."

THE WAVES CRASH into the wet sand, setting the soundtrack for my melancholy mood.

Usually, the sound of the ocean brings me peace, but for some reason, all it's doing is heightening my anger, my irritation . . . my confusion.

And the note from Pops my mom just gave me? It's burning a hole in my pocket, begging me to read it.

I can't.

Legs propped up, I lean my arms on my knees and lower my chin, when my phone beeps with a text.

I glance at my phone that's on a piece of driftwood and see that it's a text from River in our friend group text.

River: *Anyone else want to die from boredom, knowing we won't be reporting back to practice soon?*

Needing the reprieve from everything else going through my head, I type back.

Crew: *Trying not to eat my feelings.*

Hollis joins in on the conversation, pulling the smallest smile from me.

Hollis: *I'm going to lose my abs over break, I can tell already.*

River: *As if you had a manly figure to begin with.*

Hollis: *Fuck off.*

I don't answer right away. Instead, I find myself staring at the phone, contemplating whether I should tell them about Germany.

River: *Crew, where are you? You're normally coming in hot with a comment about owning the best body out of the three of us.*

Hollis: *Kind of worried now.*

Crew: *Sorry, just got a bunch of shit piled on me over here.*

River: *Hollywood got shit on? This I have to hear.*

Crew: *My Pops left me a trip to go on.*

Hollis: *Damn, really? To where?*

Crew: *Germany.*

River: *And you consider that being shit on? I know we grew up differently, but, dude, that isn't being shit on.*

Hollis*:* *Hate to be insensitive, but he's right. A free trip to Germany? What's the problem?*

What *is* the problem?

I lay back on the sand, not caring about it sprinkling in my hair or on my skin. At this point, I've worn the beach home so many times, it feels like a second skin.

Crew: *It's a trip planned by my Pops. It meant something to him, and he wants to send me on it.*

River: *So, you're just going to sit on your ass all winter break and do nothing instead?*

Hollis: *Germany sounds more fun.*

Just then, I hear footsteps behind me and catch Hutton with two Sprites and a bag of Funyuns in hand. I sit up and brush the sand out of my hair as he takes a seat next to me. He offers me the bag, and I take it and mindlessly stuff a Funyun in my mouth.

"You should go, man."

I chuckle, but it lacks humor and fun. It's almost a dry, sad laugh. "That's what River and Hollis just said."

"Did you read the note?"

How does he know about the note?

Hell, Hutton probably knows more about this trip than

I do.

"Not yet. Do you want to?"

"Nah, man. You should do that. Maybe that will give you a form of closure, or something."

Closure. I still don't really know what that is. I don't want something that makes the death of Pops so . . . final.

"I feel like I'm being forced to open a wound I'm not ready to rip open."

"Will you ever be ready? I know how much you miss him."

"No," I say softly.

Hutton cracks open the drinks and hands me one. "I've never lost someone important in my life, so I can't quite relate to what you're going through. But what I do know, from seeing friends go through the same grief, is that you're going to have to face the loss of a loved one at some point. Maybe this shit season you had was a blessing in disguise. Maybe it's given you a moment to gather yourself before the combine. We both know your last season isn't going to be held that heavily against you. That if you clear your mind and show up, you still have a great chance. But you have to clear your mind first, man."

My phone buzzes and I glance down to see the preview of texts from Hollis and River.

Hollis: *Dude, you there?*

River: *If I were you, I'd seize this opportunity. Take it.*

"Shit," I say, rubbing my palm over my right eye.

"You know I'm right." Hutton bumps his shoulder with mine. "Look, I have no clue how a trip to Germany can bring you . . . peace or closure, but what if what Pops wanted comes true? What if it gives you a place to find yourself? To end up feeling grateful and not angry?" *What I wish is that Pops had spoken to me about this. Told me these words rather than write whatever is in his letter.* But at least he took the time to write something.

"Yeah. I guess. Maybe you're right."

"I'm always right." He snags a Funyun from the bag. "You

should know that by now. And when you text River and Hollis back, let them know just how right I am."

That makes me chuckle. "Never going to happen."

He scoffs. "Always depriving me of my glory." And before I can respond, Hutton wraps his arm around me and pulls me into a hug, giving me a good slap on my back. "Love you, man."

I return the embrace, not ashamed of showing one of my best friends affection. "Love you too, man."

After a few minutes of silence and staring at the ocean, Hutton takes off toward the house to go to the bathroom. "I'll be right there," I say.

When he's out of sight, I reach into my pocket and pull out the note. Bracing myself, I unfold it and read.

Hey Kiddo,

Because I know you well, I know you're probably angry at me and your parents for not telling you about my sickness. But I didn't want you to lose focus on your goals. And you know what? I'm sad I won't get to hug you one more time too, because you give the best hugs. I'm sad I won't be able to sit beneath the oak tree with you one last time, sharing bad jokes and wise anecdotes. But I'm not sorry you're not seeing me deteriorate. We had so many great times together, and if there is one thing I'm thankful for in my life, it's you.

Please go on this trip and enjoy seeing a part of the world I wanted to show you myself one day. Please open your eyes and see the bigger world through a wider lens.

Love you.

Pops

Chapter Two

CREW

"Did you get something to eat?"

"Yes, Mom," I say with a sigh into my wireless earbuds as I walk through LaGuardia International Airport.

"And did you go potty?"

"How old do you think I am?"

"Not old enough for me to stop worrying."

I find my gate—Munich, Germany, written above the door. "You were the one who encouraged me to go on this trip."

"That was your father. I was willing to hold you to my bosom until everything was okay."

"I'm twenty-two, Mom. Being held to your bosom is far too disturbing in so many ways at this point."

"Marley, let the boy live," Dad says in the background.

"He's flying across the world, so I'm allowed to worry," Mom shoots back, and then her voice softens when she repeats, "Did you go potty?"

"Nope, planned on wetting myself on the airplane."

"In that case, you'll be thankful for the extra pair of pants and underpants I made you pack in your backpack in case you soil yourself. I'm always looking out for you, Crewy Bear."

"Do you realize how ridiculous you sound?"

"Do you realize how much I love you?"

"Yes," I sigh, remembering the tears she shed this morning when she and Dad dropped me off at LAX. Mom clung to me for what felt like ten minutes until Dad pried her off me. She then texted me all the way up to my takeoff and then called when she knew I'd landed in New York. I had an hour layover, got off the phone to grab some food—went to the bathroom—and called Mom back to let her know I would be boarding soon. Pops sprung the extra buck and put me in first class for the trip from New York to Munich. Could not be more grateful for that since the flight is a red-eye and the seats in first class lie all the way down.

From the overhead speakers, an airline attendant says, "We'll now start boarding our first-class passengers for United 182 to Munich. Please proceed to our first-class line."

I see a line of people start to move toward the gate door and take that as my cue to get off the phone.

"Hey, Mom, they're starting to board."

"Oh . . . okay." She pauses and I can imagine her trying to get herself together. "Well, I packed you some gum in the small pocket of your backpack, you know, in case you have to pop your ears. I know you always have to deal with that when flying."

I smile softly to myself. Of course she did. We've made the cross-country flight to New York several times a year ever since I can remember, and every flight, I always need to pop my ears. It became tradition that Mom bought me a new pack of gum for every trip.

"What's the flavor this time?"

"Polar Ice. Figured some fresh breath wouldn't hurt, and the mint will calm any nerves you might have."

"You saying I have stinky breath, Mom?"

She chuckles and I can hear her tone grow lighter. "Not my Crewy Bear, freshest breath in the country."

"And I shit gold, too. Right, Mom?"

"Twenty-four karats."

I laugh this time and then sigh into the phone. "Okay, well, I should get going. I love you, Mom."

"I love you, baby boy. Enjoy yourself, you hear me?"

"I will."

"Good. Call me when you land."

"Okay. And, hey, Mom?"

"Yeah?"

I swallow hard and stare at the black sign, Munich digitally written in red. An adventure standing right in front of me, the unknown just over the threshold into an airplane. "Thank you, you and Dad, for pushing me to do this."

There's silence on the other end of the phone. The seconds stretch, and I'm about to ask if she's there when I hear Dad clear his throat. "Your mom is an emotional basket case."

"Porter," I hear my mom chastise, making me laugh.

"But you're welcome, kid. Have fun and remember to text us, okay?"

"Okay. Love you, Dad."

"Love you, my son."

I hang up and take a deep breath, staring at the picture on my lock screen. It's a picture of me and Pops from a visit during Christmas when I was fifteen. I'm the definition of gangly with braces, Justin Bieber-flipped hair across the forehead, and a flannel button-up over a graphic T-shirt. I was all kinds of cocky, but in this picture, I'm showing nothing but innocence as I hold up a fish I caught ice fishing with Pops at the lake near the farm. Pride beams in his eyes as his hand grips my shoulder and he smiles at the camera, wearing a shirt I made him for Christmas one year.

What the Herbert Hoover are you doing?

I chuckle, distinctly hearing his voice yell out the phrase. He was known to swear by using presidents' names, and when I gave him the shirt, he rolled over in laughter and put it on right away. It was his favorite shirt of all time. In this picture, it still looks new, but as time wore on, so did the collar and the hems, but he continued to wear it proudly.

Smiling, I quietly say, "Ready for this, Pops?"

It might sound stupid, and I might be imagining it, but in that moment, as I walk toward the gate with my boarding pass in hand, I can feel the firm grip of his large hand on my shoulder, guiding me.

I STICK my phone in the console next to my head and adjust the headrest of my seat. Since I'm six-foot-four, I need it a little higher than the average person.

And thank God for the legroom, because I don't know what I'd do for seven and a half hours in the air if I was cramped back in the economy seats.

Soft instrumental music plays overhead, blue lights line the tops of the baggage storage bins, and I hear the shuffle of travelers working their way down the aisle, eyes drifting from their boarding passes to the numbers above, checking for their seats.

The occasional whisper of how nice it would be to fly in first class drifts through the quiet cabin. Children ask their parents if they can have a snack. A father hisses at his kid not to touch people, and flight attendants welcome boarding passengers in German.

Guten Tag.

Hallo.

Servus.

"Oh, ma'am, you dropped this," a familiar voice says. I glance over to see a woman with warm red hair cascading over her face handing the woman in front of her a pair of headphones.

"Thank you," the stranger says. "I would be bored without these."

"I totally get it. So would I." The woman pushes a wave of red hair behind her ear as she looks up at the seat numbers overhead.

"Hazel?" I ask, my heart tripping at the sight of an old friend.

Her warm, caramel-colored eyes snap to mine, her face registering shock. "Crew?" A small smile pulls at her lips. She checks her seat number and then her ticket again and smiles even larger. "Would you look at that? Seems as though we're seatmates."

"Holy shit," I say as she takes a seat and beams at me.

"How are you, Hollywood?"

"Better now." I wrap my arms around her and pull her into a hug.

Hazel Allen.

Born and raised in the neighboring house to Pops' farm, this outgoing ball of sugar and spice was a staple of my childhood ever since I can remember. Her grandpa, Thomas, was best friends with Pops, and she worked on the farm from a very young age. Whenever I visited, she always made fun of me and my latest West Coast style as she strutted around in overalls, a tank top, and rubber boots. Her hair was always tied up on the top of her head, with a rolled-up bandanna around the crown to hold back any stray hairs.

Down to earth, fun, and a jokester, Hazel was one of my best friends growing up.

Pen pals.

Long-distance friends.

And of course, each other's first kiss.

When we pull away, Hazel lifts her hand to my face and presses her palm to my cheek. "God, you just keep getting more and more handsome."

I chuckle.

"And this scruff. Now you're really looking like your DILF of a dad."

"Can you not refer to my dad as a DILF? It really creeps me the fuck out."

"Ahh, but he is a hot piece of dad ass. Sorry." She shrugs, sets her backpack on the floor, then turns in her seat to face me. "When my Grandpa told me about this trip, I had an inkling you might be my traveling partner, but I wasn't sure." She takes my hand in hers. "God, I'm so glad it's you."

"The feeling is mutual, Haze," I say, taking in her rosy, freckled cheeks and the way her hair softly falls over her forehead. *Thank you, Pops*. How easy it will be to travel with one of my best friends.

Eyes softening, she asks, "How have you been? I saw your season . . ." She winces.

"Yeah," I huff out, staring down at the way her small hand fits in mine, the callouses on her fingers from all the hard work on the farm reminding me just how different our lives are, despite a lot of the variables being the same. "Wasn't my best show on the field. Just wasn't in it mentally."

"I can understand that." She squeezes my hand and then says, "But we're not here to talk about all of your interceptions, and I mean all of them . . ." When I glance up at her, she's smiling a Julia Roberts smile. I poke her side and she laughs, her head falling back as she pushes my hand away.

"How have you been, Hazel?" God, I've missed this girl.

"Oh, you know, just living the life out on the farm. Got caught up in some mourning, ate way too much pumpkin pie this past fall. Did you get your fair share of pumpkin spice lattes?" She nudges me. "I know what a basic bitch you are."

I laugh. "Yeah, I had a few."

"A few? I remember senior year in high school when you were drinking one a day. At least, that's what you wrote to me. Then again, it has been almost four years . . ."

"Has it?" I ask, knowing damn well it's been nearly four years since I've really seen her. Since . . . hell, since I ran from her. Sure, I technically saw her at Pops' funeral but I wasn't in the right head space to talk to anyone.

"Clearly you haven't been counting." She lets out a sigh and then slaps on a smile. "Enough with the catch-up, we can do that throughout the trip. We're here to celebrate Pops."

There's hesitation in her eyes and I want to address the elephant in the room, the thing that we were probably both thinking the minute we saw each other, but before I can do that, she leans forward and pulls an envelope from her backpack. The familiar handwriting on the front says *The Plane.*

"Is that—" I swallow hard. "Is that from Pops?"

She nods and fans her face with it. "Yup, I've been entrusted with the letters. Apparently, Pops didn't trust you to not read them all at the same time."

"There's more?"

She nods slowly. "Oh yeah, there are more." Her head tilts to the side. "How much do you know about this trip?"

"Practically nothing. Just that we're going to Germany."

"Well, I don't know much either, but what I do know, I'm excited about."

"What do you know?"

She taps her chin.

I'm in a good mood from her exuberance and the familiarity of having Hazel Allen in my sights again. It's like running into a warm hug when you see her. Positive, encouraging, always smiling and laughing—she's a breath of fresh air.

Damn, looks like Pops knew exactly what I needed.

An old friend.

"You know, I think we should just enjoy this flight and catch up. Let the letters lead us." She winks and then holds the letter up between us with two fingers. "Want to read it together?"

Hell, I'm not sure I'm ready, but then again, knowing Hazel, she's going to open it either way. Another reason why I think Pops planned out this whole thing. He knows Hazel's going to push me outside of my comfort zone. She's going to challenge me, and we're going to have one hell of a time doing it.

Nodding toward the letter, I say, "Open it."

A satisfied smile passes over her glossy lips as she tears open the envelope and unfolds a piece of notebook paper.

I never thought I'd see his writing again. It makes me feel more connected to him as I stare down at the familiar chicken-scratch scribble. In my mind, I can see exactly what blue pen he used, too. The same pen he used for everything. A classic Bic with the blue top, a top he always tended to lose.

Where the Franklin Pierce did I put that blasted thing?

The memory of him slamming his head on the kitchen table while ducking under to look for the pen cap flashes through my mind, putting a smile on my face.

"Want me to read it out loud, or should we read it to ourselves at the same time?"

"Read it to ourselves," I say.

She holds it between us and I prepare myself.

Hey Kiddos,

So, you made it on the plane. My guess is Hazel, you packed up immediately and waited by the door, ready to take off as soon as you found out. And Crew, you put up a bit of a fit, only to be dragged to the airport while your mother cried the whole time, am I right?

My nostrils flare and Hazel snorts while looking at me. "Oh my God, did you throw a fit?"

I shift in my seat and say, "I wouldn't call it a fit."

She laughs out loud and reaches over to grab my hand. "Oh, Crew, always so unruly."

She turns back to the letter while I try not to curse Pops out in my head.

Sure, I gave my parents a bit of a hard time, but then again, I had my reasons . . .

Either way, you're both reading this now (you better be) and you must be wondering why I'm sending you on a trip to Germany. It's simple . . . you'll find out along the way.

I shake my head. Typical Pops.

But until you can piece the puzzle together, I'll say this. I love you both and I wish I could physically be there with you while you travel the beautiful countryside of Germany. Just know, I'm up above, laughing my rear end off at you two nitwits as you try to figure out how to drive the German roads and understand their signs.

Hazel chuckles next to me and so do I.

Attached is an itinerary. When you reach your first destination and check into your hotel, the staff has been given another itinerary to hand to you. There's no straying from the itinerary. I'm spending my final days putting this together, so you better not go rogue on me.

All I ask is that you sit back, breathe in the moment, and truly enjoy yourselves.

I love you both. Stay tuned for more.

Forever Your Pops,

Bernie

Fuck.

I suck in a sharp breath and lean my head back against the airplane headrest, a bout of emotions traveling through me like a wave of despair. I hold back the tears that start to well in my eyes and attempt to turn toward the window, but Hazel catches me before I can hide myself.

"It's okay to cry, you know," she says, squeezing my hand. "Just as long as you're not snotty and crying the entire trip."

That makes me laugh. I turn toward her and she reaches

out and wipes away a tear from under my eye. "I'm glad you're here, Haze."

"Me too." She gives me a soft smile.

"Can I get you something to drink before we take off?" a flight attendant asks.

"I would love a Sprite with a touch of cranberry juice, please," Hazel answers. "And just a regular Sprite for the big guy over here."

"Sure thing," she answers before weaving expertly through the boarding passengers.

"What if I don't want a Sprite?"

"Who are you kidding?"

Sighing, I lean back in my chair. "Yeah, you're right."

ONCE WE'RE up in the air and the fasten seatbelt sign is off, Hazel unlatches herself and turns toward me. "So, tell me everything." She props her elbows on the console between us and rests her chin on her hands, her eyes batting at me, waiting for an answer.

One thing I know about Hazel is that she's the master of avoidance. If she doesn't want to talk about something, she will divert, she will change the subject, or she will shift the focus. And that's what I feel she's doing right now.

You don't go nearly four years without talking to each other and act as if nothing happened, unless you're Hazel Allen.

"Everything?"

She nods. "Start with the good stuff."

"Uh, and what would be the good stuff?"

"You know." She wiggles her eyebrows. "I want to know all about the women in your life."

Why the hell would she want to know that? Not what I was expecting when it came to conversation, but then again,

Hazel has always been slightly off the wall. She used to ask me the strangest questions when we were cleaning out the barn or feeding the animals, just to pass the time. Questions that always came out of nowhere. Her approach might be abrasive to others, but at this point, it's comforting because I've missed this girl so damn much.

I laugh. "Yeah, no women in my life."

"Liar." She pokes me now. "You're telling me, big man on campus, Crew Smith, doesn't have girls knocking on his door every night?"

"You fail to remember just how bad my season was this year."

"Oh, I remember. It was painful looking at the number of interceptions you threw, but you're still a handsome mother effer. Pretty sure girls aren't looking at your stats."

I shake my head. "No girls."

"Ugh." She pushes back. "You're no fun. I was hoping that would fill at least a good portion of our trip."

"What kind of sex life did you think I have?" I ask.

"A vibrant one. Clearly I was wrong."

Very wrong.

"What about you?" I challenge her with a nod her way.

"Oh, you know how it is living the farm life. Once you wipe the stink off, you're exhausted and barely have enough energy to go to the local bar and flaunt your goods."

"You paint quite the picture."

She chuckles. "I was dating this guy, but he turned out to have a foot fetish. It was fun at first, but then it just got creepy when all he wanted was my feet touching him. I passed."

"He wanted you to touch him with your feet?"

She nods slowly. "Oh yeah. He'd pay for me to get pedicures and then I'd rub my feet up and down his chest. Fascinating to see how hard he'd get."

I study her. Truly study her as I try to process what she's

saying. "I don't believe you," I finally say, knowing Hazel well enough to understand when she's trying to pull my leg.

"Okay, fine, he didn't have a foot fetish." She rolls her eyes. "But he was kind of weird and I did touch his penis with my foot once and it leapt in excitement, which was cause for concern."

"You'd be surprised what can get a penis going," I say, keeping my voice down.

"Do you have a list of things that makes you hard?"

I pause. Hazel has always been outgoing, a bit of a neat freak, and very organized. She's a hard worker, has no problem getting dirty when she needs to, and is very loving. Her relationship with her grandpa mirrors mine, and it's one of the reasons I always felt drawn to her when visiting Pops. That and her ability to just have fun.

But this side of Hazel, this . . . sexual side. Call me a prude, but I never expected it from her.

Ehh, scratch that, I didn't expect it that quickly.

Umm . . . hmm . . . maybe I should have. Yeah, this actually almost feels right.

Have you ever masturbated?

Do you think pigs have crushes?

Why do you think they call it a hoof?

Her questioning falls in line with her personality.

She pokes my side. "Don't go shy on me now."

"Not going shy, just think I need something stronger than a Sprite for this conversation."

She laughs. "You might be right." She takes a deep breath and exhales, then picks up the menu showing food options for the first-class passengers. "Wow, duck on an airplane? Bet it tastes like rubber. Where's the pizza?"

"Back in economy, probably."

"Pops would have scoffed at duck." Setting the menu down, she continues, "This is supposed to be about Pops, so let's talk about him."

"You know, I don't really want to talk about Pops right now."

"Why not?"

"Not something I want to dive into on an airplane."

"Fair enough." She reaches for her backpack and pulls out an old, tattered notebook and two pens, one purple, one green. She playfully hands me the green pen and says, "Are you up for the challenge?"

"A green pen?"

"Not just a green pen, but THE green pen."

"Are we about to take a trip down memory lane, Haze?"

"I mean, if we take a detour down memory lane while on our way to Germany, then why not?"

Chuckling, I nod at the notebook that's seen its fair share of better days, the same notebook that Hazel used to carry around the farm, looking to best me. "Did you print out game boards, cut them up, and tape them inside the notebook?"

"I'm not a monster," she replies, flipping the notebook open to a new section full of empty gameboards.

"You really have thought of everything, haven't you?"

"Would it even be visiting with each other if we didn't play Dots and Boxes?"

"It wouldn't." I pick up the notebook and flip through the pages. Game after game of purple and green fill the notebook. I turn to the front page and chuckle. "Remember this, the romantic pact we made?"

She leans over and takes a look at it. "Oh God, I don't."

Hell, I do. I remember this pact vividly, especially after that kiss. The kiss that caught me by surprise. My mind immediately went to this pact and how we just broke it.

How she broke it.

How I was shocked that she did.

Because if anyone was bound to break the pact, I swore it would have been me.

Angling the notebook toward her, she reads out loud.

"Hazel Allen and Crew Smith agree to never get romantically involved ever and swear to be best friends forever." She chuckles. "Look at your signature. Oh my God."

I laugh out loud. "It doesn't look like that anymore." I flip through the pages some more and review games claiming a purple victory and some claiming a green victory. Even have a few with the label "Cheater" written across the top in Hazel's handwriting. "I still think the jury is out about these games where you assumed I cheated."

"You did," she fires back. "You cheated multiple times, distracting me with Funyuns and then adding an extra line when I wasn't looking."

"You think I would sink so low as to cheat at Dots and Boxes?"

"Uh . . . yeah." She folds her arms across her chest. "You couldn't stand losing to a girl, especially a scrawny ass like myself."

"Not true." She eyes me and I laugh. "You were pretty scrawny."

But she isn't now.

I always saw her in the summers. Christmas time, she flew to Indiana to be with her mom's side of the family, so we always missed each other during the winter.

So, it's been a few years since we've spent time together. But she's . . . uh . . . matured. A late bloomer—she was always scrawny, flat-chested, and very innocent looking.

Now, she has some curves, her lips look plumper than I ever remember, and her brilliant red hair is woven through with blonde highlights that creates a wave of color my hands are crazily itching to touch.

And those eyes of hers, now highlighted by a coat of mascara. They're large, almost doe-like, and bright, full of life and excitement. She's . . . hell, she's beautiful. The kind of sun-kissed beauty that comes naturally with her well-placed freckles and warm-toned skin. But it's that smile that's endless and mesmerizing, a smile that has always been a solid comfort in my life.

So why did I stop writing to her?

Because I'm a self-absorbed ass.

Because I was scared.

Yeah, that sounds about right.

"Scrawny on the outside, huge muscles on the inside." She attempts to flex her arm, and through her tight-fitted long-sleeve, I see a tiny hill in her bicep, but that's about it. "Can't judge a book by its cover. Remember, I almost beat you in a hay bale throwing contest."

"Uh, almost beat me is a stretch."

"We were neck and neck there for a while. I can still hear Pops's booming laughter over his grandson losing."

"Once I figured out how to use my hips, I beat you."

"Took you far too long." She smiles.

"Doesn't matter, I still beat you." But she did give me a run for my money. I was out of breath by the end of the competition. And I thought it was going to be a cakewalk. Boy, was I wrong.

She flips the notebook over to the front page and reveals our running tally of wins. "Despite your attempts at cheating, looks as though I'm in the lead. Care to play some Dots and Boxes?"

"Same rules?" I ask.

"Would we ever play differently?"

I uncap my pen and say, "Not at this point. Let's go, Allen."

A huge smile stretches across her face as she flips to an open game. "Rock, paper, scissors to see who goes first?"

"Obviously." I hold my hand out, and together we say, "Rock, paper, scissors," and throw down.

I go in with a classic rock and she tumbles over me with paper.

"You're so predictable." She grabs my fist with her

"paper" and uncaps her purple pen. "Okay, get ready to lose, Smith."

She makes the first mark and then, in silence, we go back and forth, connecting the dots with lines. Boxes start to form, strategic moves are made, and we don't say a word to each other, the white noise of the airplane surrounding us.

With every move she makes, I counter, culminating in a long, narrow section that will make or break the game. I count ahead, looking at the marks I have to make in order to score the most boxes and . . .

Fuck.

She must realize it at the same time because now every line she makes has an extra sass to it, a little gusto to her pen strokes.

"Shit," I mutter, making the final line, which grants her access to make enough boxes to not only take the lead, but take the win.

"Ahh, look at all these purples boxes," she says, rubbing it in as she scribbles purple all over the gameboard until all the boxes are filled. When she's done, she looks up at me and says, "As per the rules, I'm allowed to ask you anything, and you have to answer."

"I think we should revisit those rules."

She caps her pen and shakes her head. "No way. You agreed to the terms before we played."

"That's because I didn't think I was going to lose. Now that I lost, I want to revisit the rules."

"Warm towel?" a flight attendant asks, standing in the aisle with a tray of warm towels.

"Uh, sure." Hazel accepts a towel, then hands it to me and quips, "Something to wash away your shame?"

Together we wipe our hands, really unclear about the whole towel thing.

"You know you're living the fancy life when you're given a

towel to wipe your hands off before a luxurious meal of airplane duck."

I chuckle. "Good thing we asked for a pizza from economy class."

"Food choices are much better back with the peasants," Hazel whispers. "Pringles and pizza—sign me up."

When the flight attendant came around to ask what our choices were for our three-course meal in first class, Hazel and I asked if we could get a pizza and Pringles instead. The flight attendant gave us a wink and said, "No problem." Thank God, because the "escargot" the gentleman across from us is eating looks less than appetizing.

The flight attendant retrieves the towels and hands us our drinks and mini-cans of Pringles. We each pop them open and take a bite. I catch the man next to us give us a look, and I'm pretty sure I see jealousy in his eyes as his attention falls back to his escargot.

"Okay, how many games do we plan on playing?" Hazel asks before popping a chip in her mouth.

With the pillow provided by the flight attendant wedged between my back and the airplane window, I can comfortably sit facing Hazel. She folds into her seat easily with her small stature, but it's a little trickier for me, given my long legs and larger frame. But I've found a comfortable position and I'm riding it out until I start cramping up.

"Why do you ask?"

"Because I have a long list of questions I want to ask you and I need to pick and choose the right ones depending on how many games we play."

"Who's to say you're going to win the other games?"

She gives me a *get real* look. "Puh-lease, I could have won that game a lot sooner, but I took it easy on you. And stop trying to distract me. You owe me an answer."

"You haven't asked a question."

She takes a Pringle out of her can and taps it against her

lips. "Okay . . ." A devious smile pulls on the corner of her lips and I fear what she's going to ask me. "Tell me, Crew, the day you 'accidentally' grabbed my boob while in the pond. Was it really an accident?"

"Oh, Jesus."

Chapter Three

HAZEL

Crew Smith.

I was hoping he was going to be on this trip with me.

Praying, actually, because I couldn't imagine doing it with anyone else. Or going it alone.

The day Pops passed away, I was by the barn, washing down the horses. My grandpa sped up on one of the farm's four-wheelers. His eyes were red, his face distressed, and his voice breathless. He didn't have to say anything. I knew. I dropped the hose and rushed back to the house with him.

Pops had been sick for a while. It's why I was busting my ass around the farm, trying to take care of my normal chores, plus his. Being a tourist farm has its pros and cons. The farm has always brought in good revenue, but during summer and fall, we worked our tails off from sunup to sundown preparing for apple and berry pickers. Fall is our most lucrative season, with pumpkins patches, tractor rides, barrel rides, corn mazes, live folk bands, homemade apple cider and apple cider donuts, food trucks all along the picnic area, and, of course, the famous pumpkin cannon. It's a lot of work and Pops put me in charge. This past year was overwhelming, to say the least, and being in charge of the staff while he was sick was even tougher. I let the ball drop many times, and I wound up going to bed in a heap of tears, knowing damn well that I was failing him.

So, when Grandpa Thomas presented this trip from Pops to me, I didn't even ask any questions, I took it. I needed it. We were at the tail end of our small Christmas season and everything was under control, so I granted myself permission to go on this trip. I was also nudged by a note from Pops.

All it said was "You need a break. Take it."

He was right.

And I'm thankful Crew is the one I'm taking the trip with. Except for the last few years, he's been a huge part of my life. Every summer I looked forward to Crew and his parents visiting. I prepared a world of activities to do, and when he arrived, we hit the ground running.

Being here with him on the plane, playing Dots and Boxes—it feels so natural, it feels right.

I poke him with my pen. "Come on, answer the question."

"You really think I touched your boob on purpose? There was nothing to touch." He smirks and my mouth falls in feigned outrage.

"Crew Smith, how dare you?"

He laughs as I poke him some more with my pen.

"There was boob there. It might have been miniscule, but there was boob."

"Sort of like a pebble in a shoe. You know it's there, but you can't really find it."

"Well, you must have studied my chest closely then, because you found it."

He shrugs. "Lucky guess."

"Aha. So you admit to grabbing it on purpose."

"I admit to being quite concerned for you and wanting to make sure there was something there."

"You're such a liar." I laugh while he lays on that charming smile of his.

Crew Smith is one handsome man. Pretty-boy looks with plump lips, perfect bone structure with an angular jaw, and that boy-next-door messy hair. He's devastatingly tall and broad, his hours in the weight room evident in the way his sleeves cling to his biceps. He's always been attractive, and over these last few years, he's become positively striking. Thankfully, I'm immune to his charm.

Well, for the most part.

His smile can still cause butterflies to erupt in my stomach.

He takes the top off his pen again and says, "Come on, next game. I have some questions of my own."

"Okay, good luck."

He loses the faceoff again for who goes first, and I snicker to myself while he grumbles. I start the game off and he quickly adds a line, trying something new with a spot in the corner. We go back and forth, I let him have some boxes, he messes up a few times, and before we know it, I'm scribbling in purple again and calling the win.

"Damn it," he huffs. "Are you playing this game in your spare time?"

"What spare time?"

He shrugs. "In between chores?"

"Yup. That's exactly what I'm doing." I roll my eyes.

He points his pen at me. "I knew it."

"You're being ridiculous." With a smirk, I tap my chin playfully and say, "Now, what question do I want to ask this time?"

"Oh, I'm sure you have something brilliantly embarrassing up your sleeve."

"I have many."

Just then, the flight attendant brings each of us a tray

laden with a small pizza, a salad with accompanying dressing, a dinner roll with a foil-wrapped pat of butter, a glass of water, and silverware wrapped in a black cloth napkin.

"We'll be bringing the dessert cart around in a while. Let us know if you need anything else."

"Thank you," Crew and I say at the same time.

When she's gone, I lean toward Crew and say, "This is fancy."

"I see why we had to wash our hands with that towel now. We're fine dining, Twigs." He winks, using the nickname that Pops and Grandpa Thomas used to call me all the time.

"You're used to this, Hollywood."

"Nah, you know me better than that." He begins to spread butter on his roll.

"True. You'd rather be seen at a dive restaurant than a fancy one."

"Fact," he says before taking a big bite from his dinner roll.

I unfold my silverware and lay my napkin on my lap before cutting up my pizza and placing a small bite in my mouth. "This is good. Is it weird that it's so good?"

Like the man that he is, Crew lifts the pizza off the plate and takes a large bite. He chews and swallows before nodding and saying, "Yup, it's good. I think it might be the altitude affecting us."

"That or we have immature palates, and we should be ashamed."

"Maybe a little of both."

"How about we make a pact for the trip?"

"Another pact?" he asks, one brow lifted.

"Yeah. How about, during this trip, we step outside our comfort zones and experience the essence of all things German? I say we try all the food we come across that we've never had before."

"Immerse ourselves in the culture."

"Precisely."

"Okay, I can agree to that." He winks and takes another bite. "But when we're in the air, we eat what we want."

"Agreed. There's an ice cream sundae calling my name and there's no way I'm passing that up."

"Same." He chuckles. "Now, are you going to ask me your question, or keep me waiting in suspense?"

"Keeping you waiting sounds like fun."

"Or, we can ask each other two questions while we eat."

"Umm, how is that fair? I won the game."

"Fine. You ask two, I ask one."

"I still don't see how—"

"Humor me, Hazel," he says in a pleading tone, with those brown puppy-dog eyes of his. Ugh, the devil himself would relent to those eyes.

"Fine. I'll go first," I say, giving in with barely a fight.

"Lay it on me."

"What ever happened with Pearl? All you said was you broke up, but I don't believe there wasn't more to it. You were infatuated with her."

"Why did I know you were going to ask about her?" he practically growls in frustration.

"Because you know I'm nosy and I've been holding on to that question for years, waiting for the right moment to ask you." I stab my fork through my salad. "You know, Pops never liked her."

"I know," he says softly.

Pearl was Crew's high school girlfriend. She came to visit with them one summer, only for a few days, not the entire time that Crew and his family came to visit, and she was freaking awful. Wouldn't get dirty and help with the chores, refused to brush the horses, and didn't even attempt to eat the food Pops prepared. She was insulting, to say the least.

"So, what happened with her? All I know is one day Pops

came barreling out of the main house, arms waving in the air, yelling in excitement about the breakup."

"Of course he was a showman about it." Crew dabs his face with his napkin. "Honestly, I thought she was going to be the girl who waited for me while I went through college. She wanted me to stay somewhere local in California when it came to college, but I wanted to go wherever I got the best education and a chance at growing in my sport. When she found that out, she said she wouldn't wait for me, and I told her not to. That was that."

"After four years, that's how it ended?" I ask, surprised.

"Yup. Although, I think it was starting to go sour before that. My senior year was fun without her."

"I could have told you she wasn't the one after her visit to the farm. She wasn't really kind . . . to anyone. Especially to me."

Crew rubs the back of his neck. "Yeah, that's one of the reasons why I started to see the real her, because who couldn't like Hazel Allen?"

"That's what I'm saying." I pretend to primp my hair. "I'm an absolute delight to be around."

"Especially after a hard day shoveling horse shit."

"If I could bottle up that smell, you know I'd give you a lifetime supply."

"Thank God you can't."

I butter my roll. "Okay, your turn. What's your question?"

Turning toward me, he forces me to look at him by pressing his finger to my chin and turning my head. "Are you mad at me?"

See, this is why I knew I shouldn't have agreed to his terms. He presses until he gets what he wants, and that's what he's doing now.

"Mad at you? For what?" I ask, playing nonchalant. I was hoping he'd ask me something stupid and simple like I've asked him, something about the past, something that didn't have much substance behind it. But he goes and asks the hard-hitting question.

"Don't play with me, Hazel." His voice booms with authority. Reminds me of Pops. "Are you mad at me?"

I nibble on my lower lip while I set my silverware down on my tray. I fold my hands in my lap and tear my eyes away from his. He won't drop this. I know he won't, so there's only one thing to do. Tell the truth. "A little," I answer.

"Why?"

I shake my head. "You only get one question."

"Hazel."

"I'm serious. One question. That's it."

"I'm serious too. I'm not about to go on some crazy unknown journey through Germany with you while I know you're mad at me." He tugs on a loose strand of my hair playfully. "Come on, Haze, talk to me."

"I don't want to do this here, on an airplane."

"What better place to do it? We can have a fresh start, right here."

He's right. Carrying around this anger can't possibly be good, even though I've done a good job at hiding it so far. I've caught myself a few times reverting to the deep-rooted anger that's been weighing me down for the past few years.

"You really don't know?" I ask, nerves fragmenting my muscles and causing my bones to shake.

"I mean, I have an idea."

"And what would that idea be?" I twist so I'm facing him entirely now, both our trays of food ignored.

"Not coming back to the farm the past few summers."

"That's just a small part of it, Crew." A very small part, but I'm not sure I'm brave enough to talk about the biggest issue. I stare down at my hands, twisting them together. "You forgot about me."

"What? Hazel, I could never forget about you."

"Really?" I glance up at him, my eyebrow quirked. "How

many times did I email you? Only for those messages to go unanswered? After a year of no response, I just stopped writing you, and then you stopped coming back to New York for the summers. You forgot about me, Crew."

Distressed, he pushes his hand through his hair but stays silent. Is he thinking about what might have pushed him to run? Because it's all I can think about right now.

"As much as I love seeing you right now and think that going on this trip with you is going to be fun, I still have this sick feeling in the pit of my stomach that maybe . . . I don't know, maybe you think you're too good to hang out with the farm girl, now that you're this big football player."

"Jesus, no," he says quickly. "No, it's not that. It's . . . hell." He sighs and takes my hand in his, lacing our fingers together. "I'm just a shit friend, Hazel. I wish I could give you a reason, but I'm a shit friend. I lost sight of a lot while training. Wanting to be the best, wanting to prove my worth on the field." He laughs sarcastically. "Look where that got me. But I'm not ashamed of you, not by any means. You're a fucking badass and someone who puts a smile on my face without even trying. You're . . . hell, when you're around, I actually feel at ease, as though I'm home. I'm so grateful you're here with me."

"Yeah?" I ask, feeling a smidge better.

"Yeah, and I'm sorry. I'm really fucking sorry I never wrote back. I did read your letters, though, and I guess . . . hell, I guess I just thought after a while, you didn't want to hear from me because I'd been such an ass. I actually wrote a long email to you this summer after Pops passed, but I was too chicken to send it."

"What did it say?"

He licks his lips and then takes a sip of his water. "Talked about Pops. About football. About some of the guys on my team and how I think you could throw hay bales farther than them despite them being big, burly men."

I chuckle.

"But mainly, it said how much I missed you. Really missed you."

"I missed you, too, Crew." I give him a soft smile, and he reaches out and pulls me into a strong hug. His arms are familiar, but the broadness of his corded chest is new. Still warm and inviting, but new.

His hand cups the back of my head as he holds me tightly. "I'm sorry, Hazel. I swear, from here on out, I'll never let you think you're forgotten, ever again."

I pull away and ask, "Do you mean that? That you'll never forget me again?" There's a joking tone to my voice, but my heart is one reopened wound away from bleeding.

It's *not* that easy. The feelings of hurt and anguish rest heavy on my heart and they're not going to disappear with one simple apology. Forgiveness takes time and, right now, on the airplane, it's not the time. Not sure when the time is but this surely isn't it. I want to believe him . . . *but—*

"Swear on Funyuns," he says with a boyish grin.

I clutch my chest. "That's the holy grail of all promises."

"It's why I said it."

"Okay." Wanting this to be an easy trip and focused on Pops, not us, I say, "I guess you're forgiven, but we're still on a trial basis here. If you don't measure up to the boy I used to know, then I want a refund."

He laughs. "Don't worry, I'm already starting to feel a little like myself. Looks like Pops knew." He swallows hard, his voice growing thick with emotion. "Looks like he knew I just needed a little Hazel in my life again."

Then why did you forget about me?

"Everyone needs a little Hazel." I wink. "But thank you for apologizing. It's going to take me a second to get my mind straight, you know, let those sad feelings dissipate, but I appreciate you apologizing. It means a lot to me." I bite the corner of my lip and ask, "And just to verify, you're not ashamed of me?"

"No, but I'm ashamed of myself. That's for damn sure."

"Okay." I squeeze his hand and turn back to my tray. "You know I adore you, Crew, even if you were an ass ignoring me."

"And you know I think you're one of the best people I know, even if I'm an idiot and a shit of a friend."

"I'm glad we agree on that." I spear another piece of pizza and calm my racing heart. Keep it light, keep it breezy, keep it fun. "Ready for my last question?"

"Not really. The last two were tough."

"I'll make it easy on you, then." I sip some water, clear my throat, and ask, "The day I jumped into the pond—"

"Oh, come on, Hazel."

I laugh out loud, drawing some attention from our fellow passengers. "Did you or did you not see my top come off? Because shortly after my top came off, the boob grab happened, and I know you said you saw nothing, but I'm ninety-nine point nine percent sure that was a lie. So, did you see my boobs that day?"

He slowly nods his head. "Yeah, I saw your boobs."

"I freaking knew you did. No boy turns that red and claims to have seen nothing. Which is why you didn't want to get out of the pond right away. Probably took a trip to bone town, right? And then the slip-up of grabbing my boob—it's because I flashed the goods with an ill-fitting bathing suit top, and instead of being a window-shopper, you wanted to give them a test drive as well. You dirty, dirty boy."

He laughs, the sound like a bass hitting me directly in the chest. "I was in the prime of hormonal insanity. I probably would have wanted to grab a cow's udders if it flashed me."

"That comparison's . . . disturbing."

"You know what I mean. I was a horny idiot. I saw your

boobs when you jumped into the pond and I wanted to see if they were . . . real."

"Real?"

"Sure, that makes me sound less creepy."

"No, the whole thing is creepy. Not only were you my first kiss, but you were my first boob grab as well. I feel like, looking back, I could have done better."

"Hey." He laughs.

"At least I lost my virginity to an upstanding citizen. Lasted all of three seconds. I've chosen some real winners."

"Three seconds?" He cringes. "When I lost mine, I lasted at least ten." He smirks and I laugh.

"Wow, giving me a taste of humility. Why, Crew Smith, have you grown up?"

"Some might say I have." He tips my chin up. "God, I really have missed you."

"Damn right you did, so don't forget it. Your life will always be best with a little bit of Hazel in it."

"It will be." He pauses for a second, then asks, "So who did you lose your virginity to?"

"You don't know him. A guy in town. I was nineteen. Thought it was a good idea at the time. It wasn't. Boring and I barely had fun. It was almost like something to check off on my life list." I make a check motion with my hand. "Virginity, gone."

"Please tell me you've had more fun since."

"A little here and there. Nothing mind-blowing." Shyly I glance over at him. "Pearl rock your world?"

"I mean, it was good at the time."

"Good at the time." I can't stop the smile from crossing my cheeks. "That's a nice way of putting it."

"That's what I am . . . the nice guy."

"Probably why you don't get that much ass in college."

He laughs. "Yeah, that and my stats."

"CREW?"

"Yeah?" Crew asks from his reclined position.

We spent the last hour and a half watching *Love, Simon* together, on separate screens, but we still pressed play at the same time, and then we got ready for bed. The airline provided us with a nifty bedtime kit, as well as pillows and blankets. We both brushed our teeth and then laid down our seats. The pods aren't a five-star hotel, but they're much better than sitting up straight and trying to get some sleep.

"Are you nervous about the trip?"

He lifts himself up and rests his arms on the console between us while looking down at me. His eyes have a heavy, sleepy look to them, and he must have run his hand through his hair a few times while getting comfortable, because it's messy but adorable.

"Yeah, I am."

"Me too."

"Why are you nervous?" He lowers his hand and swipes a piece of hair off my forehead.

"I miss him," I say, my voice growing tight. "I'm scared, and I guess I just hope to find a connection on this trip, the strength I've been trying to find for the last couple of months."

Crew's brows pull together. "Scared? Why are you scared?"

"The farm is a lot of work, and I'm nervous I'm going to drop the ball. Grandpa Thomas has been helping me with operations, but it's overwhelming." A small tear cascades down my face. Crew quickly wipes it away.

"I didn't know you were feeling that way."

"Well, how could you?" I say before I can stop myself. "Sorry, I shouldn't have said that."

"No, you should have. I should have been there. I could have helped."

"How, Crew? If you haven't noticed, you're kind of on track to become a professional football player."

"I would have at least listened." He pauses and shakes his head in shame. "I should have listened. You needed a friend."

"I did." My lips tremble and I hate that I'm getting emotional. "Pops was one of my best friends."

"Me too," Crew says. He reaches over and takes my hand in his. "I miss him so fucking much. I honestly didn't want to go on this trip at first, knowing how it was going to make me feel. Having to revisit all these feelings and figure out how to say goodbye. I'm just grateful I don't have to do it alone."

"I'm grateful, too." I sit up and wrap my arms around Crew, burying my head in his shoulder. He squeezes me tight and, instead of pulling away quickly, he holds me. Tight. His hand cupping the back of my neck, his chin resting on top of my head.

"I'm sorry I wasn't there for you, Hazel."

"I'm sorry you threw so many interceptions this past season."

He chuckles, and the rumbling sound of his laugh puts me at ease.

When he pulls away, he tips up my chin and says, "Such a smart-ass."

"One of the reasons you love me so much," I shoot back.

"Ehh, love is a strong word. How about tolerate?"

"Tolerate—that works, since it mirrors the way I feel about you."

Chuckling, he pushes me down on my "bed." "Get some sleep, Allen. Who knows what's in store for us when we land?"

"Goodnight, Crew."

"Night, Haze."

I turn on my side and lower the sleeping mask the flight

attendants provided. I curl up and adjust my blanket, ready to get some sleep.

Tomorrow, an adventure begins. The unknown, guided by one of the most important men in my life. I have so many questions, though. Why Germany? Why now? Why with Crew? Why this trip?

Why did Pops have to be taken away from us?

I think the last question is one I'll never understand. Hopefully the others will be answered along the way.

Chapter Four

CREW

"You're insane. There's no way you're driving."

"Uh, why not?"

"Because you're a *terrible* driver," I say, holding the keys to the rental car we just picked up.

After we got off the plane, I called my mom to let her know we landed, even though it was the middle of the night for her. She then spoke with Hazel for a while, Hazel laughing the entire time and eyeing me. She reassured my mom that she had no problem not only keeping me in line, but protecting me from any locals trying to get my goods. I could hear my mom's laughter coming from the phone. They always got along.

She told us there was a reservation for a car waiting for us and once we got the car, we were to head to the Beyond Hotel, where we are expected.

Simple.

Especially since we have no idea where we're going.

Arms folded over her chest, Hazel says, "Are you saying I'm a bad driver because I'm a woman?"

"No. I'm saying you're a terrible driver because *you are.* You can barely drive the tractor on the farm in a straight line, and need I mention how you drove Pops' truck into a ditch?"

"I was sixteen. I'm much better now."

"Yeah, I won't be taking my chances. I'll be the responsible one taking us carefully through the roads of Germany."

"If you think this entire trip will consist of you bossing me around, you're in for a rude awakening."

"Trust me, I know you're the one who's going to be doing the bossing," I mutter. I go to her side of the car and open the door. "Get in, Twigs. I'm growing hungry and impatient."

"Starting the trip off with joy, I see."

I press my hand to my forehead. "You're right. I'm sorry." Plastering on a smile, I sarcastically say, "Dearest honey bunny, will you please get in the car?"

Smiling, she moves past me and presses her hand to my chest. "Much better, sir. Thank you."

Shaking my head, I shut her door, round the back of the car, where I make sure our luggage is secure, and shut the trunk. We were rented an Opel Corsa, a car I've never heard of before in my life, but it looks like a four-door Volkswagen hatchback. I'm assuming I'll be driving from the backseat, but hey, as long as I can get us from A to B, we should be good. I will admit I'm nervous to drive these unfamiliar roads, and wish I had my Range Rover.

When I sink into the driver's seat, I grip the steering wheel and take a deep breath. "You ready?"

She nods. "I hope this isn't a road trip."

I snort. "Okay, do you not know my family at all? Of course this is a road trip. Pops wouldn't have it any other way. I just hope we're not driving across Europe." I pull my phone from my pocket and type the hotel address into my navigation app. "Forty-three minutes. Okay, that's not too bad."

"You're sure you don't want me to drive? You look a little tired."

I adjust my ballcap on my head, the bill facing backwards like always, and say, "You're not driving. The car is under my name, my name only. We don't need to take the Hazel coaster to death."

"You drive one truck into a ditch and you never hear the end of it," she mutters.

"As it should be." I turn on the ignition and ask, "Are you ready for this?"

"Barely." She turns toward me. "Don't kill us."

"I won't." I swallow hard.

Pops, if you're listening, please don't let me crash into anything. After all, this is your fault.

"GUTEN MORGEN," a valet attendant says, opening my car door.

"Hello," I say, not quite confident enough to throw down a *Guten morgen* as well.

"Möchten Sie einchecken?" the attendant asks.

"Um. I'm checking in. Name is Crew Smith."

The attendant's eyes light up. "Ah, yes, the front desk has been expecting you. Let me help you with your luggage."

Someone else helps Hazel out of the car, and our luggage is put on a luggage cart. "Oh, we can handle that."

"*No.* We are here to take care of you. My name is Elias. Allow me to show you to check in."

Hazel joins me at my side and we both walk into a gray building with windows extending up to the roof, a combination of modern and old-century architecture. In the distance, Christmas music plays, and the chill in the air reminds me that I'm not in California anymore. Thank God I brought a winter coat.

When we cross the threshold of the hotel, we're greeted by a festive lobby. Pine garland is beautifully draped along the walls with glass baubles hanging precariously throughout the garland. The lobby is sleek with dark gray tones and underlighting that highlights the sharp edges of the front desk. Modern, sophisticated—something I never would have assumed Pops would pick for us.

"*Guten morgen*," the hotel attendant says.

"Berdine, this is the Smith party."

Berdine's eyes light up as well, and she says, "We have been anticipating your arrival." From behind her, she grabs a small package and sets it on the counter in front of us. "We were told to hand this over to you when you arrived. We already have a card on file. I will just need a form of identification."

I fish my wallet out of my pocket and remove my ID.

"Ah, from California. I've been once. Quite lovely. Is this Mrs. Smith?" Berdine asks, directing her attention to Hazel, who snorts and shakes her head.

"Oh no, I'm Hazel Allen. Friends. Just friends."

Sheesh, could she sound more insulted?

"Ah, my apologies." Berdine types away at her computer and then says, "Elias. Room 410 please." Elias nods and takes off with our luggage. After a few more seconds, Berdine says, "You will be staying with us for one night, it seems."

"Honestly, we have no clue." I laugh. "This whole trip is a surprise."

"What a wonderful way to spend your holiday. On a whim, as they would say." Looking between us, she asks, "How many keycards would you like?"

"One should be fine, right?" I ask Hazel.

"Yeah, don't plan on going anywhere without the big guy." She thumbs toward me.

"Great." Berdine makes a keycard for us and then hands me my ID before explaining the amenities of the hotel. "Our kitchen is open for breakfast, lunch, and dinner. We've quite a list of wines, if you're interested. Just outside the hotel is the Marienplatz, also known as St. Mary's Square. It's full of vendors right now for the Christmas Market. Stalls line the space and are filled with holiday treats and souvenirs. We have a concierge if you have questions about the area." She hands me a card. "You're on the fourth floor, room 410. The room overlooks the Marienplatz and Alter Peter. It's quite breathtaking. Take the elevators up to the fourth floor and then make a right. You'll find your room quite quickly. Do you have any questions?"

I shake my head and Hazel does the same. "Thank you so much," I say.

"Of course. We hope you enjoy your stay, and if you need anything, please let us know."

I smile and then we head to the elevator bank, where we press the *up* button.

Leaning in, Hazel says, "I honestly wasn't expecting a hotel like this. I half-expected a shack with plaid wallpaper."

I chuckle. "Yeah, me too. I wasn't aware Pops even knew swanky hotels existed, given all the beaten-down cabins I've stayed in with him." The elevator arrives with a ding, and we hop in and press the button for the fourth floor.

"Not going to lie—I'm tired and it's only ten-thirty in the morning." Hazel yawns.

"Yeah, I don't think jetlag is going to be our friend, but I heard we have to power through, not give in to wanting to sleep during awake hours."

"I read the same thing."

The elevator dings and the doors open. It takes us a few seconds to find our room, and when we do, Elias is waiting by the door. He smiles as we approach.

"Your luggage is in your room. Please let us know if you need anything else." I reach for my wallet, but he holds up his hand. "No need to tip, Mr. Smith. Enjoy your stay." He pushes open the door and Hazel walks in first.

"Oh, wow," she says on a hushed breath.

Oh, wow is right.

Panoramic views of the beautiful Munich architecture greet us, and it's what I'm drawn to first. Across the square, there's an opulent cathedral with gothic-style pinnacles and corbels decorating the front. You don't find these in America, especially in California. Below is a widespread marketplace, every last inch covered by white tent tops and contrasting green garlands. Christmas lights are strung along the space. It must be a beautiful place to walk through at night.

"I don't think I've ever seen anything like this," Hazel says, one hand pressed against the window. "It's gorgeous. Do you think Pops has been here?"

"I don't know. Want to look at the let—" My words fall short when I catch a glimpse of the bed. "Uh, are we supposed to share a bed?"

Hazel turns around and she spots the single queen-sized bed in the center of the far wall. It's covered with a white comforter, fluffy white pillows, and a yellow throw blanket. It's calling my name, beckoning for me to take a nap, but my mind is buzzing with the idea that I very well might have to share a bed with Hazel.

"Huh, I think so." She shrugs and goes to the open bathroom where she picks up a mini shampoo bottle and takes a sniff. "These smell amazing."

"Uh, aren't you concerned about having to share a bed?"

"No. Are you?" she asks, her brow crinkled.

"I mean . . . maybe?"

"Why?" she asks as if I'm crazy. "It's just a bed. We're grown-ups. We know the no-touch zones."

"I guess so."

She sets the shampoo down and walks over to the bed to run her fingers along the mustard-yellow throw. She playfully looks up at me and asks, "Are you afraid you might fall in love with me if we share a bed, Crew?"

"No."

"Afraid you might wake up horny?"

I clear my throat. "No."

She laughs, her head tilting back. "Liar. You're nervous about a little morning wood." She waves her hand at me. "Don't worry, I won't judge. I'll let you have the shower first so you can whack off." She flashes a smile, and I truly wonder how the hell I went three years without *this* Hazel. A lot changes when you don't talk to your friend for a while.

"Thank you?" I say in a question.

She pats my chest. "You're welcome, Hollywood. Just keep the moaning to a minimum."

I flop down on the bed. "You've changed, you know that?"

"That's what happens when you grow up. You change. You'd have known that if you wrote back to me."

"How many times am I going to have to apologize for that?" I ask, lying back on the bed and removing my hat. *Just let me shut my eyes for a few seconds.*

"Oh no, you don't." Hazel jumps on the bed next to me and shakes my shoulder. "No sleeping. We have things to do, letters to read, envelopes to open."

"Come on, let me just get like twenty minutes in." I roll to the side and rest my head on her lap. She leisurely strokes my hair, and fuck, does that feel good. All it does is make me want to fall into a deep . . . dark . . . slumber . . .

"Crew, look alive," Hazel shouts, causing my eyes to spring open.

"Hell," I groan, pressing my hand to my forehead. "You're relentless."

She taps my cheek. "Go take a shower, a cold one. I'll order us some food and coffee to wake us up, and then we can open the envelope together. How does that sound?

"Fine," I grumble, lifting up from the bed.

She slaps my back. "Attaboy."

I walk over to the bathroom, and that's when I realize there's no wall to the bathroom, just a piece of glass that exposes everything.

"Uh, there's no privacy in here."

"You afraid I'm going to sneak a peek?"

"Yeah," I say.

She chuckles and then walks into the bathroom, moving me to the side. She presses a button and the glass wall tints with a frost, granting privacy.

"Now I won't see your little man bits." She walks to the sitting area and sits in one of the two upholstered captain's chairs. She picks up a folder from the coffee table in front of the chairs and says, "Ooo, bratwurst."

"They're not little."

"The bratwurst? I didn't think they were."

"No, my . . . uh, man bits. They're not little."

In an exasperated tone, she says, "You're such a man, always needing to defend the size of your penis."

"You were defending your boob size," I point out.

"Uh, because you said I didn't have any. It's not as if I offered my condolences to you for not having a dick."

"I'm too tired to defend myself right now, and you're too witty. I'm taking a shower."

She kicks her feet up on the coffee table. "Smells like a good idea."

I TAKE A DEEP BREATH, feeling refreshed, and emerge from the shower. Hazel pushes me into the wall and runs to the toilet, shamelessly pushing down her pants.

I turn away just in time.

"Jesus, take a long enough shower? I really had to pee."

Slightly stunned, I grip the towel that's wrapped around

my waist and say, "You could have gone to the bathroom before I took a shower."

"I didn't have to go then, and thanks to your supreme modesty, I didn't want to barge in on your man time." She sighs in relief. "God, I would have been humiliated if the first thing I did in Germany was pee my pants." She gives me a smooth once-over and says, "Nice muscles."

I glance down at my bare torso and then back at her. "Uh . . . nice thigh."

She smooths her hand over her exposed thigh and says, "You like that? I have two of them." She wiggles her eyebrows.

Fucking ridiculous.

"I think we've reached a new level of our friendship."

"Never seen a girl pee before?"

"Probably my mom when I was small, but recently, no."

"Ah, well"—she motions to her body—"soak it all in. A real sight to behold. But I'll tell you this, I would appreciate some privacy while I wipe. Don't need you watching the intricacies of drying off my crevices."

"Jesus, don't call them that." I turn away and head to the living area, where I lift my suitcase onto the bed and fish out a clean pair of boxer briefs. I slip them on under the towel, then whip off the towel and drape it over my head, tousling my hair. I turn toward Hazel. "Did you—"

"Uh, excuse me," Hazel says, hand thrown across her chest as she sits on the toilet now topless and her pants still around her ankles.

"What the hell are you doing?"

"About to take a shower. What does it look like?"

"I don't know. You're still on the toilet. For all I know it's some weird woman ritual where you sit on the toilet topless."

"Please don't tell me you're that clueless about women," she counters.

My back toward her, hand in hair, I say, "I'm not. I just

wasn't expecting you to be topless. I swear, and I really mean it, no lies—I didn't see anything."

"I know you didn't. I heard your mammoth stomping on the way over here. You're not a silent walker, Crew."

"You're not very subtle, Hazel."

"Have I ever been?"

No. She hasn't.

Relaxing, I ask her, "Why are you topless, though? I know you're going to take a shower, but do you usually undress on the toilet?"

"Killing two birds with one stone, Crew. While I attempt to drip dry—"

"Never mind." I shoot away from the bathroom and call out, "Did you order food?"

"Yes, sheesh. I'll be quick. Don't worry."

The shower turns on, and I take a seat in one of the captain's chairs. What the hell was Pops thinking? Sharing a hotel room, a bed? It almost seems as if he's trying to work some magic from beyond the grave.

I glance up at the frosted bathroom glass and regret it immediately as I catch the silhouette of Hazel's body. There's no definition, just smooth curves, an outline of a woman's curves—but what a fucking body. She's standing next to the shower, waiting for it to warm, and she's running her hand through her hair, her breasts sticking out, the curve of her back leading to her ass. Hell, Hazel really has grown up.

Thanks a lot, Pops. This should be a real joy for the next week.

"I CAN'T STOP SMELLING my hair." Hazel is wearing one of the hotel robes, her wet hair hangs around her face and shoulders, and I have to keep reminding her to tighten her robe because it continues to gape open too much.

I haven't seen anything, but we've had a few close calls. It's difficult to reconcile the curvy woman with my *scrawny* friend, Hazel. Maybe if it hadn't been months since I've been with anyone, I wouldn't find her shape so distracting. *Or be tempted to allow the gaping.*

There's a knock at the door, and before I can attempt to move, Hazel pops out of her chair and goes to open the door. A gentleman in a white button-up shirt, black vest, and black tie pushes a cart into the room. "Where should I put this? In the sitting area?"

"That would be great," Hazel says.

He hands her a black folder and says, "Could I grab your signature, Mrs. Smith?"

Instead of correcting him, Hazel goes with it this time. "Of course. Newlyweds, you know." She nods toward me. "This old ball and chain is showing me around Germany for our honeymoon. What a guy, huh?"

"A nice man, ya?."

Hazel quickly scribbles on the receipt, then snaps the black folder shut and hands it to the guy where he waits patiently at the door. "Have a good one," she says, waving her hand.

He nods and leaves, the door clicking shut behind him.

"Old ball and chain?" I ask, one brow raised.

"Oh yeah. You have ball and chain written all over you. Clingy and needy—you're the definition of a ball and chain."

"When have I ever been clingy and needy?"

She takes a seat and lifts up the food cloches, revealing . . . what looks like worms in a yellowish sauce.

"What's that?"

"Well, remember our pact on the airplane? Trying new foods? Well, this is Käsespätzle. I looked it up and it's supposed to resemble mac and cheese to us uncultured Americans. Thought it was an easy first step."

"I thought you were going to order bratwurst."

"You have all the time in the world to snack on wieners. I

went with something a little more surprising. Now, shall we eat first and then read the letters, or read and then eat, or do it at the same time?"

"Eat first."

She unfolds her napkin and lays it across her lap, but her eyes stay fixed on me the entire time. "You know, for someone who just lost his grandfather, I thought you'd be more interested in the trip he planned on his death bed."

The comment hits me harder than I expected, and when my bleary eyes glance at her, she catches my trepidation.

"That didn't come out right," she says quickly.

"No, it's okay. I know what you meant, and yeah, I'm avoiding opening anything right now."

She picks up her fork and spears one of the worm-like noodles. "Want to talk about it?"

"Not really. Just the same old bullshit of not wanting to let go of something that's already left my life."

"That's not bullshit. That's a valid feeling. But unfortunately, you're on a trip with me, and I'm not going to let you hide from your feelings." She smiles at me, and then, from her side, she lifts the white envelope we were given at the front desk.

"Why do I feel as though you're about to rip off a Band-Aid?"

"Because I am." She comes to take a seat on the arm of my chair.

"You can't hide from the loss of Pops, but you can start to learn to accept it, and there's no time like now to do that."

She tips the envelope over and a letter falls out, along with a picture and a map. I pick up the picture and immediately smile. It's a picture of Pops and his wife, Gloria, who I never got to meet, but I've heard about many, many times.

They're standing in front of a Christmas tree. Pops proudly has his arm around Gloria, and they're both smiling at the camera.

"Oh my God. Look at Pops' plaid pants. Those are killer," Hazel says.

I chuckle. "I never knew he had it in him to pull off something so stylish."

"You think that's stylish?"

"Back then, I believe they were."

Hazel leans in. "Gloria is so beautiful. She reminds me of your mom so much it freaks me out."

"She does," I say softly. "They look really happy in this picture."

"They do," Hazel agrees and then picks up the map and unfolds it. It's a printout of the Christmas market and the best way to visit each stall. "Well, this is well thought out."

"I wonder how much time he worked on this."

"Let's see." Hazel looks in the envelope and then gasps.

"What?" I ask.

She slowly pulls out a wad of Euros. "Uh, he just had this sitting at the front desk?"

"Holy shit," I say, thumbing through the bills. There has to be at least eight hundred euros in here. "Why would he give us so much money?"

"I have no idea."

I nod at the envelope. "Is there anything else in there?"

She looks in the envelope. "Nothing. Oh, wait—duh—the letters are in my backpack." Hazel runs over to her backpack where she sifts through the letters and then holds one up in the air. "Here we are." She takes a seat next to me again and hands me the envelope. It's labeled "Munich. Letter #2." Hazel nudges me with her shoulder. "Read it out loud."

"Not making this easy on me, are you?"

"Nope. Come on, time to rip."

Sighing, I open the letter and unfold the paper. I instantly take comfort in seeing Pops' very familiar handwriting.

Clearing my throat, I read the letter out loud. "'Hey kiddos, glad you made it to Munich—at least, I hope you did.

How was the drive? Crew, I hope you took the wheel. Knowing Hazel's track record, you two could have ended up in a ditch.'" I laugh out loud while Hazel protests.

"It was one time. Good God, you can't hold that against me for life."

"I think we can," I say before turning back to the letter. "'Anyway, welcome to Munich at Christmastime. It's unlike anything you'll ever experience, and this is where your road trip starts. Yes, road trip. Did you think I would send you on anything else?'" I look up at Hazel. "Told you." She just rolls her eyes. "'You're probably wondering why I sent you on this trip, and the answer is . . . something you'll find out later, but the real road trip hasn't started quite yet. This is a small detour until you get up to the starting point. For now, I want you to take the night—don't let sleep take you over—'"

"Ha, told you." Hazel nudges me.

"Congratulations, you were right about one thing."

"Uh, I was right about you opening this letter." She pokes my cheek. "See? You're smiling and enjoying it."

Damn it, I am.

Ignoring her, I go back to the letter. "'Immerse yourself in the holiday culture today. Spend time walking through the stalls, taking in the intricacies of all the handmade works. Buy yourselves a trinket, something to remember these moments by. That's what the cash is for. That and food and drinks. Find things that mean something to you, things that will remind you of each other, of me, of your families. Munich is about reconnecting.'"

Hazel drapes her arm over my shoulder and gives me a good squeeze.

"'You might have thought I didn't notice, but I did. I noticed how you two grew apart. Don't worry, Twigs, I place all the blame on my idiot of a grandson.'"

Hazel laughs, and I chuckle as well, imagining Pops' look of displeasure over me ignoring Hazel's emails. He'd have smacked me on the back of the head and asked, "What the Abraham Lincoln were you thinking?" And honestly, I wouldn't have had an answer for him.

"'Some of the greatest moments of my older years were watching you two get together during the summer and goof around. I always thought there was a deep-rooted connection between you, and to see that connection slowly disappear to the point that, Hazel, you didn't even know some of things I told you over the last year about Crew . . . it hurt my heart. As we know, we've such limited time here on Earth, which means you need to make the most of the moments you have together.'"

I pause and take a deep breath. Glancing up at Hazel, I say, "I'm really sorry, Haze."

"I know you are." She bites her bottom lip, something I've seen her do when she's holding in her emotions, trying not to cry. *God.* She taps the paper. "Keep reading."

"'Munich is that moment to iron out any of the wrinkles you might have in your friendship. To clear the air, to make sure that, going forward, you're both on a clean slate. I would love for you to go through the Christmas stalls, but if you instead think you should stay in the hotel and work out any differences you might have, do it, because for the rest of the trip, I want you to be able to enjoy your friendship. Got it? I love you both. Pops.'"

I sigh and set the letter down as Hazel goes back to her seat and picks up her fork. Silently, she pierces the dumpling noodles and takes a bite. I study her the entire time, wondering if there's any resentment toward me left in her heart.

She accepted my apology so easily. If I were in her position, I don't think I would have been as forgiving as she has been.

"Hazel?"

"Hmm?"

"Do you still hold resentment toward me? I know I apologized, but anger doesn't just go away. And I know you. You laugh things off because it's easier that way, but you still take them to heart. There are always the lingering effects."

I can tell that I'm right because she grows eerily silent.

She twirls her fork around her dish now. "I just . . ." Her beautiful, light eyes connect with mine. "I don't understand how you could just ignore me. I don't know what I did wrong."

Okay, finally she's ready to dig deeper. This is what I wanted on the airplane. But now that we're alone in our hotel room, she seems more comfortable.

"You did nothing wrong, Haze. Nothing. I honestly can't give you a reason why I didn't write back. I read each letter, though. I cherished each communication."

"Was it because of what happened the last summer I saw you?" She bites her bottom lip. "I told you it was an accident. I don't know what I was thinking."

"It wasn't—"

"Crew." She gives me a pointed look. "I kissed you, and you could not run fast enough away."

Fuck.

I push my hand through my hair, remembering that moment. We were down by the horses. I'd just gotten into a fight with my dad about focusing too much on football and not taking a second to breathe. He told me I was going to regret not having fun during the few summers I had left to visit the farm, and I told him there was no way the professionals took breaks on their way up the ladder, so why should I?

I was steamed, and I needed Hazel to lighten things up.

But when I got to the barn, my fun, easy-going friend was gone, and in her place was a nervous, fidgeting girl. We were brushing Titus, one of the stallions on the farm, when I turned to Hazel for advice and she kissed me.

I was shocked, stunned. I had no idea she saw me like that. That she had any sort of romantic feelings toward me. Hence the romantic pact she drew up for us. And like the coward I am, instead of talking to her, I backed away, trying to comprehend what the hell just happened. My mind whirled, my body froze, and then I felt it . . . I felt the rapid pound in my heart, the urge to press my lips against hers. I wanted more, and that fucking terrified me, so I ran.

That was the last summer I spent at the farm.

That was the last time I remember communicating with her.

"You know, we're never going to get past it if we don't talk about it," she says quietly.

"Yeah, I know."

"So then let's talk about it." She shrugs, posing as the calm and collected one. "I kissed you. You thought I was a dragon. You ran. Okay, your turn."

"I did not think you were a dragon," I answer, guilt swimming around me like a swarm of bees ready to strike.

"Could have fooled me."

"That wasn't it at all." I grip the back of my neck, trying to figure out how I can tell her exactly what happened without making things exceedingly more uncomfortable.

"Was it because I smelled like a horse? Did I smell like a horse? Honestly, I don't even know at this point."

"You've never smelled like a horse, Haze. Always like flowers." Summer flowers in a large field. When we were in high school, I'd take a whiff when she walked past me, committing the smell to memory.

Still rambling, she says, "I mean, it wasn't my best kiss in the world, but it wasn't sprint-away worthy. There was literally fire coming out of your shoes you moved so fast."

"There wasn't fire."

"You tripped over a rock and still ran." Her brow raises.

"I was testing out my balance and ability to catch myself."

"I'm being serious, Crew," she says, annoyed.

"Are you? Because it seems as though you're cracking jokes to avoid the awkwardness, like you always do."

"Fine. You don't want the jokes? Then here's the truth. I kissed you. I was feeling something at the moment and foolishly acted on it when I shouldn't have. You ran away, things were uncomfortable after that, and then I never saw or heard from you again. So, yeah, I might be feeling a little weird toward you even if I'm trying to laugh it all off as nothing. Even if I'm trying to pretend everything is okay when it's really not." Her eyes brim with tears and she bites her lip.

Shit.

"You didn't have to run away. You could have just said you wanted to be friends, and just friends, Crew. But pushing me out of your life, that . . . that really hurt."

"Hazel." My lips press together, knowing the truth is the only way to explain this, to make her not feel dejected and worth less than what she actually is. "I wanted to kiss you back."

"What?" Her eyes grow confused.

"I did. I was shocked at first, but then I wanted to kiss you back, and that fucking terrified me. So, fight or flight kicked in, and I ran. I ran as far away as I could because I knew if I stayed around, I would have probably got lost in something I shouldn't be getting lost in. I needed to focus, to train, to keep my head straight. Much luck that did me, given how shitty I played this season, but that was still the end goal."

"I wasn't trying to distract you, Crew."

"I know."

"It was a weird, spur-of-the-moment thing, and I regret every second of it."

"Don't regret it, Hazel."

"Don't?" She raises a brow as she drops her fork and crosses her arms over her chest. "Why wouldn't I? I lost one of my best friends over it. You have no idea what it's like to grow up in a small town, Crew. You have no idea the kind of reputation my mom had around town. It's why I hung out at Pops' farm all the time, just to get away from the talk. We didn't have much, and my mom did anything she could to make money . . . everything. And everyone knew it, too. You were an outlet for me."

"I had no idea," I say, that guilt intensifying. Why didn't Pops tell me? Probably to keep Hazel separate from her mom.

"Yes, I had friends growing up, but they all knew my dirty laundry, and they all judged me for it. I was Patricia Allen's daughter, which meant the apple probably didn't fall far from the tree. The looks I got, the sneers. It was suffocating at times, but then there were the summers. Every summer there was a wave of fresh air that came to the farm and it was you."

"Hazel, I—"

"Let me finish." She takes a deep breath. "I counted on seeing you every summer, on spending lazy Sundays on the pond with you floating on innertubes. I looked forward to driving the four-wheelers in the back woods, or racing to the house for homemade pie, or even cleaning out the pigsty with you because we always made it fun. But then you took it away. You ignored me. You stopped coming. It was . . . devastating. You made me believe that I'd ruined everything we'd built."

"You didn't, Hazel. I did. This is my fault."

"Coming on this trip, I wanted it to be you who was my travel buddy. I was begging and pleading in my head for it to be you and for you to show up. Just so I could say sorry. So that I could see you and make sure that you weren't . . . repulsed by me."

A tear falls down her cheek, and I can't take it anymore. I stand from my chair and pull her from her seat as well. Hand in hand, I bring her to the bed, where I sit next to her. I cup her cheek and say, "I'm not repulsed by you, not in the slightest. To be truthful, I've always had a mini-crush on you. I mean, you're Hazel Allen, the girl who can toss a hay bale on a truck without breaking a sweat."

"It's disturbing that me heaving hay bales is a turn on." Her voice is light with humor but there's still sadness in her eyes.

"You know what I mean." I shift. "But once I felt the pressure of my future, I started to have tunnel vision. Nothing else mattered to me at the time except training and making something of myself. And, fuck, do I regret that on so many levels." I push my hand through my hair. "I hurt you. I hurt myself because I didn't have you to talk to. And I didn't . . ." My voice grows tight. "I didn't give myself those last summers with Pops, too." I let out a long sigh and place both my hands in my lap. "Fucking biggest mistake of my life so far. I can never get back that time, ever."

Hazel's hand falls to my back and she leans against my shoulder, giving me a soft hug.

"Will you forgive me, Haze?" I ask, my voice coming out pathetically sad.

"Only if you can learn to forgive yourself during this trip."

"That doesn't seem possible at this point."

"Make it possible," she says simply. "You know how to reach a goal. That's evident through your football career. Maybe in order to move forward with everything else, you're going to need to forgive yourself first."

"When did you become so wise?"

"Oh, you know, I did grow up while we weren't speaking."

"Yeah, I noticed," I say before I can stop myself.

"Was that a nod to my newfound bosom?"

"Can you not call it that?" I ask in a tired tone.

"No, it's more fun to annoy you." She nuzzles my shoulder. "Come on. I'll forgive you if you start to forgive yourself. Remember what Pops said—clean slate. This is an opportunity to reminisce, to remember, and to say goodbye. It's time that you work on your emotional health, rather than your physical." She squeezes my bicep. "Because oh boy, do you have the physical down."

I chuckle and wrap my arm around her, bringing her in close. "Okay, I'll work on it."

"Promise?"

"Promise on Funyuns."

She lifts up and looks me in the eyes seriously. "The golden promise. You better mean it."

"I wouldn't have said that if I didn't."

"Good." She stands from the bed and heads back over to the cart of food. "I'm hungry. Let's eat."

Still on the bed, I call out, "Haze?"

"Yeah?" Her fork is loaded.

"I wish I kissed you back. One of my biggest regrets."

Smiling shyly, she says, "Glad to hear it." She then winks and points to my plate. "Get to work on that food. We have some wine to drink tonight, and I can't have you acting like a lightweight because you didn't eat anything."

I walk over to the cart and take a seat. Having spent the last ten hours with Hazel has made it glaringly obvious what I've missed. She's intelligent, witty, direct, and she also knows me well. Football did become my life, but despite the friendships with the guys, there have been times I've felt alone. And I was surrounded by people. Who did Hazel have? *Pops.* The farm. Working it. Now she's worried she'll let Pops down, and she's probably had no one to talk to about it.

Munich is about reconnecting. We've such limited time here on Earth, which means you need to make the most of the moments you have together.

That's what I want to do more than anything now. Still staring at her, I add, "I couldn't imagine being on this trip with anyone else."

"Damn right, Hollywood."

Chapter Five

HAZEL

"Are you ready for this?" I ask Crew, who's finishing tying one of his boots.

Hollywood has style. On the farm, he's always dressed casually in athletic shorts and T-shirts. He wore jeans occasionally, but that was rare.

So I'm not used to seeing him dressed up like this.

Jeans that hug his hips and legs in all the right ways are cuffed just above a pair of brown boots. The jeans rest low on his hips, where his maroon shirt dances along his waistline. He paired the outfit with a gray knit cardigan and slouch beanie that hangs off his head in that sexy kind of way that Ryan Gosling can pull off.

Yup . . . he's hot.

Deathly hot.

Making-me-reconsider-my-begging-and-pleading-to-be-on-this-trip-with-him kind of hot.

"Ready." He pats his legs and stands. With a smile, he

walks over to me and tugs on one of the braids peeking out from under my white knit hat. "Your hair has gotten long."

"Grew it myself." I smile.

"All by yourself? Wow. You're quite the phenom."

I laugh and push at his stomach—his rock-hard stomach. *Gulp*. "Are you mentally prepared for this? It's twenty thousand square feet of Christmas market."

"I'm actually excited."

"Yeah?"

He nods and goes to the window, where he looks down at the market. We spent some time eating our food and getting ready. We played a few rounds of Dots and Boxes, both agreeing that we wanted to explore after the sun went down to take in the nighttime magic of the Christmas market.

Now that the sun has set, the twinkle lights down below are lit, and the large Christmas tree in the middle is sparkling with cheer; we're ready.

"Christmas was Pops' favorite holiday. You were always visiting your mom's parents but there was something about Christmas that put Pops in an unwavering good mood."

"Tell me more," I say, walking toward the door of our hotel room and strapping my purse over my shoulder like a messenger bag.

Crew pulls on his jacket and opens the door for me, and together we make our way to the elevator.

"Did you ever get to have a cookie-making day with Pops?"

"No, but I did eat a lot of the cookies he made."

"Man." Crew chuckles. "It's a big production." We get into the elevator and Crew hits the button for the lobby. "The process starts in the beginning of November."

"What? November?"

"Oh yeah. That's when he starts looking for different ways to improve the cookie selection from the year before. He had a binder full of pictures from cookies he made in years past with attached recipes and any notes he might have taken to help better the recipes the next year."

"Stop. I didn't know this."

The elevator doors part and we walk into the lobby. Berdine waves to us from the front desk and Elias holds the door open for us just as a blast of cold wind pierces us.

"Holy shit," Crew says, zipping up his coat.

I chuckle. "Do you think your California skin is going to make it in this weather?"

"No." He stuffs his hands in his pockets. "Did we fly into the artic? It wasn't this cold earlier."

"Ah, yes, that's because the sun was up. Now that it's set, it's much colder."

"I already feel the cold seeping to my dick."

I laugh out loud and say, "It's not that bad. Don't be so dramatic, or I might have to start calling you Uncle Paul."

"He'd be having a world-class fit about how cold it is if he were here."

"I don't doubt it." I slip my hand through his arm and draw my body close to his, hopefully offering him some body heat, even though he's much taller and larger than I am. Every little bit counts. "Try not to focus on the cold. Tell me more about the binder."

"Wait, which way are we supposed to go, according to the map?"

"Far left and then work our way through in a zigzag motion."

He nods and leads us to the left. "So, this binder—it was his baking bible. No one was allowed to touch it but him and there was absolutely no flash photography allowed near it."

"Oh my God. I can so see Pops saying that."

"Every Friday after Thanksgiving, Pops called me and ran through a list of possible cookies that would make the lineup for the year."

"You were that involved?"

"Oh yeah. I was his helper every year. Those butter cookies that were perfectly iced with mini chocolate chips for snowman's eyes? Those were frosted and decorated by me, with a pair of tweezers reserved for cookies only."

"Wow, Crew, I'm impressed. Did he ever let you come up with a new cookie to add to the lineup?"

"Never, and he wasn't ever sorry about it either. He made it quite clear where I stood when it came to the cookie lineup. I was there to help. My opinion was heard, but ultimately, Pops made the decisions."

We make our way down to the far left, where the very first stall is filled with homemade glass ornaments. Beautifully designed and handblown ornaments dangle from wooden pegs. The lights catch off the glass, giving the stall an enchanting ambience. I'm drawn to the ornaments and pick one up, the lightness of it surprising.

"There's no way this would make the trip back to New York," I say to Crew, who shakes his head.

"Shame though, my mom would love these. She collects glass ornaments. Her most prized possessions are her hotdog ornament collection."

"Shocking," I say sarcastically. "The McManns liking hotdogs? That's completely unheard of." I set the ornament down and slowly look over the rest. "So, when it came to your visit, did Pops put you straight to work?"

Crew nods. "Yes. He gave me the night to gain my bearings, but first thing in the morning, he was waking me up, slapping an apron on me, and pushing me toward the kitchen."

"You had aprons? Please tell me they were matching."

"Unfortunately, they weren't. Pops had a simple black apron—"

"What? That's so unlike him. I would expect a funny apron—you know, something obnoxious, or even an apron that said 'I'm making Mother Franklin D cookies.'"

Crew throws his head back and laughs. "Shit. Why didn't I ever think about making him that? That would have been an amazing Christmas gift. Maybe it was because I was so distracted that he'd wear a button-up flannel shirt and a tie to bake."

I pause on my way to the next stall and turn toward Crew. "He wore a tie to bake cookies?"

"Oh yeah. I'm telling you, he took it very seriously. He'd have the ingredients out on the counter, a lineup of the cookies to be baked and in what order to bake them on the chalkboard of the kitchen, and we were allotted a certain amount of bathroom breaks and hands were always to be washed in the kitchen as proof of proper sanitization."

"I never knew so much went into making his famous cookies."

Crew smiles sadly and slows his steps. "I didn't even think about the cookies until now. My senior year in high school was the last time I made them with him. College football doesn't lend itself to long Christmas breaks if you're actually having a good season."

"Maybe it was good then, you know, that you threw all those interceptions."

"You really know how to kick a guy when he's down."

I chuckle and bump his shoulder with mine. "You have to look at the glass as half full. A bad season isn't the end of your career. You and I both know that."

"I don't know. I could have just dug the grave of my football career." He shakes his head. "That's not something I want to talk about right now."

"Fair enough. Tell me what your least favorite cookie to make was."

We wander among stalls that sell ornaments, each specializing in a different medium. As we stroll by a stall with windowpane-like ornaments, I pause and take a look at the different designs sorted by rainbow color, all catching the light in their glass, and hung by delicate red and white strings. Some of the ornaments are square blocks with colors swirled through the middle, and then there are others that are designed to look like an object. Like a Christmas tree, snowman, nussknacker . . . a bratwurst.

"Linzer tortes," Crew says, examining one with a tree in the middle. "They were incredibly delicate and difficult to make. Lots of steps, and Pops was all about perfection. Not only did his cookies taste good, but they had to look good as well. He never allowed for a burnt edge or a cracked corner."

"It's why they were so popular on the farm. Tasty and pretty. Some might say they resemble me."

Crew sets the ornament back down and chuckles. "The pretty is obvious, the tasty—well, I can't comment."

"Such a shame," I playfully say, moving to the next stall, which is decorated in intricately carved pieces of wood. "Oh, wow, look at these." I run my hands over handcrafted cheese boards. "The wood grain is positively beautiful."

"I recall you making a cheese board for Pops once and him using it every day as a plate, not quite sure what it was."

I laugh out loud and nod. "It went over his head. Not much of a charcuterie man, but he sure did love using that board as a lunch plate. Fit his sandwich perfectly."

"Remember when he used to grumble about his grapes falling everywhere and he finally stopped taking them off the vine and instead would put the bundle on the board so they didn't roll?"

"So many presidential swear words thrown around during the grape-rolling days," I say.

We keep moving along, and the farther we walk, the more I see Crew's shoulders creep up to his ears.

"Where's your scarf?" I ask him.

"Didn't bring one."

"That wasn't very smart, was it?"

"I'm lucky I remembered a winter coat," he says.

Just then, I spot a stall selling hand-knitted items. I grab him by the hand and stand him in front of the stall. "I think it's time we buy our first souvenir." I pull down a gray knitted scarf and hold it up to him. "What do you think?"

Talking quietly, he asks, "Is it scratchy?"

I chuckle and remove one of my gloves so I can feel the yarn. "Yeah, a little."

"I'd rather be cold."

I hang it back up and pull down another gray one. This time, it feels extra soft. "Oh, this is nice."

"Yeah?"

"Mm-hmm. Very soft, and, hey, look, matching gloves. Hold up your hand." He removes his large hand from his pocket and I fit the glove over it. "Shocking. They fit."

He clutches his hand, testing out the glove, and slowly nods. "Yeah, this is nice."

"You know why booths like this exist?"

"For suckers like me?" he asks.

"Precisely." We turn toward the shop owner and hold up the scarf and gloves. "We'd like to purchase these, please," I say.

"Twenty euros," the man shouts over the noise of the crowd. What a deal. I reach into my purse, grab a twenty, and hand it over to the man.

"We don't need a bag," I say when the owner goes to hand us one. "Thank you." I give him a wave before pulling Crew to the side and putting the remaining glove on his other hand.

"You know, I'm capable of putting on my own gloves."

"Yeah, but I'm being a good friend." I place the scarf over his head and around his neck. I tuck it into the collar of his coat and then take a step back to look up at him. "Ugh."

"What?"

"Most everyone else when they wear winter gear look like puffed-up marshmallows walking around, but not you. You make winter look good."

"You flirting with me, Haze?"

"Ha, you wish. Your chance at all this is gone," I say, motioning up and down my body.

"Damn. Now I'm really regretting my choice to run away like a giant dick." He pulls on his bottom lip with his teeth, and I swear a wave of butterflies hits me hard.

It's hard not to be affected by anything Crew Smith does. He's the epitome of an All-American boy. Tall, devastatingly handsome, athletic, funny, and has no problem with being affectionate. He's been my rock for so long. He's been the boy I've measured every other man against. No one will ever be as good as Crew Smith in my eyes and my heart. And even though he puts butterflies in my stomach, it's his heart and friendship that matter more to me. Would I want to be with someone like him? Yes. But be *with* Crew? No. Our lives don't intersect naturally, and I'd hate to lose his friendship again by pushing for something that can't evolve. He was my solace. My safe haven. And I'm okay with that going forward. *Even if he's hot.*

Turning a corner, I see the base of the large Christmas tree in the middle of the market. Towering over the stalls, it reminds me of the tree in Rockefeller Plaza, minus the skating rink below. Beautifully colored in white lights, its height almost seems impossible to capture in one picture, and the soft pine branches are a wonderful contrast against the ornate architecture of the Neues Rathaus Courtyard, which is Munich's New Town Hall.

"Crew, we need to take a picture in front of the tree. Just like Pops and Gloria." From my pocket, I take out the picture Pops included in the package and show it to him. "Same backdrop, different tree. It would almost be as if we're taking the picture with him—just many, many years later."

"Let's do it."

We walk up to the tree, and thankfully there's a small line where people are patiently waiting their turn to take their picture in front of the tree. Luckily, there's a nice attendant who's managing the line and taking the pictures.

"What's that smell?" Crew says, glancing around while we wait in line.

"Nuts," the gentleman in front of us says.

"Excuse me?" I ask.

He turns and points to a stall off to the right with a sign that reads *Hot Nuts*. "Some of the best hot nuts you'll ever have," he says with an English accent. "My wife and I travel to Munich this time of the year for the Gebrannte mandeln and an annual picture in front of the tree."

"Oh, wow. Well, looks as though we need to get some nuts after this," I say.

"It's a must." The gentleman smiles kindly. "Are you two on your honeymoon?"

"Yes," I answer automatically and snuggle up to Crew. "Can you tell we're in fresh wedded bliss?"

He nods. "You have a glow about you. You picked a nice place for your honeymoon. I hope you enjoy."

"Thanks," Crew says, and there's humor in his voice.

"Ah, we're up." The man turns to the side and says, "Bella, darling, it's our turn."

From the left, a woman in a wheelchair rolls up next to him and says, "I was just talking to a lady over there about the nuts. Told her she must get some."

I chuckle as I hear the gentleman say how he just told us the same thing.

"He was nice," I say.

"So, are we going with the whole honeymoon thing now?"

"Does it offend you?" I ask, a wave of insecurity crawling up my back.

"No." He shakes his head. "Just want to make sure we're on the same page."

I shrug. "Just seems easier than explaining that we're on a

trip that your dead grandfather and my dead pseudo-grandfather planned for us while he was sick."

"Yeah, I think you might be right about that." He yawns and covers his mouth. "Shit, sorry."

"It's okay. I'm feeling tired as well. I had plans to drink all the mulled wine I came across tonight, but I have a feeling that might be a bad idea. I might pass out in the giant tree."

"I might join you. And now that you have a—as you like to call it—bosom, I could find comfort in your chest as a pillow."

"Aren't you funny." It's our turn and I tug on his hand. I hand the attendant my phone and then position us in front of the tree, hoping I have the right angle to mimic the photo of Pops and Gloria. Crew drapes his arm over my shoulder and pulls me in tight. I place my hand on his chest and, together, we smile.

The attendant takes a few pictures, and when we're done, we step aside to look at them.

I pull out the photo of Pops and Gloria and compare it to the one on my phone.

They're almost identical, besides the people in the pictures.

"This looks so good." I smile up at Crew. "This might be my new favorite thing."

"Send me that picture, will you?"

"Oh, sure, just let me try to guess your phone number."

"Wait, you don't have my phone number?" he asks, a crease to his brow.

"Nope. Just your email address. Remember? Pen pals."

"Jesus, okay." He takes my phone from my hand and sends himself a text of the picture. I have free International roaming, which will make sending photos to each other easy. "There, now you have it. Feel free to abuse it as much as you want."

"Watch what you say, Hollywood." Nodding toward the

nuts, I say, "Want to try these famous nuts? See what all the talk is about?"

"Can't say I've ever been excited to get my teeth wrapped around some nuts before today, Allen."

"YOU OKAY?" Crew asks, walking up behind me as I stare down at the Christmas market.

"I can't stop thinking about the nuts."

He chuckles, the rumble of his chest feeling like the beat of a bass drum, shaking my bones. "Want me to run down and get you some more?"

"You'd do that?" I turn to find him in nothing but athletic shorts. God, this man's chest. It's unlike anything I've seen in person, having only seen similar on the covers of health magazines and romance novels. Thick in his pecs, defined in his shoulders all the way down to this waistband. Swallowing hard, I add, "You'd go down there wearing that?"

"It would bring a new level to cold, but I do need to make shit up to you, so if Twigs wants more nuts, she can have more nuts."

"Why does it feel as though when you say nuts, you're talking about a man's balls?"

"Uh . . . because apparently you've become perverted over the last few years."

"I guess that's what happens when you lose your virginity, huh? You unlock a perverted side."

"Ah, I was perverted way before that."

I pat his chest and instantly regret it as my palm is met with rock-hard muscle. "Different for boys." In my pink silk pajama top and matching shorts, I walk over to the bed just as he snags my hand and twists me back toward him.

"Seriously, do you want the nuts?"

I chuckle. "No, I think the three bags we ate was enough."

"Because I would really go get them for you."

"I believe you, Crew. But I think I'm about two seconds from passing out."

"Me, too," he says in relief and lets go of my hand.

While I get comfortable in the bed, Crew turns off the entry light to the hotel room and locks the door. Then he walks toward the bed and I catch a glimpse of him in the light from outside. Sleepy eyes, drooped shoulders, but there's the smallest smile on his lips as he crawls into bed next to me.

I face him, and when he's settled, he faces me as well.

"Never thought I'd get Hazel Allen in bed with me, but dreams do come true."

"Might want to pinch yourself. This very well might be a dream."

He chuckles and his eyes drift shut.

"Hey, can I ask you something?" I ask with a small poke to his hand.

"Mm-hmm," he says, eyes closed.

"Are you going to pay attention or just fall asleep?"

His eyes open. "I'm listening, Haze. I'm always listening."

Well, not always, but we won't get into the blackout period again.

"Did you think we did a good enough job honoring Pops today?"

"What do you mean?"

"I just felt as though we didn't immerse ourselves into the Christmas market today. We barely got through half of it before we dragged our bodies upstairs and got ready for bed."

"Yeah, I feel a little guilty about it."

"You do?"

He nods and adjusts his hands under his pillow. "I mean, the map he wrote was intense, and I keep thinking, what if there was a clue along the way? What if there was something he wanted us to see and we didn't see it?"

"That's what I keep thinking." I nibble on my bottom lip. "Do you think we should go back out there?"

Crew thinks about it for a few seconds. "No. Do you know what I think would be best?"

"Hmm?"

"Getting sleep. We still have six more days here in Germany. Pops even said this wasn't the start of the road trip. I think we take tonight to catch up on some sleep and recharge for tomorrow."

"So we can hit the ground running?"

"Exactly. And, hey, we did do something that was very important today. We took that picture. Reading between the lines and looking back at the envelope he left us, I think he wanted us to experience something together that we'd both never done. To create new memories with him as . . . as our guide. Enjoy the atmosphere. Something so different from home, you know?"

"YEAH, I THINK YOU'RE RIGHT."

"Come here." Crew lifts up and pulls me into a hug. The side of his head presses against mine and he squeezes me tight. "I don't think we should put pressure on ourselves to make this perfect, or else we're not going to enjoy it." He pulls away and smiles at me. "Let's just have fun, make it a part of Pops and a part of us as well. Okay?"

I nod. "That sounds perfect."

We both lie back down and get comfortable. I scrunch my knees up and curl into a ball, accidentally grazing Crew in the process.

"Sorry," I mutter.

"No need to apologize. I've a feeling we're going to have to get used to sleeping in a bed together for the rest of the trip. Let's just call it like it is. We're going to bump into each other."

"As long as hands don't try to grab for a free feel again."

Crew chuckles. "It was one time."

"Yeah, and driving a truck into a ditch was one time, too."

"Uh, two completely different things. My hand grazed your boob. Your mistake had to be pulled out by a tow truck. Apples and oranges, Haze."

"They both seem like little mistakes to me."

"Of course they would." He closes his eyes. "Goodnight, Hazel."

"Night, Crew."

Chapter Six

CREW

"Come on, Crew. I'm sure your hair is perfect. We're wasting time."

I finish tousling my hair and step out of the bathroom. "I spent like a minute doing my hair, unlike you, who spent ten minutes blow-drying yours."

"If your hair was as thick and as long as mine, then yes, you'd be spending ten minutes on it."

"You never used to," I counter.

"And how do you know?" she asks, arms folded.

"Because it never looked that damn good."

Her eyes widen in surprise as her hand falls to her long locks. "Are you saying you think my hair is pretty, Crew?"

"Gorgeous, actually," I say, taking a seat next to her on the bed and snagging the "DAY TWO" envelope from her.

"Okay, winning back some brownie points."

"When did I lose them?" I ask, opening the envelope.

"When I rolled out of bed and you laughed at me. Morning appearances should be a no-judgment zone."

"Sorry." I chuckle. "But you looked like you slept in a dumpster the night before rather than our comfy bed."

"Wow, aren't you pleasant?"

"It was endearing."

"Yeah, sure sounds like it." She taps the envelope. "Just get on with it so we can move along to the next place."

"Want me to read it out loud again?"

"If it weren't for the dumpster fire comment, I would tell you that your voice adds a certain charm to the letters, but I'm going to skip that now and just say, yes, read it."

"That's fair." I take the letter out and smile. Clearing my throat, I read, "'Hey kiddos. How was the Christmas market? Spectacular, right? Oh, wait . . . let me guess, you made it to a couple of stalls and then passed out. Am I right?'"

"Oh my God, how did he know that?" Hazel whispers as if Pops is in the other room listening in on our conversation.

"Seems as though he knows us a little too well." Turning back to the letter, I continue. "'It's okay if you did. I expected that. Although, if you made it through the entire market, color me impressed. But my gut is telling me you didn't. As long as you stopped by the Christmas tree and took a picture.'" Hazel squeezes my arm and I know she's feeling just as relieved as I am. "'I hope you got some sleep last night, because this is where the trip picks up. Today you're headed to one of my favorite places in Germany during the holiday season: Nuremberg.'"

"Sounds exciting," Hazel says, leaning into me.

"'Nuremberg not only has one of the most enchanting Christmas markets you'll ever visit, but it's also widely known for its gingerbread. Word on the street is, when you think of Christmas in Germany, you think of Nuremberg Lebkuchen —their gingerbread. And we're not talking about the stale gingerbread recipe I never seemed to be able to master. This is different. It's nutty and full of spices and flavors that will keep you coming back for more. Every Christmas, before my dear Gloria passed away, she had some Nuremberg Lebkuchen shipped to the house. It was a staple of our holiday for a long time. Now, I would love for it to become a staple of your holiday. But instead of buying it, you're going to learn how to make it.'"

"What?" Hazel says, excited. "We're making gingerbread?"

Continuing with the letter, I read, "'The bakery is expecting you. It's the small hole-in-the-wall bakery where we purchased our gingerbread every year. They know you're coming today. Do me a favor and learn from the unique experience, so when you have children or grandchildren of your own, you're not swearing up Ronald Reagan's name in the kitchen with every burnt or foul-tasting piece of gingerbread you attempt to make.'"

I laugh as tears spring to my eyes. Shit. I miss him.

I take a deep breath and Hazel quickly wraps her arm around my waist.

"Sorry."

"Don't apologize. I get it. Feel free to cry anytime you want."

I chuckle lightly. "I'll attempt to keep it together." Going back to the letter, I continue to read. "'After that, I expect you to check in with the hotel and then get ready to spend your evening at the Christmas market, and this time, no clocking out early. Eat some gingerbread, get a bratwurst, drink the wine . . . literally, drink the wine. Enjoy the music and, before you retire for the night, make your way to the Schöner Brunnen. The fountain is a rather large statue wrapped in gold and protected by an impressively built iron fence. But off to the side, in the fence, there are two bronze rings dangling from the iron. Legend has it that it's good luck to spin the brass rings. I spun them with my Gloria when we were in Germany, and I'd say I was a very blessed man through my lifetime. I can only hope the same for the both of you. Give it a spin and know that I'm there with you in that moment. Addresses that you'll need and hotel information is attached. Have fun. Love you both. Pops.'"

I rest the letter on my lap as Hazel grabs her phone and opens up her directions app. She types in Nuremberg. "Two-and-a-half-hour drive. Think you can handle it?"

"You're not driving."

"I wasn't going to suggest it."

"Liar." I playfully push her back on the bed and then get up, taking the note and sticking it in my backpack carefully, where the other notes and maps are.

"It's not nice to push. Didn't you learn that when you were younger?" Hazel comes up next to me and bumps me with her hip. I don't even move. "God, that's frustrating."

"That you can't move me?"

"Yeah." She turns toward me and gestures with her hands, "Face me."

"Face you?"

"Yes, face me."

Confused, I turn toward her, only for her to place her hands on my chest and start pushing, digging her feet into the brown hotel carpet.

I don't move an inch.

"What are you, made of stone?"

"Pretty much." I pat the top of her head and then set her upright. "Looks like you need to throw more hay bales."

"Apparently." She takes a deep breath and then says, "Are you ready to spend two-and-a-half hours in the car with me?"

"Depends." I shoulder my backpack and take out the handle to my suitcase. "What's on your playlist?"

"Good music."

"Yeah?" I raise a brow at her.

"Really good music." She winks. "Anticipating such a

moment and knowing the importance of music during a road trip, I made a playlist. I made two, actually."

"Two? That's dedication."

She blushes and says, "Well, I did two because I wasn't one hundred percent sure of who I would be traveling with. So, I made a generic one with classic road trip songs, and the other, well, the other is more for you and me."

"You made a playlist just for us?"

"Yeah."

"Well, then." I move closer to her, those innocent eyes cutting me deep, and I say, "Let's get going so I can hear this playlist."

"OH, SWEET JESUS, THESE ARE GOOD," Hazel says, humming over a German *puddingbrezels* we picked up from one of the stalls outside of the hotel. Berdine told us before we left that we had to grab one for the road. Being that we're going with the flow, we bought a few, along with a cup of *heiße schokolade*, also known as hot chocolate. We learned that it's not made from a powder or a mix, but rather an actual chocolate bar melted in milk. Hazel couldn't order fast enough.

Still familiarizing myself with the car, I pick one up from the box and take a bite, ready to put it back down, but think twice when the flavors hit my tongue. Driving can wait. I need to eat this now.

"Holy shit, they *are* good."

"Dare I even try the hot chocolate? The guy said there's an entire chocolate bar inside. I'm not sure you're ready for Sugar High Hazel."

I laugh. "As long as you don't turn into, as you like to call it, Sicky Belly Hazel from eating too much sugar."

"I can't be held accountable for what happens today with my consumption of food. If later you find yourself lying next to me on our new bed, rubbing my stomach while I cry tears of sugar, then so be it." She takes another hefty bite of her *pudding-brezel* and moans softly. "I really think I might start crying now."

"I might drop the whole football thing and go for food-and-travel blogger instead." I take another bite of the *pudding-brezel*, savoring the flavors.

"I think I'll join you in that endeavor. We could pitch a show to the Travel Channel. Who wouldn't want to watch Hazel and Crew travel the world?"

"Crew and Hazel," I correct her, putting my name first. "My idea, after all."

"Ugh, don't be that guy." She takes a sip of the hot chocolate and her eyes widen in surprise. She lets out a long, drawn-out moan.

"You know, the moaning doesn't have to be part of the eating process."

"Are you insane? Of course it does. That's how you express how great something is . . . you know, like sex." She grants me a beaming smile, and I just shake my head.

"That's exactly why you shouldn't be moaning."

She licks some of the pudding out of the pastry and asks, "Are you getting turned on, Crew?"

"Why did I know you were going to go there? Oh yeah, you've turned into a pervert."

Arms spread as far as she can in our small car, she says, "This is how I am. Take it or leave it."

I pick up the hot chocolate as well, and before sipping, I say, "I guess I'll take you as I can get you, and that's only because I've missed this—missed us."

"I've missed us too." She smirks and then we both clink our cups.

Together we sip and then . . . moan.

Shit, this is really fucking good.

She eyes me over her cup. "See? It's totally moan-worthy,

but you don't seem ready to pull my pants off and bang it out."

"Why are you the way you are?" I ask.

She pauses, giving it some thought. "Honestly, I think I spent too much time with the chickens. The hens chip-chirping all the time does something to your conscience."

I shove the rest of the *puddingbrezel* in my mouth before starting the car. Once I chew and swallow, I say, "At least you can recognize where the issue might have stemmed from." I nod toward the radio. "Hook us up with some tunes, Haze. We've some road to cover."

WHEN HAZEL SAID she made us a playlist, she wasn't kidding. Back in high school, we used to send each other emails that consisted of songs we needed to listen to. Hazel tended to drift toward Indie music I'd never heard of, whereas I would pull up oldies that my mom and dad always played on Sundays when we'd clean the house together as a family. I was the only kid in my school who spent Sundays cleaning. Everyone else had a cleaning service that cleaned their house every week. Even though Mom and Dad easily have the money, they always kept things "normal" with me. They said I would thank them later.

Haven't found that gratefulness for dusting just yet.

"I can't get enough of his voice," Hazel says. She pulled her legs up to her chest earlier on in the car trip and has kept them there ever since. She's small enough and flexible enough to fit curled up on the seat. I would look like a buffoon if I tried to mimic her position. As it is, my chair almost hits the backseat, it's pushed so far back.

"I remember the first time you sent me a Lumineers song. I was skeptical initially since it was once again another band

I'd never heard of before, but the moment I heard Wesley Schultz's voice, I was sold."

"I had such a big crush on him."

"Really?"

"Oh yeah." She nods as the melodic sound of one of my favorite songs by the Lumineers, "Nobody Knows," plays in the background. "It's the voice that captured me."

"Did you have a poster of him on your wall?" I ask, and then something strikes me. "You know, I've never seen your room, actually. Isn't that kind of weird?"

From the corner of my eyes, I catch her shake her head. "No, it was planned that way. Mom and I didn't have much when it came to a home, and I actually slept in a blanketed-off section that was supposed to be a dining room. I never had anyone over."

"What? Seriously? Did Pops know?"

She nods. "Oh yeah. He tried to get my mom and me to live with him quite a few times. Grandpa Thomas—my dad's dad—didn't have any room for us in his cabin, or else he'd have helped us out. Mom wouldn't take Pops's help because she didn't ever want to take charity. There were a few nights, though, when Pops would have me stay the night because I was working late. Those were my favorite nights, because I felt such comfort in the bed—" Her words stop short and I can see her start to retreat.

"Feel comfort in what?"

"Nothing." She shakes her head. "It's stupid."

"No, it's not. What did you feel comfort in?"

"It's going to sound really stalkerish."

"Try me," I say.

Sighing, she says, "Felt comfort in knowing it was the same bed you slept in when you were visiting."

"How is that stalkerish? I mean, unless you were trying to smell the pillow to find any sort of essence I might have left behind."

"Don't be an asshole."

I laugh and nudge her leg. "Seriously, though, you said it yourself—I was a comfort to you, especially during the summer. Why wouldn't you want to cling to that, especially when you were going through a lot of shit at home?"

"I know but saying it out loud feels creepy."

I reach over the console between us and take her hand in mine, lacing our fingers together. "It's not creepy, Haze. It makes sense."

"Thanks for getting me."

"No need to thank me. We've gotten each other for years." Instead of removing my hand from hers, I continue to hold it, not just because I want to, but because I feel as though she needs it right now.

I came into this trip thinking I was the only one needing to find acceptance with losing Pops, but it seems we both have to accept his passing, but in different ways. Pops was my cheerleader, my inspiration, my guiding light. A best friend.

But to Hazel, he was more than just a second grandfather—he was a safe place, a shelter, someone she could rely on when things got hard. And from listening to her on this trip, it seems as though things were hard often.

Which brings me to think . . .

"What are you doing now?"

"Uh, sitting here, listening to the Lumineers."

"No, I mean, on the farm, in life. What are you doing? Are you still living with your mom?"

She grows silent and I glance her direction to catch her looking out the window. She slowly lets go of my hand and shifts in her seat.

"Um, right now, things are kind of hard."

"What do you mean?" When she doesn't answer right away, I say, "You can talk to me, Hazel."

"I know. It's just hard to talk about, is all." She takes a deep breath. "Around June, Pops asked me to go to the house in the morning to have a conversation about the farm. I thought it was going to be about the upcoming fall season. But that's when he told me he was sick with pancreatic cancer. Stage four." She grows silent again and I can hear her sniffle. "I wasn't expecting it. I had no idea he was even sick. I felt stupid for not recognizing the signs and overwhelmed with what was going to happen to the mini empire he'd built with the farm."

"I can't believe he told you and not me."

"He didn't want to ruin your season," she says softly. "At least, that's what he told me."

Well, it was ruined anyway.

Continuing, she says, "He brought me in to talk because he wanted me to start taking over operations. He then asked me to take up the guest room as well, to help him around the house."

"You helped him while he was sick?"

"Yeah," she says softly.

Hell. Hearing that, knowing that she was making things easier on Pops during his final days, it changes something in me, almost as if I'm seeing Hazel in a completely different light, and it's confusing and alarming, all at the same time. *If I'd kept in contact, would she have told me? Even though Pops hadn't wanted me to know? Would Hazel have given me the chance to say goodbye to him?*

I clear my throat. "So, is that where you've been staying?"

"It is. I'm not sure for how long, though. Grandpa Thomas said things might be changing when I get back from the trip and after the New Year. He wasn't quite sure since Pops left a will, but he hasn't heard any details yet. Not sure if they plan on selling or leaving the farm to your mom. I started thinking about what I was going to do for a job, you know?"

"If the farm is left to my mom or Uncle Paul, you know they would never make you get a new job."

"Maybe not, but I can't count on it. I've been working

pretty hard on woodworking, which has always been a passion of mine. But that doesn't make a lot of money—"

"Wait, you're into woodworking? You made that charcuterie board for Pops. You made more?"

"Yup."

"When . . . oh, let me guess. Something you learned while I wasn't talking to you?"

"Had to keep my wandering mind busy with something. Do you know those wooden bowls your mom got from Pops last year?"

"You made those?"

"Yeah. Took me forever, and Pops definitely overpaid, but, yeah, I made them."

"Hazel, those are my favorite bowls. They're my popcorn bowls." I laugh.

"Well, looks as though I'm going to have to make you some for when you become a big football player. You can eat popcorn and remember the simple days."

"Not sure I'm going to be a big football player."

"One season isn't—"

"No, I'm not sure if it's what I want now."

"What do you mean?" she asks, shifting toward me now and turning down the music. "You've worked so hard, Crew. Why wouldn't you pursue it?"

"I don't know. This past season didn't feel right, and with Pops gone, it doesn't feel the same. You know, it was his dream first and it quickly became mine. But with him no longer with us, it almost feels making it pro doesn't even matter anymore."

"What would you do if you didn't go pro?"

"That's the problem. I've no idea. All I've known is football, so I'm not quite sure what I would do other than that."

"When is the combine?"

"February."

"Oh, I didn't realize it was that soon."

"Yeah, it is." I sigh, thinking about how soon it really is.

"Well, you'll have some time. But I'm guessing that's not something you want to talk about right now."

"Not really."

"So, then tell me something about yourself that I missed these past few years. Something funny. We need to recharge the mood in here. It slipped into Depressedville and we're supposed to be celebrating, right?"

"You're right." I shake out my shoulders, keeping my eyes on the straight road in front of me. Something that's been surprising is how normal it looks here. I half expected to be driving down some medieval highway, but it looks like anything I would find in upstate New York, with snow banks and leafless trees on either side of the Autobahn. "Okay, something funny. You probably want embarrassing."

"Embarrassing would be ideal. Utterly humiliating would be absolutely perfect."

"Well besides my final season—"

"Enough with the season. You sucked; we get it."

I laugh. "Okay, okay, no need to get angry. Hmm, embarrassing. Let me think on it for a second. You know, it's hard to think something up because I'm so perfect."

"Perfect, huh? What about that season?"

"I thought we weren't talking about it."

"Just tugging you out of the clouds, Hollywood," she says with humor.

"Always there to ground me. I wouldn't expect anything less."

"So . . . embarrassing story."

"Yes, okay. Uh . . ." My mind goes through a reel of memories as I try to think of the perfect story, and then it hits me, and I start laughing. "Oh, shit. I have the perfect story for you. It might be too perfect."

Hazel rubs her hands together. "Oh, I'm here for it. Whatever it is, I'm here for it."

"Okay, but this has to stay between us. You can't tell my parents. They would never let me live it down."

"That good, huh? Okay." She holds out her pinky. "Promise I won't say anything."

Like old times, I hook my pinky with hers and we shake on it.

"It was my sophomore year in college, right after the season was over. At that point, everyone on campus knew who I was. My buddies, River and Hollis, thought it would be a good idea to hit up our favorite bar in town—it's called The Truth is Out There—to celebrate. And normally, yes, this would have been a good idea."

"Why wasn't it a good idea this time?"

"I'm in a fraternity with River and Hollis, and one of our frat brothers was a baker. A really good baker. Well, we were at the house pre-gaming and he showed up with a batch of brownies for the crowd."

"Uh-oh . . ."

"Yeah, 'uh-oh' was right. I was high as a fucking kite that night and didn't realize it until the next day. The brownies tasted normal, really fudgy actually. I had three."

"You had three?"

"The season was over, I was letting loose, and, like I mentioned, they were really fucking good."

"So, you were high at the bar. Is that the end of the story?"

"Fuck, I wish it was." I chuckle some more. "And honestly, the only reason I know this happened is because River and Hollis grabbed video of it on their phones. Don't ask me how it happened or why, but I wound up wearing nothing but a pair of boxer briefs with little footballs on them."

"Football boxer briefs? Of course you'd wear those. So douchey."

"Hey, my mom got them for me."

"Of course she did." Hazel chuckles.

"Do you want to hear the rest of the story?"

"Yes, sorry. Please continue."

Huffing, I grip the steering wheel and say, "So, I don't know how I ended up in nothing but boxer briefs and socks, but there I was on the bar, thrusting my pelvis into the air while 'We Didn't Start the Fire' played in the background."

"Stop. Please tell me you were singing."

"So off-key, you could hear dogs howl in the background. But that wasn't the worst part."

"No? Oh, please tell me the worst part."

"So, this bar, it's X-Files themed, and they have . . . paraphernalia all around. You know, like UFOs and aliens and shit like that? Well, there was this alien head that was on the top shelf of the bar. I decided that it was my time to wear it."

"Did you fall and break all the alcohol?"

"No, that would have been better, I think. I grabbed the alien head, put it on my head, and then proceeded to take the soda gun from the bartender, drop down to my knees, and shower myself in Sprite. And when I say shower, I mean I lifted the waistband of my boxer briefs and drenched my dick in Sprite while shaking my head back and forth."

"Oh my God . . . does this video still exist? Because I'm going to need to see that."

"I'm sure River and Hollis both have it saved on their clouds."

"When we get to Nuremberg, you're going to need to text them."

"For you, I would do it."

"Damn right," she says with humor.

CREW: *Do you have the video of me at the bar with the alien head?*

River: *I have it saved on my cloud and in my Google drive.*

Hollis: *I made multiple copies on a thumb drive and secured it in a safety deposit box at five different banks.*

Crew: *Can one of you send it to me?*

River: *Why would you need that video? Are you losing it, man?*

Crew: *Hazel wants to see it.*

Hollis: *Hold up. Who's Hazel?*

River: *Hazel sounds like a girl name. Are you in Germany with a girl?*

Crew: *She's one of my best friends from my childhood. She was very close to Pops. He sent us on the trip together.*

Hollis: *Sounds like a love connection to me.*

River: *Your pops is totally setting you up.*

Crew: *It's not like that. We're friends. Good friends. Friends that have to share a bed.*

River: *They're totally going to fuck.*

Hollis: *Yup.*

Crew: *We are not going to fuck.*

River: *Is she hot?*

Crew: *What does that matter?*

Hollis: *It doesn't, but it'll help us understand the timeline of when you'll fuck.*

River: *He's right.*

Crew: *I'm not answering that.*

Hollis: *Shit, she's hot.*

River: *Really hot. I give it two days.*

Hollis: *I would consider that an accurate guess.*

Crew: *Just send me the damn video.*

River: *Sure, but if you're thinking this video will impress her, you're wrong.*

Crew: *I'm not trying to impress her.*

Hollis: *Oh, I get it. He's trying to repel her so he doesn't slip up and try to have sex with her. If she thinks he's a fool, then there's no chance she'll give in to his advances.*

River: *Smart move. The video acting as woman repellant is clever.*

Crew: *Just fucking send it.*

River: *Cool your dick, man. Finding it now.*

Hollis: *River's angle is better, but if she wants an angle of your back, let me know. I'll send mine.*

Crew: *You're such good friends. Sarcasm.*

River: *We know you love us.*

Hollis: *Kisses, boo bear.*

Crew: *<Middle finger emoji>*

"ARE you sure this is the way we go?" Hazel asks, clinging to me.

"Nope." I laugh. "Honestly, I've no idea where we are."

"Hole-on-the-wall bakery was right."

"I think we missed a turn back there. The man at the hotel said if we saw the shoe repair shop, we went too far." I point ahead of me. "I think that's a shoe repair shop."

"Well, it has shoes in it so I guess you'd be right. Honestly, I've never seen a shoe repair shop in person. This is going to sound awful, but I feel as if we're in EPCOT. The music playing in the far distance, the quaint shops, and half-timbered houses with intricate detailing. It's throwing me off."

I turn us both around and head back down the narrow street. "You're not alone in that thought. I was thinking the same thing. They really did pull all the details, but it makes me feel as though it isn't real here."

"Agreed. Walt Disney is distorting our image."

"Damn him." I laugh, and when we reach the fork in the road again, we take the other route, and that's when I see the bakery. "There it is. Remember? They said there would be a maroon wooden sign hanging over the door."

"Yes." She stops me and faces me. "Before we go in there, can I ask you something?" She's serious, which puts me on edge immediately.

"Sure."

She takes my hand in hers and looks up at me, those endearing eyes connecting with mine. "Did your friends send the video?"

"Jesus," I say, laughing and pulling my hand away. "I thought you were going to ask something serious."

"This is serious. We're talking about a video of you shooting Sprite down your crotch."

I roll my eyes. "They sent the video."

"Really?" She lights up and bounces up and down. "Let me see it."

"No. This isn't the time. I'm saving it for later."

"Crew, come on." She tugs on my arm. "I can't wait until later. I'm impatient. You know this. Just show me now and then we can focus on the gingerbread."

I reach out and pinch her chin. "Let's work on patience today, huh?" I wrap my arm around her shoulder and lead her toward the bakery. "Just think how much fun it'll be to eat gingerbread in our hotel room while watching the video over and over again."

"That does sound appealing."

"And you'll be able to turn the volume all the way up, which totally adds to the experience."

"Ugh, I hate that you're right."

I give her a squeeze.

"Fine, we shall wait. But I'm warning you—if that video isn't the first thing I see when we hit our hotel room, I'm not going to be pleased."

"Hazel not pleased? Well, we wouldn't want that." I open the door for her and we both walk into the tiny bakery. The walls are old wood slats, both rustic and charming, and the floor is made up of stone pavers. There's a single bakery case in front of us full of gingerbread, but not the kind I'm used to. Instead of the little men and women with the hard royal icing decorating their outline, what's in the case are round, dome-like cookies. Some have what looks to be chocolate glaze on them, some with nuts decorating the top, and some with powdered sugar.

"Oh my God, it smells amazing in here," Hazel says just as an old woman walks through an archway that leads to the back of the shop. She's wearing a white apron over a dress with burnt-orange, puffy sleeves that complement the fiery hue of her hair.

"Hallo. Kann ich Ihnen helfen?" She waves with a small bob of her head.

"Ah, hallo. Hello," I say, placing my hand on Hazel's back. "I'm Crew Smith and this is Hazel Allen. I believe we're supposed to have a baking lesson with you today?"

"Ja. Stunde." She nods and waves for us to join her as she trails into the back of the bakery.

Hazel gives me a look over her shoulder and I shrug my shoulders. "I think we're supposed to follow her."

"I gathered that, but what if there's some nefarious slaughterhouse in the back? I'm not ready to end my life, are you?"

"You really think there's a slaughterhouse in the back?"

"I mean, it does smell pretty potently of gingerbread in here. Maybe they're using the smell to cover something up."

"You're being ridiculous." I push her along, and we file through the archway toward the back, Hazel first, because, you know, just in case something does happen, she'd be the first to go.

What a gentleman, right?

When we reach the back, we're welcomed by the old woman, who is sitting at a table with bowls and several ingredients in front of her. Next to her is another fair-skinned woman, wearing the same outfit and almost the spitting image of the woman next to her, but younger.

"Welcome. My name is Petra, and this is my mama, Monika. We've been expecting you."

"Petra, it's nice to meet you," I say, waving awkwardly. "I'm Crew, and this is Hazel."

"Hi," Hazel says, giving the back kitchen a smooth once-over.

It almost feels as though we've stepped back into the world of *Lord of the Rings*, and we're in a Hobbit-hole. The walls are made of clay, and large wooden beams span the ceiling. There are a few ovens off to the right, but they're not the typical ovens you'd find in America; instead, they're clay ovens, big enough to hold a few cookie sheets. I know this because there are cookies baking in them right now. It's so far from anything I ever expected that I'm starting to feel the energy of Pops. He'd have loved this.

Hell, maybe he did. Did he say he visited here? Now I can't remember. Maybe this is where his love of baking cookies came from. That would make sense as to why he sent us both here.

"It smells so good in here," Hazel says. "I don't know if it's good being here as I might eat all of the cookies."

Petra laughs. "Have as much as you want, and take home as much as you want, as well. But before we eat, I think we should learn how to make the cookies first, ja?"

"Yes, we'd love that," I say.

"You will have to excuse my mother. She doesn't speak much English, so if she seems quiet, it's because she either might not understand you or she's just trying to konzentrieren . . . ah focus on understanding the language as you speak it." Pointing behind us, Petra continues, "There is a sink behind you where you can wash up, and I will grab you some aprons while you do that."

We turn around to find a cast-iron sink carved into wood countertops, and below it, and instead of cabinet drawers, there's a red-and-white checkered curtain covering up the pipes.

"This place is so cute," Hazel says quietly.

I whisper, "See? No slaughterhouse."

She playfully elbows me, and we wash our hands. When we're done, we're greeted by Petra holding up two frilly white aprons. She smiles and says, "Hope you don't mind, Crew."

"Nah, I'm manly enough to wear this and rock it." I take the apron from her and drape it over my neck, only to find out that I'm far too tall and large for the apron, so instead of it somewhat fitting, it actually looks like I'm wearing an apron made for a child.

Hazel catches sight of me and is barely stifling a laugh. "Oh, we're going to need a picture together."

"Do I look pretty?" I ask with a curtsy.

"The prettiest in all the land." Hazel digs her phone out of her purse and asks Petra, "Could you please take a picture of us? This is a moment I want to capture forever."

"And use as . . . eh, blackmail?" Petra asks.

"Oh, yes. Very much so." Petra and Hazel laugh together. I really don't mind, because seeing that smile on Hazel's face, genuine and happy, makes me okay with being the butt of the joke.

Petra holds the phone up and takes a few pictures. When Petra hands the phone back, Hazel doesn't check the pictures, but instead puts her phone away and steps up to the worn wooden table in the center of the room.

Rubbing her hands together, Hazel says, "I'm excited. Let's make some Lebkuchen."

"Ah, you said it rather perfectly."

"Thank you. I was practicing on the drive."

"She was," I say, my eyes widening. "I'm pretty sure I'll be saying Lebkuchen in my head for the next few days."

"It's a good word to know, especially in Nuremberg, where we are known for our Lebkuchen." Petra reaches out and hands us a bowl. "You two can work together while I will work with my mama on an orange cardamom batch. Don't worry, you'll be making a traditional batch."

"Wonderful," Hazel says.

Monika starts moving around, picking up different types of jars, while Petra does all the talking. "Now, something you need to know before we get started is you're about to bake a miracle cookie."

"Miracle cookie? Really?" Hazel asks.

Monika starts placing jars and spices in front of us, as well as measuring spoons and cups.

"Yes. You see, back in 1720, it's believed, one of the master bakers of Nuremberg had a daughter who fell incredibly ill. No doctor around could cure her. Desperate to save her, he baked a secret Lebkuchen recipe that contained not one sprinkle of flour, but instead he loaded it with ground hazelnut and spices."

"Did it cure her?" Hazel asks, hands clasped together.

Petra smiles. "It did. The baker named the recipe after his daughter Elisabeth and called it Elisenlebkuchen. To this day, you can only call your Lebkuchen Elisenlebkuchen if there is less than ten percent flour in the recipe, and that is the law."

"Really?" I ask.

Petra nods. "*Ja*. It's the mixture of nuts and spices that pulls the cookie together, and the modern Lebkuchen has taken on more flour for a stable hold. But here, in our bakery, we stick to less than ten percent flour, sometimes none at all, by using ground hazelnuts and almonds in its place, offering a very rich and nutty flavor to our Lebkuchen."

"Is that what we'll be making?" Hazel asks.

Petra nods. "We don't make anything else in here. We use our base ingredients and then add what's necessary to change the flavors."

"What's your most popular flavor?" I ask.

"The *Elisenlebkuchen*," Petra answers. "And that's because no one else can make it like us." She smiles, and I love how much pride she takes in their quaint bakery. She claps her hands together and says, "Let's get started. In front of you,

you have a combination of walnuts, hazelnuts, and almonds all ground together. We'll keep the exact ratios to ourselves. We have to keep some things secret." She winks.

"Smart businesswoman," I say.

"And then we have a combination of spices—we'll keep the ratio for that to ourselves as well—but in the jar, if you give it a sniff, you'll hopefully detect some cloves, cardamom, ginger, coriander, allspice, and fennel."

Hazel opens the small jar and we both give it a sniff. "Oh, wow. That smells like Christmas in a jar," Hazel says, bringing it up to her nose again.

Petra laughs and repeats what Hazel said in German. Monika smiles and says, "*Ja*. Christmas."

"And then the rest of the ingredients, which are quite important, are candied orange, citrus peel, and honey. And then of course a few other things. Are you ready to bake?"

"We are," Hazel says, smiling up at me. I smile back, and I swear, I can feel Pops here with us, leaning over my shoulder, watching intently. *He'd be saying, "Don't Harry Truman stuff up."*

As Petra guides us through the steps of adding ingredients and mixing, I say, "My pops tried to make the American version of gingerbread cookies and failed miserably every time. This, though—I think he could have handled this."

"Easily," Hazel says as she stirs the mixture together.

Petra moves to the back of the kitchen and then brings out some metal tools. The only way to describe them are a metal pedestal with a place for your hand to grip under a flat surface and then a flat "shaper."

"These will help you shape the Lebkuchen into their famous dome shapes. Watch Mama as she demonstrates the perfect technique." We turn to Monika, who's sitting on a stool and gracefully working in peace. "Observe carefully and do what she is doing."

The room falls silent except for the soft sound of Monika working the dough into a dome, the metal of the shapers clattering in a soothing manner. She's smooth in her movements, purposeful, and it only takes her a few seconds to shape each one, but you can tell she cares about every single cookie.

In silence, Hazel and I attempt the same motions as Monika. Hazel magically gets it before me. Her cookies are smooth on the edge, sticking to the paper placed on the metal shaper. She's a pro. When I can't seem to figure out the right angle, Hazel lends a hand and helps guide me. Despite feeling both Monika and Petra watching us carefully, I allow myself to fall into the moment and the gentle touch of Hazel's hands.

"Yes, like that," she says softly, her hands on top of mine. "Smooth it out right there. Perfect."

"Thanks," I say as our eyes connect, the moment slowing down to a snail's pace as the corner of her lips turn up. Happiness reflects in her eyes and, fuck, my stomach releases a swarm of butterflies I was never expecting.

Yeah, Hazel has always been beautiful. She's always had a certain charm that, now that I think about it, I've looked for in other girls but never found. But in this moment, there's something more, something I can't quite put my finger on, but it makes me want to live in this moment forever, to savor it. To memorize the way her dainty but calloused hands eclipse mine, or the way her lithe body presses into my side, or the smell of her sweet perfume that I know she only saves for special occasions. This moment feels magical, almost as if something is starting to bloom. Something new and exciting. Something—

"Wo man Liebe sät, da wächst freude," Monika says, looking at the both of us.

Petra grips her mom's shoulder and says, "Das stimmt, Mama."

With the back of her hand, Hazel pushes a stray hair behind her ear and says, "Can I ask what she said?"

Monika nods and Petra translates for us. "'When you sow

love, joy will grow.' Mama sees something special in you two. As do I."

Unsure of what to say, I smile, because honestly, that's all I can do right now when it feels as though my heart is wildly trying to beat out of my chest.

When you sow love . . . joy will grow.

Is that what's happening right now? The love Hazel and I have for each other, not necessarily romantic love, but love for each other as friends, are we growing it back together, from the tear I put in it?

Thinking over the last forty-eight hours, I would have to agree. That's exactly what we're doing, and from the smile on Hazel's face, I'm comfortable saying our joy is growing.

Chapter Seven

HAZEL

"What are you doing?" Crew walks up to me and pats my stomach right before catapulting his large body on our bed that I'm lying flat on. As if we're on a trampoline, I bounce up and down from the impact of his weight.

"Thinking about what a peaceful life Monika and Petra must have. They seemed so content, didn't they?"

"They did," Crew says, turning toward me.

While the Lebkuchen baked, we sat with Monika and Petra and asked them questions about their life, the family traditions of their bakery, and they even spoke about Pops and how they enjoyed sending their cookies all the way to America. Once the Lebkuchen was done, we let them cool and delighted in eating a few. It was such a pleasant way to spend an afternoon that I feel enriched, as if instead of just feeding my stomach, I feel like I fed my soul as well.

When it was time to go, we packaged up our Lebkuchen, and they offered us a few other flavors that we took with us graciously. There was no way in hell we were about to turn down more of the delightful treats.

I turn toward Crew and look at him. "Think you'll ever find that kind of happiness in your life?"

"I don't know," he answers. "I hope so, but given how things are right now, I'm not entirely sure what *would* make me happy. I don't even know if I've been happy for a while. Even though we've only been here for two days, I'm starting to realize that I've been going through the motions of life rather than living it."

"What brought you to that realization?" I ask.

He smirks and reaches out, tucking a piece of hair behind my ear. The gesture is sweet . . . comforting. Being around Crew again is soothing, as though with him next to me, all my worries are slowly starting to float away, and it's just me and him like it used to be. And that scares me, because I don't know what's going to happen after this trip, when we go our separate ways. Is he going to stay in touch with me? Or will he forget about me again when he returns to bigger and better things? The thought of not talking to him for years fills my stomach with a sick feeling, especially when he's looking at me like he is right now.

With love.

With affection.

With tenderness.

"Being here," he answers. "I don't think I've laughed like I have since being here in a long time. There's this lightness in my shoulders, like I'm not carrying the weight of the world on them. I feel free."

"You don't think it's all the Lebkuchen that's making you feel that way?"

He chuckles. "Maybe. Since I'm on such a strict diet during the season, all the sugar might be sending me into a high." Nodding slightly, he says, "What about you, Haze? Are you content?"

"Right now, I believe that I am."

"So that means you plan on drinking with me tonight?"

"I mean, it's required, isn't it? According to Pops, we have to let loose?"

"I believe so." He reaches out and rests his hand on my hip, his palm warming the left side of my body with just one touch. "But I think I need one of those bratwursts wrapped in a pretzel before I drink anything."

"You saw that stall, too?" I ask, excited. "When we were walking to the bakery, I made a mental note to make sure I read that correctly. Pretzel-wrapped bratwurst."

"Yup." He nods. "I need it."

"Then let's get going." I sit up and so does Crew. When he stands, he takes me by the hand and pulls me up off the bed into a hug. "What's this for?" I ask, my cheek resting against his chest.

"Just catching up on lost time." He lets go and then pushes me back on the bed so I'm flat against the mattress again. "Let's go, Twigs."

"Ugh, you're such an ass," I say while standing up.

He laughs, throwing his new scarf around his neck and then zipping up his jacket. I join him, punching my arms through the sleeves of my jacket, and when I'm set, he reaches out and takes me by the hand. "Off to the market."

Hand in hand, we head out of our hotel room and into the cold, Christmas-filled air.

"Oh wow," I whisper in awe. This place is incredible. The intricate detail on the ancient buildings, the square lit with bright, twinkly lights that illuminate the sweet red-and-white candy-cane-striped roofs of every stall in the market. *It's magical.* The Church of Our Lady serves as the backdrop of the charming town, while string bulbs travel from tall stake to tall stake, creating an ethereal border along the edge of the Marktplatz. At the front desk we were told that Nuremburg is known as Christmas Town, and I can see why now.

It's an enchanting ambiance where you can practically taste the joy in the air.

"I just got a huge smile on my face," I say in a whisper.

"Me, too." Still holding my hand, Crew weaves me through a small crowd gathering near a beer stall and straight to the bratwurst stall, where he orders us each a bratwurst pretzel. Instead of talking while we wait for our food to be ready, we take in this remarkable city. The sound of Christmas melodies being played by a live band in the background, the laughter of children as they needle their way through the crowd of adults, and the comradery coming from those who have dipped their wallets into several cups of wine.

When our brats are done, Crew takes both of them and nods toward a mulled wine booth. "Want to get a souvenir cup?"

I look over at the stall and see that there's a ceramic mug, designed especially for the Christkindlesmarkt. A combination of a beer stein and a coffee mug, it sports a wonderfully illustrated depiction of the market in all its Christmas glory, and all I can think of is if I don't have one of those, I don't think I'll ever forgive myself.

"I need one of those mugs in order to live."

Crew laughs out loud and hands me the brats. "I'll grab us each one. Head toward the Ferris wheel and get in line."

"You want to ride the Ferris wheel?"

"Can you think of a better way to enjoy our brats and wine?"

"I guess not."

He walks toward the stall, and I weave my way to the Ferris wheel, where there's a decent line but nothing too long. I count out the people and the chairs on the Ferris wheel, and from the looks of it, we'll be able to ride the next round.

The Ferris wheel is adorable—tiny, white with Christmas-themed seats. It almost feels as though it belongs in one of those ceramic Christmas villages that grandparents display on their credenzas.

In a matter of minutes, Crew walks up to me and hands me a mug of wine while taking back his brat.

"Oh, this is so freaking cute. I think I might be in love with a souvenir mug."

"To each their own." He chuckles and takes a sip of the wine. His eyes widen as he smacks his lips together. "Oh, shit, this is dangerous."

"Good?" I ask.

He nods. "Really fucking good."

I lift the mug and take a sip. A wave of cinnamon, citrus, and cloves hits my tongue as the smooth, warm liquid trickles down my throat. "Oh, wow. That's dangerously good." I laugh. "Uh-oh. If we're not careful, I think this could be the death of us tonight." This is especially potent, given I'm still feeling jetlagged.

He clinks his brat with mine and says, "Then we better eat up."

Just then the line moves, and we're the last ones to hop into a red chair. The attendant locks the safety bar in place and steps aside, and we slowly start rotating toward the midnight sky. The ride isn't very fast—actually almost at a snail's pace—which gives us enough time to take in the sights while we eat our brats.

"Look," I say, after swallowing this delicious concoction. "Isn't that the fountain we're supposed to visit?"

"What? That's a fountain? It looks like a mini cathedral," Crew says.

"I know. I was looking at pictures of it on our drive here. I wanted to make sure we knew what we were looking for. Isn't it pretty?"

"Very. I was worried we wouldn't be able to find the rings, but from the look of it, there's a little line off to the side. I bet that's where you spin the gold rings."

"Most likely." I take a sip of my wine and then inhale in a

sharp, cold breath. "I feel like getting lost under the twinkle lights tonight."

"Then let's do it. That's what we're here for—to get lost."

"And drunk, right?"

"Of course, drunk." He holds up his mug. "To Pops."

I hold up mine as well and we clink our mugs together. "To Pops."

"DO WE MAKE A WISH?" I ask Crew as we move closer in line to the gold rings.

"I don't think so. Pops just said it's supposed to give you good luck if you spin them."

"Want to spin it together?" I lift my mug to my lips. We're both on our second cup of mulled wine, which has kept us fairly warm on this cold winter night.

"I thought that's what we were doing," he says, wrapping his arm around me and holding me close.

God, I love being wrapped up in his arms, this close to him. It reminds me of warm summer days, of carefree days. It reminds me that I'm not alone—that at least for a short period of time, I'm not alone.

When it's our turn, we step up to the fountain and I realize that I can barely reach the gold ring. Crew laughs, and without even thinking about it, turns around so I can climb up on is back. He hands his phone to the person in line behind us, and together, we reach out and touch the gold ring, smiling at the camera. Then we turn it together, one full loop.

Whispering, Crew says, "That was for Pops. Now one full turn for us."

Smiling, we turn it one more time and then collect our mugs and phone.

We stand to the side and take a look at the picture. Behind us in the picture is a light orb from one of the bulbs strung along the stalls, but I can't help but think how it might be Pops, joining us.

"Another keeper," Crew says before pocketing his phone.

"Make sure you send me these photos, Hollywood."

He rolls his eyes. "Of course I will, Twigs. Can't have you missing out on my handsome self in your phone."

I laugh. "Ass."

Bringing his mug up to his lips, he asks, "What should we do next?"

"I think it's time to get lost."

"Then let's get lost together."

Once again, he takes my hand in his, and we walk into the thick of the Christkindlesmarkt stalls.

"CREW," I whisper and laugh at the same time.

"Hmm?"

"Look at that stall over there." I point to the left.

"Where?"

"There."

"Where?"

Laughing, I grab him by the chin and force him to look where I'm pointing. Four mugs of mulled wine in and we're starting to feel the effects.

"Look at the dolls with no pants playing instruments."

He blinks a few times. "Are you sure they're not wearing pants?"

"Positive. See, that tuba player has a carved bum."

"I'm going to need a better look at these." He walks up to the stall and I follow closely behind him, giggling the entire time, because that's the maturity level I'm at right now. Crew picks up the tuba player and examines it. "Huh, no pants. Look at his little butt crack." Crew runs his finger along the seam and says, "Smooth."

"Uh, you're fingering the bare butt of a pant-less tuba player, I think you need to check yourself."

He pauses and watches how his finger is moving up and down. "You know, I really am. And for some reason, I'm still doing it."

"Is your finger short-circuiting?"

"I think it is."

To save him from the humiliation of butt-fingering a ceramic doll, I pull the figurine from his hand and set it back down on the table.

"Thanks," he says in relief.

"Of course. I really think that was uncomfortable for everyone."

"Were people watching?"

"I don't know, but I'm afraid to look around," I whisper now, keeping my eyes trained on him.

Leaning closer, he asks, "Are we drunk?"

I dab my finger on my tongue and then hold it up to the chilly night air. I pause, letting the wind whip around my finger, and then I nod. "Yup, we're drunk."

Crew clutches his heart and lets out a sigh of relief. "Shit, I feel accomplished."

"Me, too," I say with pride, my chest puffing. "We did it. We got drunk and we're not passed out in our bed."

"Some might say we're killing this whole vacation thing."

"Some might say that." I slowly nod. "Oh, look. This one is playing the violin." I hold up another figurine and Crew takes it from my hands to examine it.

"Why do they have the Ken-doll crotch? And look at their faces, they're all cherub-like. Is this supposed to be a pant-less child playing music? If so, are all these figurines prodigies? I don't know much about kids, but what I do know is that they're not great at playing instruments unless they're prodigies. But could there really be that many child prodigies all in one area?"

"Maybe it's a convention? Maybe all these pant-less, cherubic children are at a convention for the musically gifted."

Crew thinks on that. "Is the uniform shirts only?"

"I mean, if we were to assess the scene properly, I would say, yeah, it's a shirts-only convention."

"But they have shoes," Crew points out, a crease in his brow. "And socks. Tube sucks. They have shoes and tube sock and no pants." Whispering, he says, "Where are their goddamn pants?"

"Honestly, I have—"

"*Kann ich dir helfen?*" the stall owner asks as he comes over to us.

Startled, Crew holds up the figurine and says, "I'll take two."

"What?" I try not to laugh.

He grabs the tuba player and hands it and the violinist to the owner.

"These are awesome. Love the no-pants angle."

The owner gives him a weird look but walks over to the bagging area and starts wrapping up the figurines.

"What the hell are you going to do with two of those?"

He shrugs. "Give them to River and Hollis." And then, as if a lightbulb goes off in his head, he says, "Oh, shit, can I get one more? Hutton needs one of these as well." Crew picks up another figurine, but this one is playing the flute.

I stand there next to him, giggling the entire time, trying not to be disrespectful, but honestly, he's about to give his friends pant-less, instrument-playing cherubs with Ken-doll crotches. I would love to be a fly on the wall when they open those gifts. After paying and receiving a carefully wrapped paper bag, we head down the aisle of stalls, arm in arm.

"I know about Hutton, especially since he came to the farm that one summer."

"Oh, yeah, you were so jealous at first."

"Was not." I sway.

"To hell you weren't. You were so mad you had to share time with me, but he was only there for a week before he went home. You changed your tune after that."

"You just surprised me, that's all. I was expecting Crew, and instead, I got the California twins. Yeah, I might have felt a little left out."

"Ah, see? You were jealous."

Rolling my eyes even though he can't see me, I say, "So, tell me about River and Hollis. Are they hot? Want to introduce me to them?"

Crew stops and turns to face me. "Excuse me?"

I laugh. "What? You don't want to play matchmaker with your friends?"

"You're not available."

"Oh, I'm not? Since when?"

"Since we're friends again. Friends don't date each other's friends. You're off limits unless I approve."

Hope falls for a second in my foggy brain. For a second there, I thought I was off limits because he was claiming me.

Silly, silly drunk girl.

"You don't approve of your own friends?"

"Uh, no." He shakes his head as we walk past yet another Lebkuchen stall. I think that's the fifth one we've seen tonight. And yet, every time, I'm tempted to buy more.

"We Wish You a Merry Christmas" plays in the background, and a light dusting of snow starts to fall over us, but thanks to the wine, we're warm, feeling good, and have no need to retire to the hotel just yet.

I stop us both and look up toward the sky, letting a snowflake fall on my cheek. I take a deep breath and relish in the moment. We're in Germany, in a famous Christmas market, surrounded by joy and laughter, music serenading us while it snows. I don't think this moment could be more perfect. *Well, unless Pops was here with us.*

"What are you doing?"

"Taking in the moment," I answer. I look up at him and smile.

He smiles back and then shakes his head. "Yeah, you're definitely not available."

With that, he continues to walk me down the aisle, and a little part of me does believe that he means that in a more romantic way. That he might be seeing me a little differently. It might be the booze talking, but that shared gaze, his words—they make me feel . . . all warm and fuzzy inside.

"Hollis and River are the reason I made it through this last season," Crew says, quietly. "It was a shitty season, but without them, I never would have gotten through it."

"Because of Pops?"

He nods. "Yeah. They carried me through the semester. They made sure I woke up and got out of bed to train, to hit up my classes, to continue moving forward even though I didn't want to." He taps his bag. "This is a thank-you for all of that."

I laugh out loud, and he chuckles too. "What a wonderful thank you gift."

"I'll be sure to write a passionate card to go with the figurines so they think I'm serious and, therefore, they're obligated to keep the figurines as a token of my appreciation."

"Maybe you should add something in there like, 'This reminds me of that one special time we shared together,' but don't be specific, so they're truly confused."

Crew laughs a little harder. "Hell, that's perfect. Yes, I'm going to do that. We can send them out tomorrow before we take off again. Maybe they'll get them before Christmas if we pay extra." He sighs. "In all seriousness, I'm glad they're in my life for many reasons, but one of the biggest ones was having them this past semester."

"I'm glad they were there for you," I say. "I wish you'd have let me be there for you too."

"I know." He holds me a little tighter and then stops. "What's that?"

I turn to the right to spy a wave of fire erupt from a stall while the people around it clap with exuberance.

Oooh . . . fire.

"I don't know, but I need to find out."

Entranced, we walk over to the stall and watch as a man hovers over a giant cauldron, pouring what seems to be liquid over a spicket of sugar and fire. On the side of the stall, I see a sign and read aloud, "Fire tongs punch."

"What's that?"

I pull out my phone and type it into my web browser. I click on the first thing I see and read it to him. "A traditional German drink during Christmas and New Year's. It's a rum soaked sugar loaf set on fire that drips into mulled wine."

"Oh damn. Mulled wine and rum—should we?"

I hold up my empty mug and say, "I *am* thirsty."

He holds up his as well. "Me too." He clinks his mug to mine.

"Then I think we have our answer."

"Rum and wine, the perfect combination."

"OH MY GOD, CREW, GET UP," I say, laughing so hard I can barely catch my breath.

"These hallways are so small. How am I supposed to logroll to our room if I can't fit in them?"

Crew is lying on the ground, in a fetal position, trying to roll down the hallway, but keeps bumping into wall after wall while I hold all the things we bought at the Christmas market, including the cherubs, our mugs, and some more Lebkuchen, because there were heart-shaped ones the size of my head and I needed it.

"Try a somersault."

"Oh, that's a good idea."

Crew tucks himself into a somersault position and then flings his body forward, only to go crooked just as his legs fly out and kick open a hotel door, scaring the ever-loving shit out of a woman in a robe.

Screaming, hands clutched to her chest, the woman yells bloody murder for help while Crew scrambles to his feet and tips into the wall drunkenly.

"Excuse me." He straightens up. "Uh, sorry about that, ma'am, just . . . uh, you know, looking for Santa Claus. Heard the sneaky bastard was lurking around here. By chance, have you seen him?"

"You have two seconds to move along before I call hotel security."

"I'm going to take that as a no."

"Go," she shouts, slamming the door and locking it.

Hand to his heart, Crew says, "Holy shit. I think she's hiding him in her closet. Didn't she look guilty?"

I can't even respond, I'm laughing so hard tears stream down my face.

I push him toward our hotel room, and he opens the door with the keycard from his pocket. Together we stumble into the room where I carefully set our stuff down on the dresser and then sink to the ground resting my head against the wall.

"Oh no, I think I might pass out here." Crew tears his winter clothes off and stumbles against the wall before gaining control of his legs. "I don't think the punch was a good idea."

"Nope." I shake my head. "It went downhill from there."

"So why did we get another glass?" He laughs.

"Because our mugs told us to."

"Ahh, that's right." He leans down and grabs my hand. "Come on, Twigs. Brush your teeth and then throw yourself in bed. You don't want to sleep on the floor."

"I'm protecting the door from that bastard of a jolly man, just in case he comes to our hotel room."

"It's not Christmas yet."

"Oh . . . right." I nod and let him help me to my feet. Together we brush our teeth and then make our way to the bed. Crew flips the covers back and then reaches behind him, grips his sweater, and pulls it over his head, revealing his toned torso.

For some reason, I decide to do the same. From behind, I grab my sweater and attempt to pull it over my head. Let's just say, men make this move look flawless . . . me, on the other hand . . .

"Are you stuck?" Crew asks.

Stomach bare, arms sticking straight out in front of me, head tilted down, I flail about, trying to release myself from the confines of a cable-knit sweater.

"What's happened?" I ask. "Where's the exit?"

"Keep pulling."

"How? My arms are stuck."

Laughing, Crew leans on the bed, takes the sweater in his hands, and yanks it off me.

After I tilt my head back and scatter my hair out of my eyes, I earnestly tell Crew, "You just saved my life."

He dusts off his shoulder. "All in a day's work."

Standing again, he takes off his pants and socks, leaving him in nothing but a pair of boxer briefs with bananas scattered all over the fabric.

"You have banana underwear?"

He flops down on the bed and places his hands behind his head. Wow, his body is really nice. Defined in all the right places, a well-indented *V* at his hips, muscular thighs, and yup, a bulge.

Don't stare at the bulge.

Remove your eyes from the bulge.

Divert. Divert.

"Are you staring at my dick?"

"What? No?" I look away. "Just making sure they were

bananas and not birds." I take off my pants and socks as well, leaving me in nothing but a bra and underpants. Nothing sexy over here, just a regular black bra and black full-butt hipster underwear.

Yup, eat your heart out.

"They're bananas. My mom thinks it's funny to get me interesting underwear. They're a nice surprise. Not that many people see me in my underwear." He turns to look at me and his eyes focus on my chest. "Nice tits, Haze."

"Thank you." I poke the top of each breast. "They have bounce to them."

"Some might say they jiggle," Crew offers.

"I always wanted a jiggle to my boobs. Look at me, all grown up." I smile lazily and climb into the queen-sized bed that Crew seems to be far too big for. "I'm rather impressed with the way my boobs turned out."

"Me too. They seem as though they would be a good handful."

"They are." I nod. "Here, feel." I take his hand and place it over my breast.

His eyes go lazy as a goofy grin spreads across his cheeks. "I'm holding your boob. And this time, it's not on accident."

"It's merely to see the difference from the last time."

"Uh-huh." He gives my boob a squeeze and I swat at him, both of us laughing. Tearing his hand away, he says, "That's a superior tit, Hazel. Congratulations."

"Why, thank you."

He sighs and drapes his hand over his forehead. "That made me horny. Thanks."

"What? Just a boob grab? Aren't you too drunk?"

"Apparently not. Don't worry, I'm not hard or anything. Just got a stirring in my groin."

"Oh my God, don't say stirring in your groin. What's wrong with you?"

"Many things." He turns to his side, facing me, and then

wraps his arm around my stomach and pulls my back up against his chest.

I freeze, unsure of what's happening, but when he snuggles in and pulls the blankets over us, I realize he just wants to spoon.

Right?

Honestly, I can't really tell. My mind is mush and, oh yes . . . he's so warm.

"Are you spooning me?"

"Yeah. Consider it drunk comfort. You okay with that?" he asks, his breath tickling the back of my neck.

"Totally okay," I answer, my voice sounding desperate, but I don't really care.

"Good." Crew's hand splays across my stomach as he holds me closer, my ass pressed up against his crotch. "I had fun tonight, Haze."

"Me, too." I shift, my butt rubbing against him.

"Not too much of that," he says, his voice sounding hoarse. "You'll get me excited."

I laugh. "You mean, not too much of this?" I grind into him, and his hand lands on my hip, halting me in place.

"Hazel Marie Allen."

I laugh even louder as I grind again, unsure what's come over me. "Sorry, didn't mean to do that."

And as he holds my hip, my backside against his pelvis, I feel him harden. My eyes widen.

I suck in a sharp breath when my hips shift again, feeling him even more.

"Goddammit," he mutters. "Look what you did."

I laugh some more, thinking it's funny more than anything.

Thank you, rum and wine.

I continue to move my backside against Crew until he groans against the back of my neck, and that's when I still.

That's when I feel the first spike of arousal hit me. That's when I start to regret everything I just did.

Chuckling, Crew says, "Did you just get horny?"

"No," I lie.

"Such a bad liar." His hand travels up my hip lightly and across my stomach, his fingers dragging along my skin near the waistband of my underwear. "You just got hot, and your skin broke out in a sweat."

"I'm hot."

"And bothered," he adds, his voice playful, doing nothing to calm down my libido. "What are you going to do now, Twigs? Finish something you started, or tuck in for the night?"

"Wh-what do you mean . . . finish?"

"You tell me," he whispers, and I swear the feel of his seductive voice along the back of my neck sends a wave of goosebumps down my arms and legs.

Then I'm lifting up from the bed and turning toward Crew where I push him on his back, because right now, right the hell now, I need something hard between my legs. That tingly feeling needs to be tingled. *Now. By him.* Could be a giant mess, but I don't care. Need. Him. Now.

He licks his lips, his eyes full of drunken lust, and I straddle him, my pelvis to his. He smiles and grips my hips.

"What are you doing, Haze?"

"What does it look like?" I ask, moving my hips along his.

"Looks as if you're trying to get me off."

I shake my head. "No, I'm trying to get myself off." Keeping my hands to myself, I smooth my center over his erection and revel in the feel of his hard cock beneath my warmth.

God, that feels good.

So freaking good that I get lost. He's gripping my hips tighter and tighter, or trying to pull me down closer to him, but my focus is on the feel of my arousal gliding over his length, two pieces of fabric being the only barrier. *Yes. This is what I needed.* It's erotic.

It's sensual.

It feels so freaking wonderful that my hips move faster and faster.

"Yes," I whisper, my hands in my hair now.

"Shit, Hazel," I hear Crew say from what sounds like the far-off distance, but it does nothing to pull my focus away from our connection.

From this euphoria.

From this moment that I'm pretty sure I won't remember tomorrow morning as my head fills with haze, with lust, with the need to let go.

"God, yes," I moan, moving faster and faster.

"Fuck," Crew gasps just as my hands fall from my hair and onto his chest, where I prop myself up and grind harder. "Ahh . . . hell," he cries out. "Hazel, you're going to make me come."

I'm right there, his words miles away. I can feel my arousal spike to a crescendo. My orgasm climbing and climbing up the backs of my legs until it hits me right in the core. A wave of spasms takes control of me all at once as my back arches and my body takes over.

"Yes, yes . . . yes," I cry out as I grind harder and harder until . . . "Oh my God," I cry out, my orgasm pushing through me like a freight truck. Beneath me, I feel Crew go rigid as he comes as well, a groan falling past his lips, his fingers digging into my thighs.

We ride out our pleasure until we're both sated, and then I roll off him in a heap of satisfaction.

Our breathing syncs together, and all I remember after that is hearing him say, "Now I have to go change my goddamn underwear."

Chapter Eight

CREW

"Do I smell coffee?" Hazel asks, her voice groggy, the sheets wrapped tightly around her body. I know this, because not only is she in a cocoon, but I woke up freezing my ass off since she'd stolen all the blankets.

"Yeah," I say, my head pounding with a roaring headache, my body aching from the cold, and a distant recollection of Hazel straddling me. Was that a dream?

She pushes the sheets down and reveals her face, her mascara faintly streaked down her cheeks. Her hand sticks out from the covers and her fingers wiggle about. Chuckling, I hand her my cup and then serve myself another cup from the room service tray I ordered the minute I woke up. While I waited for the food, I took a shower, hoping to warm up my body. It barely worked.

Carefully, Hazel sits up and brings the mug to her lips. "Jesus Christ, what happened last night?"

"I think there was rum involved," I answer, my voice still groggy.

She presses her hand to her head. "What time is it?"

"Eight."

"Eight?" she nearly shouts. "Why are we up so early?"

"I woke up because I was freezing my dick off."

That's when Hazel looks down at the covers and sheets wrapped around her. "Oh no. Did I steal all the blankets?"

"Yup." I stir my coffee and then bring it close to my lips, ready to heat me up.

"Crap. I'm sorry, Crew." She sits and groans. "Did we do a lot of walking last night?"

"I mean, a decent amount. Why?" I ask, as I catch the sheet fall down her shoulder, revealing the strap of her black bra. Something flashes in my mind, a glimpse of her in that black bra, on top of me.

Jesus, I dreamed about Hazel last night, straddling me, riding me. It almost feels as though it were real as another memory flashes past me, my hands gripping her thighs, her mouth parted open as she rides me.

I blink a few times, trying to wash away the image.

What was in that rum?

"My inner thighs are sore." She sits up farther, and the blankets slip even more so her bra is completely exposed. And fuck, her tits are all plump and sexy . . . "Oh, shit. Sorry." She quickly covers herself as my eyes snap up to hers.

She tilts her head, studying me.

I study her.

I imagine the confused look on her face is mirrored on mine.

"I slept in my underwear last night," she states.

"So did I. Probably why I was freezing my ass off."

She continues to look at me weirdly. I stare back and I have another flash of her grinding on top of me, but this time she's coming and I'm coming and . . .

"Holy shit," I say, just as her eyes widen as well.

"Oh my God," she whispers, lifting up the covers and looking at her body and then back at me. "We didn't . . . uh, you know . . ."

Lips pressed together, unsure of what to say, I give it some thought. Did we?

No. I woke up with boxers on. If we did it, I would have been naked.

Then why do I have such vivid images of her riding me?

I'm thinking this wasn't a dream.

"Uh, I don't think so," I say in an unsure voice.

"Then why are your eyes all freaked out?" She presses her hand to her head. "And why am I in my underwear?" She glances around the bed, the floor, and nightstand. "Are there any, you know, wrappers?"

"I don't have any, so, no."

She nods. "Okay, okay." Her eyes meet mine. "How does your dick feel this morning?"

"What?"

She swallows hard. "Does it feel . . . satisfied?"

"Should it?"

She pushes her hand through her hair. "Honestly, I don't know. I keep having these images of me on top of you, grinding." Her cheeks flush to a bright red. "Was that a dream?"

"I don't think so, unless we're both having the same dream."

"Oh God," she says quietly, bringing the coffee to her lips. "I'm—oh God, I'm sorry, Crew." She shakes her head. "I think I dry humped you last night."

And then it all comes together.

Me spooning her.

Telling her she has great tits.

Hazel rubbing her ass against my crotch.

Hazel straddling me.

Me encouraging her.

Hazel's pelvis grinding me.

My hard cock begging for more.

Haze . . . *coming on top of me.*

"Oh hell," I mutter.

"I want to die a slow death." She pulls the comforter over her head and hides from me.

I don't blame her. If I had a comforter, I'd be hiding, as well. I don't remember the finer details of last night, but what I do remember is encouraging her with my hands, watching as she writhed above me, undeniable passion in her expression. And I remember enjoying it. I remember a feeling of electrifying euphoria washing over me as Hazel came right on top of me. *Fuck. It was sexy as hell.*

It's been a long time since I've been with a girl, a really fucking long time, and even though our interaction was dry humping while drunk, in my mind, it was better than any sexual interaction I've had in a long fucking time.

And that's scary.

But what's scarier is that we have *many* more days left together and we can't hide from each other. We have to move past this—possibly move forward.

What does it all mean? Does she like me like that? She admitted to having a crush, unlike me, who has kept that aspect of my feelings completely secret because I refuse to let my mind wander in that direction. Although, it seems as though my alcohol-laden brain broke open that floodgate and allowed me to indulge.

And look where we are now.

I'm staring at a mortified, comforter-covered Hazel who can't even look at me.

Sighing, I move to sit next to her on the bed. Carefully, I pull down the comforter, revealing her tearful face.

Immediately, I jump to concerned. I set my coffee mug on the nightstand and quickly wipe away her tears. "Hey, why are you crying?"

She sucks in a sharp breath. "I'm so embarrassed."

"What? Why?"

"Uh . . . I humped you last night, Crew."

"Yeah, and you didn't hear any protesting from me."

"You were drunk."

"So were you," I counter. Taking her mug from her hand, I set it on the nightstand as well and then take her hands in mine. "Listen, let's just chalk it up to some drunken fun, okay?"

"Not a drunken mistake?" she asks, looking down at our hands.

I tilt her head up and force her to look me in the eyes. "Do you think it was a mistake?"

"Only if it makes things weird between us."

"It'll only be awkward if we make it awkward." I sit back and smile at her. "I had fun. And, yeah, my dick does feel better this morning."

"Oh God." She covers her face with her hands, but I pry them away.

"Nope, you can't hide from me. Come on, Haze. We're adults. We can talk about this stuff. You talked about it easily at the beginning of the trip. How is this any different?"

"Because I dry humped you, Crew. And you came. And I came. We both came."

"Which in my eyes is a successful dry humping." I smirk, and she pushes at my face.

"Why are you not horrified?"

I shrug. "Because it was hot. From what I can remember, at least. Because I had a good time, and because I'm not going to let this change anything between us. You're my Hazel, I'm your Crew, and that's that."

"So, you're not thinking that I'm some desperate farm girl trying to get any kind of ride out of the hunky, popular athlete?"

"Uh, no. I'm thinking, 'Hell, Hazel rode me last night and

it was hot as shit. I hope she doesn't hate that I have an image of her riding me on replay in my mind.'"

"Oh my God." She flops her body to the side and buries her head in the pillows.

I tear the covers off her, leaving her curled up in her bra and underwear, and then I give her ass a big slap. With a yelp, she jackknifes off the bed and swirls around to look me in the eyes, fury striking in them.

"You did not just spank me."

"I think I did."

"You're going to regret that." She stands on the bed, and before I know what's happening, she's launching herself at me, flattening me on the mattress, her body straddling me once again.

"Aw, memories," I say while gripping her thighs.

Her nostrils flare. "You think this is funny?"

I let out a loud laugh. "I do."

"So, if I start moving my hips again . . ." She shifts, and I quickly toss her off me and push myself to my feet.

"Don't you even fucking think about it."

She launches her body at me and clings to my chest, wrapping her legs around my waist. I can't do anything but grip her and try to steady us as she sticks to me like glue, her hips once again grinding against mine.

"If you think it's so funny, then I'll keep doing it."

I arch my pelvis away from her, trying to keep her crotch from meeting up with mine. "Hazel, stop. You're going to make me hard again."

"But it's funny, Crew."

I see what she's doing. Well, two can play at this game.

I spin around and lay her on the bed, grabbing her hands and locking them above her head, then I move my pelvis against hers. This time I'm the one taking control.

"Okay, then. Let's laugh about it," I say.

Her eyes widen and her breath catches in her chest.

"Crew, I was . . ." She bites her bottom lip and I watch her eyes slowly start to close and her legs begin to fall open.

Shit.

Fuck.

SHIT!

My hips thrust slightly harder, and her fingers entwine with mine.

"Hazel," I whisper. Her eyes barely flutter open, and when they do, I ask, "What are we doing?"

"I . . . I don't know."

"Want me to stop?"

"Yes and no."

I chuckle. "That's not an answer."

My cock hardens rapidly as I move against her some more. She rotates with me, and we both pick up our strokes.

"Do you want to stop?" she asks.

"Not really," I answer hoarsely. "But I feel as though we should. I don't want you being weird with me."

"I don't want to be weird either."

"Okay, then I should stop."

"Yup."

But I don't. Instead, I keep moving, faster and faster, and I realize if I don't stop soon, I'm going to come in my pants for the second time in twenty-four hours.

"I should really stop," I say, my teeth clenched, the pleasure that's pooling at the base of my cock way too fucking good to give up.

"Yeah," she says breathlessly, moving her hips faster. "Oh God, yes, you should stop."

"Shit, Haze, are you close?"

Her large round eyes connect with mine and she slowly nods, her teeth biting down on her bottom lip.

"Don't let this be weird between us. Please," I beg her. "Because, fuck, I need this release, but I need you too."

"I won't let it be weird."

"Promise?"

She nods, her breath picking up. "Yes . . . promise." Her hands grip tighter, her back arches, and her core matches up to mine. And fuck, her tits. God, they're fucking gorgeous. *She's gorgeous. Sexy as hell.* "Yes, Crew, right there," she whispers, and it's my fucking undoing.

I plant my legs and thrust hard, my cock rubbing against her arousal, causing her to moan louder and louder until she arches so high I can see the point of her nipples pebbling against her black bra as she comes, her hips wildly seeking out every last ounce of pleasure.

The pressure at the base of my cock builds, my balls tighten, and, before I know it, I'm coming once again, riding out the pleasure with her until we both slow down our hips and stare at each other.

We're silent for a few seconds before she starts laughing.

"Not the kind of reaction a guy likes after he makes a girl come."

"I'm sorry, but . . . we must be really freaking horny if we're dry humping like teenagers."

I laugh. "Yeah, well, it's been a really long time for me, so I can't be responsible for what my dick does." I grip her hands tighter. *In fact, when was the last time I had sex?*

She laughs and sits up. "I think I should take a shower and you should clean up."

"Yeah . . ."

She nods. "And the letter. Can't forget the letter."

"You're right." I start to lift up but then pause. "Promise we're good."

She nods again and bites her bottom lip. *Not helping, Haze.* "Nothing changes, right?"

The pleading in her eyes—the desperation—sends a wave of disappointment through me. *Nothing* changes? Not even a little? A part of me wonders—what if things did change, what if we did make some moves forward, progress whatever this is between us—would it be so terrible? I love Hazel. She's one of my best friends. It almost seems as if we'd be missing out on something if we didn't give this a try.

Then again, from the way she's looking at me, I'm going to guess that she might not be thinking the what I am. That even though these feelings and emotions bubbling up inside me are strong and they're making me act out, she might not feel the same way.

She might not want to invest in something romantic. Not when my future is unknown, not when we live so far apart. I can understand the hesitation.

Swallowing my pride and the resurgence of feelings, I nod. "Nothing changes, Haze."

"Still friends?"

"Always friends."

She looks between us and asks, "Given that your shorts are all, um, gooey—"

"Jesus."

She chuckles. "Maybe you should clean up first, yeah?"

"Probably smart." I glance down, my dick still semi hard, a wet spot on my shorts. "Think you could look away?"

"You're making it weird."

"Uh, I think it would be weirder if you got a shot of what's going on down below."

"You're right." She covers her eyes. "Go ahead, walk away from me, take care of your man problems."

Rolling my eyes, I lift off her and go to my suitcase for another pair of boxers. We're going to have to do laundry at this rate.

When I'm in the bathroom cleaning up, I hear Hazel from the other room. "Wow, quite the spread. There are so many pastries and sausages to choose from."

Chuckling, I say, "I am quite the gentleman, after all." *And I know Hazel likes her sausage.*

"OKAY, are you ready for this letter?" Hazel asks, coming up next to me, freshly showered and fed.

"I am if you are."

When she said nothing would be weird, she meant it. Ever since our second humping, she's been the normal one. Teasing me, playing around, singing Christmas songs while getting ready for the day, even if she has a pounding headache, as she's announced many times. I'm the one who's feeling weird. I'm the one who's trying to act normal now. I'm the one who doesn't feel right in his own skin.

My mind is foggy.

My heart is racing.

And my body is aching for more. So much more.

I can't stop staring at her lips and wondering how they might taste.

I can't stop checking out her ass every time she bends over.

And I can't take my eyes off her tits in that sweater.

"Then stop staring at me and grab the letter," Hazel says, pulling me from my haze.

"Yeah, right."

I lift the envelope from the nightstand and start to open it, when Hazel's hand stills mine. "Are you sure this isn't going to be weird?"

"Why? Am I making it weird?"

"You're acting a little weird," she admits.

"Sorry." I let out a slow breath. "Everything is cool. No worries."

"Are you sure?"

I nod. "Yup." I hold the letter up and say, "Let's find out where we're going." I flip the envelope over and start to open it, but the whole time, all I can think about is Hazel's sweet moans.

Shit, maybe the second dry hump wasn't a good idea,

because at least the first time almost felt like a dream, a distant memory. But the second time when I picked up the scent of her arousal, when I saw her eyes roll back in her head in bliss, where I heard every moan—yeah, that's vivid as shit in my head, and I think it will be for a while.

I pull out the letter and unfold it. Clearing my throat, I read out loud. "'Hey, kiddos. How was the Christkindlesmarkt? Did you try the fire tongs punch? I hope you did. Gloria and I had a little too much fun while drinking it.'" I pause and look at Hazel. "Looks as if everyone has fun drinking it."

She smirks. "Wonder if there's aftereffects the next day for others as well."

"Probably tradition, actually."

"So, you think it's customary to dry hump your friend after drinking fire tongs punch?"

"I think I read somewhere that it's a German tradition."

"Well, you know what they say: when in Rome . . ." She shrugs, and I swear, I don't understand how she can go from a horrified wreck, burying herself under the covers, to being so casual about what happened that it doesn't even seem like a blip on her radar.

I'm a goddamn mess inside. Why isn't she?

"Right." I chuckle, even though I don't want to, and then turn back to the letter. "'This morning—hopefully it's morning for you—you're off to Würzburg. The drive is only an hour and a half, so you won't be spending too much time in the car, but Würzburg is the start of your real journey. Many, many years ago, I went there with Gloria. She fell in love with Germany, and I fell in love with her. Friends at the time, we weren't romantically involved, but this trip changed my life forever as we travelled down the popular route called The Romantic Road.'" I swallow hard. What the hell was Pops thinking?

"Everything okay?" Hazel asks.

"Yeah, sorry. Throat is a little dry."

"Here." She hands me a water and I take a sip even though I'm not thirsty. No, I'm freaked out, because in a short amount of time I've been reconnected with my good friend—and I mean short—I've started to see her in a different light. *I can't seem to keep my hands to myself when around her.* I've *had to* hug her, kiss her forehead, hold her hand . . . I crave her laugh and her smile, and I fucking dry humped her. And, yes, technically, she did the humping first, but we were drunk last night. I was fully alert for every grind, every pound of pleasure that passed through us this morning.

And now Pops wants to send us on some sort of romantic trip?

Is this what he was trying to get at the entire time? To get me to fall for Hazel? Because from the grave, he's doing a damn good job.

"Better?" Hazel asks.

"Yes, thank you." I turn back to the letter. "'Now, I'm not saying for you two to fall in love.'" Well, there you have it. He's not trying to play matchmaker. "'But what you get from this trip is based solely on you. It's about reconnecting, about finding your passion, about sitting back and reflecting on your lives and where you want to go from here. This trip is to give you time for soul-searching, and the sights you'll come across will be magnificent, unlike anything you've ever imagined. The rich history will blow you away. The image of Germany wrapped up in a blanket of snow will leave you breathless, and by the end of this road trip, down a romantic fantasy of castles and half-timbered houses, I hope that you leave with an appreciation for the simple things, for the ease of making hard decisions because you follow your heart instead of your brain, and that you're refreshed with a new understanding of one another. You aren't anyone in this world without the people around you. Both of you need to remember that. Hazel, my dear Twigs, you can't do everything on your own, so please stop believing you should. And, Crew, my moronic grandson, you can't leave the people who've been there for you your entire life behind, so stop believing you could.'"

Shit. That last comment hits me hard.

But instead of recoiling, Hazel turns in toward me and rubs my back while resting her chin on my shoulder.

Finishing up the letter, I read, "'In the envelope, there's a map of the Romantic Road and where you'll be stopping for the night. You won't be stopping in every town along the way, but you're welcome to, if you want. The Romantic Road isn't very long at all. You could drive the length of it in a day. But the point of traveling this road is to appreciate the beauty of it. Immerse yourselves in the culture, don't second-guess one thing, and for the love of God, just enjoy yourselves.'" I smile. "'Today, when you reach Würzburg, you'll go to a wine tasting. Germany is known for their beer, but little do people know, they're proficient winemakers as well, and that's what you'll be enjoying today. Directions and other vital information are attached. Have fun. Love you, Pops.'"

"More wine?" Hazel asks. "I'm going to have to eat more bread to get through that."

"Let's just hope there's no rum in it," I joke.

She nods. "For your underwear's sake."

"RIGHT THIS WAY, Mr. and Mrs. Smith," Ingrid, our sommelier, says, guiding us toward an archway that leads to a staircase.

"We're not married, actually," Hazel says, surprising me. "Just friends."

"Ah, my apologies." Ingrid gestures toward the stairs. "Follow the guiding lights into the wine cellar and we'll be right down."

"Thank you," Hazel says. Taking a step forward, her foot

gets caught in the wood, and she falls forward. I quickly grab her by the hand and keep her from tumbling down the stairs.

"Oh, are you okay?" Ingrid asks.

"I got her." I hold up our connected hands. "Don't worry."

The staircase is dark, only lit by sconces, which are somehow secured to the cave-like walls that form the tunnel we're descending into. "Wine cellar" is right. It almost feels as if we're entering an entirely different world—the underworld.

As we descend, Hazel removes her hand from mine. That's the third time today she's shied away from my touch. Call me paranoid, but I feel like it has something to do with what happened last night and this morning, but then again, she's *still* acting more casual about the whole thing than I am.

"Everything okay?" I ask her.

"Yeah, great," she answers with a little too much pep in her voice. "I mean, this staircase is a little creepy, but if there's wine at the end of the tunnel, I'm not going to let mood lighting scare me."

Not wanting to get into it with her, I drop the topic and say, "While you were in the bathroom, I did a quick search on the Romantic Road, and it really is only a two-and-a-half-hour drive, but Pops has us on the road for six more days."

"Are you complaining about spending more time with me?"

"No," I say quickly as we reach the bottom of the stairs and turn right into a dimly lit wine cellar. Barrels of wine are held up by iron racks and span all the way down the long tunnel of the underground. To the left is a taste-testing area where bar-height tables and stools are scattered throughout the space, with strings of bulb lights offering a delicate ambiance while keeping the atmosphere cozy and intimate.

"I wonder where we'll be for Christmas," Hazel says, dragging her fingers over a barrel of wine. "I've always gone to my grandparents' for Christmas, so this will be new for me. We don't even have any Christmas cookies."

"Not true. We have all that Lebkuchen."

"True." She glances at me. "I've never spent Christmas with you. Do you have any traditions I should know about?"

"Nothing that I think we could do here."

"Like what?"

We're walking down the long aisleway of all the wine, barely taking in the different years and flavors. Honestly, I'm completely inept when it comes to wine. I only know if it tastes good to me, and that's about it. I'm more of a beer guy. I know that doesn't shock anyone, given I'm in a fraternity and I'm a student athlete, but thought I'd put it out there.

"Christmas Eve, we'd do the traditional thing of wearing matching pajamas and then take pictures in them. Pops always read *'Twas the Night Before Christmas* to us which, when I got older seemed kind of weird, but I know it's something I'm going to miss terribly this year. And then, when I *was* older, Pops would sneak into my room at midnight and whisper, 'Merry Christmas,' and together, we'd have a Christmas cookie before he went back to his room. Christmas morning was meticulously planned out. It wasn't a free-for-all. We all sat around the tree and opened up individual gifts while everyone watched. Took hours to get through the presents, and we always paused to refill on hot chocolate or hot cider. A tray of donuts, turnovers, and cookies was always in the middle of the coffee table to add to the sugar high of the day. Christmas music played in the background, there was always some sort of argument going on between my mom and Uncle Paul, and Dad would just sit back, coffee in hand, and take it all in. If magic was real, then it would be Christmas morning at Pops's house."

"I love that," Hazel says just as Ingrid comes up behind us.

"Your wine is ready if you'd like to take a seat at your table."

"Sure." I hold my arm out for Hazel to take but either she doesn't see me, or she ignores it. She walks in front of me with Ingrid as I trail behind her.

Yup, something is off, and I'm not sure she's going to let me pry deep enough to figure out what it is.

Hell, I don't need to figure it out. The problem is still at the forefront of my mind. I dry humped my friend, and now things are awkward. That's what happens when you cross that line and have no plan of action for the repercussions afterwards.

Really smart, Crew.

COMFORTABLY SEATED in our bar-height chairs, I stare at the three bottles of wine in front of us. Are we supposed to drink all of that?

If so, I'm thinking we might have a repeat of last night. There's also accompanying bread and a butter spread, but I doubt that's going to soak up all the alcohol.

Standing beside our table, Ingrid holds a towel over her arm, acing the butler vibes as she speaks to us. "There are three types of wine to know about."

Shit, I hope there isn't going to be a test after, because all I know is white and red. That's it.

"Some might tell you there's more, but here at our winery we believe there are three types: the New, the Classic, and the Great."

"Oh, I thought you were going to throw down some different classifications of wine." Hazel laughs.

"Ah, everyone does. But let me show you what I mean." She gestures to the first bottle. "To us, this would be listed under the New. This would be considered for everyday drinking. A Bacchus wine. Something you mindlessly pop open while making dinner, or that you share with your friends during a gossip night while the best of Shawn Mendes plays in the background. Simple, gets the job done, and good."

Hazel chuckles. "Got to love the sweet combination of a bottle of wine and Shawn Mendes."

"*Oh ja*, a great combination." Ingrid points to the middle bottle. "This is the Classic. Also known as a dinner party wine. A Sylvaner. You would buy this for your birthday or if you are trying to impress your boss while attempting to earn a promotion."

"Ah, the give-me-a-raise wine," I say, pulling a smile from Hazel. "Take notes, Twigs."

"And the third." Ingrid lifts up the bottle carefully and holds it so gently that I actually believe she thinks it might break if handled too roughly. "This is the Great. This is a once-in-a-lifetime wine. A look-but-don't-touch. A dream-about-but-never-open. This is saved for the most special of occasions, like wine tasting in an old wine cellar in the heart of German wine country." She winks and sets the bottle down. "Shall I start you off with the New and work you up to the Great?"

"I couldn't think of doing it any other way," I say, bringing my glass closer to Ingrid. Hazel does the same while Ingrid opens the bottle.

"Now, here in this winery, we pour wine the old-fashioned way."

"How's that?" Hazel asks. Her hands are folded on the table, but her eyes are intrigued.

"It's called 'over the top.'" Ingrid pours the wine into the tall, round glass, filling it all the way to the brim. She sets the glass in front of Hazel and says, "Always to the brim." She takes my glass and does the same, emptying out the bottle. When done, she rests the bottle between us and then takes a step back from the table. *"Prost."* She takes off, leaving me with Hazel and a giant glass of wine.

Hazel and I connect eyes and then we both chuckle as we look back at our wine glasses.

"We're totally fucked if we don't like this wine," I say. "What kind of assholes would we look like if we don't drink it all?"

"Like American assholes."

"Exactly." I carefully lift up my glass, the white liquid teetering close to the edge. *"Prost."*

"*Prost* . . . whatever that means."

I tilt my head back and laugh. "Pretty sure it means 'cheers' in German."

"Ah, okay." She lifts the glass, and I watch her take a small sip, letting her be the guinea pig. When she doesn't flinch or grimace, I take a sip as well.

A little dry, but not so dry that I feel as though my tongue is shriveling up. It has a smooth flavor that glides over my taste buds and straight down my throat.

"Huh, not bad," I say, surprised. "I could totally see this as an everyday wine." I take another sip.

"Oh, yeah. This is one of those wines that you don't really savor. You just guzzle because you're an adult and you can."

"Yes, exactly." We both take another drink, our sips growing bigger and bigger. "Wow, I can see how people could get drunk quick at a wine tasting, especially with glasses full to the brim like this."

"Yeah," Hazel sighs. "I'm going to be wasted by the end of this."

"That a bad thing?"

She eyes me over the glass. "No, it's probably a good thing."

"PROST," Ingrid says, stepping away from the table after filling up new wine glasses with the Classic.

She didn't return until we were done with our glasses of the New, which means we need to drink up in order to get to the Great. This isn't a tasting, this is a guzzling. False advertising.

There should be a sign outside warning, excessive wine guzzling in the cellar, proceed at your own risk.

Already starting to feel a little warm and relaxed inside, I lean back in my chair and slowly twist the bottom of my wine glass.

"Are you ready for the Classic?"

"I'm ready for it," Hazel answers. "I need to know what kind of wine gets me a raise, that's if I ever work a corporate job."

"Do you see yourself doing that?" I ask. "Leaving the farm and pursuing something else?"

She slowly shakes her head. "No, I don't think I could ever leave the farm, unless someone kicked me out. I have too much of my life attached to that acreage. I want to see it succeed, flourish."

"You're pretty awesome, Hazel, you know that? I really admire your loyalty and dedication. I remember when I was a senior in high school, going into my freshman year of college, Pops was talking to me on the phone about you and how hard you worked around the farm. How he thought of you as one of his own. He really loved you, bragged about you all the time."

Her smile becomes teary. "Yeah?"

I nod. "Yeah. He did."

"That's nice to hear. Thank you." She holds up her wine glass and I lift mine, as well. Delicately we clink our glasses, and we don't have to say it out loud to know who we're toasting to. This is for Pops. It's all for Pops.

"THAT'S the fourth time I've gone to the bathroom," Hazel says, sitting back down on her seat. "How are you keeping all this wine in?"

"I've no idea. I've only peed once and, frankly, it's concerning." I lean forward and whisper, "The longer I hold it in, the drunker I get."

"I don't think that's a thing."

"I think it might be," I say, staring at the Great. "There might be research out there that proves it."

Neither one of us has touched the Great; instead, we've been eating bread and going to the bathroom, our laughter growing heavier with every minute that passes.

"Is it me, or does it feel as if the room is slowly, and I mean centimeter by centimeter, turning counterclockwise?" Hazel's eyes track the walls.

I take in the room, and yeah, I think it is. "You know what? I think we might be on some kind of German ride and don't even know it."

"Right? I'm pretty sure the entryway to the tasting room was at least six feet to the left."

I look over my back and take in the entryway. "At least six feet, if not seven or eight." I glance over her shoulder. "And that group of barrels over there, I think they've moved, too."

"The ones behind me?" Hazel shakes her head and holds up her hand. "Don't even get me started on the barrels behind me. Those have been different every trip to the bathroom." She leans forward and says, "What if this place is haunted and the ghosts are floating around, fucking with the drunks?"

"Hell, that's what I would do if I was a ghost."

"It smells like a ghost down here," she whispers.

"You've smelled a ghost before?" I ask, picking up another piece of this delicious bread, leaving out the butter this time.

"I mean, haven't you?"

"Can't really say if I have or haven't. I mean, probably, but who am I to know if it was a ghost?"

"Fair. Fair." She nods. "Well, this cellar smells like a ghost. Take it all in for future ghost-smelling references."

Setting my bread down, I brace my hands on the table and then take a giant whiff of the room, telling myself to commit the smell to memory. "Fruity and bready with a little hint of dinge—that's what ghost smells like. Got it."

Hazel taps her temple. "Keep it locked in. Now you'll know, whenever you run across this smell, you'll understand there are ghosts around you, so if any freaky shit happens, like rooms turning and barrels moving, you'll know . . . ghosts." She whispers the last word.

"God, I'm so glad I'm here with you. I'm learning so much."

"That's what I'm here for." She holds up her glass as if it's the holy grail. "To the ghosts."

I hold up mine as well and clink. "To the motherfucking ghosts."

We take a sip and . . . holy fuck. We lock eyes with each other—as best we can while spinning slowly—and that one look, that's all we have to silently say. Yup . . . this is the Great.

This is once-in-a-lifetime wine.

And I get to enjoy it with Pops's Hazel.

My Hazel.

My girl.

"WHOA, WATCH YOUR STEP," I say, laughing as Hazel tumbles into a wall.

Hands planted against the old stone wall, she says, "Where the fuck did that road come from?"

I help her to stand. "We've been walking on it this whole time."

"Are you sure? Honestly, I thought we were riding on a bus a few seconds ago."

"No, you galloped on a short wall. I took a picture." I hold out my imaginary phone, pretending my palm is the screen. "See, you're galloping."

"Look at that posture." She sends her finger to the sky. "Give me a horse award."

"I don't think that's what they're called."

"Doesn't matter." She taps the spot above her heart. "Pin that blue ribbon right on me."

"If I had one, I would." I reach into my back pocket and pretend to pull one out. "Oh, wait, look, I have one in my back pocket for just such an occasion."

"You clever, clever bastard," Hazel says, swaying back and forth. "Go ahead, pin her on me."

Reaching out, I pretend to pin a ribbon on her, and then I pat her chest, to make sure it's secure. "There, our prize-winning galloper, decorated in glory."

"I don't think it's secure. You need to tap it some more."

"Oh, shit, really?" I reach out and tap her chest a few more times. "There, is it on there?"

She looks down and then back up at me. "One more time."

I pat a little harder, her soft breast taking the brunt of my patting. "There. Good?"

"Satisfactory." She salutes me and then starts to walk away.

"Hazel, you need to hold my hand."

"Why?" Her nose scrunches.

"Because we're about to walk over the old main bridge of Würzburg. It's tradition to hold hands."

"Where did you hear that?"

I sway. "One of the stenchy ghosts whispered it to me before we left." I hold my hand out to her but she doesn't take it. "Hazel, don't make me come after you and force you to hold my hand."

"That hand is dangerous."

I lift it up to my eyes and give it a good look. "How so? It doesn't have any medieval spikes coming out of it."

"It's a tempting hand. Gets me into trouble." She walks toward the bridge, and I catch up to her, standing in front of her, the wine in my belly sloshing dangerously. I steady myself before I speak, because, hell, I'm drunk.

Hands on her shoulders, I force her to look me in the eyes. "Hey, is this because of the dry humping? You haven't wanted to hold my hand all day. We always hold hands."

"I know, and I don't want you thinking I'm some desperate girl."

"What?" My brow creases. "I would never think that."

"But I was the one who tried kissing you and you ran away, and then I humped you while you were drunk. It's not looking good on my end."

"Uhh . . . do you not remember what happened this morning?" I ask. A few people walk by us, bundled up, with concerned looks on their faces. I smile at them and say, "Just talking about our morning escapades. *Guten tag*."

Talking quietly, Hazel says, "It was a lapse of judgment on both of our parts."

"Is that what you really think?"

"Don't you?" she asks, her eyes watery from the wine, her lips a tinge of red, looking more kissable than ever before.

I shrug. "I thought it was pretty cool."

"Pretty cool?" She laughs. "Oh my God. What's wrong with you?"

"I'm a guy. I think getting off with a gorgeous girl is pretty damn cool, no matter how it happens."

"But I'm Hazel."

I nod. "Yes, you are. And I would hump you right here if I could get away with it."

Rolling her eyes, she pushes her gloved hand against my face and knocks me away.

Laughing, I snag her hand and hold it tight. "Stop being

ridiculous and just hold my damn hand as we walk across this bridge. We have that letter to read from Pops. You know, the one that said 'Old Main Bridge'?"

"Oh, yeah. Think you can read it? You're drunk."

"So are you."

"Maybe we can read it together."

"Nah, I got this. I'm the official narrator of this trip."

"What?" She turns toward me. "I never voted."

"Didn't need a vote, it just happened. Plus, my voice is closer to Pops's."

"Because you're his grandson?" she asks, a little irritated.

"Well, that and because I'm a man. I mean, no offense, Haze, but you have a girl voice."

"I can have a man voice." She clears her throat, and in a deep tone she says, "See, I can speak man."

"You sound like a caveman."

"Which means it's a step up from you," she counters, and, damn, if I wasn't so drunk, I think I could come back with something, but she has me.

And she knows it. She snatches the letter from me and opens it up as we lean against a thick stone pedestal that holds a statue of some person, likely important, given the historic area.

Clearing her throat, she holds up the letter but doesn't say anything. I wait.

A few more seconds.

A few more.

"Uh, are you okay?"

Groaning, she slaps the letter to my chest. "My eyes are all out of whack from the wine. You read."

Chuckling and holding back the "I told you so," I read the letter. "'Hey kiddos. Hope the wine was good. Did you have the Great? Life changing, huh?'"

"Yup, life changing, all right. Now I can't read."

I nudge her shoulder and she chuckles. "'I'll make this

note short and quick. I brought you to this bridge because many years ago, and I mean many, I brought Gloria here. We walked along the stone bridge, marveling at the statues and the beauty of the two sides of the town connecting. It felt so majestic, but it was what Gloria said that day on the bridge that changed my life forever. She said, 'Take a look at this bridge, how weathered and worn it is, and yet, it's one of the most magnificent things I've ever seen. It may have its battle scars, but it's sturdy, a strong foundation, and that's something love should be built on.' She was right. There were scars in our relationship, some battle wounds, but underneath the cosmetic features of our friendship was a sturdy foundation that love could be built on. Love you. Pops.'"

I stare down at the letter, my mind whirling, trying to comprehend.

Is he hinting at me and Hazel?

I mean, why else would he bring us here? And write about that? He knew damn well that we've had our moments—my lack of communication being a big one—but we still have a solid foundation.

Pocketing the letter, I glance at Hazel whose eyes are turned down, and she's nibbling on her lip.

"Hey, you okay?"

She looks up at me and asks, "Was he talking about us?"

"I think so," I answer.

She nods and then reaches out and takes my hand. Our palms locked together, we make our way over the rest of the bridge in silence as it starts to lightly snow. Once we reach the end, we walk back, and we keep walking until we reach our hotel. Through the entire walk, we don't say a thing. We don't giggle. We don't laugh. It's almost as if with the snap of his finger, with that one letter, Pops sobered us up.

A foundation to build love on.

Love.

Fucking hell.

Chapter Nine

HAZEL

The worst part about day drinking is that you sober up by nighttime and you have to nurse a hangover before you go to bed, and that's exactly what I'm doing.

Ever since we got back to the hotel, we've been quiet.

I don't know what to say.

Crew clearly doesn't know what to say.

Things have become incredibly awkward.

The dry humping—which I know you know already, but there's that, then the awkward conversations about holding hands.

Pops's letter . . .

Love.

Foundations.

Battle scars.

What?

Jesus. I feel as though I can't think straight, and it doesn't help that Crew has decided to sequester himself on the couch and read a book on his e-reader while I sit here on the bed all by myself, legs tucked into my chest and my head spinning with uncertainty.

Knock. Knock.

Crew perks up. "That must be the food."

"Thank God," I mutter. "I'll get it." I open the door and make small talk with the delivery person and then roll the cart over to where Crew is sitting. "Mind if I sit next to you?"

"Why would I mind?" he asks.

"I don't know. Just seems as though you want to be alone. I could eat my dinner on the bed if you want."

"Don't be ridiculous. I don't want to be alone. I was just giving you space because you looked so freaked out."

"Not freaked out."

"Okay. Then sit next to me," he says.

"Fine. I'll sit next to you." Turning to the food, I lift the lids and don't bother shifting the plates around since we both got a simple burger. Trying to keep things normal, I ask, "What are you reading?"

He doesn't answer right away, and as I dress my burger, I can feel his eyes on me, debating what he should say. I pray that he just moves on. Thankfully, he clears his throat and says, "*The Witcher*."

"Like the Netflix show?"

"It's actually a book and a video game. Netflix came last."

"Oh. I didn't know. Is it good?"

"I mean, I'm not much of a reader so it's taking me longer to read it, but it's neat getting details that you don't get from the video game or show."

"You play the video game?" I ask. "Are you a gamer?"

"No." He spreads mustard on his burger bun. "I play with the boys on occasion, but I spend most of my time studying for school or for football."

"You don't take a break?" I ask, wondering what Crew is like at school.

"I do. That's when I'll hang out with River or Hollis, or go out to our favorite bar. But I don't get too caught up in video games because I know I could easily become addicted." He sets the bun on his burger and then cuts the whole thing in half. "When you have the kind of goals that I do, there's no room for error."

"Oh, so your goals are more important than other people's goals?"

"What?" He turns to me. "I didn't say that."

"You implied it."

"No, I didn't."

"You said your goals don't leave room for error. Do other people's goals leave room for error?" I question him.

"Why are you trying to pick a fight with me?"

"I'm not."

"Uh, yes, you are." He sets his burger down and turns to completely face me. "You're intentionally starting an argument with me. Are you trying to push me away? Is that the goal? Because there's room for error on that, as well. You fail to realize I won't let you."

"I'm not trying to push you away, and if I was, I would succeed because I learned from the best." *Fuck. She looks pissed as hell.*

"Oh, wow, okay." He takes my burger out of my hand and puts it on my plate, only to push the cart away. "You want to get into this, even though I thought we'd made peace with that? Fine, get into it."

"Get into what?"

"Whatever hostility you're harboring toward me."

I shake my head. "There's no hostility."

I reach for the cart but he stops me. "Do you want me to apologize for what happened this morning? Do you want me to say it never should have happened? Because I won't. I fucking liked what we did, okay? I liked it too goddamn much to regret it.

Stunned, I lean back. "That's not what—"

"Want me to apologize over and over again for how I stopped talking to you? Fine, I'll apologize every fucking day. I'm sorry, Hazel. I shouldn't have ever stopped talking to you. If I've learned anything on this trip so far, it's how much I've missed you in my life. I was a fucking moron, a self-absorbed asshole. Okay? And I'll keep admitting to that every day until you can finally, *truly* accept my apology." He grips my hands. "I'm sorry. But I won't apologize for what happened this morning or last night."

"I don't need you to apologize."

"Then what do you need from me?"

"I . . . I don't know." I remove my hand from his and push it through my hair, trying to understand these obscure and foreign feelings rushing through me. "I don't know what I want, Crew. I feel . . . weird."

The anger in his expression softens. "What do you mean, 'weird'?"

"I mean, I want to hold your hand even though I know I probably shouldn't. I want to joke around with you, but I don't know if things are strained between us now. I want to be able to sleep in the same bed tonight and not worry if I need to cuddle or put a pillow between us. Things are just weird and I don't know how to handle it."

He blows out a heavy breath. "Yeah, I don't know how to handle it either. But I do know I want to hold your hand. I want to take pictures with you as we travel around Germany. I want to joke around and sing songs in the car and not be afraid to touch you like I always have."

"You want things the way they've always been, before . . ."

"Yeah, but—" He turns away. "Hell, I don't know, Haze." He shakes his head, almost as if he's trying to dismiss the thoughts in his head.

"What, Crew? Just say it. Say what's on your mind."

Head tilted down, he turns ever so slightly so I can catch

the strain in his eyes, the torment that's flashing through him, as if our situation is taking a serious toll on him. "I like you, Haze. But I'm afraid *that* type of liking you might fuck up everything we have already, and if today was any indication of that, then I don't want things to change."

"Are you saying you want more?" I ask, my chest filling with anticipation and nerves at the same time.

"I don't know," he says, looking down at his hands. "I think I'm right there with you in that I don't know what I want, what I should do. It doesn't seem as though passing this off as nothing is possible. Not with you, Haze."

"I was thinking the same thing. I tried to act normal today, but it just felt weird. I found myself pulling away, not wanting to look clingy or needy."

"You'd never come off as clingy or needy to me," he says, and I can see the truth in his eyes as he looks at me. "Just because you made the first move doesn't mean that you're clingy or needy."

"I know, but it's just how I feel." Groaning, I lean back on the couch. "Do you think this is what Pops wanted? Do you think he was playing matchmaker?" I pick up the bridge letter from the coffee table and look it over. "Am I simply being overly sensitive, or does this actually seem like a matchmaking trip?"

Crew drags his hand over his stubble. "I'm beginning to think that was the case. The bridge letter practically solidified that hypothesis."

"Now that I'm not drunk, I look at the letter and feel like I should be reading between the lines. Or this entire trip—how we have to keep sharing a bed, the romance of the wine tasting. The Romantic Road . . . I mean, I think I'm feeling the pressure."

"The pressure of what?"

"You know." I pull my legs up to my chest. "The pressure

of having to make something of this trip. Of us. And I don't know how to navigate that."

"Hey, we don't have to make anything of this trip other than what we want to get from it."

"And what do you want to get from it?" I ask.

Instead of answering right away, Crew picks up his water and takes a sip. Finally, he says, "Closure. I think that's what I really need out of this. I never got to say goodbye, and that kills me every goddamn day. Coming on this trip, I wanted to get my head on straight and figure out where I was going with my future. Put some closure to the past and move forward, you know?"

"Yes, I can understand that," I say, feeling odd and out of place. I can't put my finger on it—I can't quite comprehend these thoughts going through my head—but it almost sounds as if he wants closure for *everything* to do with Pops.

And I'm not sure if that includes me.

Maybe teenage friendships can't transfer to adult friendships because of the reality of our very different lives. *Even if Pops thought otherwise.*

"What about you?" Crew asks.

I pull the cart close to us again and, this time, he doesn't push it back, so I pick up my burger and take a bite. What *did* I want from this trip? After I swallow, I say, "Just one more moment with him. I wanted to see if he left anything behind, any hints, any clues, anything to help guide me. I feel lost and unsure, and I was hoping that maybe this trip would help me find what I was looking for. And it just seems like a grand scheme at a love connection."

"You're not looking for a love connection?" Crew asks with humor.

"I mean, are you?"

"Wasn't on the list of things to do," he answers.

"Yeah, me either," I say, even though that doesn't feel like the truth. Coming on this trip, I wanted Crew to be my partner in crime and there has to be a reason for that, more than just reconnecting. I think after what happened last night and this morning, I have my answer.

I like him.

I've always liked him.

And I've never gotten over him.

This trip is just making that more and more clear with every second we spend together.

What's even more clear is that Crew isn't in the same headspace as I am. Yeah, he might have initiated what happened this morning, and he said he didn't regret it, but he's also a guy. Guys won't regret anything that allows them to come. Might be vulgar, but it's true. They can detach their hearts from their heads.

Some women can do that, as well.

What I'm learning is that I'm not one of those women.

Not even close.

"How about this," Crew says. "How about we erase everything that we did. I know I said I didn't want to forget it, but it seems like a giant, pink elephant in the room that we need to kick out. So, let's just get rid of it. Acknowledge that we were intimate for a second, but we're more focused on repairing our friendship."

Ah . . . friendship.

Maybe a month ago I would have been happy to hear that, but being here with Crew, seeing him, holding his hand, Crew laughing at my jokes, reminiscing—*the feel of his hard cock between my legs*—I know that it's not just friendship for me. It's so much more, and that's terrifying.

"No pressure from Pops. He might think he's trying to hook us up, but little does he know, we value our friendship more."

I swallow hard, pushing back the emerging feelings. "Yes, focus on the friendship."

"You're sure? We're not going to have any more awkward moments?" He lowers his head so he can catch my eyes.

Braving a smile, I say, "No more awkward moments. Just you and me."

"Good." He pulls me into a hug. "Come here, Twigs." He presses a kiss to the top of my head and it feels so brotherly, nothing like what I experienced this morning with him. "No more weirdness."

"No more weirdness," I answer, feeling my throat tighten. Needing to get away before I lose it, I say, "Don't squeeze me any harder. I have to pee."

"Oh, shit." He releases me with a laugh. "Don't need you peeing your pants while eating dinner. That would bring on the weirdness, and we're trying to get rid of that."

"Exactly." I quickly get up and run to the bathroom, where I shut the door and then lean against it, squeezing my eyes shut.

Pops, what were you thinking?

Crew has never liked me as more than a friend, never will. This just seems cruel.

I try to catch my breath and still my racing heart.

It'll be okay. *You'll be okay, Hazel.* Five more days. *You totally can do this.* Don't be weird. Smile, laugh, and try to enjoy yourself. And after it's done, Crew will return to his life, probably play pro, get married and have a full, error-proof, goal-driven life. And I'll . . . I'll return to the farm, to the town ridicule, to never knowing if I'll ever succeed in meeting Pops's expectations. I'll be too busy to find a husband, and life might just pass me by. But there are five days with Crew that I need to endure . . . *enjoy*. I can do that.

Deep breaths.

CREW IS NEXT TO ME, asleep on the bed. After finishing our dinner, we played some more Dots and Boxes, and then broke off to do our own reading. He went to sleep pretty quickly, but I can't seem to find any need for sleep, so I turn away from him and reach for my phone where it's charging on my nightstand. Knowing my friend, Mia, from back home will be in her florist shop, pruning away, I send her a text.

Hazel: *Hey, do you have a second to talk?*

God, I hope she has her phone next to her like she normally does.

Mia: *Uh, yeah. Sheesh, I've been waiting to hear from you. Last thing I heard was that you landed in Germany and confirmed it was Crew you were on the trip with. I need all the details now. Is he with you?*

Smiling softly, I consider how grateful I am for Mia. We've been friends for a few years now. Her husband, Johnny, moved them back to our small town to help out his parents, and she wound up opening a florist shop while he's a social studies teacher at the K-12 school. We became fast friends, and it's been really nice since she doesn't know much about my background other than what I tell her.

She does know about Crew, though, because she was there for me when he started ignoring all my emails and attempts to reach out. She's also been a steady shoulder to lean on as things have gotten tougher on the farm.

Already starting to feel some of the anxiety ease, I text back.

Hazel: *Sorry, things have been crazy. We're nonstop moving around and attending activities Pops set up for us. And when we're not doing something, we're passed out from exhaustion.*

Or drunk, but I don't say that.

Mia: *Sounds thrilling. I've loved the photos you've posted on Insta. It looks like a story book coming to life. Is that what it feels like?*

Hazel: *Yes, it's kind of crazy how unreal it feels. The buildings resemble something from* Pinocchio, *and it's hard for my brain to wrap around the idea that I'm actually in a real place.*

Mia: *I wonder if people from other countries think the same about America.*

Hazel: *Probably. But yeah, it's been fun. Drank a lot, visited some beautiful places, had some gingerbread, dry humped Crew, and we're on a road trip now.*

Mia: *Wait . . . what?. You dry humped Crew?*

Mia: *Don't think you can just slip that little detail in there and not get called out for it. Deets!*

Hazel: *We were incredibly drunk and it just happened. I don't remember much of it, but what I do remember is the morning after and doing it again.*

Mia: *Oh my God! You dry humped twice?*

Hazel: *Yes.*

Mia: *Why the hell are you keeping your clothes on?*

Hazel: *It's not that easy. I think I like him.*

Mia: *Like . . . *like* him, like him?*

Hazel: *Yeah, and I know he doesn't feel the same way about me, and this entire trip is built around our relationship and Pops trying to play matchmaker. We're sharing a bed in every hotel, we're partaking in romantic wine tastings, and we're on a road trip called the Romantic Road, for fuck's sake. It's messing with my head and I don't know what to do.*

Mia: *How do you know he doesn't feel the same way?*

Crew stirs next to me and I hold my breath, waiting to make sure he doesn't wake. After a few seconds, I type Mia back.

Hazel: *He told me he's here for closure, not for a relationship.*

Mia*: Ouch. Okay, that's a bit of a blow.*

Hazel: *Yeah, tell me about it. I acted as if it didn't hurt me and then ran to the bathroom, where I nearly hyperventilated.*

Mia: *Aww, Hazel, that makes me so sad. I wish I could be there to give you a hug.*

Hazel: *I could use one right about now. One that isn't from Crew. God, Mia. He's . . . he's more than I remembered. Outgoing, fun, charismatic. Sweet, loving. I don't understand what Pops was thinking.*

Mia: *Maybe he was thinking that you two were meant to be together.*

Hazel: *We could not be more polar opposite. He's an All-American college football star about to go off to the combine and try out professionally. I'm a farm girl with nothing to really show for it. Plus I have my sordid family.*

Mia: *That's not true, and you know it. You're not just a farm girl. You have helped change McMann Farm into the bustling tourist attraction it is today. People drive up from all over during the fall season just to go to the farm. You helped create that.*

Hazel: *And I've no clue what's going to happen to the farm at this point. It could be bought out. I could be shit out of luck with no job.*

Mia: *What's really bothering you, Hazel? Is it the farm, or is it Crew?*

Hazel: *The unknown. These unknown feelings. The unknown of what's waiting for me at home when I leave this dreamlike bubble in Germany. It's like, after what happened this morning, I can't find a way to relax around Crew. I can't find a way to have fun and enjoy the time here. I can't find a way to connect with Pops and ask him for advice.*

Mia: *Maybe this time, you have to figure it out yourself.*

Hazel: *That's what I'm afraid of. Once again, being alone.*

Mia: *You're never truly alone. You know that.*

Hazel: *I know. I just . . . I miss him, Mia.*

Mia: *Pops or Crew?*

Hazel: *Both.*

Mia: *And you're dreading the end of the trip because you're not sure when you'll ever see him again.*

Hazel: *I can't even think about it.*

A lone tear slips down my cheek. I quickly wipe it away as my heart aches for what's to come in a few short days. Another goodbye that I'm not ready for.

Mia: *Easier said than done, but I think you need to focus on the amazing opportunity Pops gave you. Enjoy being in Germany with Crew Smith. Focus on honoring Pops. And then when the time comes to say* *goodbye, you let your emotions take over. And, yes, that will be hard, but at least it won't be every day you're there.*

Hazel: *You're right.*

Mia: *Usually am. And text me when you start to feel sad again. You know I'm here for you.*

Hazel: *Thanks, Mia.*

Mia: *Anytime. Now, tell me more about this dry humping.*

"GOOD MORNING," I say as Crew lifts his head from his pillow and looks around. I'm already showered and ready to go for the day, thanks to my restless sleep last night.

I spent the early portion of the morning on the couch, looking out our window at the snow-covered rooftops of Würzburg, deciding how I'm going to handle the rest of this trip.

Yes, I have feelings for Crew. That's obvious. There's no stopping those.

Yes, I miss Pops, and am so thankful for his generosity in sending me to Germany.

Yes, I'm scared of what's to come after this trip and what's supposed to happen to the farm.

But . . .

I'm in Germany.

With a boy who has been a part of my life for as long as I can remember. A friend. A comfort.

I'm getting glimpses of Pops through letters and pictures and maps.

I'm exploring a place I've never seen before.

So, I decided I can either sit and be depressed with all the rapid and unsure feelings I'm trying to drift through.

Or, I can block them out, and like Mia said, enjoy the opportunity.

I choose to enjoy the moment, even though there might be

heartache at the end. I would rather enjoy the here and now, and not worry about the latter.

"Are you showered?" Crew asks, bringing his palm to his eye, rubbing it carefully. His hair is twisted and pulled in all different directions. It's one of my favorite parts of the morning, seeing what kind of hair he's going to wake up with. Today has not been a letdown.

"Yup, and I already picked out what I want for breakfast."

"Well, hell." He sits up farther so the comforter falls from his chest, exposing his bare and toned torso. "I should probably get in the shower then, huh?"

"It would be helpful if you smelled nice while we travelled together."

His eyes land on mine. "I see you're back to your sarcastic self."

I hold my fingers up, pinching them closely together. "Just a minor speed bump yesterday, but all good here. Ready to give you shit all day."

"Lucky me." He smirks and then throws the covers off. He stands and stretches his arms above his head and, shamelessly, I watch as his abs flex from side to side. "What are you getting for breakfast?"

"Sausage and eggs," I say, quickly pulling my eyes away from his body. "I figured I'd order the same for you."

"That would be awesome, and some coffee, please. Given you're already a spitfire this early in the morning, I'm going to need it."

"I suggest an espresso to handle me."

"Oh, shit." He chuckles and heads toward the bathroom. "I'll be quick."

While he's in the shower, I order us food and then start packing up my suitcase for the next hotel. At this point, I leave as much as I can in my suitcase and only take out what I need to because the packing and unpacking is starting to get tiresome. Got to play this road trip smart.

From my backpack, I pull out the envelope marked "Day Four." I can't believe it's only been four days. Feels so much longer than that, as if we've been in Germany for two weeks. Possibly from trying to face all these unspoken feelings and emotions.

Staring at the envelope, I quietly say, "What do you have planned for us today, Pops? More romantic shit?" I shake my head. "You were always a romantic."

The bathroom door opens and I look up to find Crew walking out in nothing but a towel wrapped around his waist and droplets of water hanging from the tips of his unruly hair.

Yup, thanks a lot, Pops. *Why can't your grandson be average looking?*

"Is that the letter for today?" Crew asks while digging through his suitcase. He pulls out a pair of boxer briefs—these have little hot dogs on them—a pair of jeans, and a long-sleeved Braxton College shirt. It's a simple outfit, but he'll still look really good in it. He always looks really good, doesn't matter the time of day.

"It is," I answer as he slips on his boxer briefs under his towel. It's not the first time he's performed the magic trick of getting dressed in front of me without showing any private parts. He must do something like it at college to be such an expert and to be so comfortable changing in front of me.

"Have you opened it?" He slips his jeans on, followed by his shirt, and then he grabs a pair of socks.

"No, I wouldn't do that without you."

He nods at the envelope and says, "Read it."

"I thought you were the narrator of this trip," I tease.

"Nah, you should read one. Have at it, Haze." He smirks and sits on the bed to put his socks on.

It's disgusting how quickly guys can get ready for the day.

With my index finger, I open the envelope and take out the letter. I unfold it carefully and smile to myself as I read out loud. "'Hey kiddos, hope you had fun in Würzburg. Being the start of the Romantic Road, it holds fond memories for me. Crew, it does for your parents as well, as they went on this trip many years ago. I think you were conceived there.'"

"What?" Crew grimaces, causing me to laugh out loud.

"Just kidding," I say. "I added that myself."

Crew points a serious finger at me. "Hey, no improv allowed, or your privileges will be taken away."

"Understood." I smirk and go back to the letter. "'Today you're headed to Tauberbischofsheim.'"

"Glad I didn't have to read that." Crew laughs, coming over to me and taking a seat next to me. "Glad I didn't have to read that after three full glasses of wine, too."

"'This is the home of Germany's first nunnery, which makes it seem fitting to go to St. Martin's first thing. It's a beautiful church in the center of town with gothic architecture that you'll hopefully appreciate while walking through the quiet and peaceful halls. I know you two aren't heavily religious, but I do ask that you go into the church and light three candles. One candle for the past—the memories we have with each other, the ones we'll always cherish. Think of a past memory in that moment, one that brings joy to your heart. Secondly, I want you to light a candle for the present. For the moment you two are able to share on this journey. And the third candle, light that for the future, and what's to come.'" I look over at Crew and ask, "Have you ever been to a Catholic church before?"

He nods. "Many times, with Pops. I've lit candles before too. I'll guide you."

"Thank you." I return to the letter, reading out loud. "'After you offer a little peace and blessing into the world, it's time to put your competitive hats on because you're going fencing.'"

"Fencing?" Crew asks, confused.

"'Tauberbischofsheim isn't just another beautiful stop on the way down the Romantic Road, but it's also well known in

Germany for housing the most famous fencing club in the world. Currently, it's a training base for Olympic athletes, and I've arranged for you to take a lesson and then go to war. This is where you're to take out any leftover aggressions you might have with each other. Hazel Girl, I know you're going to destroy Crew. All I ask is that you take it a little easy on him.'"

"What? No way. I'll annihilate you."

"What makes you think that?" I ask, challenging him.

"Uh, my superior athletic genes. Pretty sure you don't even know the difference between a baseball and a tennis ball."

"With insults like that, you're only adding fuel to the fire of my gloating when I do beat you."

"It's cute that you're so confident."

"It's throw-up-worthy that you're so condescending." I turn back to the letter and finish it. "'All the information you need is attached. Winner gets to pick the other's dinner. You got this, Hazel Girl. Love you, Pops.'"

"Oh, I can't wait to pick the worst thing on the menu for you tonight." Crew rubs his hands together.

"You're woefully cocky."

"Of course I am. This is going to be a piece of cake."

There's a knock on the door, indicating our breakfast has arrived. I stand to answer the door, and as I pass Crew, I pat him on the shoulder and say, "You might want to add a few extra prayers while we're lighting candles. You're going to need them."

Chapter Ten

CREW

"I've been in my fair share of Catholic churches, especially while on road trips with Pops. He always liked to stop in one and light a candle for Gloria." I study the high, pitched ceilings and elegant rose-colored stone that offers height to each pillar. "But I don't think I've ever seen anything like this before."

Polished wooden pews are lined up row after row, leaving just enough room for an aisle down the middle. The altar is beautifully carved wood with depictions from the Bible highlighted in gold, with stained-glass windows on either side, and a dome-like ceiling. It's grand, but also humble, with its white plaster walls. A contrast of rich history and architectural detail you don't see in America.

"I know I haven't," Hazel says in awe, staring up at the tall ceilings. She turns slightly and then says, "Look at the organ."

Behind us is a choir balcony with a pipe organ set as a

backdrop. It's grand, and I can only imagine the acoustics they would have in a place like this.

"I can understand why Pops loved this church so much. He was never a strict Catholic, but he did appreciate a place of worship. Any place—a temple, a synagogue—didn't matter what was worshipped in between the walls, just that there was love and joy and understanding in every space. This seems like a place where Pops would identify those types of emotions." Spotting the candles over in the right corner, I point to them and say, "That's where we need to go."

"Okay." Hazel walks slowly, taking everything in. "Pops has been here, right?"

"That's what the letter said."

She nods. "Is it weird to say that I can almost feel him with us?"

"No. I've felt him many times on this trip, just didn't want to say anything and sound . . . I don't know . . . weird."

"That's not weird at all. I can feel him." She smiles up at me, those captivating eyes nearly gutting me with one look.

Last night, hell, I don't even know what we argued about. I was trying to give her some space. I thought she needed it, but boy was I wrong. That's not what she needs at all. Instead she needs communication, she needs the small touches, the hugs, the jokes. Hell, I need them too.

This morning, waking up to her smiling face, it was a relief to know I didn't utterly fuck things up. The trip to Tauberbischofsheim was fun. A short trip, but we listened to some music, took in the sights, and kept things simple. Normal.

That's how it's been ever since, and I'm grateful because I was nervous that we'd lost our connection, that she was pulling away. It's no wonder Pops loved her so much. And right now, I cannot ever imagine not having her in my life again. She's so beautiful, inside and out, and I know I'm a lucky bastard to experience this adventure with her. *Thank you, Pops.*

When we step up to the candles, I pull out a long match from a glass jar and take her hand in mine. "We need to kneel." Together, we kneel on the kneeling pad, and with her hand in mine, I hold up the stick and I say, "Take it with me." She reaches out her other hand, and we hold it together. "Now we need to light it." We dip the stick in the candle in front of us and watch the tip ignite. "Pops said three candles. Let's start with the past. Be grateful for the past, be conscious of how it shaped us, and always keep a memory close to your heart. Do you have your memory?" She nods and, together, we light a candle. "For the past," I say quietly.

"Now the present, right?" she asks.

I nod and hover our hands over the candle that's next to the one we just lit. "This is for the present, for this moment of being connected again and for connecting with Pops once more." We light it and then we move over to the third and final candle. "For the future and what's to come. Let Pops always be there with us and let us always be there for each other."

"You and me?" Hazel asks.

"Yes, you and me, Hazel. Let us always be there for each other." We light the third candle, and then I lift the stick and blow out the end, depositing it with the rest of the burnt-out sticks.

We don't get up right away.

Instead we kneel silently in front of the candles, and I take this moment to be grateful. To remember that it was a rough year, that I lost my grandpa and my season, blowing my career chances tremendously. I'm lost. I'm sad. I'm unsure of what's to come, but what I do have is a girl who's willing to hold my hand in sad times such as this, in meaningful times. I have friends who care about me and my future. I have parents, an uncle and aunt, and five cousins, who would do anything for me. I have a fulfilling life, even if things aren't going the way I expected. Life might have thrown me some curveballs, but I need to be grateful for what I do have.

And what I do have should be enough to make any single human happy.

Friends. Family. A future, no matter what it might be. It's there, waiting for me to take hold of it.

Hazel squeezes my hand and when I look over at her, I catch tears in her eyes.

"You okay?" I ask her quietly, our voices easily echoing in the vast space.

She nods and wipes a tear off her cheek. "Yeah, I'm good."

"Ready to go?"

"Mind if we just sit in one of the pews for a second?"

"Not at all." I help her to her feet and we walk over to pews that are off to the side but still offer a picturesque view of the baroque altar. We take a seat and Hazel doesn't let go of my hand. Instead she sits close enough to me so she can rest her head on my shoulder. I wrap my arm around her shoulders, then I link my other hand with hers.

Comfortable silence falls over us as we sit in this awe-inspiring church, the only visitors, taking in the serenity the space offers.

"It was a humid as hell day," she says, surprising me. "I was playing out by the big oak tree with that sprinkler that Pops attached to the hose. You know which one."

"Yeah." I chuckle. "Meant for the crops, but he'd hook it up for us and we had to keep enough distance to not get blasted in the head."

"That one. I was jumping around, just doing stupid kid things when Pops came up to me with a glass of lemonade and a plate of cookies. He asked me to sit with him and take a break. Cookies of course got my attention. But what he told me stole the attention away."

"What did he tell you?"

"We were staring out at the cornfields and he told me that his grandson was going to visit during the summer and that he expected us to be best friends."

"He said that?"

She nods against my shoulder. "Yup. He said that his grandson from California was my age, and that I needed to teach him what it meant to grow up on a farm. To show him how to ride a horse. To do chores, to appreciate the little things like a gust of wind bristling through the leaves of an oak tree. And in return, he said I would gain one of the best friendships of my life. I had no idea what he was talking about at the time, but I knew when you showed up, I would do exactly what Pops said because I was grateful to him. That was the first summer I got away from my mom and spent time on the farm with Pops and Grandpa Thomas. That summer changed my life and that's the memory I'm the most grateful for. I didn't know it at the time, but he was right. I was about to meet a lifelong friend and I'm so glad I did."

I lean over and kiss the top of her head. "I'm glad you did too." Little does she know, I'm so grateful she took me in that summer. Grateful she decided to be my friend, because not only was it life-changing for her, it was life-changing for me.

"You don't have to share your memory with me. I just thought you'd want to know."

"It was a humid day," I say, and she chuckles. "I just flew in from California, where there's dry heat, and I remember thinking, why is it so wet outside even when it's not raining?"

She laughs some more.

"That night, Pops told me about this girl and how she was going to be my buddy all summer. I remember thinking a girl . . . no thanks."

She chuckles some more.

"And then he introduced me to you and, God, I was enamored."

"Stop. You weren't old enough to even know what that means."

"I wasn't. I am now, though. I followed you around like a sad puppy, begging for attention. Whatever you did, I wanted to do. And I wanted to do it better."

"Of course you did." I can practically hear the eye roll.

"But that was the moment I thought about from the past, one that I know changed me for the better. Every summer, you grounded me, brought me back to reality, and I think I'm a better person for it. Hell, I know I'm a better person for it."

"Damn right you are," she teases and lifts up, placing a kiss on my jaw.

It isn't an intimate or sexual kiss, it's supposed to be a comforting kiss—I know that's how she intended it—but having her that close to my mouth, feeling her lips on my skin, ignites my entire body with a wave of heated awareness.

I can feel the imprint of her lips on my jaw, the soft, plumpness of them confirming everything I've been feeling since I've been with Hazel again.

I like this girl.

I've missed this girl.

I could see having so much more with this girl.

But how does one even cross over the line of friendship to something more? We tested the waters yesterday and we all know how that went over. She's skittish, and I can't seem to read her mind. Does she want this? Does she not? Either way, I don't think it matters because, like I said, we're here to enjoy ourselves and figure out what we're doing next. I need to stay focused, and make sure Hazel has a wonderful time, putting aside any thoughts of whether or not we've a *romantic* future.

"Are you ready to go?" I ask her, quietly.

"Yeah, I am."

Together, we stand, and I guide her from the pew into the center aisle. As we walk down the aisle together, her hand in mine, I have this weird thought cross my mind.

Me in a tux.

Her in a white gown.

Family cheering for us as we make our way down the aisle as mister and missus.

The image is so clear in my head, so perfectly visible, that it gives me pause.

I stop in the middle of the aisle, my heart racing, and just as quickly as the vivid image popped into my head, it floats away.

"You okay?"

I look at Hazel, noting her worried expression.

What the fuck was that? I glance back at the candles, the future candle seeming to glow brighter than the others. Tall, more prominent.

My heart's racing, my mind's swirling.

I swallow hard and look into Hazel's gorgeous eyes.

"Yeah, everything is fine."

"DO you think you are ready to spar?" Jörg, our instructor, asks.

"Oh, I'm so ready." Hazel lifts her mask and shakes her head, pushing some stray hair out of her face.

I bet she's ready. Ever since she was handed her foil, she's been itching to hit the mats and have a "whack" at me. Jörg has had to remind her a couple times that you don't whack in fencing, but rather, you lunge.

She continues to say whack, and frankly, it's concerning.

During practice, I was impressed with how quick she was. I thought I'd be lighter on my feet, but for some reason, I'm dragging today. I don't know if it's because my head isn't in it again or what, but I am not having an easy time.

"Yeah, we can give it a go," I say, hearing trepidation in my voice.

"Are you scared, Crew?"

Yes.

"Pfft, no. Remember what I said in the hotel? I'm going to destroy you."

"We do not destroy in fencing," poor Jörg says.

"Yes, we lunge to death," Hazel says, fixing her mask back on her head, giving herself a good pat on the top of her head.

I'm pretty sure Jörg is ready for this lesson to be over, so instead of correcting Hazel, he steps between us, and lacking luster, he says, *"En garde."*

Hazel and I both raise our foils into position. I can't see her eyes through the mesh of the mask, but I know if these were clear windows, I'd see utter determination. Hazel has always been tenacious— in everything we've done together— especially if she felt as though I had the upper hand. Little does she know, I don't feel confident in my skills as a fencer at all.

Not when I keep getting flashes of her in a white wedding gown.

"Allez," Jörg says, and before I know it, Hazel lunges at me, poking me dead-on in the crotch. Thankfully, I'm wearing protective gear, so I don't crumble in pain. *What the hell?*

"Oh God, I got you in the manhood. Are you okay?" Hazel asks as Jörg offers her a point.

I hold my hand up and nod. "Yeah, just caught me by surprise is all. Nothing is damaged. Maybe aim higher next time."

"Sorry." She chuckles. "You're just so tall. Your penis is at lunge level."

"Lucky me." I stand and shake out my limbs.

"You ready?" Jörg asks. I nod and so does Hazel. *"En garde."* We get into position. *"Allez."*

Once again, Hazel lunges, and her foil hits my inner thigh with a double jab to my crotch.

"Jesus," I mutter, bending over.

"Point Miss Hazel."

"Did I get you in the junk again?"

I'm curled over slightly as I nod at her. "Yeah."

"Does it hurt?"

"No." I shake my head, even though the jab to the inner thigh was definitely surprising. "Just making sure everything is in place."

"Okay, well, I'm ready when you are."

"Yeah, I'm ready." *Focus, Smith.* Allez *means go, that's when you're supposed to lunge, not just stand there and let her continue to poke you in the dick.*

"En garde." We get into position, and I swear, I catch a glimpse of a smile on Hazel's face through all the mesh. *"Allez."* Is she planning—

She jabs me again, harder this time, and I crumble to the floor.

"Goye . . . my balls."

"Point Miss Hazel."

"Yes, we know," I groan. "Don't kick a man while he's down, Jörg."

Hazel walks up to me, her shoes coming into my view as I kneel on the floor, curled into fetal position.

"Ooops. Did I get you in your precious zone again?"

I slowly turn my head to look up at her. Her mask is off, hanging in her hand, and there's a sinister smile on her face.

"You . . . wench."

The corners of her mouth tilt up even higher while her foil presses against my chest. "I hope this serves as a reminder to you to never underestimate me. I might be small in stature, but I'm quick, smart, and I can tear down your behemoth body any day." She tilts her chin up and walks away.

Talk about being bested.

"YOU ARE A CRUEL, CRUEL WOMAN."

I stare at the Pepto-Bismol pink sludge that's in between two pieces of bread as she laughs.

"You go and stab my testicles multiple times and then order me a herring salad sandwich." I poke the sandwich with my fork and try not to flinch from the ooze of whatever this thing is made of.

"It sounded so appetizing. And Pops did say I could pick what you eat tonight. Why wouldn't I pick a sandwich filled with herring, beetroot, gherkins, and mayonnaise? All on a lovely piece of dark rye bread. It was screaming your name."

I eye her and she tries to hold back her smile, but I can see that it's impossible.

"You do realize you have to share a bed with me tonight, right?"

"Yes."

"And if I have any sort of repercussions from my digestive system not being able to suffer through a new type of food, you're going to have to deal with the consequences."

Her smile falters. "What kind of digestive repercussions?"

I shrug. "Who knows? Could be a series of ungodly events."

Her eyes narrow. "You're just trying to make me change my mind about this."

I eye her pretzel-bun bratwurst, jealousy coursing through me.

"Nah, I'd never do that. I'm a man of my word. I lost, and I'll eat what you place in front of me. Just wanted to make sure you know what might happen if I do."

She crosses her arms over her chest and says, "I'm willing to take my chances."

"Okay." I shrug and pick up my fork and knife so I can cut into the sandwich. There's no way in hell I'm going to pick the sloppy thing up and allow whatever pink juice is coming out of it to slide down my hands and arms. The less contact the better. I cut a small piece and spear it with my fork then hold it up to her. "Cheers to your victory." Without giving it a second thought . . . or smell, I place it in my mouth.

Holy.

Fucking.

Hell.

My nostrils flare.

My taste buds revolt.

My stomach churns.

And, yup, just as suspected, that is not good.

I chew as if the food is on fire, my teeth colliding in a rapid rate, then swallow and reach for my beer. I take a big gulp, gargle, and swallow. That's the kind of class I'm showing right now. I slap my hand on the table, eyes wide, and I catch my breath.

The entire time, Hazel is gripping her chest, laughing her sweet little ass off.

"Oh my fuck," I say on a deep breath, right before taking another swig of my beer. I smack my lips together, trying not to wince from the aftertaste. "Wow, that was . . . a fucking delight."

Hazel throws her head back and laughs some more. "Oh God, I might wet myself."

"Please do. That would make up for whatever you just made me eat."

"What? Are you saying you didn't like it?"

"It tastes like fishy pickles and—" I burp and nearly throw up from the taste on my tongue, as I bring my fist to my mouth, causing Hazel to laugh some more. "Shit, you ruined gherkins for me."

She wipes under her eyes, tears of uninhibited joy forming on her lids. "Oh Jesus." She picks up her phone and quickly takes a picture of me, the light flashing in my face, nearly blinding me.

"What the hell was that for?"

She looks at the picture and laughs even more. "Oh God, I really am going to pee my pants." She shrinks in her seat. "I needed to remember this moment forever. Best part of the trip so far."

"I'm so glad my pain is your joy."

She picks up her napkin and dabs under her eyes. "I'm not even sorry."

"I can see that. There's not one ounce of remorse on your face."

"Not even a gram." She takes a deep breath and settles down. When she's finally not laughing so hard, she picks up her bratwurst and says, "Well, are you going to finish?"

I shake my head. "No way in hell."

"Going to bed hungry?"

"I'd rather not eat at all."

She shakes her head. "Food waste is a big problem in this world."

"Blame yourself." I push my plate away. "You knew I wasn't going to finish that shit."

And then I watch her take a large bite of her brat.

"Oh yeah," she moans. "This is so good. Tastes just like victory."

Such a goddamn wench.

HOLDING MY BREATH, I slowly lift from the bed, keeping my eyes on Hazel the entire time.

I've waited what I consider an appropriate amount of time for her to fall asleep. An hour, to be precise. After dinner—well, her dinner—we came back to the hotel room and played cards. We kept it simple with Kings in the Corner and some California Speed, both games we used to play as kids all the time. I beat her every game in Speed—wished that was the game we played instead of fencing when it came to the dinner choice bet—and we split the games for Kings in the Corner.

After that, we called my parents and told them about the trip so far. Hazel then called her friend Mia, who I talked to for a few minutes on speaker. She sounded pretty cool, and when I watched Hazel talk to her, she seemed relaxed. Made me happy.

We then got ready for bed, and I've been waiting for this moment to sneak out and hit up our snack bag.

Because I'm a starving motherfucker.

I mean, serious stomach pains.

I've no idea how those people on survival shows go without food for so long. I'm hours into no food and I'm at starvation level ten—can't walk, need to crawl across the floor for food because I'm so weak.

I'm almost out of the bed when my phone lights up on my nightstand. I glance at it, and see that it's a text from River.

The food bag is across the room. Maybe if I answer this text, it'll give Hazel more time to fall into a deep slumber.

River: *How are you fuckers doing?*

Before I can answer, Hollis types a response.

Hollis: *Please, for the love of God, don't ask.*

River: *Same, dude. Same.*

Crew: *That bad?*

Hollis: *Are you saying you're faring better than us?*

I glance over my shoulder at Hazel, peaceful in her slumber. God, she's pretty. I have an overwhelming urge to drag my fingers over her soft cheeks but I refrain, remembering exactly why I'm awake right now.

Food.

My stomach wants food.

Crew: *It's not terrible.*

River: *That's because you're humping your friend.*

Hollis: *^^Facts*

Crew: *We haven't humped since. It was a two-time thing.*

River: *That's what you say now. I bet you two are banging on Christmas Day.*

Crew: *Trust me, that's not going to happen. She wants to keep things platonic.*

Hollis: *Oh shit. She threw on the chastity belt. That stings, man.*

River: *Doesn't seem like she was too impressed with the dry humping.*

Crew: *She was impressed. She got off. Twice.*

River: *Just because she got off, doesn't mean she was impressed. Just means she has an easy trigger.*

Hollis: *Yup.*

Crew: *Why am I texting you two?*

River: *You're addicted to us.*

Hollis: *Can't get enough of us.*

Crew: *Yeah, sure, that's it. *Insert eye roll**

River: *What happened to making progress?*

Hollis: *Trying.*

Crew: *Speak for yourself. I think I'm making progress.*

River: *Yeah? Figured out what you're going to do with the combine? Been able to find closure?*

I think on it, the memories of our trip sliding through my mind. Some good, some bad.

Crew: *I think I'm coming close to closure.*

Hollis: *That's cool, man.*

River: *Seems like Germany is where you're meant to be.*

Crew: *Yeah, I guess it is.*

Smiling, I set my phone down and very slowly lift off the bed. When Hazel doesn't stir, I walk quietly to the snack bag, where a container of pretzels awaits my munching.

Breath caught in my chest, not wanting to do anything to wake Hazel, I carefully lift the canister out of the bag, slowly pop open the top, reach into the canister—

"What do you think you're doing?"

Out of sheer terror, I toss the canister in the air, scattering pretzels all over the hotel room while a very unmanly squeal falls past my lips.

I spin around on my heels and catch Hazel sitting up on one elbow, staring me down.

"Jesus Christ. I thought you were asleep."

"Yeah, right. You think I was going to fall asleep before you?" She shakes her head. "I know you, Crew Smith. I knew you were going to sneak off for some food."

"I wasn't sneaking off for some food. I thought I heard something in the pretzel canister. A mouse. As the bigger one in this hotel room, it's my duty to take care of any rodents that might threaten our food supply."

"Did you think up that lie while waiting for me to fall asleep, or come up with it on the spot?"

Succumbing to being caught, I say, "Thought of it on the spot. Impressed?"

"No. It was lame."

"Wow, thanks," I say sarcastically while picking up the pretzels and tossing them in the trash, because a hotel floor doesn't really scream cleanliness.

She laughs, and even though she's awake, it sounds sleepy. "Just keeping it real, Hollywood."

"You're really going to let me go to bed hungry?"

"If you're hungry, eat something."

I stare her down, not trusting that smirk of hers. "You're going to think less of me."

"You do what you think is best."

I chuck a pretzel at her and she laughs. "You're mean." I finish picking up the pretzels and then climb back into bed.

"Aw, are you upset?"

"I'm hungry," I say, pulling the covers over my bare torso.

She faces me in bed and smiles. "Then eat something."

"No. I refuse to eat something in front of you when you have that knowing look on your face. I'd rather go to bed with hunger pangs."

She reaches out and turns my chin toward her. "Are you really that hungry?"

"Starving."

Hopping out of bed, she trots to the snack bag and grabs a bag of Kettle chips then brings them back to the bed. "What if I have a snack and just happen to offer you some?"

"You'd share?"

"Not much of a nighttime snacker, but I could eat something right now."

"Then, yeah. I mean, I wouldn't want you to snack alone. That wouldn't be fair. I'd take one for the team and eat with you."

She chuckles and pops open the bag. "What a knight in shining armor." She picks up a chip and holds it out to my mouth. Without giving it a second thought, I snatch it with my teeth, and she yelps, shaking her fingers out. "You nearly bit my fingers off."

"Careful around a beastly man like me when I'm hungry."

She rolls her eyes and picks up a chip for herself, then she feeds me another and another. And I let her. I want her to be the one in charge of dividing up the chips.

"Who were you texting before you tried to sneak over to the snacks?"

She places a chip in my mouth and I chomp down on it. "How long were you awake?"

"The whole time."

"Seriously? That's some stealthy feigned sleeping."

She casually shrugs and gives me another chip. "Pretending to sleep was a much-needed super power growing up, especially when mom brought someone home and I was on the couch. I knew it was—" She swallows hard. "It was important for Mom that I stayed quiet. So, I did. I learned how to lie so still, unmoving, that no one thought twice of me being there."

My heart aches as I picture Hazel lying on her couch, a peaceful look on her face while she's tormented inside.

"Jesus, that makes me physically ill just thinking about it."

"Sorry, I was just—"

"No." I reach out and place my hand over hers. "It makes me ill thinking of you lying there, trying to be quiet while your mom did who knows what. It makes me sad for the innocent childhood you missed out on. I wish I could have been there more for you."

"You were there enough. You were there during the most important time of the year when I didn't have school to distract me."

"Well, I'm glad."

I don't want to get into a debate again about the years I regret, so I'm not raising my stupidity again.

Nudging me, she asks, "So who were you texting? Late-night booty call?" She wiggles her eyebrows, lightening the mood.

"Nah, none of that shit for me. It was River and Hollis, just checking in. They asked how I was doing with closure."

"What did you say? If you don't mind me asking."

"I said I was getting there." She offers me another chip and I take it. "I think I'm slowly starting to find that closure. Very slowly."

"Doesn't matter how slowly. As long as you're moving forward, that's all that matters."

"Thanks, Haze."

"Why are you thanking me? Besides the chips." She winks and places another in my mouth.

"Just thank you for everything."

"No need to thank me. Just get me something good for Christmas."

"Already have."

"What? Really?" she asks in surprise. "Did you seriously get me something?"

"Yup. And it's good."

"When did you get it?"

"In Nuremberg. At the Christmas market while you were peeing."

"Crew." She pushes my shoulder. "I didn't get you anything."

"You don't have to. You being here is enough." I snag a chip from her and smile while chewing.

Yeah, I can't wait to give her the gift I got.

Chapter Eleven

HAZEL

"Merry Christmas Eve," Crew says, lifting up from the bed to find me walking out of the bathroom, freshly showered and clothed. His hair is rumpled and he has a lazy smile spreading across his face—he's completely and utterly adorable.

"Merry Christmas Eve, Crew." I take a seat on the bed. "I'm assuming you just woke up, but did you get a chance to take a look at the weather?"

"No. Cold today?"

"Snow for the next two days. Calling for heavy snow tonight leading into tomorrow."

"Oh, shit, really?"

I nod. "Looks as though it'll be a white Christmas in Germany."

"Think Pops planned that?"

"Probably." I bring my foot up to put my sock on and say, "I think we should consider spending the day where Pops has planned, and tonight, we drive to the next stop. If the hotel is close we can just head to whatever Christmas location we're supposed to be at."

"Yeah." He pushes his hand through his hair. "That might be a good idea." He tosses the covers off him and goes to my backpack, where the letters are. He picks up the letters for today and tomorrow. "I feel weird opening both."

"I know. Maybe we can just look at the itinerary and not the letter for tomorrow."

"Oh, that's a good idea." He opens up the letter for today and sits next to me on the bed, draping his arm casually over my shoulder as he reads. And because he's just woken up, he's so warm. I swear, male skin does not work properly. His tempting warmth has been hard to steer clear of at night in our bed, because all I've wanted to do was snuggle into him. *But that's dangerous.* "'Hey kiddos. Merry Christmas Eve. How was fencing? If I could guess who won, my money is on Hazel Girl.'" I needle Crew's side and he squeezes me tighter. "'Next on the trip you're headed to one of the most popular stops on the trip, Rothenburg ob der Tauber. Why is this town so popular? A few reasons: it's one of few walled medieval towns left in Germany, meaning the entire town is circled by a large stone wall. But most importantly, you'll find the Plönlein, a yellow, crooked timber house at the entrance of the spital quarter. It's a house that sits in a fork of the town's cobblestone road, and it's the inspiration for Disney's *Pinocchio*. You'll see that Gloria and I took a picture in front of the famous house that splits the town's two towers. I suggest you give it a look, take a picture, and marvel at how a building can be crooked and majestically, can still stand tall. Makes me believe we're all a little crooked in our own way, but with a little support from our friends, from our family, we can still stand tall.'"

"God, that rings so true," I say, missing the advice Pops always offered.

"Truer than I think you know," Crew says softly before continuing. "'I suggest from there, you walk around the wall. There are staircases at the entrance that allow you access to the top. It's the best view of the town you'll get, but note—cars aren't allowed in town, so look for parking outside the walls. Since it's Christmas Eve, and I wouldn't make you drive on Christmas Day, this is a day trip. After you have walked around, maybe pick up a beer stein from one of the souvenir shops, get back in the car for an hour drive to Nördlingen. There will be a package waiting for you at the hotel. Love you. Pops.'"

"I guess we don't need this letter, then," Crew says, holding up the Christmas Day one.

"He really thought of everything." I glance at the letter. "I wonder how long it took him to put this all together."

"Probably a long time." Crew stands from the bed and hands me the letter. "I'm going to take a shower, and then we can get going. If we're driving to two towns today, I want to get a head start so we make sure we spend an adequate amount of time in Rothenburg."

"Sounds good." As he starts toward the bathroom, I call out, "Are you nervous about the package at the hotel?"

"I don't know if I'm scared or apprehensive. Either way, I feel as though I'm not going to be able to appreciate the town we're supposed to be visiting today."

"Same."

"Don't worry about breakfast, by the way. We can pick up some egg sandwiches and coffee from that place downstairs."

"Sounds good."

He ducks into the bathroom, and I sit back up on the bed, pulling out the picture of Gloria and Pops. It's faded—the colors almost all seem to mesh together—but their smiles are clear and so is the crooked building in the background. I wish I'd met Gloria, but she passed away before we were even a thought. Seeing this side of Pops makes me wonder if I'll ever experience the love they did. He was so kind and thoughtful, romantic with his beautiful wife, and sensitive to two young kids who needed his wisdom. *Still* need his wisdom. Makes me wistful.

According to the many stories Pops shared about Gloria, she and I share the same vivacious attitude and hate being told we won't achieve something we set out to do.

Maybe that's why Pops liked me so much, because I reminded him of his Gloria.

I rub my thumb over the picture, smiling to myself.

"What do you think, Gloria? Think I'm crazy to like your grandson?" I sigh. "Yeah, crazy stupid."

"THANK YOU," Crew says to a fellow tourist who took a picture of us together in front of the Plönlein.

"Of course," the guy says before walking off with his boyfriend. While we waited in line, we struck up a conversation with them and found out they were on their first official trip together as a couple. We took a picture for them and they were kind enough to return the favor. "Enjoy your stay." They wave and we wave back.

From my back pocket, I pull out the picture from Pops and hold it next to Crew's phone. We compare the pictures and, once again, it feels like Pops is here, looking over our shoulders, enjoying the picture with us.

"My mom will love this picture." Crew sends it to her and then he stuffs his phone in his pocket. He brings his hands to his mouth and blows in them. "Fuck, it's cold out today. Usually the sun helps warm things up, but with a storm coming, I feel as if my dick is turning into an icicle."

"That's a visual," I say.

"I don't know if I can stay outside too long."

I pat him on the back. "That California blood of yours is really showing."

"You're telling me you're not cold right now?"

I shrug. "It's cold but I'm not going to be dramatic about it."

Crew's head swivels to face me. "Are you calling me dramatic?"

"Yes."

He nods, nostrils flared. "Okay, I see how it is."

"Good. Glad you can recognize the truth." I loop my hand through his arm and say, "Let's go into that shop over there. It has beer steins."

"I'll go anywhere as long as it's not outside."

As we walk toward the shop, I ask, "Am I going to have to get you something warm to drink in order to make it to the wall?"

"You might."

"Why aren't you wearing the scarf I bought you?"

"Left it back at the car."

"Well, that wasn't very smart, was it?" I ask as Crew opens the door to the shop for me.

We're instantly hit with warmth, and Crew groans. "Oh, that feels fucking good."

Turning toward him, I say, "That sounded really sexual."

"This very well might be a sexual experience for me," he says, rubbing his hands together.

"You're pathetic."

"I'm aware." He laughs, and I guide us over to the quirky beer steins.

"I want to get something for Mia and Grandpa Thomas." I pick up a stein and nearly choke on the price. "Holy shit, these are expensive."

Crew picks one up and takes a look at the price. "Sixty euros isn't bad."

"Says the boy who grew up outside LA in a house that overlooks the ocean," I say, the tone of my voice snarkier than before.

"Hey, I didn't mean to be insulting."

"I know. Sorry. I was just surprised is all."

"You know we still have a huge dent to make in the money Pops left us."

"I'm not using that money to buy gifts for Mia and Grandpa Thomas."

"Why not?" He casually picks up another stein. "I used it to buy those pant-less cherubs. He said to use the money however we wanted."

"You used it for the cherubs?" I ask, feeling as though it might be okay for me to use it since Crew did.

"Hell yeah."

"Okay." I nibble on my bottom lip. "But I still don't want to pay sixty dollars for a beer stein."

"This one is thirty." Crew holds up a more decently sized one.

"Really?" I take it from him and examine it. "Think you can fit a normal-sized beer in here?"

"Do you expect Mia and Grandpa Thomas to actually use them?"

"Why not?"

Crew examines the bottom of it. "I don't know. I thought they were meant to be decorative."

"No, I think you can drink from them." Not being shy at all, I walk up to the register and ask the store clerk, "Hello, I was wondering if you could drink from these?"

The elderly woman with her hair in a crown braid smiles softly and nods. "Ja. Hand wash."

"Thank you." I turn to Crew. "See? You can drink from them."

"Huh." He scratches his chin. "I wonder if I should have got the boys beer steins instead of pant-less, musical cherubs?"

I shake my head. "No way. The cherubs are so much more fun. Think about their reactions. They're going to see they got a package from Germany, know it's from you, and expect something like a beer stein, but instead find a cherub and a heartfelt card telling them how much the figurine reminded you of them."

"Oh, shit, I forgot about the cards." He chuckles. "You're right. I just wish I could see their reactions when they open them."

"I'm sure they'll be the *what the fuck* expressions you have in your mind."

"Especially River. Pretty sure Hutton will love it, though."

"Hutton seems like the type who would marvel in such a present."

Crew chuckles and picks up another beer stein, giving it a good look. "Yeah, he's the kind of guy who will probably leave it around the house he shares with other athletes to try to freak them out."

"Oh, yeah, that's what I'd do too."

He nudges my shoulder with his. "See? You two would be great friends. You don't have to be salty about him."

"I'm not salty about him anymore. Actually, he's hot. Why don't you set us up?" I ask jokingly, but the smile on Crew's face falls.

"He's taken."

"I was kidding, Crew."

"It wasn't funny," he says seriously, reaching out for another beer stein.

"Are you seriously mad right now?" I ask, my brows pulled together.

"Do you think my dad would like this?" he asks. "I think I want to get one for him and Uncle Paul."

I needle him with my finger. "Hey, don't ignore my question."

"Do I look mad?"

"Uh, you sound mad."

"I'm not. Just nice how quickly you've asked to be set up with all my friends, even though I'm standing right in front of you."

"Whoa." I hold my hands up. "Where's this coming from?"

"I'm sensitive," he says, and I see the smallest crack of a smile pass over his lips. "My man feelings can't take the harsh dismissal of my good looks and superior charm for other men."

I roll my eyes. "Oh my God, I really thought you were mad."

I really thought he wanted to be considered.

Ha—of course he's joking.

I'm not his type. Not his match. Not the kind of girl he could ever see himself with.

"I mean, it wouldn't hurt to have my ego stroked every once in a while." He holds up a black beer stein with the Plönlein carved into the cylinder.

"You get your ego stroked enough by everyone else around you. What you need from me is reality."

"Oh yeah?" He tucks the black beer stein into the crook of his arm and picks up a matching one. "And what's my daily dose of reality going to be today, Twigs?"

I find a green stein that has a white castle carved into it that I know Mia will love. She's all about the fairy-tale romance. "Reality is you're stuck in Germany with me for Christmas, and unless you want it to be an awkward Christmas, I suggest you don't ask for your ego to be stroked."

Wiggling his eyebrows, he asks, "Can I ask for something else to be stroked?"

I press my palm to his face and push him away. "You wish."

He wraps his arm around my waist and pulls me into a hug. "Ah, only in my dreams, right, Haze?"

The press of his chest against my back combined with the feeling of his words dancing across the back of my neck has me catching my breath quicker than expected.

"You tell me," I say, feeling breathless.

"Do you need help with those steins?" the store clerk asks, walking up to us, looking concerned at how Crew is holding me. Probably doesn't want anything to break.

Crew releases me and says, "I'm going to take these. What about you, Twigs?"

I hold out the green one, trying to appear as casual as possible, even though there's a wave of butterflies in my stomach from his touch, from his words, from the suggestion in his tone.

"Uh, this green one. Thanks."

The clerk takes the steins from us, and I right my jacket as Crew moves past me, his arm brushing against mine as he makes his way to the glass ornaments.

I steady my breath and follow closely behind. "Look at this. It's a pretzel." Crew holds out an ornament, acting as if everything is normal.

"Do they have an RV? That would be a cool one for your mom."

He sets the pretzel back on its hanger and then searches around. "No, but not sure how popular an RV ornament would be in Germany."

"Too bad they don't have a Funyun bag."

He chuckles. "Now that's an ornament I would buy for everyone, including you . . . even though I already got you something."

I sigh. "Stop rubbing it in. I feel like I need to find something to give you."

"Nah, I'm just teasing you. You don't need to get me anything."

"What are you going to open tomorrow?"

He shrugs while looking over some baubles. "Maybe Pops left something."

"Maybe." Taking in the rest of the shop, I ask, "Are you good in here?"

"No, I think I want to stay a few more hours."

I playfully push at him. "You're braving the cold. I don't care what you say."

"Brutal."

"HOW ARE YOU DOING?" I ask as Crew cuddles up to his large coffee.

"Surviving."

"You're so strong," I say sarcastically as we make our way around the town, walking on top of the stone wall. It barely fits two people side by side. Thankfully I'm smaller than Crew or else we'd be having a hard time walking next to each other. On the outer side of the wall, it extends up and connects to a wooden roof, providing shelter from the freshly falling snow. It's light, but it's starting to increase. And the town side of the wall is blocked off by a wooden split-rail fence that I don't think could take the weight of Crew if he fell into it.

"How much longer do we have?"

"We're almost back to the start. Glad you could enjoy this once-in-a-lifetime stroll with me instead of counting down the minutes."

"I'm sorry," he says quickly. "I don't know what's with me today. It's the lack of scarf. Shit, okay." He shakes his arm out and puts it around me. "What do you want to talk about?"

"Are you using me as body heat?"

"I wish that was an option, but you're so goddamn small it makes it impossible to steal any warmth from you. Just trying to show you that I'm enjoying our *stroll.*"

"You don't need to put your arm around me to do that. You could tell me what you like about this town."

"Honestly, I think this has been my least favorite place we've visited."

"Really?" I ask, surprised. "It's a very popular destination. Why is it your least favorite?"

"I just don't feel Pops here. I don't know. Maybe it's because we've just walked around and there hasn't been an activity. But I don't know, it hasn't really struck me."

"Is it because you're itching to get to the hotel and open the package waiting for us there?"

"Maybe," he says quietly.

"I can understand that. You're distracted so you can't appreciate the beauty of Rothenburg ob der Tauber."

"I guess not."

"Then let's pause for a second." The entrance to the stairs and the town are right up ahead, so we don't have much farther to go. I turn Crew toward the town and we both look out over the carbon-copy red roofs and timber houses. "Can you imagine what life was like back then, living in the circle of the town, barricaded by a wall to keep you safe, never knowing if anyone would come and attack you?"

He joins me and leans against a pole. "No, I can't. Honestly, I don't think I'd survive."

"Why do you say that?"

"Spent my whole life working on throwing a football. That wouldn't have gotten you anywhere back in the day. Now, you—you, on the other hand, would be able to hold your own on many accounts. Even fencing." We both chuckle. "I would have to marry you, keep you by my side, be your homemaker while you took care of the dirty work for our household."

"Is that so?" I ask, the thought of marrying Crew churning my stomach with nerves.

"Yeah, and I'd be one hell of a homemaker. You'd always come home to fresh bread."

"Do you even know how to make bread?" I challenge him.

"Hell yeah, I'm the baker in my frat. The boys call me . . . uh . . ." He pauses, his nose scrunched up. "Uh, who's a famous baker?"

My head falls back as I laugh. "Duff Goldman."

"Who's that?"

Rolling my eyes, I say, "Never mind. So, you can make bread?"

"Yeah. And as we both know, I am accomplished at making cookies, thanks to Pops."

"True. What about dinner?"

He takes a sip of his coffee and says, "Well, I know how to grill. I know, I know—typical frat-guy cooking. But we do a lot of barbeque. I made a chicken noodle casserole once that was pretty good. I also know how to make homemade cornbread, and I can roast veggies."

"Okay, that's a pretty good start. Now when I came home after doing all the—as you called it—dirty work, would I find my husband looking pretty, put together, and in an apron?"

"Is that what the wife would require?"

"It is." I take his coffee from him and sip as well, feeling a little colder now that we're not walking, but loving this conversation.

"Then, yes, I'd look like a smoke show for you every day when you got home so you'd have no choice but to want to jump in the sack with me."

"But the food would get cold," I suggest.

He taps his chin. "Good point, and since we're in the medieval times, we don't have access to an oven to keep it warm, just a fire. I'm not proficient with fire cooking to know if the food will stay warm or burn. Hmm . . . oh, how about we eat naked in bed?"

"Naked with you?" I give him a smooth once-over—or at least I attempt a smooth one. "Eh, I think I'll pass."

His eyebrows shoot up to his hairline. "Excuse me? You've seen what I have to offer."

"Is that supposed to impress me?"

A smile creeps over his lips. "You little shit." He pulls me against his chest and I laugh as he kisses the top of my head, something I'm starting to love.

We were always tactile with each other growing up, but it

was more about lighthearted jabs and taunts rather than affectionate touches and kisses. *He's changed. And I like that.* Especially since Pops used to kiss my head, too, whenever we shared a story or moment together. Another thing I miss. Thank God for Grandpa Thomas, who still greets me with a hug when I see him.

Who will hug me when he's *gone?*

Affection wasn't something my mother ever doled out to me—there was never anything left for me—yet it's clear it's something I love. *Need.*

And that's not the best revelation to grasp right now, Allen.

Crap.

The rest of the walk down the stairs is easier. Lighter somehow. We share his coffee, handing it back and forth, and when we reach the entrance of the town, I spot a bakery to the left. "Want to grab something for the road?"

"If you're asking if I want a pastry, the answer is yes."

"That was the right answer."

We walk over to the bakery and Crew opens the door for me like the gentleman he is, and not only are we hit with warmth again, but also with the delicious smell of fried dough. The shop is lined with glass cases full of differently colored fried dough-like balls. Some dipped in chocolate, some white chocolate, some pink, some green, some covered in powdered sugar, some in candy. There almost seems too many to count all at once. To the right is a baker rolling out dough behind a sheet of glass. Next to him is a large fryer, where there are sticks poking out from the hot oil.

"What kind of heaven is this?" Crew asks, his hand pressing against my back as we walk up to a case.

"Schneeballen," I say, reading a sign. I pull out my phone and look it up quickly. "Fried dough in a ball, basically, and it seems as though they've gone wild on the toppings and different flavors."

Crew rubs his hands together now and says, "This is where I lose the definition in my abs."

"If you were going to lose definition, I think it would have been with the copious amounts of Lebkuchen you've eaten."

"Nah, that's all nuts. Healthy."

I laugh. "Okay, Crew. Pretty sure you'll never lose definition in your abs."

He raises a brow in my direction. "And here I thought you were unimpressed with what I have to offer."

Damn it.

He chuckles, knowing he got me. Taking my hand, he leads me to the register and says, "Hello. We'd love six Schneeballen with accompanying mallet and board to break them open."

"Of course. What flavors?" the clerk asks.

"FUCK, THAT WAS NOT FUN," Crew says, letting out a long breath as we make our way down the hall to our hotel room.

After purchasing our Schneeballen—cranberry for Christmas, an original, chocolate-covered pistachio, and a strawberry, we decided to head to our next destination.

Instead of eating the Schneeballen on the trip, I helped Crew navigate to the hotel, the both of us tense the entire time from the snow and the unknown roads. I tried to keep him as calm as possible, but I could tell he was incredibly tense and trying to be careful.

"No, but we're here now," I say as he opens the door to our hotel room.

Instead of walking in, he pauses at the door.

"Everything okay?" I ask.

"Yeah, it's just really small. I think it's the smallest room we've had since we started our trip." He walks in and I follow behind him. The ceiling is slanted on one side to go along with the triangle shape of the roof. There are two twin beds mashed together under the slanted ceiling. On the other side is a dresser/desk combination and a mounted TV. There's about four feet of space, if that, between the beds and the dresser/desk, and I'm pretty sure Crew's legs might fall off the end of the bed.

"Those aren't regulation-sized twin beds," Crew says, setting his suitcase to the side and then taking mine from me. I have the Schneeballen in my other hand and set that down on the desk.

"Looks as though we'll be nice and cozy for Christmas Eve."

"Yeah, seems that way." He sets his backpack down just as there's a knock at the door.

I answer it, and it's Anja from the front desk. "Here is the package that was sent for you." She looks past me and into the room. "Is everything to your satisfaction?"

"Yes, thank you."

"It's great," Crew says from behind me.

The hotel is quite small. It's better known as a restaurant with some rooms on the upper floors, and the owners seem quite nice, especially to house people on Christmas Eve and Christmas Day.

"Let us know if you need anything. We will have the dinner you ordered sent up soon, and tomorrow morning you said you woud like your Christmas brunch at nine in the morning?"

"Yes. That would be great. Thank you."

Anja gives me a curt nod and disappears as quickly as she showed up. Package in hand, I take it to Crew and hand it to him.

He stares at Pops's handwriting that reads "Open Christmas Eve."

"Are you going to be okay?"

He nods. "Yeah. You? This isn't just about me, you know."

"I know, but I never spent Christmas with Pops. This seems more important to you."

"Well, now you get to spend Christmas with him." He sets the package down and says, "Let's get settled and then we can open it. How does that sound?"

"If that's what you want." I'm trying to be extra sensitive, as I know Crew has been nervous about this package, so I'll follow his lead.

Silently, we move around the hotel room, almost like clockwork now. We set up our suitcases, I pull out a few toiletries, placing them in the tight-fitting bathroom. Then I gather my pajamas, quickly change, and wash my face. When Crew is in the bathroom, I plug my phone in on the right side of the bed, the side I've been sleeping on since the start of the trip, and check my messages. I have a few from Mia that I quickly answer. I send her a few pictures, tell her I got her something, and that I can't wait to see her to tell her all the details.

When Crew emerges from the bathroom, he almost looks somber as he moves around the room and then finally takes a seat on the bed, where the package waits for the both of us.

"You sure you're okay?" I ask.

"Yeah." He takes a deep breath and picks at the tape. It takes him a few seconds, but he tears the tape off and opens the box. At the very top is a piece of construction paper in bright green. It says, "Play Christmas music."

On my phone, I pull up my music app and search for Christmas music. "Do you want instrumental or traditional? Pop Christmas? Country Christmas?"

"Crooner Christmas," Crew says. "That's what Pops always used to play. That and Mannheim Steamroller. God, he loved that music so much."

"Should we play Mannheim Steamroller, then?"

Crew gives it some thought. "Yeah, actually, I think that's what we should play."

"You got it." I look up their most recent Christmas album, select random play, and the warm sound of the xylophone fills the room as "Carol of the Bells" floats into the room. *Perfect.*

Looking a little less sorrowful, Crew lifts up a handful of shredded newspaper to find an envelope. I scoot closer so my shoulder is now pressing against his and I can hold his hand if need be.

He opens the envelope and reads out loud. "'Hey kiddos. If you're reading this, you made it to Nördlingen. The hotel is quite small, but I chose this hotel for its more intimate atmosphere. The staff was very accommodating when I spoke to them on the phone, and said you'd be taken care of when you arrived. Being away from home for Christmas I know is going to be different, especially for you, Crew, but I figured I'd try to bring a little bit of Christmas to you. Lift up the tissue paper. I'll wait.'"

Crew reaches into the box and lifts up the tissue paper, revealing two sets of matching plaid Christmas pajamas with tiny reindeer printed in the fabric. Immediately Crew laughs out loud as he pulls them out.

"Oh my God, matching PJs," I say, unravelling one that seems to be a long-sleeved thermal nightgown. "This must be mine." I unravel the other, and it's just a pair of pants. "Unless you think you can fit into the nightgown."

Crew snags the pants. "Over my dead body." He goes back to the letter. "'Can you imagine there aren't a lot of options for Christmas PJs in the summer? So, hope you guys like them. Lift up the tissue paper.'" Crew removes more tissue paper, revealing two wrapped boxes. "'These are for Christmas, so don't open them just yet. Just something small. And the pop-up tree is so you have a place to put them.'"

I take out the crepe-paper decoration and expand it, forming a small paper tree, and secure it back to itself. "This is perfect," I say, placing it on the dresser near the window, where we can see the snow falling. Our very own little Christmas. When I move back to the bed, Crew stops me, sits me on his leg, and wraps his arm firmly around my waist. Knowing he needs this comfort, I don't protest; instead, I loop my arm around his shoulder.

"'I wish you had cookies of mine to eat tonight, but I doubt they would have been good after such a long wait. Instead, I asked the hotel to provide you with the best cookie platter they have. Finally, lift up the last bit of paper.'" Crew lifts the paper and I hear him suck in a sharp breath. His hand releases the letter and he reaches into the box, pulling out a small recorder and a tattered version of *The Night Before Christmas*. "No fucking way," he whispers, shaking his head. "No . . . fucking way."

"Is that the book Pops read to you every Christmas Eve?"

Crew strokes the cover almost reverently and nods. "Yeah. It was the one he read from when my mom was young, too. I can't believe he sent this." Crew sucks in a deep breath. "Fuck." And then I catch him wipe under his eye.

"Hey." I tilt his head up toward mine and catch the tears in his eyes. "Want me to read the rest of the letter?" He nods. I pick it up and find where he left off. "'One of the greatest treasures of spending the holidays with you was passing down the traditions I shared with your mom and uncle Paul to you. I can only hope you'll do the same. But for this last Christmas, let me . . .'" My voice trails off as I suck in the tears as well. "'Let me read to you one last time.'"

Crew covers his eyes, and I quickly hug him as tears fall down my cheeks. He grips me tightly, his body shaking. He presses his face against my shoulder, and I can feel the tears as they soak through my top. Together, we hold each other, not saying a thing, just letting the moment hang over us.

After a few minutes, Crew pulls away and takes a deep breath. "Should we get changed?"

I nod. "Yeah." I take the nightgown into the bathroom and quickly change into it, realizing just how skintight it is, and it's shorter than I thought, hitting me mid-thigh. It's comfortable but revealing. I contemplate changing, but knowing Pops planned for us to wear matching PJs, I suck it up and step into the room, where Crew's wearing his low-slung pajama pants and his chest is bare.

Jesus.

I know he always goes to bed shirtless, but for some reason, seeing the waistband of his boxer briefs peek past his pants has my nipples hardening, which doesn't bode well for me since I'm braless and this shirt clings to me like skin.

Crew spin towards me, taking me in, and I watch as his eyes travel up my body, pausing at my breasts. His hand goes to the back of his head and he looks away.

"Uh, want to listen to the book?" he says, still looking away.

"You want to do that now?"

He nods. "I'd rather get all my crying out before dinner and then enjoy the rest of the night."

I chuckle. "Okay." I move to the bed, and Crew joins me. We lean against the headboard with the book and the recorder. The nightgown barely covers my legs as I take a seat, and I can feel Crew's eyes on me.

"That nightgown is something else." He laughs.

"Yeah, pretty sure he got the size wrong. Or forgot the pants."

"You can change if you're uncomfortable."

I shake my head. "No, these are our Christmas PJs and I will wear them."

"Fair enough." He opens the book and says, "Okay, press play."

Taking a deep breath, I press play, and it takes a few seconds, but Pops's deep, burly voice sounds through the recorder. "'Twas the Night Before Christmas . . ."

And let the tears begin.

Chapter Twelve

CREW

"These cookies are really good," Hazel says. She's lounging across the bed and eating a cookie. Her face free of all makeup, hair cascading around her shoulders, wearing that goddamn nightgown as if it's not showing off every curve of her body, she's stunning. Her nipples have been hard for the past two hours, and I know this because *I can't stop myself from looking*.

Shameful, man.

But, hell, look at her. She's fucking gorgeous, and I don't even think she knows it. She has no clue the effect she has on me. She has no idea what it meant to me that she allowed me cry into her shoulder freely. I felt no judgment. Sharing in the moment of listening to Pops read to us was the best thing Pops could have given me. And she has no idea what it means to me to have her here, holding me, letting me hold her, reminiscing about Pops and sharing this Christmas together.

I'm itching to hold her again, to touch her, to . . . fuck, I want to kiss her. I've wanted to kiss her all goddamn day, especially when she was making fun of me for how cold I was. I loved the smile on her face, how she couldn't believe this *strong, muscular man* could be such a wuss in the cold weather. I loved everything about it.

And now that we're in this tiny hotel room, the snow falling outside, covering every rooftop and window in a blanket of Christmas, my restraint is starting to dissolve.

"They are good," I say, peeling my eyes away from her tits once again.

"The almond thing is my favorite." She examines the cookie, completely clueless of my leering.

I'm emotionally exhausted. I don't think I could take one more surprise from Pops at this point. I'm mentally drained as I attempt to figure out what the hell I'm going to do with my life, on top of navigating these strong, unforeseen feelings I have for Hazel . . . while trying not to scare them away. And I'm physically tapped. There's only so much I can do to keep myself from not touching her, but I still end up touching her anyway. I love the feel of her soft hand in mine. I love having her lined up against my side as she holds me around the waist. And I love that she understands. She's living through the pain with me.

"Yeah," I say mindlessly.

Her foot nudges my leg. "You're not being all Christmas-y."

"I know. Sorry." I blow out a hard breath and push my hand through my hair. I catch her eyes rake over my chest. That's not the first time that's happened. No, while I've been catching glimpses here and there of her, she's been doing the same thing, but after every glimpse she takes, her tongue peeks out and wets her luscious lips.

With every minute that passes, the attraction just grows heavier and heavier.

I swear it's these pajamas. What was Pops thinking?

Hell, he was probably hoping something like this would happen, that the sexual tension would be so thick it's almost stifling.

"My head is all muddled right now," I say honestly.

"Anything you want to talk about?"

"Nah." I take a sip from my water and ask, "What were your traditions at your grandparents' house? Did you do anything special?"

"Well, nothing like you, but we did have this one stupid tradition that we did every year."

"Why is it stupid?"

"Because it's not, you know, all warm and cozy like baking cookies and wearing matching pajamas."

"But it reminds you of Christmas, right? Of good times?"

A small smile passes over her face as she rotates so her stomach is flat against the bed and her legs are propped up behind her. "Yeah, it never felt like Christmas until we did this."

"See, it's not stupid. What is it?"

"Promise you won't laugh?"

"Promise," I say, full of sincerity. She's made this a safe place for me to open up, and I want to do the same for her.

"So, you know how TBS plays *A Christmas Story* on loop?"

"Yeah."

"Well, we play it Christmas Eve, watch it late into the night, and then when we were opening presents, we'd have it on in the background. We tried to count how many times we'd see Ralphie stroke his hand up the soft glow of electric sex—the leg lamp."

I burst out in laughter—not because of her tradition, but her description. "Oh, hell, he does say that, doesn't he? The soft glow of electric sex?"

She nods. "Oddly, my favorite part of the movie."

"Don't blame you. Fra-gee-lay has got to be one of the best parts, as well."

"Yes." She chuckles. "I think every person who has a love for A *Christmas Story* pronounced *fragile* like that at some point in their life."

"Hell yeah, I know we did. Hey, want me to grab my iPad and we can watch it?"

"You have it?" she asks, perking up.

"I'm sure I can find it on one of the subscription services I have. How about we clean up, get ready for bed, and then watch it?"

"That would be perfect. You don't mind?"

I shake my head. "Hell no, it'll be fun—bringing our traditions together."

She smiles. "Yeah, that would be nice."

We take care of the food and set the tray outside our door like we were told to do. We're saving the Schneeballen for tomorrow and ate the cookies tonight in honor of Pops. We both take turns going to the bathroom and brushing our teeth. While she's finishing up, I grab my iPad and start searching for *A Christmas Story*. Thankfully, it was easy to find and I cue it up.

Hazel emerges from the bathroom and turns off the overhead light, leaving only the nightstand light to illuminate the room. I try not to stare, but I can't take my eyes off her as she lotions her hands and walks toward me, her small but curvy frame perfectly accentuated in her nightgown.

Hell.

"Did you find it?" she asks.

"Huh? Oh, yeah, I did."

"Perfect." She slips under the covers with me and squeezes into my side, immediately resting her head on my chest, so I drape my arm around her and pull her in tight. "Are you going to judge me if my laughter is obnoxious?"

"No. It'll probably make me laugh harder." I press play, and she snuggles in even closer, tangling her top leg with mine.

The smell of her lotion lulls me with a sense of comfort, but the feel of her warm body against mine sends me into a tailspin of lust.

Instead of focusing on her, because that's going to get me nowhere, I turn my attention to the movie and try to get lost in the comedy.

But with every inhalation of her lotion and rub of her leg against mine, my mind drifts to something else, and I can't focus on what Ralphie's saying. All I see is him moving about the little screen, but the words? They're drowned out by the beat of my own heart.

"God, I love the dad," Hazel says, her hand falling to my stomach, where her fingers slowly glide across my skin.

Fucking hell.

"Yeah, he's . . . funny," I say on a swallow as awareness shoots straight to my cock.

Does she realize what she's doing to me? Does she realize the slightest touch has my skin burning for more? Does she know that ever since I saw her on the airplane, I've wanted to bury my hand in her hair and bring her mouth close to mine, making up for my missed opportunity?

Does she know how fucking turned on I was when she was on top of me, riding my cock, seeking her own pleasure? And the morning after—does she know how much I wanted to stay in our hotel and repeat what we did over and over again, but this time, let our lips meet?

Does she know that when she wakes up in the morning, she's the most gorgeous thing I've ever seen, and when she walks into the room, I can't help but smile?

Does she know she's my person?

"Do you like meatloaf?" she asks, her fingers trailing up my chest.

"Huh?"

"Meatloaf—do you like it?"

"Um, I'm not sure I ever had it."

"Really?" She sits up to look at me and I catch myself getting lost in her beautiful, expressive eyes. "Pops made it for me a couple of times. He never made it for you?"

"No, but a loaf of meat sounds appetizing. Why do you ask?"

She tilts her head to the side, a humorous scrunch in her nose. "Uh, because that's what they're eating in the movie."

"Oh, right, yeah."

She studies me some more. "Are you even paying attention to the movie?"

"Yeah, why wouldn't I?"

I swear she can see straight through me, her thoughtful gaze penetrating down to my soul. "You're not paying attention."

"How dare you call me out on such a thing? Of course I'm watching a Christmas classic."

She pokes my bare stomach. "You're such a liar."

"Well . . . you're not watching right now either."

"Because you aren't. What were you doing?"

"Nothing," I answer quickly. The universal cover-up of *I don't want to talk about it.*

"That's convincing." She sits up completely, pausing the movie and looking me in the eyes. "What were you doing?"

"You know, if we're going to finish this movie before Santa comes, we better press play."

"Crew, I'm serious. Did you really not want to watch it?"

I sigh. "No, I did. I'm just . . ." Jesus Christ, how do I say this without sounding like a total pervert? "Just lost in my thoughts."

"About Pops?"

"No." Shit, I should have said yes. That would have been an easy escape out of this inquisition.

"Then what were you thinking about?"

"What is this? Twenty questions?" I laugh and attempt to pull her back to my chest. "Let's just enjoy the movie."

She studies me for a few more beats before she lies back down—on my chest—her hand *going right above the waistband of my pants*. I can feel the warmth of her palm seeping into my skin. I swear to God, she's doing this on purpose—trying to tease me—and if that's the case, maybe I should do the same.

I attempt to pay attention to the movie, but instead, my mind is plotting what I can do to drive her crazy, what could I do that would—

Fuck.

Her fingers are slowly stroking my skin. So fucking deliberate that I feel I'm going to die a slow death of anticipation, of wondering what it would feel like if her hand inched lower with every stroke she made. Then her foot glides up my calf and then back down.

Yup, she's fucking with me.

She has to be.

And, yup, I'm pretty sure I can feel her little pebbled nipples pressing against my chest and side, as well.

But what can I do? One hand is positioned at the iPad, holding it up and steady, and my other hand is draped behind her. I feel almost trapped. Not being able to make a move without being obvious. The only option I have is my hand behind her back.

Her fingers dip closer and closer to my waistband, and my groin is stirring.

Now or never.

My fingers trail over her side close to her stomach and then back to her hip. She sucks in a sharp breath and stiffens beneath my touch, and I almost apologize, but then she relaxes with one more pass over her side.

Good.

Smiling, I continue to glide my fingers over her side, and with each drag up, her nightgown rises higher and higher.

I trace the curve of her side, down her hip and dangerously close to her ass. Her hand on my stomach pauses, and her breath catches. That tiny breath turns up the heat in the room, and I'm not sure either of us are paying attention to the movie at this point.

I continue to draw circles over her side and back, continuing to slowly pull her nightgown farther and farther up until it's barely covering her ass. Is she wearing a thong? Regular underwear? Something . . . sexy?

Nah, Hazel wouldn't wear anything sexy. She doesn't seem the type. At least, not to wear something sexy with her nightgown. Not that it matters at this point. If it were up to me, underwear is underwear—it's supposed to be coming off anyway, so who cares what it looks like?

"Could you imagine growing up in this era?" she asks casually, her pinky finger dipping just barely under the waistband of my briefs.

I bite down on my lower lip and squeeze my eyes shut tightly, trying to not show my excitement, trying desperately to kccp things undcr control.

"No," I answer strained.

And she catches my tone, because she glances up at me, her pinky sliding farther. "You okay?"

Is she kidding me right now?

Not being able to hold back anymore, I ask, "Does it look like I'm okay?"

She chuckles. "No. It looks like you're turned on."

"Hmm, I wonder why that is. Maybe because your hand is down my pants." I call her out and her cheeks blush in the most perfect way ever.

"My hand was not down your pants. You were the one who was practically stripping me out of my nightgown."

"Uh, because you were playing feather fingers on my stomach."

"Feather fingers?" She laughs. "What's that?"

"Oh, come on," I scoff and then lightly drag my fingers over her arm. "That's feather fingers."

Her brow creases. "I wasn't purposefully doing that. I guess it was just subconsciously. Sorry."

"Sorry? You're sorry?"

She chuckles and so do I.

"Unbelievable, Twigs." I fold the cover over the iPad and say, "Movie time is over. It's time for bed. We'll have the movie playing on repeat tomorrow to make up for tonight. But for now, we're to return to our respective sides and go to sleep."

"You're just going to boss me around like that?"

I set my iPad on my nightstand and answer, "Yup. Goodnight, Twigs." I turn my back toward her and take a deep breath, willing my body to settle down.

"Hey." She pokes my back. "Crew." *Poke.* "Crew." *Poke.*

"Stop it."

She laughs and pulls on my shoulder.

I don't know what comes over me, but I flip around and pin her to the mattress, her arms by her side, my torso covering half of hers.

Her eyes widen as I lower my head toward hers. "What do you want, Haze?"

Her tongue peeks out and wets her lips as her eyes search mine. But she says nothing.

"You clearly want something if you're going to annoy me and poke me."

"No. Nothing in particular," she says, swallowing hard.

"Okay, so if I turn around, you're not going to poke me again?"

She shakes her head. "You don't ever sleep turned away from me."

I softly smile. "You want to look at my handsome face to put you to sleep? That's fair."

She rolls her eyes and I lift off her, missing the feel of her soft body under mine immediately. I settle myself on my pillow and then turn toward her. She does the same, and instead of the usual foot or so of distance between us, she's closer.

Because of her proximity and my large body, to make it more comfortable for me, I rest my hand on her hip under the covers. I give her a playful squeeze and she smiles at me.

"That better, Twigs?"

"Much better."

"Then Merry Christmas, Haze."

"Merry Christmas," she says quietly. Her hand creeps up to my chest once again and she places her palm against my skin. But she doesn't move. She just leans into her touch, almost as if she needs to feel me in order to fall asleep.

And I do the same, holding her at the hip, gripping her just tight enough to remind me that she's still here with me, and she's not going anywhere.

Lying there, eyes closed, I steady my breathing and try to calm my mind so I can drift off to sleep, but my hand itches to move along her hip, making it impossible to shut off my brain.

Just one little stroke.

One small touch.

Just for a second.

Slowly, I rub my thumb over her hipbone, holding my breath, waiting for any kind of noise to fall past her soft lips.

But nothing.

No inclination of noticing, so I move my hand over her ass—not clutching, just resting.

Nothing.

So I move my thumb.

After a few strokes, she shifts closer to me but continues to stay silent. During her shift, her nightgown crinkles under my palm, indicating it shifted up. Wanting to know just how far up, I move my hand farther down. She sucks in a sharp breath when I connect with the hem.

I hold still, my breath growing heavier, my eyes still shut, my mind whirling with how far I should go. She hasn't told me to stop and she hasn't pulled away, so she must be okay with this. *Does she want me to touch her? To go higher?* Following her cues, I drag the nightgown up a little farther until I can feel it gather around her waist. That's when I lower my hand back down to her backside and my hand connects with something lacy.

Fuck.

She's wearing sexy underwear.

I was not expecting that.

And from how high they rise, I'm guessing they're cheeky panties, and those fucking haunt me in my dreams. Just enough ass exposed to be tempting, but not enough to give everything away.

I expand my fingers over her backside, and I can't help myself when I pull her in a little closer. I slip my hand under the lacy fabric of her underwear and then I pause there, my thumb grazing over her skin very lightly.

This is perfect. I can be happy with this.

I can settle down and sleep, knowing I at least have this moment.

I start to relax and attempt to drift to sleep again when I feel Hazel's fingers press under my chin, pulling my head forward gently. I open my eyes and find her staring at me. Her eyes look unsure as she continues to guide me closer and closer.

I slide my hand farther over her ass.

She licks her lips.

The tension between us grows as she slowly brings her head closer as well.

She wants to kiss me and, fuck, do I want to kiss her.

So goddamn bad.

I want to tear this nightgown off her and spend hours worshipping her body, memorizing it, loving it.

"Hazel."

"Yeah?" she asks softly, her bottom half scooting closer so

her leg drapes over mine and my hand moves over the middle of her ass. My fingers splay, slowly caressing beneath her panties. Right. Near. Her. Pussy. *Fuck.*

"I want to kiss you. Really fucking bad."

Her eyelashes flutter as she says, "You do?"

"Isn't if fucking obvious?" I laugh, my cock already hardening from the prospect. "I want this. I just need to know that you want this."

Her teeth roll over her bottom lip as her eyes fall to my mouth and then back up to my eyes. "I can't tell you how long I've wanted this."

"Fuck," I say, right before I close the distance between us and my mouth crashes down on hers.

Sweet, plump lips meet mine and, fuck, is her mouth perfect. Not at all tentative, but demanding. Hungry. Needy. Desperate for more.

She slides over more and rolls on top of me as I roll to my back. Her ass lines up with my growing cock, and as she leans her pebbled tits against my chest, her hips roll over my arousal, reminding me how easily she can get me off without any penetration.

It's that fucking easy with her. *But I want inside her. Her heat. Her wet warmth.*

She gathers her hair to one side and drapes the long locks over her shoulder, then grips one of my hands, locking our fingers together and raising it above my head as she finishes lowering her mouth to mine, capturing my lips.

My free hand trails up her thigh as her mouth works mine. I move it to her hip and then to her stomach. When I reach the spot just below her breast, she sucks in a harsh breath, and I feel her stomach hollow out. I glide my thumb along the underside of her breast and she groans, grinding down on my cock. *Hard.*

Jesus, yes.

I stroke her again, this time moving higher until my thumb rubs against her nipple.

Her mouth lifts from mine, she releases my hand, and before I know what's happening, she grips the hem of her nightgown and pulls it over her head, only to drop it on the floor.

Mother . . . fucker.

I stare at Hazel, topless, wearing nothing but a pair of lacy underwear, her tits plump and round, with dark, rose-colored nipples, hard and turned on.

She reaches out and takes both of my hands and places them on her stomach. As she drags them up to her breasts, she says, "I've always wondered what it would feel like to have your large hands hold my breasts, squeeze them, do whatever you wanted with them." She brings my palms to cup them, and her head falls back as I squeeze them. She rocks back on my cock.

"Fuck, you're gorgeous," I say. "So goddamn perfect, Hazel." She rotates her hips over and over again, matching the pressure of my squeeze, or the way I carefully roll her nipples, seeing if that's something she likes. I realize that's exactly what she likes when her mouth falls open on a gasp. Her hands fall to my stomach as she starts to ride my cock. "Are you getting close, Haze?"

She nods, not saying a word, but instead pulling on her lip with her teeth.

"Then take what you want."

Her eyes pop open and she says, "I want you. All of you."

With that, I rise up and press my hand to her back as I carefully lay her down on the mattress, her head toward the end of the bed. And that's when it hits me.

"Fuck," I say angrily.

"What?" she asks, her eyes flashing in concern.

"I don't have condoms. Didn't really think I'd be having sex on this trip."

"It's okay," she says, stroking her hand down my face. "I'm on the pill."

On the pill . . . Holy shit.

"I've never gone unprotected, Haze, I'm clean."

"I trust you."

Understanding the moment, the permission she's giving me, I lower my head and take her lips with mine, showing her how much I want this. How much I want *her*. After a few seconds, I lift up and stand at the edge of the bed. I hook both my thumbs in my pants and briefs, and I push them down, exposing my hardened cock.

Hazel's eyes widen as she sits up on her elbows and gives me a once-over. I reach down and grip my cock tightly, my fist relieving some of the pressure that's been building for days. And she watches me. She seems intent on keeping her eyes on my hand as it moves up and down, and I watch her, mesmerized by the fascinated, innocent expression on her face.

Giving her a show, I pump my cock, squeeze the tip, then bring my hand back down to the base, where I perform short fast strokes, pumping myself hard.

Her eyes are wild, hungry, and I watch as she snakes her hand down to the spot between her legs, where she slips beneath her lacy underwear and starts moving her fingers under the fabric.

Shit, that's hot.

Really hot.

So hot that I feel a surge of excitement rush through me, and my cock grows thicker, harder.

"Take your underwear off," I say.

Removing her hand from between her legs, she slides her underwear down, then she spreads her legs for me and moves her hand over her wet pussy.

Yes.

Fuck . . . yes.

Wait, she can't be doing the work. That's my job. I need my mouth on her, my hands turning her on.

Releasing my cock, I grab her by the ankles and pull her so her ass is at the edge of the bed, and then I drop down to my knees and spread her legs even wider.

The room falls silent, nothing but our wild breath setting the mood for what's about to happen, that and the dim glow of the streetlights outside bouncing off the snow.

"You're so fucking wet, Hazel."

"You've been teasing me for far too long."

"Me, teasing you?" I shake my head. "Other way around, gorgeous." I press my lips to her inner thigh and glide them so close to her pussy that I feel her tense in anticipation, but I move over to her other leg instead. "You've been torturing me all night, and you fucking know it."

I glance up and catch a smile on her beautiful lips.

"And now it's my turn to torture you, but in the best way possible." I glide my lips all the way down her legs and then reach up with my fingers and part her. And that's it. I hold still and glance up at her. Her ample breasts rise and fall as she takes deep, labored breaths, waiting for my next move. Her auburn hair pools on the mattress and her hands grip the comforter beneath her.

"What are you doing?" she asks, clearly already tortured.

"Letting you enjoy this moment—of me, this close to your greedy pussy, waiting for me to pleasure you."

"I would enjoy it more if you did something," she complains.

"Like what?" I lean down and lightly flick my tongue over her clit. "You mean like this?"

"Holy God, yes, like that." She shifts under my hold, her legs parting even more. "I need this, Crew. I need this so bad."

"When was the last time you had sex?"

"Can't remember," she says right before I bring my mouth

to her pussy and start lapping at her. "What . . . about . . . you?"

"Can't remember either. No one has been good enough . . . until now."

I work her pleasure, pulling it out with long, languid strokes of my tongue, and then I set it on fire with short flicks. I repeat the process over and over again, watching as she slowly starts to lose control, as her brain shuts off and her body takes over, writhing and shaking under my touch.

I feel her tighten, her orgasm right on the edge, and that's when I pull away.

With a gasp, she curls up and stares me down. "Crew, what are you doing?"

I reach my hand to her chest and press her down onto the mattress. "I'm letting you build, Haze."

"I don't want to build. I want to come."

I chuckle and lower my mouth back to her center. I kiss her pubic bone and all around, slowly, with purpose. Each press of my lips is supposed to drive her more and more wild, and it seems to be working as she shifts and groans beneath me.

"How many times have you thought about me doing this?"

"Too many," she answers honestly.

"Me, too."

I spread her again and press kisses to her clit. Her legs squeeze against me, and I pause, sliding my hands up her thighs and slowly pushing them open again, while I run my hands up and down her soft skin.

"Please, Crew," she begs in a strained voice.

"You want to come, Haze?"

"Badly."

Smiling, I lower my mouth again, and this time, I press one of my fingers inside her. She instantly accepts me and rides my finger by rotating her hips. God, she's tight. Wanting to make sure she can take me, I press another finger inside, and she seems to like that even more by the way her back arches off the mattress.

I curve my fingers up and stroke while lowering my mouth back to her clit. This time, I want her to become unhinged, so I keep my mouth steady and I lick her—short, quick strokes over her little nub over and over again.

Her breathing picks up.

Her hands crumple the sheets beneath us.

Her moans grow louder and louder.

Her legs spread even wider, if possible.

Her mouth falls open, eyes shut, and she moans as she comes on my finger and tongue. Her body spasms, her hips rock, her bouts of pleasure rocking her to the point of exhaustion as she slowly falls into a heap of joy.

"Oh . . . my . . . God, Crew." The disbelief in her voice should bother me, as if I could perform any worse, but I actually find it cute.

Chuckling, I kiss up her stomach to her breasts, and I finally take one in my mouth. I lightly nibble on her nipple, not giving her a chance to slow down. She gasps, and her hands go to the back of my head, sifting through my hair.

My cock falls between her legs, so goddamn ready for release, but I don't take it, not yet. I need to spend more time learning her body, memorizing it.

I move my mouth to her other breast and spend time there. Licking. Nibbling. Sucking.

And when I get comfortable, playing with her tits, I feel her hand creep down between us and find my erection, pressing hard against her leg. She takes it in her palm and squeezes.

A sharp breath escapes me as I pause the work on her tits.

"I want you in my mouth," she says, pushing at my chest.

"And I want to play with your tits."

She lifts my chin up and presses a kiss to my mouth before saying, "It isn't always about you, Crew."

With a wink, she pushes at my chest, and I allow her to press me against the mattress. My cock falls heavy on my stomach, straining for more. Straining for her.

"Your body is so sexy." One of her hands roams my chest as her other hand floats under my dick and rubs a finger in each divot of my lower abs. "I've wanted to touch you so badly this entire trip. Every time you walked out of the bathroom in a towel, I wanted to strip it off and kneel in front of you. Take your dick in my mouth."

"Jesus," I mutter, feeling my arousal spike to another level.

She kneels on my right side, giving me access so I can still play with her tits. I take one in my hand and roll her nipple as she lowers her mouth. I wait in anticipation for her hot mouth to take me in, but instead, she presses kisses around the spot where my cock rests, and I swear to Christ, she's going to make me come without even touching me.

That's how horny I am.

That's how much she turns me on.

I've never felt like this with anyone else, never in my goddamn life. But there's something about Hazel that has me on the edge of losing control.

"Hazel, I want to come inside of you."

"I know." She lifts my cock and licks the tip.

"And . . . fuck, I think I might be quick on the trigger with you touching me."

She chuckles. "That's not boding well for your stamina."

"Haze, watching you come on my tongue turned me on so goddamn much that I could have come with you if I'd allowed myself to. Now, you touching me, it's inevitable."

"Then I'll have to be slow." She lowers her mouth again and presses kisses along my length, to the base, and then gently cups my balls and kisses those, too.

Fuck, this is glorious torture. She's not doing enough to make me come, but she's doing enough to build the pressure at the base of my spine, to the point that I feel as though I can't breathe, the tension taking up all the space in my chest.

"Fu-ck, Haze."

She moves her mouth back to the tip, then very slowly opens her mouth and sucks me in, not all the way—just a small amount—and then she rotates her mouth.

I need her to pump my length, I need her to apply more pressure. I need . . .

"Fuck, I need to come, Hazel."

I move away from her and then pin her down on the bed.

"I need inside you." My words come out choppy, caveman-like, but I don't care. I'm losing all sense of reality as the room around us blurs and turns into nothing. I stare at the only thing that matters—Hazel.

Me and Hazel.

"I need you inside me too," she says, taking my cock and guiding it to her entrance.

"You sure?"

She nods. "Go slow. I know you need me, but I need to adjust."

"I'd never hurt you." I lean down and press a kiss to her lips. The hand not holding my cock grips the back of my neck and keeps me there.

And then slowly, I push forward, entering her warm, tight heat. And, fuck, it's the best goddamn thing I've ever felt.

So fucking good.

So fucking perfect.

Nothing compares.

I feel her every muscle pulling me in, accepting me, adjusting to my girth, to my length.

Her mouth pulls away for a brief moment as she catches her breath. Whispering, I ask, "Are you okay?"

"Yes." She brings her mouth back to mine and I feel her relax, so I push a little farther.

And a little farther.

My muscles strain. I'm barely hanging on.

I want to let loose. I want to pound into her, explore this deep warmth I've never felt before. I want to lose control and take her with abandon, but she wants slow.

So I'll give her slow.

She continues to make out with me, her tongue diving in and out of my mouth, and with each pass I feel her relax more and more, allowing me inside her until I bottom out. I pause, letting her adjust.

"So . . . full." She exhales shallowly as I give her one small pump of my hips. "You feel amazing, Crew."

She has no idea how great this feels. Like I'm on cloud fucking nine and I'm never coming back down. In this moment, I know it won't be like this with anyone else, because this is Hazel. I'm neither saint nor monk, but it ought to mean something when a woman allows a man inside her body. It's a privilege. I like to connect with a woman emotionally before sex, and with Haze, the connection is years deep. Significant. *Priceless.*

Testing the waters, I start to rock my hips. Her kisses grow more frantic, and I take that as a sign to keep moving, so I set a steady pace with my thrusts. Just enough to feel how tight she is, but not enough to set me off.

"Yes," she whispers, her breath trailing over my spine, raising the hairs on the back of my neck to attention. "Yes, Crew." Hearing my name fall off her tongue like that, it spurs my hips to go faster. "Yes." Her hands fall to my back, where they grip tightly, her fingers digging into my skin.

I pick up my pace, feeling her, only her, as I plunge deeper, harder, listening to her pleasure whisper into my ear.

"More," she says before taking my mouth with hers.

Her tongue swipes against mine.

Her fingers dig deeper.

Her pussy tightens around my cock.

She moans into my mouth.

"Oh my God," she says, before pulling her legs up higher. "Oh . . . Crew. Yes, oh God, yes," she says, her moans growing louder and louder. "Right there, yes. Oh my God, I'm going to come."

I push harder, feeling her pussy contract just as she arches against me. Her moan tumbles out of her as she comes, and it feels next to impossible to continue my thrusts as she spasms around me, but I push and push and . . . Jesus Fucking Christ . . .

"Ahhh, motherfucker," I groan as my body tightens up, and I come. I still, my cock spasming inside her tight warmth, everything around me turning black as I get lost in this feeling.

As I get lost in Hazel.

Fucking explosive—that's the only way to describe what that felt like.

I collapse on top of her. Her arms wrap around me and she kisses my forehead while I catch my breath.

Together, we take deep breaths, our bodies settling until we're completely sated. She strokes my hair and I hold on to her tightly, never wanting to let go.

Finally, I ask, "Are you okay?"

Her hand runs over my hair and she says, "Perfect."

"I didn't hurt you?"

"No. Not even a little."

I lift my head up and press my lips to hers, and we slowly make out for a few seconds, until I finally pull out of her and go to the bathroom where I clean up quickly and then grab a warm washcloth for her. I'm about to take it to her, but instead run into her in the bathroom.

She chuckles and when she sees the warm washcloth, her eyes soften.

"Okay, you just earned brownie points."

I smile at her and step aside, giving her the washcloth and some privacy in the bathroom.

I return to the bed, where I flop down on the mattress and stare up at the slanted ceiling.

I just had sex with Hazel Allen.

No, not just sex, but mind-blowing, earth-shattering, life-changing sex. Sex that means something. The kind that you're not supposed to forget about. The kind that alters your life forever.

Chapter Thirteen

HAZEL

Hazel: *I had sex with Crew.*

Mia: *Well . . . Merry Christmas to you.*

Hazel: *Yes, Merry Christmas, blah, blah, blah. Crew and I did it last night.*

Mia: *You're lucky I'm awake right now. What's Crew doing?*

Hazel: *He's sleeping.*

Mia: *Okay, so are you freaking out? Are you happy? Are you wishing you were anywhere else but sharing a bed with that fine piece off ass?*

Hazel: *LOL. I'm . . . I don't know, happy?*

Mia: *Is that a question or a statement?*

Hazel: *A statement, I think. I'm still trying to figure it out.*

Mia: *How many times did you do it?*

Hazel: *Four.*

Mia: *Jesus. Okay. Wow. I don't think I've ever done it two times in one night, let alone four. Are you able to walk this morning?*

Hazel: *Haven't tested it out yet. From just shifting around, I can tell I'm sore.*

Mia: *The best kind of sore.*

Hazel: *What do I do, Mia?*

Mia: *What do you mean? How did you leave it last night? Was it intimate or just carnal?*

Hazel: *Both. The last time we did it though, it was really slow, and then he held me until we both drifted off to sleep.*

Mia: *Well, that right there tells me what happened last night wasn't just sex. It was so much more.*

Hazel: *You think so? I honestly don't know how to act this morning.*

Mia: *Act normal. When he wakes up, tell him Merry Christmas, and see what he does. If he reaches out to kiss you, that sets the tone.*

Hazel: *And what if he doesn't kiss me?*

Mia: *Uh . . . I don't know, I'm kind of expecting him to kiss you.*

Hazel: *That's not helpful.*

Mia: *He's going to kiss you.*

Hazel: *You don't know that.*

Mia: *And you need to stop freaking out. You know Crew better than I do, Haze. It seems as though he's been tentative with you, so maybe he doesn't know what you feel for him.*

I think about that for a moment. Crew was surprised when I said I'd wanted him for so long, but he wasn't uncertain when he told me how desperately he'd wanted me. From what he's mentioned, he's not a one-night-stand guy. Does he need me to show him that I want more?

Hazel: *My heart's already attached. It has been for a while.*

Mia: *Then perhaps his has been too.*

Crew stirs next me, and setting my phone on the nightstand, I hop out of bed to retrieve my nightgown. I quickly put it on so I'm not walking around naked as I make my way to the bathroom to take care of business and brush my teeth. When I exit, I run right into Crew, who's wearing his pajama pants now, scratching his chest, and looking adorably cute.

"Oh, hi," I say, my nerves itching at the back of my neck.

"Morning, Haze." He gives me a lopsided grin.

We stand there, staring at each other, and I wait.

I wait for him to kiss me, but he doesn't make that move. Instead, he nods to the bathroom and says, "Uh, can I use the bathroom?"

My heart tumbles in a spiral as I step aside. "Sure, of course."

"Thanks, Twigs." He steps into the bathroom and shuts the door.

Well . . .

I consider texting Mia, but I'm honestly stunned and don't have it in me. He didn't kiss me, which makes me teary.

You're being ridiculous. Maybe he needed to pee. Maybe he was tired.

And maybe I'm emotional because I'm tired from not sleeping much last night—*thank you, Crew, for sensational sex*— and it's Christmas morning and I'm not with my family. If I was, we'd be sitting around unwrapping presents and listening to *A Christmas Story* as background noise. But I can't let Crew see me upset or he'll worry, and he doesn't need that this morning. This is a hard day for him too, and his first away from *his* family.

The door to the bathroom opens, and my heart stills, tears welling in my eyes, and I curse myself for being too sensitive.

Pull it together, Hazel.

"There's my girl," Crew says. He charges toward the bed and pushes me back on the mattress, shocking me as he cups my cheek and presses his lips to mine. "Mm, Merry Christmas, Haze."

"M-merry Christmas," I say as a tear slips down my cheek.

"Hey, why are you crying?"

I wipe it away and take a deep breath. Everything is fine. Stop with the emotions.

"Nothing." I smile up at him. "Did you sleep okay?"

His brow is still pulled together as he studies me. "Yeah, but I want to talk about what has you upset."

"It's really stupid and I'd rather not say."

"When has that ever gotten you out of telling me the truth?" He presses another kiss to my lips, his minty breath matching mine. "Talk to me, Haze."

"It's really, really stupid." Another tear falls and I curse myself.

"Clearly not stupid enough. Spill."

Sighing, I press my palm to my eye, rubbing it. "I expected you to, I don't know, be all kissy this morning."

"Uh, I thought I was kissing you. Shit, have I been kissing you wrong this whole time?"

"See, I told you this was stupid."

"No, it's not. I won't joke. Go on."

I bite on the corner of my lip, looking to the side, and decide to just go with the truth. "Last night meant a lot to me and I wasn't sure if it meant the same to you. I thought if you woke up this morning and acted as if nothing happened that maybe it was just a night to you. When we ran into each other outside the bathroom, I guess I expected you to kiss me is all, and you didn't, which made me think that last night was just fun for you, and that's fine. It was fun for me too—"

He presses his hand to my mouth, silencing me. Looking me in the eyes, he says, "It meant so much to me, Hazel. Last night, was . . . fuck, I don't even know how to describe it. It shifted my whole world on its axis, and I woke up this morning fucking happy. Excited. Thrilled. I didn't kiss you right away because I wanted to brush my teeth first. But tomorrow morning, when you wake up in my arms, I'll be sure to just go for it, minty mouth or not."

His thumb strokes my cheek, and I swear, in that moment, something cracks opens in me. I can feel it in my chest, a burst of . . . of . . . hell, of love.

I love him.

I know I do. It's so easy for me to admit that to myself. I think I've loved him for a very long time, and this moment right here, with him staring at me, touching me intimately as if I'm the most precious thing he's ever held—it confirms those feelings.

I'm not just infatuated with Crew Smith, but I'm in love with him.

"You okay, now?" he asks.

I nod. "Yes. Sorry for being a girl."

"I'm not sorry you're a girl. Pretty happy about it, actually." He chuckles. "You know, because of your amazing tits."

I push at him but he pins my hands to the sides of my head, and he moves his body so it lines up with mine. He lowers and presses his mouth to mine. I open up, accepting, enjoying every aspect of this man.

"Why did you get dressed?" he asks, moving his mouth to my jaw and then my neck. "You know I'm going to need you naked for the remainder of this trip."

"I'm not going outside naked," I protest as he lets go of my hands and drags my nightgown up and over my head, exposing my naked body.

"That's what I like to see. I still can't believe I'm getting to see you naked, Haze. You're so goddamn gorgeous." His large hand starts at my neck and slowly drags down my body until it reaches the spot between my legs.

I don't even have to think about it at this point. My legs just fall open for him, and he presses his palm to my pubic bone.

"Do you want to open presents first, or do you want to come first?"

"You let me come first every time last night."

His dark eyes turn into molten lava as they sear me with lust. "Ladies first always," he says, right before lowering his hand and fitting two fingers inside of me. "Already wet for me. You're making this too easy, Haze."

"I'll remember that for next time."

He strokes me leisurely, building me up slowly, but enough that if he stops, I wouldn't know what to do with the ache he'd leave behind.

"Do you realize how amazingly gorgeous you are?" He brings his mouth to my stomach, where he presses a few light kisses. "You don't even know how much you affect me. How much I've wanted to kiss you. I've wanted to strip you down and worship every last inch of you."

My thoughts tumble aimlessly out of my head as his mouth lowers farther and his other hand spreads me.

"You've been driving me crazy. But what's been driving me the craziest is that I had a chance at feeling your soft lips. I had the opportunity to taste you, and like the fool I am, I chickened out." He flicks my clit a few times. "Fucking stupid man." His fingers curve up and his tongue rapidly fires between my legs, shocking me as my orgasm bursts out of nowhere.

"Oh my God," I moan, pressing my hand into his hair and riding his tongue, my hips rocking with him, seeking out every last bit of pleasure.

My nerves feel like they've been set on fire as I fall from bliss, floating gracefully, bringing me back to reality.

"So sexy," he says, kissing his way back up my body until he reaches my lips. He presses a chaste kiss there and then stands, his erection pressing desperately against his pants.

Smiling, I pull him down on the mattress and lower his pants, freeing his erection.

"Hazel, you don't have to."

"Yeah, but I really, really want to."

"THANK you for letting me borrow one of your shirts," I say, loving how his extra-large shirt drapes like a blanket over my shoulders. "That nightgown was constraining."

"I liked it." Crew is propped against the headboard, shirtless and wearing a pair of boxer briefs, looking all kinds of hot with his rumpled hair that I've combed my fingers through multiple times.

Food is on its way, we're both satisfied—for now—and we have presents to open. I don't think I could imagine a better Christmas at this point.

I walk to the bed and he quickly pulls me across his lap, making me laugh as his lips find my neck again.

"Crew, you can't be serious."

"What?" He chuckles against my skin. "Have you seen you? You can't blame me."

"You can't be that turned on all the time."

"You wearing my football shirt? Yeah, I'm turned on."

I move out of his arms and crawl across the bed, only for him to catch me and spin me around so he's hovering above me.

"Where do you think you're going?"

"Trying to make sure your dick doesn't fall off. That would be a detriment to both of us."

His eyebrows raise. "Hey, you saying you like my dick?"

I smile. "I really like your dick."

Once again, his eyes darken, and he spreads my legs with his knees, but this time I stop him.

"Food is on its way—"

"You and I both know I can make you come in seconds."

"Take a break, big guy. We still have plenty of time for me to ride your yule log."

Chuckling, he kisses me and capitulates. "Fine. But if I pass out from being banned from your pussy, it's your fault."

I roll my eyes as he helps me sit up. "You're not banned."

Knock. Knock.

I point to the door. "See? I told you food was on the way."

"If you hadn't been talking, I could have made you come."

I pat his cheek and say, "You're good, Smith, but you're not that good."

As I stand from the bed, he gives me a playful whack on the ass and then falls back on the mattress, hands behind his head.

Food, Hazel. Get the food.

After some pleasantries and Merry Christmases, I tip the hotel attendant very well and take the food to set it next to Crew, who's smiling like a fool.

"What?" I ask him.

"Just really like you in my shirt," he says, pulling on the hem.

I feel my cheeks blush and I fall onto his lap, looping my arm around his shoulder. His hand travels up my thigh to my hipbone . . . and he notices I'm not wearing any underwear.

"Hazel . . ."

"What?" I smile mischievously.

"You really think this is going to keep me away?"

"Are you really that big of a horndog?"

"When it comes to you, yeah, I am." He drags his hand up my body to my breast, where his thumb rubs over my nipple, and it takes everything in me not to sigh.

"Breakfast, presents, sex."

He lets out a loud groan while his forehead meets my shoulder. "That's too many things."

"You also promised me we'd watch *A Christmas Story*."

"I did, didn't I?" He thinks about it. "You know, I'm not opposed to having sex while Ralphie shoots his eye out. Might be nice background music."

"You need help." I hop off his lap and go to the other side of the bed, making the food a divider between us—giving me enough space from his grabby hands.

Honestly, I know I could go again with him. After I was

done sucking him off, I was ready for more, but I also know that I need a break, even if my libido thinks otherwise. A part of me wants to know if this is more than just sex for him. I want to ask him a million questions that pertain to what happens after we leave Germany, but that would ruin the mood, and I can't let my mind wander in that direction.

"Are these crepes?" Crew asks, picking up a napkin and silverware.

"They are, and this is mushroom spaetzle. Some egg and mushroom yumminess."

"So, what you're telling me is that we're going halfsies on these dishes."

I chuckle and nod. "Yeah, that was the plan. But the coffee is for me, the tea is for you."

"I don't need coffee to wake me up, just your tits." He wiggles his eyebrows and I roll my eyes.

"You're ridiculous."

Dividing up the plates, he responds, "You're ridiculously hot."

"Crew, it's breakfast, presents, sex—that order won't change."

His lips flatten but he continues to divide up the plates. "Well, you're still ridiculously hot, and I love that I can finally say that out loud *and* do something about it." He glances up at me and winks.

Yup, I'm in trouble.

"THAT MUSHROOM SPATTLE is the best thing I've ever eaten," Crew says, licking his fork, and if he wasn't sincerely enjoying the dish, I would swear he's licking his fork on purpose, to tempt me. Note, it's working. But I hold strong.

"It's called mushroom spaetzle."

"Whatever it's called, that shit was good." He sets his fork down and then leans back on his hands. "I still think you should have let me eat the crepe off your naked body. You know, since you didn't get me a Christmas present, that could have been your opportunity."

"Oh, but I did get you a Christmas present."

"Really? When?"

"When you weren't looking."

"You mean when I was freezing my ass off trying to buy more coffee yesterday?"

I smile knowingly. "Maybe."

"Way to take advantage of the situation. But seriously, Haze, you didn't have to get me anything."

"I know, but I wanted to." Motioning to the tray, I ask, "Are you done with this? I can get it out of our way."

"I can take care of it." He stands from the bed and takes the tray to the hallway, where he sets it down and then shuts the door behind him. He rubs his hands together. "Present time."

"Should we open up Pops's presents first or the things we got for each other?"

"Pops's first." He grabs them off the dresser and sits on the bed next to me. They're the same shape and size, and I have a general idea of what they might be.

Together we open the wrapping paper and reveal picture frames. My eyes immediately well when I see the picture inside. It's me, Pops, and Crew sitting under our favorite oak tree, drinking lemonade and enjoying cookies. I rub my hand over the picture, remembering the years of great times we had under that tree, the crazy and terrible granddad jokes, and also the deeper, serious conversations we had, especially as we got older.

I look at Crew, and he's holding the same picture. He glances at me and smiles softly before reaching out and pulling me close with a kiss to the top of my head. "One of my favorite places in the whole world is under that tree."

"Mine, too," I say, quietly. "I just can't get over how much thought Pops put into this for us, Crew. He knew us both so well, and I now wonder if he also knew how much we valued him?"

"I think he did, Haze. After all, doesn't that show in his attention to detail and planning? He knew we'd appreciate him and value this time because it's from him."

I nod. He's right. Bernie McMann was an exceptional man. Caring and thoughtful beyond his time.

"There's a letter to open. Shall we read it?"

I nod and Crew opens the letter. It's a short one. "'Merry Christmas, kiddos. This is one of my favorite pictures of all time and it means the world to me to be able to share it with you. All those times we spent under that tree. They hold a special place in my heart and I'll never forget them. I hope you never forget either. Enjoy today, and tomorrow, you'll be moving on to the last leg. Love you both. Pops.'"

Crew folds up the letter and quietly sets it down while staring at the picture frame. "Remember the time we decided to have a lemonade stand under the tree?"

"And Pops was trying to set up for all the apple pickers. He was dying of thirst and bought a cup from us."

"A cup full of lemonade mixture and lemon juice and squeezed lemon, because Uncle Paul said no one likes lemonade that just tastes like water."

I laugh. "I still have the image of Pops with his cheeks sucked in and his eyes ready to flutter out of his head from how sour it was."

Crew joins me in a full-on belly laugh. "And he drank the whole thing. Now that's a good grandpa."

"And then he offered his constructive criticism and told you to never listen to your uncle Paul again."

"Brilliant advice that I still hold to this day." Crew sets his frame down and asks, "Did he ever give you advice that you took to heart?"

"Tons."

"Anything in particular?" Crew asks.

I think back to this past summer when he was sick, how he was training me for I don't know what, but he spent the summer making sure I knew everything.

"He told me to trust my gut because I knew more than I thought I did."

"And have you trusted your gut?"

"Well, I'm here, aren't I?" I ask.

Crew rests his hand on my thigh. "You are, and I'm really fucking glad that you are." He leans in and I reach up, placing my hand on the back of his neck as he kisses me.

It's not the kind of kiss that leads to more, nor is it a friendly kiss. It's a kiss that offers comfort and support. A kiss that makes you think you have so much more time with the person kissing you, rather than a few days. A kiss that speaks of friendship, love, and knowledge, and one I'm so thankful to be part of.

His hand grips my cheek, and he parts my mouth with his tongue and I let him explore, getting lost in the feel of him, in the feel of us, and just as I'm ready for him to lean me back against the mattress, he pulls away.

"Presents."

I blink a few times, snapping my attention back to reality. "Right, presents."

He chuckles. "And here I thought you were the one doing all the reminding."

"I can only be strong for so long. You wore me down."

He goes to his backpack and pulls out a present wrapped in protective paper. "This, Hazel Allen, is for you." He holds out it to me and says, "Merry Christmas."

Butterflies fly around in my stomach. In all the years I've known Crew, he's never gotten me a gift. Not for Christmas, not for my birthday, and I've done the same. We didn't have to get each other anything. All we needed was letters. Lots and lots of letters.

So, right now, it almost feels odd receiving a gift from him, but I push that feeling away quickly as happiness envelops me.

Carefully, I unwrap the long butcher paper until I reveal a miniature carved figurine, no bigger than my hand. It takes me a second to realize what it is, but once I do, tears hit me and I'm a blubbering mess.

Crew somehow in the midst of the mass Christmas market found me a carved farmer with angel wings.

"It's so you have a little piece of Pops with you. When I saw it, I thought it was meant to be, especially because when I was waiting for you, someone bumped into me rather hard, sending me into a woodcarving booth. I was about to yell at the person for being so goddamn rude, but that's when I spotted this guy. I knew I had to get it for you. And I know you enjoy carpentry and woodwork, so I knew you'd appreciate the craftsmanship."

I hold it close to my chest. "I love it so much, Crew." I wipe at my tears. "Thank you. This means a lot to me." I reach up and grip his jaw, bringing his mouth to mine. "Thank you, Crew."

"Of course." He gives me another kiss and all I want to do now is get lost in these lips, in this man. "Now, where's my gift?"

Oh yeah.

"Uh, mine isn't as thoughtful as this. I thought maybe you got me something creepy like one of the cherubs, even though I know you said you didn't."

He laughs. "I would cherish one of those cherubs. I'm sure whatever you got me, I'll love."

Standing from the bed, I walk over to my backpack, pull out the souvenir bag, and hand it to him.

"It's actually pretty stupid now that I think about it."

"Stop." He pulls me onto his lap and wraps his arms

around me. He takes the inexpensive keychain I got him out of the bag. It's a metal replica of a tiny beer stein with "The Romantic Road" written across it in script. Really simple, but I thought it was something that could remind him of these past few days while he's doing whatever happens in his future.

"It's so that you'll always remember this trip. Remember me."

"Hazel." He turns me toward him so I catch the crease in his brow. "I'm not going to forget about you. Or this trip, for that matter."

"Just in case. Whenever you drive around, you can think about how we drove around Germany that one time during Christmas and almost got caught in a snowstorm."

He smiles and rests his hand on my thigh. "Thank you, Hazel. I love it."

"YOU'RE REALLY TESTING my manhood, aren't you?" Crew asks, zipping up his coat.

"You act as if you've never seen snow before." I walk next to him, putting my hat on my head.

"I've been in snow before, but I've never enjoyed it."

"Then you haven't been doing it right," I say as we reach the hotel doors. I reach over and take his gloved hand in mine and lead him outside, and man, does the cold hit us.

"Fuck." He turns to walk back into the hotel, but I tug on his hand and gesture toward the empty town.

"Stop it. Come on, when can we ever say we had an entire German town to ourselves?"

After another round of sex, because that was the deal after all, we watched *A Christmas Story*, both of us drifting in and out of sleep. Once we'd shared a small lunch, because we were still full from breakfast, I told Crew we had to go outside and enjoy the white Christmas we'd been blessed with.

It took a lot of convincing, and I mean *a lot*—my boobs were involved at one point—but here we are. We borrowed some snow boots from the hotel, though they didn't have any big enough for Crew's freakishly large American feet, and we set off to explore.

"There's a foot of snow on the ground and you're making me traipse around in boots that are too small. My feet are getting wet."

I pause and look back at him. "Are you going to complain the whole time? Because if so, I'm going to explore on my own."

"Hey, sass," he teases. "Just give me a second to adjust my Californian bones." He shakes out his limbs and then plasters on a large smile. "Okay, ready."

"Good."

Together, hand in hand, we walk down the road, admiring the particular characteristics of Germany. The houses that look like something out of Snow White, the signature red-orange roofs, the stone architecture—it's all so charming, like walking through a real-life fairy tale.

"While you were getting ready, I read about the town," Crew says. "I was curious since Nördlingen has a wall around it, and I wanted to read up on it."

"Are you going to delight me with some facts?"

"Only if you want them."

"I want everything you can offer me," I say, with a wiggle of my brow.

His eyes narrow, humor pulling at his lips. "Be careful what you say, Twigs." We make a right turn, not minding where we're going, just getting lost in the snow-covered town. "If you were to look at the town from an aerial view, you'd see that it's actually a big circle, and that's because fifteen million years ago, a meteor struck the Earth here and changed the soil. When people began to settle here, the settlers thought it was the perfect shape to offer protection, not knowing what lay beneath."

"The meteor?" I ask, getting into the story.

"Well, no. They didn't realize that they built a town on a gold mine, or diamond mine, if you will."

"What? This town is built on diamonds?"

"Seventy-two thousand tons of diamonds, to be exact."

"What?" I ask, my eyes now searching every building. "Are you serious?"

Crew nods. "The buildings and streets are embedded with microscopic diamonds. Some might say this could be one of the richest towns in Germany, and yet, they don't have access to any of the riches."

"Wow, that's crazy. Man, if I lived here, I'd find a way to gather those diamonds."

"Nah, you wouldn't." Crew wraps his arm around my shoulder. "You're too loyal. You'd just brag to anyone who came to visit that you paid way less for your house than its actually worth."

"Yeah, you're probably right."

"I am. I know you, Hazel. You're not the kind of person who would sell out."

"No, I'm not."

Crew is silent for a second, and then he asks, "So, what's happening with the farm?"

"I don't know. Things have been in limbo. Something about Pops's lawyer not being available. I'm really unsure. I know there've been investors from the city who have been interested in the land."

"What? Really? I didn't know that."

"I tend not to mention it because if I think about it, I get too sick. They want the land for an outlet mall. Pops has been adamant about not selling. They also want to connect a highway, and the farm is in the way. Big-city people have been sniffing around for a while."

"Why didn't you tell me?"

"I didn't want to believe it," I say. "I didn't want to think of it as an option. I mean, what if Pops left the farm to your mom and dad? Their life is in California, their business is there, and they can't just pick up and move. And I love your uncle Paul, but he has no idea what to do when it comes to the farm. He's so far removed that I think he'd be overwhelmed. I know Pops met with some investors this past summer, but I've no idea how that went." I try not to tear up, but my eyes still become damp. "I don't know what I'd do, to be honest. I haven't been very smart regarding my future, because I thought I'd work at the farm my whole life, for some reason. I have no higher education on my resume, and there aren't a lot of thriving farms in Upstate New York looking for a farmhand my size."

"Hey, you can haul bales just like the rest of the guys, if not better."

"You know what I mean. I just don't have a lot to offer other than what I'm doing, and that scares me."

Crew kisses the top of my head. "I want you to know you have so much more to offer than you think, but I know the feeling. If football doesn't work out, I'm not really sure what I'm going to do."

"Do you want football to work out?" I ask, my pulse picking up. This is a subject I do and do *not* want to address, because it makes the future that much closer. And I like where I am right now—with Crew.

"It's all I've ever dreamed of—playing on the big stage. If it doesn't happen, I'm not sure what's left for me to do."

I nod and try to keep my voice level. "So, what happens if you do well at the combine?"

"Well, if I perform—when we get back, I have to hit the gym and the field hard to prepare, because I'll have just over a month to get myself ready—then I'll enter myself in the draft. From there, I just wait to see if a team picks me up. Last year,

I was a top-ten prospect. After this year, though, not sure where I rank. It's all up in the air."

"So then, let's say you're drafted—then what?"

"Then I go to wherever football takes me."

"Do you have a preference?"

"Yeah." He laughs. "Somewhere warm."

I try to chuckle, but it comes out forced, and he notices.

"You okay?"

"Yeah," I lie. "My lips are getting cold."

"And here I thought I was the one complaining." He turns me toward him and lifts my chin. "Let me warm them up for you."

As he lowers his mouth to mine, I realize that the sadness eclipsing my joy is because he never mentioned me while talking about his future. Not that he needed to, but it just makes me believe that while my whole heart is in this, his isn't. That's something I need to come to terms with. He might be saying and doing all the right things now, but once we're back in the States, he's going back to training and I'm going back to the farm. And the pain that slashes through my heart reminds me of the many times I stayed still and quiet, hoping not to be seen by my mother and her "guests." Making myself invisible. Nobody noteworthy. Forgettable.

And here I am again. But at least, in some senses, I have a choice to make. I can back away, try to keep things neutral again and maybe make the rest of the trip awkward, or I can go all in. I can let my heart fall and tumble for this man and deal with the pain later.

As his lips move across mine, I realize there's only one clear-cut choice.

"FUCK, HAZEL," Crew says, as he moves in and out of me, the hot water of the shower spraying down on his back. "I'll never get used to how good you feel, how good we feel together."

He has both of my hands pinned above my head while my legs wrap around his waist. The sheer power of his thrusts shows me just how fit—how strong—he is while he holds me against the shower wall, bringing us both to the brink.

"I'm going to come," he says just as my body pushes over and wracks with greedy need, convulsing around his large cock until I'm completely sated.

He lowers me, making sure I'm steady, before he lets go and presses his forehead to mine.

"So good." He breathes heavily.

"That was my first shower sex," I say, feeling a little shy.

"Really?" he asks, surprised.

"Yes. How many times have you had shower sex?"

He gives it a thought and then he chuckles. "I guess only once, and it wasn't even sex, just oral."

"Well, then, I guess that was a first for both of us."

He drags his thumb down my cheek. "We took each other's shower virginity."

That makes me laugh out loud, and he takes that moment to kiss my neck for a few seconds before turning off the shower.

Because he loves taking care of me, he wraps a warm, plush towel around me first and then dries off with his, only to wrap it around his waist like an expert. He then maneuvers me around him, grabs another small hand towel, and starts drying my hair with it.

"I've always loved your hair," he admits. "I remember being fascinated with the color when I was younger. I didn't grow up with many redheads, and the kids I did know with red hair had a more fiery red, not the warm color of your hair. It set the standard for all the girls who passed through my life."

"Did you ever go out with a redhead?" I ask as he picks up my brush and starts brushing my hair carefully, almost as if he's scared to tug too hard.

"Never. They never matched up to you. It would have felt as though I was chasing after something I could never have."

When he says things like that, it gives me hope, makes me think that there could be more. But then I remind myself of our conversation in the snow, his future laid out with me nowhere in sight.

"What about you?" he asks. "Ever date a guy with brown hair?"

"Yes," I say, making him frown. I chuckle. "Sorry, but your hair isn't really unique."

"Ouch, Haze. You could make me believe that I'm unique in my own way."

"Why would I inflate your ego more than it is? You know you're hot, that you're a stud, that you have the body of a god, and that your dick is massively impressive."

"Massively, huh?" He smirks, and I reach out and pinch his side playfully. "Don't let me stop you there. Keep the compliments coming."

"I'm not sure I'd be able to squeeze around you in this bathroom if I inflate your ego any more than I have."

"We can go into the bedroom, if that's better." His smirk just about does me in. God, I love him.

I only wish he felt the same way.

"Uh-oh, you thought of something to bring down the mood."

"Huh?" I ask.

He presses his finger between my eyebrows. "There's a crinkle there, which means you're thinking about something you shouldn't be thinking about."

Trying to keep it light, I say, "You're right. I was trying to figure out how to sneak out of here so I can go hang out with

Fritz at the bar. His *lederhosen* had my nipples perking up. And his eyes—such a brilliant blue."

Crew's eyes narrow. "He's actually good-looking, so this isn't a joke to me."

I laugh. "Ah, jealous?"

"Yes, yes, I am. And I have no problem saying it. Sorry to say, Haze, but you're stuck with me."

He removes my towel and wraps it around my waist, but not before getting in a good feel of my breasts. *Of course.*

"So, what should we do for the rest of the night?" he asks, securing my towel.

"I think we should break into the Schneeballen."

"Oh, shit, I forgot about those. Hell yeah, we can order some milk—"

"Milk? You really drink milk?"

Like a complete douchebag, he flexes his arms and says, "You don't get muscles like these without it."

"You can, actually."

"Anyway . . . we can get some drinks brought up and play some Christmas music, eat some Schneeballen, and then you can eat my balls. How does that sound?"

I tilt my head back and laugh. "All sounds great but the last part. Not going to eat your balls. Sorry, dude."

"Lick them?"

I glance over my shoulder as I walk out of the bathroom. "If you're lucky."

Crew's phone rings on the nightstand and I grab it for him. It's his mom, FaceTiming. I quickly hand him the phone and step away, not wanting to be seen in a towel with her son.

"Hey, Mom," Crew says. "Merry Christmas."

"Merry Christmas, baby boy."

"Merry Christmas," I hear Porter say, his voice so similar to Crew's, it's scary. The apple really didn't fall far from the tree. Not only do they sound the same, but Crew is a carbon copy of his dad. It's why I still get a little weak in the knees around Porter Smith. Yup, I'm that girl, and I'm not even ashamed.

"Hey, Dad. How are you guys?"

"We're good. Enjoying a nice, peaceful Christmas without you," Porter says, making me chuckle.

"You really know how to speak to the heart, Dad."

Porter chuckles. "We miss you, boy. Are you having fun?"

"We are," Crew answers, including me, which I think is sweet. "It snowed about a foot here. Luckily, we were able to get to the hotel last night before it got too bad. The staff here is amazing, especially since it's Christmas."

"That's good. Pops called around a lot to make sure there'd be a place for you guys to stay during Christmas and be taken care of."

"How much time did he spend on this trip?" Crew asks, his voice softer. "Did you help?"

"I helped a little," Marley answers. "But it was mostly Pops. He really wanted to make sure you replicated the trip he went on many years ago, or at least, as close to it as he could get. Isn't it beautiful?"

"It is. It might sound corny, but it feels as though we're in a storybook."

"That's what I kept saying," Porter says.

I finish putting on my clothes, and just in the nick of time, because Crew walks out into the bedroom with the phone.

"Say hi to Hazel." Crew hands me the phone and then drops his towel, turning away from me, giving me the perfect view of his backside. Damn him. I feel my cheeks redden as his parents say hi to me.

"Hey, Hazel, is our boy treating you nicely?" Marley asks, looking pretty, as usual. She has such natural beauty, and doesn't need anything more than mascara to bring out the beautiful hue of her eyes. No wonder they produced such a handsome son.

"He's been an awful hag," I say, which pulls Crew's attention. He whips around to scowl at me, wearing nothing but a pair of boxer briefs now.

"He has been known to be a little haggish at times," Porter says, making me laugh.

"I'm not being a hag," Crew calls out. "I'm being a gentleman."

That makes my cheeks redden even more. All I can think about is him saying he lets me come first—*because that's the gentlemanly thing to do*.

"Is that true?" Marley asks me.

Swallowing hard, I plaster on a smile. "That's true. He has been quite the gentleman."

"Some might say an energetic gentleman," Crew says, wiggling his eyebrows at me as he slides a pair of sweats on.

"So, how's your Christmas?" I ask, not wanting them to respond to Crew's inappropriate comment.

"It's great. We're excited to see the both of you soon," Marley says. "And hear all about your trip."

"Oh, I didn't know I was going to see you," I answer, confused.

"Yes, we're all meeting up at the farm. Didn't Crew see that his return ticket doesn't go to LAX?"

"Probably didn't pay attention," Porter mumbles. "Just like his father."

"Wait, what?" Crew comes up next to me and takes the phone so he can angle himself into the screen. "I'm not going straight home?"

Marley shakes her head. "No, we're having a small gathering when you return. Uncle Paul will be there."

"Is this another intervention?" Crew asks, annoyance in his voice.

Porter and Marley laugh. "No," Marley says. "We want to visit the farm, visit with Hazel, see how the trip went, and see where things go from there."

See where things go from there?

What does that mean?

It clearly doesn't strike a chord with Crew, because he says, "Okay, sounds good. Well, we're going to crack into some Schneeballen."

"Oh, babe, remember those?" Porter asks. "So good. Enjoy."

We all wish each other well, then Crew hangs up and tosses the phone on the bed, only to turn toward me and say, "You're wearing far too many clothes for my liking. I demand you put my shirt back on and take off your underwear. I'm going to need easy access for the rest of the night."

Before I can say anything, he lifts me up and tosses me on the bed, only to hop on top of me and start ravishing my body once again.

Chapter Fourteen

CREW

Hey Kiddos,

This is the second-to-last town you'll be visiting. After this, it's one more place, and then you're back to Munich, where you'll be flying home. I'm sad just thinking about the trip coming to an end, but trust me when I say I left the best for last.

Today, you're on your way to Augsburg. Augsburg is the third-largest city in Bavaria, with a housing complex referred to as Fuggerei. It was built by the wealthy Fugger family and houses 147 small apartments, and the rent is—get ready for this—one dollar a year. Yes, you read that right—one dollar. But the stipulation is, you must be poor or homeless to live there, and three times a day, you must stop what you're doing and say a prayer for the Fugger family. For one dollar a year, I think I'd say a prayer every hour, on the hour.

Since this is your second-to-last place, I didn't plan anything for you to do, in case you just want to walk around and enjoy the long rows of historic facades, see ornate buildings—some of which have been standing for nearly one thousand years—or visit Schaezlerpalais for the lavish art collections. I know it'll be cold, but try to people-watch, to feel a part of the city. But I do ask that you visit one place for me: the Volgetor. It's a four-story tower that was built in the Middle Ages. The man who built it got into an argument with the city coffers, who were running low on funds. They claimed the tower wasn't built straight, so they refused to pay. Legend has it, the builder was so furious that he decided to prove them wrong. He went up the four flights of stairs, pulled down his trousers, stuck his rear end out the top window, and defecated. His feces never once hit the side of the building, proving how straight the tower was.

I know what you're thinking—"What on earth?" I thought the same thing when I read about the Volgetor. I didn't get to visit the tower, and it would fulfill a dream of mine if you would please go to the tower, go up the four floors, stick your bum out the window, and defecate. Who knows what kind of wind or other natural variables might have gotten in the way of the original defecation . . .

I'm just kidding. Please don't poop out the window of a tower in Germany, it'll ruin this wonderful trip. But at least go stand next to the tower and make up your own mind about whether it's straight or not.

Have fun. Love you both,

Pops

"I CAN'T STOP LAUGHING," I say as we walk toward the tower. I dab under my eyes, trying to get ahold of myself. "I just can't imagine using my own bowel movements as a way to prove something is straight. That would never even cross my mind."

Hazel laughs next to me. "Now you will though, right?"

"It most likely will cross my mind."

The tower is built of gray stone and set off by a burnt-red roof. It's square in shape, taller than I expected it to be, with an arch at the base for people to walk through. My eyes immediately go to the windows, and I try to picture a Bavarian man knocking down his *lederhosen* and dropping a deuce.

I chuckle some more.

"This might be my favorite landmark."

"Because of the poop?" Hazel asks, a cute scrunch to her nose.

"No, because it's a symbol of insolence. 'You're not going to pay me? Well, I'm going to shit out a window and prove you wrong.' I'd never have the balls to do something like that. I'm the person who thinks of doing something extreme, but never pulls the trigger."

"Me, too," Hazel says. "I wish I could say what's on my mind most of the time, but I'm not that person. I'm a people pleaser."

"Bullshit," I challenge. "You're always telling me what's on your mind, especially when it busts my balls."

"That's different. That's just joking around. I'm talking about confrontation. Think about it, if I really spoke my mind when it came to confrontation, you'd have heard from me a lot sooner during our time of no speaking, because I would have found your phone number and given you a piece of my mind."

I pause and think about it. "Why didn't you do that?"

"Because you clearly didn't want to talk to me. I wasn't about to go all psycho on you."

"Did you want to go all psycho on me?"

"Very much."

I pull her against me, lift her chin, and press a kiss to her lips, knowing I'll never get used to doing that. "Well, I'm glad you stuck your hand down my pants and made the first move."

Her lips still and her hand falls to my chest. "I did not make the first move."

"Yes, you did."

She takes a step back now. "No, I didn't."

"Uh, care to explain why you don't think you made the first move?"

"Easy. You wrapped your arm around me."

"What?" I laugh. "Hazel, I've wrapped my arm around you on several occasions. That never led you to stuffing your hand down my pants."

She holds up her finger while smirking. "Firstly, I didn't *stuff* my hand down your pants. I didn't even make contact with anything. And secondly, you were shirtless, in bed. What am I supposed to do with that?"

"Uh, what you did every other night we were together—not stick your hand down my pants." She shakes her head and I laugh, pulling her into my chest. "Just admit you made the first move."

"I didn't."

"Technically, if you want to dig deep here, you really did make the first move because you were the one who first kissed me years ago."

She gasps and then a sly smile spreads across her gorgeous and playful face. "Oh, so you want to dig into the past? Fine. You're the one who made the first move because you tried to cop a feel when we were younger."

Shit.

I clear my throat. "You know, actually, I'm just talking about this trip."

Her head tilts back as she laughs. "You're so full of shit." Pushing off me, she walks toward the tower. I chase after her and pick her up in my arms. I spin her around and she laughs, but then I trip over a crack in the walkway and we both tumble into a snowbank.

We laugh, and I can't think of a moment where I've felt more carefree, looser, happier. I don't think I've felt this way in a long time.

Years.

Probably since I last saw her.

And this feeling I have with her? I can't lose it. I can't lose Hazel. With the combine, the farm's future in question, how the heck do I do that, though? *And more to the point, does she want it, too?*

"THIS WAS FANCY, CREW," Hazel whispers over the secluded table we have by a warm fireplace.

"And you look beautiful."

We decided to step out for dinner rather than eating in the hotel. The concierge was kind enough to book us a table at one of the finest restaurants in town and then we both dressed up in clothes we brought for such an occasion. She's wearing a beautiful, deep-green dress with long sleeves and a deep *V* in the neckline that is making it hard for me to keep my eyes attached to hers. I opted for a pair of slate-gray chinos and a navy-blue button-up shirt. My mom told me to pack one nice outfit, just in case. I'm glad I did.

"Thank you," Hazel says, her cheeks blushing under the candlelight. "You're very handsome yourself. I had no idea a button-up shirt could cling to arms like that."

I chuckle. "It's hard to find shirts that make room for the muscles, and I don't mean that in a douchebag way. It's just true."

"I believe it. I've seen professional athletes on Instagram, walking into the stadium, their suits skintight to their bodies. It's hot."

I raise an eyebrow. "It's hot?"

"It is." She smirks.

Since we've already eaten our food and paid, we're simply enjoying the fire and finishing our wine.

"And what would you think if you saw me in one of those Instagram pictures, heading into the stadium?"

Her smile falters for a second before she picks up her glass of wine and she says, "I would think . . . meh."

"Why do you find it necessary to constantly lie to me?"

"Keeping you grounded, Hollywood." She sets her wine down, and I sense a change as she plays with her fork on the table, moving it up and down, her eyes downcast. "So, yesterday, on the phone with your mom, what do you think she meant when she said: 'We'll see where things go from there'?"

"What?" I ask, confused.

"When she was talking about visiting. She was like 'We'll visit the farm, talk about the trip, see where things go from there.' What do you think she meant?"

"Uh, probably just, you know, keeping it casual. See where things go, maybe we order pizza, maybe we don't. Who knows? Why?"

"Just wondering."

"Care to elaborate?"

"Are you going to drop it?"

"No."

She sighs and leans back in her chair. "Figured." She pushes her hair behind her ear. "I'm just nervous about the farm. I feel like we're going to find out what happens to it when we get back home."

"Why?"

"I just have a feeling, is all. Mia texted me this morning that there were some investors coming up this week from New York City. They're staying at the inn, and Brenda, the inn owner, asked her for some fresh winter arrangements to replace the Christmas one before they arrived."

"Pops would never sell the farm," I tell her reassuringly.

"You don't know that. He could. It might be easier for everyone to sell. Everyone involved."

"You can't worry about that," I say, picking up my wine and taking a sip.

Her eyes widen. "I can't worry about that? Are you kidding? This is my livelihood, Crew. This is my life. That farm is my life. I don't have a fancy college degree or a future playing a professional sport. I have the farm, and that's it. Of course I'm worried about what's going to happen. When we get back, you're going back to school, you'll get drafted, and I'm going back to the farm, wondering if I'll ever have to sink to the level of my mom to put food on the table."

"Hey," I say, feeling my brows crease. "You have me."

"What does that even mean? I have you? That sure went well the last time."

"That's not fair. I said I'd never do that to you again, and this time things are different."

"How are things different, Crew?"

Is she really asking that? Confused, I say, "Because we're together."

As if I slapped her, she rears back in her seat. "We-we're what?"

"Together," I answer, wondering if I'm missing something here. "You're my girl."

She blinks a few times and then shakes her head. "No, I'm not."

"Excuse me?" I ask, feeling my voice grow with irritation.

"What do you mean, I'm your girl? What are you expecting to happen after this trip?"

"What were *you* expecting to happen?" I ask her.

"I asked you first, Crew."

Where's this anger coming from? One second, we were ready to pounce on each other from across the table, and the next, we're arguing. Am I missing something?

"I think we should take this outside," I answer, draining the rest of my wine and setting the glass on the table. She does the same. She puts on her jacket and she heads out of the restaurant, me trailing after her.

When we reach outside, she turns toward me and asks, "So, what did you expect to happen?"

"I don't know." I drive my hand through my hair. "I just expected us to continue what we're doing."

"Do you have some sort of high-speed airplane that can

take you across the country in a matter of seconds that I don't know about?"

"You don't have to be condescending. I guess I didn't think things through."

"Because I'm not a top priority in your future, Crew. Not that I'm asking you put me as a top priority, but you have a future, you know what you want, and you're going to go take it."

"You're a priority, Hazel."

She rolls her eyes. "I'm not. I've never been. Football is your top priority, as it should be. That's what you're good at. And you should continue to pursue that, but while you've been thinking about football or how you're going to fuck me next, I've been thinking about what's going to happen when we get home."

"And what exactly do you think is going to happen?" I ask. I'm so frustrated with this conversation and angry at her for . . . hell, I don't know what, pointing out thc truth? For telling me that I put football first, which is the absolute God's honest truth? I put it first over everything. Over Hazel, over my parents, over Pops. Football has always come first, and that's a tough pill to swallow, especially when the girl you've fallen for points it out.

"You really want to know?"

"Yes, please enlighten me." *Once more.*

She folds her arms over her chest, striking a defensive pose. "We're going to go home, we'll have some visiting time with your parents, I'm sure we'll sneak off and fuck somewhere because I have no restraint when it comes to you, and then when the time comes, you'll go back to California for the rest of winter break where you can train, and I'll stay in New York. When school starts back up, you'll head to Georgia, try out for the combine, and then get drafted by some team that's far enough way for you to forget anything ever happened between us. It's not going to last. We aren't going to last."

"So, basically, you're putting this relationship in a coffin before it's even cold? How's that fair to me?"

"How is this fair to either of us?" she asks, tears forming in her eyes. "It's just not." With that, she pushes past me and starts walking toward the hotel a block away. A light sprinkle of snow starts to fall as I catch up to her in the dimly lit street.

"Hazel, you're not even giving me a chance to figure this out, to talk it out with you. It's like you've already made up your mind."

"As if you haven't made up your mind. What do you really expect to happen when you leave? Do you expect me to wait around?"

"I don't know. I didn't think about it."

"And that's the problem right there, Crew. I don't matter enough to think about."

We reach the hotel, and she charges up the stairs rather than taking the elevator. I trail behind her, my mind whirling with what to say, with answers to her questions. Answers I don't have.

When we get to our hotel room, she sheds her coat and tries to shut herself in the bathroom, but I stop her.

"You think you don't matter to me?" I say, pushing the door open. "That couldn't be further from the truth. You matter the most to me, Hazel. And I know I haven't shown that in the past, but I'm showing it now. You matter to me. And I might not have answers about *our* future, but I'll tell you what's not going to happen." I step in closer, pressing her against the wall of the bathroom. Her breathing picks up as she looks me in the eyes. "What's not going to happen is you're not going to push me away because you're afraid of the unknown. You're not going to push me away because you think it's easier that way. And you're not going to push me away because you think it'll hurt less."

I reach behind her back and unzip her dress, then peel it

off her, leaving her in a pair of matching white lace bra and underwear. *Beautiful.*

"It's not going to work, Crew," she says, sounding deflated.

I unbutton my dress shirt, and her eyes fall to my chest as I push it over my shoulders and arms. And then I step out of my pants and let them pool on the bathroom floor. I quickly take my socks off and then take her to the bed, where I lie down and pull her on top of me.

"Let me figure things out, okay?" I rub my hands up her back. "A week ago, I didn't even know I was seeing you. I didn't know Pops was giving me this opportunity to rekindle our friendship, let alone become something even more. This is all new, and I've loved every minute with you."

Her eyes well with tears, and they quickly spill over. I sit up against the headboard so we're eye to eye, and I wipe away her tears with my thumbs.

I want to tell her how I feel. I want to let her know how much I've fallen for her, that I think I've always been in love with her, ever since we first met. But I'm pretty certain she won't be able to hear that right now. She's angry. She's made up her mind about something I've not had enough time to process. Hazel is stubborn, always has been, so I need to somehow reassure her that she's important and not forgettable. That although she was right about what has always been my focus, I'm starting to realize that the future might look different than what I'd previously expected.

I wipe away another set of tears that have fallen down her cheeks. "I'm going to figure this out, Hazel, okay? I'm not going anywhere, not without you."

"How can you figure it out? I have to stay and help with the farm. No one knows what I know."

"And what if they do sell? Then what?"

"They can't sell." She shakes her head. "That would be all of our memories sold to a bulldozer, that would knock them down. They can't sell, Crew."

"Okay, shhh." I bring her into a hug. "We'll figure this out. I promise." I force her to look me in the eyes. "Do you trust me?"

She takes a second to respond, but when she does, it eases my chest. "More than anyone."

"Then let's not focus on the 'what ifs' right now, and instead focus on the present, what we can control. Can you do that for me?"

She nods, tears still falling over her cheeks.

"Aww, come on, Haze. It guts me seeing you cry like this."

"I'm sorry. I'm just . . . I'm happy, and I'm afraid it's all going to be snatched away from me." She looks me in the eyes. "You really consider me your girl?"

"I always have. You've always been mine, Hazel. That's something I realized on this trip, probably from Pops's doing, but, yeah, you're my girl. No one has ever matched up to you. No one ever will. And I'll be damned if I lose you again."

"You . . . mean that?" she asks, looking so timid and fragile that I wonder if this is the same girl I've fallen for. Where's her fierce spirit? Her tough exterior?

You smashed it to smithereens when you ignored her for years, you moron.

Realizing there must be an immense amount of insecurity where I'm concerned, I try my best to reassure her.

I cup her cheeks and look her dead in the eyes. "I mean that. I'm not letting you go. I'm not letting you push me away. And I'm not letting anything come between us. It's you and me when we get back, just like on this trip. It's still going to be you and me." I bring her mouth to mine and tentatively kiss her. When her hands slip up my shoulders, I deepen the kiss and let my hands fall down her back to the clasp of her bra. I undo it and drag the fabric off her body, revealing her round, gorgeous chest. Gripping both breasts, I lift them to my mouth, and I pull one nipple into my mouth at a time before releasing them and using my fingers to roll her hardened nubs.

"I could never leave this behind. Leave you behind, not when I'm the happiest I think I've ever been."

"You are?" she asks in surprise, her hips starting to rock over my already hard cock.

"The fucking happiest." I cup her jaw, staring her in the eyes. "I came into this trip depressed, unsure, and confused. In this short time, it almost feels as though you've opened my eyes and shown me exactly what I've been missing. And what I've been missing . . . is you."

Her teeth pull at her bottom lip, and she takes a moment to remove her underwear, as well as mine. She then climbs on my lap again; this time, she takes my cock and drags it over her aroused center.

"My life has been missing you, too, Crew. My backbone, my strength, my courage. You carry the key to all of those."

She lowers down on me and I suck in a sharp breath from how warm and tight she is. This feeling, being deep inside of her, it's not something I'll ever get used to and something I'll forever crave.

"That's not true. You're all those things without me."

"I'm versions of that person, but I'm not fully me. I haven't been fully me since you left." She rocks her hips and presses her hands to my shoulders. "You taught me what it's like to stick up for myself. You taught me how to fear nothing. You taught me how to be strong. When you left, I was never the same. Every day, every unanswered email, felt as though a part of me was slowly crumbling inside, and I didn't know how to fix it. But with you here"—she rocks a little harder and I clench my teeth, holding it together—"it reminds me just how much of an impact you have on my life. I don't want to lose that again."

"You won't," I answer. "I promise, Hazel, you won't lose me."

Her hands travel up to my jaw where she holds me tenderly and then lowers her mouth to mine. I grip her sides, helping her rock up and down, back and forth, while my tongue swipes against hers. As fucking mind-blowing as sex is with Hazel, this almost just feels like a natural extension of *us*. She's soft to my hard. *We were made for each other,* and I'm thankful to Pops for opening my eyes to that.

I don't know the future. I don't know my own future, but I do know that Hazel is part of it. And the farm? *Surely Pops wouldn't leave Haze jobless and homeless. She was like a grandchild to him.* Mom and Dad wouldn't either, so how do I convince her that she's not alone? That even if I don't see her all the time, she'll still be my girl?

I love her.

It's as simple as that.

And I'll work our future out.

So we're together.

CREW: *Something has happened.*

River: *Dude, what time is it there?*

Hollis: *Aren't you six hours ahead or something like that?*

Crew: *It's the middle of the night.*

Hollis: *So, something happened in the middle of the night?*

River: *Did you pull a David Rose and have a nighttime oopsie-daisy?*

Hollis: *I just cackled. Please tell us you wet the bed.*

Crew: *I didn't have a nighttime oopsie-daisy. Jesus. I'm trying to tell you two idiots that I . . . fuck, I'm in love.*

River: *WHAT?*

Hollis: *Uh . . . in love with a German pastry?*

Crew: *No, with Hazel. I fucking love her.*

River: *Call me crazy, but you haven't been on your trip that long. How could you fall in love with her?*

Hollis: *They did know each other before the trip.*

Crew: *I think I've always loved her. No, I don't think it, I know it.*

And being with her again, it showed me how goddamn happy I am around her. This past week has been monumentally different. It's as if a weight has been lifted off my shoulders and I've returned home. I love her.

River: *I did not expect this, but I'm happy for you, man.*

Hollis: *Last thing I thought you'd say, but seriously happy for you. What are you going to do when you get home?*

Crew: *Don't know. Tomorrow is our last full day in Germany. When we get home, there's a lot of shit we have to sift through, but I'm determined to make it work between us.*

River: *Let us know how we can help.*

Hollis: *Yeah, we're here for you.*

Chapter Fifteen

HAZEL

"I can't believe this is our last day in Germany," I say, holding Crew's hand as we drive to Füssen.

After getting ready this morning, we had a quick breakfast and read where we'd be ending our trip. There wasn't much to the letter, just Pops telling us where we're going, but there was another letter we need to open when we get to the Neuschwanstein Castle. There were strict rules set by Pops that we're to park at the base, to not bother with tickets, but to walk up the long driveway together and experience the nature around us. If we felt inclined to go inside, we could buy tickets, but Crew and I both agreed, we were more interested in listening to Pops.

"I know. I felt like it flew by. I'm going to miss how simple this has been."

"Simple?" I ask.

"No outside factors, just you and me on this trip. When we return, there will be a lot more we're going to have to face."

I nod, even though his eyes are on the road. Last night, it felt like we were making love. Our connection felt deeper, more intimate than before. And the entire time he was inside me, slowly pumping, drawing out every last ounce of pleasure, I kept hearing his voice, promising me I won't lose him. And this morning, when we woke up and he lowered his head between my legs, languidly bringing me to climax, only to slowly enter me, it felt real. Not like a fantasy, but that this could actually be my life.

That when we get back, we'll be able to work this out.

"I have a question," I say, feeling nervous but curious about the answer.

"Hit me."

"Are you going to tell your parents about us when we get to New York?"

"It might be awkward if they see us holding hands, and they ask if something is going on and I deny it, don't you think?"

His answer pulls a smile out of me. "So, just like that, huh? You're not going to hide it?"

"Why would I hide you?" He shakes his head. "Nah, you're someone I want everyone knowing about."

"I mean, I am pretty awesome," I say as a joke.

"You are, Haze." He glances at me and his smirk nearly melts me into my seat. "Now that our trip is coming to an end, tell me what your favorite part was—well, besides the sex, because I know that's chart-topping for you."

It is.

Sex with Crew is easily the best sex I've ever had. Hands down, Crew knows how to pleasure me without even fumbling. It's almost as if he can predict what I need before I need it.

But I'm not going to tell him that and inflate his ego more.

"Sex was subpar."

He laughs. "Oh, okay. It's cute that you try to lie about it."

"Who says I'm lying?"

"Uh, the echoes of your moans that are still playing in my head from this morning. Or the scratches on my back from last night when you were begging for more."

I fold my arms, removing my hand from his. "I was not begging."

In a girly voice, Crew says, "Oh, Crew, please. Please, I need more."

I playfully whack him. "Stop that."

A deep, hearty laugh falls past his lips. The sound puts a smile on my face because he almost sounds like Pops. There's a hint of the same cadence, which I love.

"Seriously, though, what has been your favorite part?"

"Hmm, that's hard. There have been so many great moments." I give it some thought, and I do have some moments that stick out in my mind, ones that remain so vivid in my memory it's as if they're laid out in front of me. "Can I have two categories of moments?"

"What are the categories?"

"Germany . . . and us."

I see his lips turn up before saying, "I like that. Approved. What's your favorite Germany memory?"

"Excluding today, because today might eclipse my favorite Germany moment, keep that in mind."

"That's fair to the castle."

"So far my favorite Germany moment has been drinking in Nuremberg and walking around the Christmas market. It just felt magical. Everything about it. The lights, the music, the wine, the company. It felt like a dream, and it's a moment I'd happily revisit over and over."

"That was fun. And the wine led to some fun things, too." He wiggles his eyebrows.

"You're such a doof."

He chuckles. "Not even sorry about it. Okay, what's your favorite memory of us?"

"That's an easy one for me." Pushing past feeling shy and knowing that we're open and honest with each other at this point, I say, "The moment you wake up in the morning. Your eyes are still sleepy, your hair is messy, but you always have a lopsided smile on your face when you see me, followed by a deep, almost gravelly 'good morning.' I think I'll miss that the most."

I know I'll miss it. Waking up next to him, feeling his strong arm wrap around my waist and pull me against his warm chest. His lips traveling over my neck and down my shoulder. I'm going to miss it so much.

"I'll miss seeing you in the morning, too, Haze. But we'll figure it out, okay?"

I nod, knowing he's made me that promise over and over again. *We'll figure it out.* Somehow, someway, we'll figure it out.

"What are your favorite moments?" I ask. "Germany and us."

"Germany—probably when you kept poking me in the dick with the fencing foil."

"That was your favorite part?" I laugh.

"Yeah, you were unfiltered, happy, proud of yourself, and I loved that. I also like that your hand was a magnet to my dick."

"You're ridiculous."

He rests his hand on my thigh and keeps it there. The hold is possessive. Something I've seen in movies, on TV shows, but never experienced myself. I was never involved with someone enough to have this kind of intimacy, and it might seem inconsequential, but it's not to me. Crew is claiming me. Even when we're alone, he's letting me know I'm his and he's mine.

"Maybe, but it still was one of my favorite moments. And then an 'us' moment—well, I think it's obvious."

"If you say the dry humping, I'm going to put on a chastity belt tonight."

He laughs out loud and shakes his head. "As much as I

love the messiness of coming in my pants, that wasn't my favorite 'us' moment."

"Then what was it?"

"The moment I saw you on the airplane."

"Really?" I ask, surprised. *And swoon. That's one of the nicest things he's said to me.*

"Yes, really. I didn't think I deserved to see you again, but it was as if Pops was giving me a second chance. I had a shitty summer, a shitty semester. And seeing you on the plane—it was a gift I didn't deserve. It was as if Pops knew exactly what I needed, and he delivered."

Tears well in my eyes again, and I swear I'm never this emotional. Apparently, it's my job to cry on this trip. Over and over again.

"Don't cry, Haze."

"Trying not to." I take a deep breath and will the tears away. "This trip has just been life-changing, on many levels, and I get overwhelmed. I just feel as if everything is going to come to a crashing halt when we get to New York."

"I know you do, but please know that it's my heart's desire that it doesn't. Let's attempt to put all our thoughts into our last day, though. Another day to be surrounded by unimaginable history and awesome scenery. Just you and me."

I press my hand on top of his. "You and me."

BREATHTAKING.

It's the only way to describe the scene in front of us.

On top of what feels like a mountain, nestled into the Alpine Foothills and against a beautiful backdrop of snow is a fairy-tale castle.

White limestone walls, blue-roofed turrets with Rapunzel-like windows—the castle screams romanticism, and is the perfect grand finale to a remarkable trip through Germany.

"Wow," I say, staring up at the awe-inspiring building.

"Pops was right. He saved the best for last." Crew takes my hand. "Shall we start walking up to the base of the castle?"

I nod. "That's where we're supposed to read the last letter."

The driveway is steep, but thankfully the sun is out, the stone is clear of snow and ice, and it's not as cold as it has been on the previous days—meaning Crew isn't freezing his cute ass off.

"Did you see the pamphlet back there? It said that Walt Disney was inspired by this castle," I say, trying to keep conversation light as we make the climb up to the end.

"Seems as though Walt was inspired by a lot in Germany."

"It's beautiful. I can see why."

"Is this your first time out of the country?" he asks me.

"The first time leaving North America. I've been to Canada a few times. What about you?"

"We've been to a few tropical places," he answers casually, downplaying his childhood.

"How many?" I tug on his hand.

"Uh, just a few."

I laugh. "Trying to downplay your rich parents?"

"No." He chuckles. "I've never been to Europe, which I feel is weird, given I've been to Bora Bora."

"Ah, yes, so odd."

He pulls at me and I laugh. "We had different childhoods, but our summers were always the same, and that's what's important."

"It is. And I'm glad our summers were the same."

"Me, too. Don't get me wrong, I liked going on trips with my parents, but I always looked forward to going to the farm, to spending time with Pops and, most importantly, spending time with you."

"You're just saying that so you get some action tonight," I tease.

"Yup," he says, causing me to spin toward him, mouth open in shock. He laughs and pulls me into a hug while tilting my chin up and placing a kiss on my lips. "You have an amazing pussy—what can I say? I'm addicted."

"Oh my God, Crew."

"It's a compliment."

I push at him and he just holds me tighter.

"You know I'm kidding. You have a phenomenal pussy."

I push away from him and he laughs even more, taking my hand again as we make our way up the driveway.

It's steep at times and I'm puffing, but Crew takes it slow with me, despite his athletic prowess and long stride.

We pause halfway up and have someone take a picture of us from an angle, so the castle is in the background. It's a beautiful shot and one that I make Crew send me right away. I save it to my phone as my wallpaper.

"Committing me to your phone wallpaper? That's a big move," Crew says.

I pause, embarrassment washing over me. "Oh, is that weird?"

He holds up his phone and shows me a picture of me and him, cuddled in close, taking a selfie. The picture was taken when we were in Augsburg. "Nah, I think it's cute. Makes me think you actually like me."

"You know I do."

We continue our trek, and when we finally reach the base of the castle, it's overwhelming. The walls seem endless, allowing us only the view of the very tops of the turrets.

"This is unlike anything I've ever seen," I say, studying the strong walls and the grand expanse of the castle. All the work that must have gone into this without modern machinery. It's impressive and hard for me to comprehend.

"Look at that archway over there," Crew says. "Want to see where it takes us?"

"Are we allowed to go over there?" I ask.

"Yeah, we're just not allowed inside since we didn't buy tickets."

"Okay."

I follow Crew through the archway and we slip into a small courtyard. When we look up, the castle comes into better view. The ground is made of stone, making it uneven in spots, and all I can think about is how heels would not be the shoe of choice here. There's a stone staircase to the right that leads up to an austere door, and to the left is a covered balcony that looks over the courtyard.

I point to the balcony and say, "Do you think that was made so the owner could speak to his servants from above? Maybe his knights."

"Possibly. It looks lavish enough to be something so ostentatious."

"Do you think all the rulers were assholes, or do you think there were some good ones out there? Ones that appreciated the people around them, and the people beneath them?"

"I think there were good people. You always have to trust that there are good people out there in the world, and even if the bad people have louder mouths, the good people have bigger hearts. And those hearts will outweigh the mouths."

I snuggle in closer to Crew. "That was really profound. I've never thought about it like that."

"I have my moments." He points to the staircase. "Want to take a seat and read the last letter?"

"I'm not sure I'm ready for it," I answer.

"I don't think I am either, but we have to bring this to an end at some point."

"I know."

We head over to the stairs and we both take a seat. The chill of the stair breaks right through my leggings and turns my butt cold. But I don't say anything, because when I look up, I realize this is the perfect view. The mountains and snow-covered pines as a backdrop, the sun highlighting the opulent stone, spreading warmth over the rather cold surface. This is where our trip ends.

Right here.

In this moment.

Crew pulls out the letter from his coat pocket and he opens it up.

"Do you think we can read it to ourselves?" I ask, looking at the people around us. It's not crowded, but we're not alone. either.

"Yeah, we can." Crew circles my shoulders with his arm, pulling me close, and then he holds the letter out in front of us so we can both read.

Hey kiddos,

You probably know at this point that this is the end of the trip and, like I said, I saved the best for last. Besides the beauty of the backdrop and the contrasting colors of the limestone and tall pines that surround the grandiose architecture, there's something peaceful about this castle. When Gloria and I went to Neuschwanstein Castle, we were in the midst of a fight. It was a stupid fight, and I can't quite remember what it was about, but we didn't drive to Füssen as a happy couple. We didn't speak a word to each other in the car. And as we made the trek up the driveway, she walked two feet ahead of me the entire time, on a warpath to prove the point that she could experience this moment without me.

I remember keeping a steady pace to keep up with her, and making sure I was always only two steps behind because I wanted her to know that even though she was mad at me, I was always there for her. But the moment we reached the base of the castle, it was as if something washed over the both of us, helping us realize that in that peaceful moment, there was no room for anger, no room for petty fights. Gloria turned toward me, looked me in the eyes, and at the same time, we apologized.

You must be wondering why I am telling you this almost inconsequential story. It's because you two need to hear it.

When I met you, Hazel, I knew you were special. I knew in that moment, this little girl with the pigtails was going to have a huge impact in my life, and you have. I've always considered you my very own granddaughter; even if we don't share the same blood, I share you in my heart. And I knew the moment you met Crew, you two were going to hit it off.

From the very first time you two played together, there was a special connection. I'm not sure if my Gloria had something to do with it, but bringing you two together, watching you grow up together over the summers, it put me at ease.

You each brought something to the table in your friendship. Hazel, you grounded Crew. My brilliant, athletic, and goal-oriented grandson. You brought him back down to reality every summer and showed him he could have fun in pursuit of his goals. And Crew, you gave Hazel Girl a foundation. In her rocky, unstable upbringing, you gave her stability.

And as you both grew up, I noticed your friendship only growing stronger. I can vividly remember one day washing the dishes and catching a glimpse of you two out the window. You were under the oak tree, reading a book together. Hazel, your head was resting on Crew's leg as he read out loud. There was comfort there. Familiarity. And I spoke to my Gloria that day. I said they're meant to be together. Their souls are connected. And it's true, no matter what you might think. Your souls are connected for life.

These past few years, missing Crew during the summer, I saw the toll it took on you, Hazel. I saw the toll it took on you, Crew. I wanted to do something, I wanted to say something, but I was reminded by your very smart Mom (Crew) that you two will always find each other someway, somehow.

Knowing my time is coming to an end on this Earth, I want to leave with the knowledge that I did my best to make sure your connection remained strong. That you didn't forget about each other.

Did I have ulterior motives by sending you on a trip that was decorated with romanticism? Yes. And as I write this, do I wish that you two can finally see through the thin veil that's been separating love and friendship? Yes. As I write this, knowing where you've been and where you are, I hope that you're holding hands, a new chapter just a step ahead when you return. But even if you're not in that frame of mind, I would at least hope that the friendship you share is intact, and when you depart Germany tomorrow, you carry your newfound appreciation for each other and hold it closely to your hearts.

You get one life. Don't waste it on mindless, tedious fights, hurt feelings, or pride. Celebrate each breath you take. Wake up every morning knowing it's the start of a new day. A new day where you can accomplish anything. And spend your life loving.

The greatest gift I ever was given was an open heart for the people around me. I loved tenderly, I loved emotionally, and I loved with passion. That love brought me the greatest people in my life, and I know, sitting in my bed, blankets covering my legs, that I will leave this Earth with a legacy. A legacy that doesn't speak of the work I put into my career, but a legacy in the people I loved.

Don't take for granted what's right in front of you.

Spend the rest of this day reflecting. What will make you happy in this life? What will bring you joy? Who will help you make the most of this precious life you've been given? My heart knows you're connected at the soul. What are you going to do about it?

I love you both.

Pops

Tears are streaming down my face, my chest is heavy with sorrow, and as Crew finishes reading, all I can wonder is how I got so lucky to have a man like Bernie McMann in my life. A man, who from the first day he met me, wanted me to experience genuine happiness. A man who saw my "rocky, unstable upbringing," and took it upon himself to provide stability and unconditional love. *Even from the grave, he's making me feel cherished.*

And I love that he saw me. That he gave me Crew. He recognized that our souls connected so much more deeply than was comprehensible at our ages. He's also so right about the legacy he left behind. Such enviable love.

His letter also brings questions. So many questions that are unanswerable . . . for now.

What will make you happy in this life? What will bring you joy? Who will help you make the most of this precious life you've been given?

I know in my heart of hearts that that person is Crew for me, and I think he sees me as his soulmate too. And I guess time will tell what we do about that.

I just hope we make Pops proud.

THE REST of the day has been pretty quiet.

After crying together, we sat on the steps of the castle for what seemed like hours. It wasn't until I started shivering from the cold that we ended up leaving. Hand in hand, we walked down the curvy driveway to our car, and we drove to the hotel in silence.

We shared an early dinner together since we have a morning flight to catch and want to get some good sleep beforehand, and even that dinner was quiet. We didn't talk about the letter. We didn't talk about Pops or what the plan is for when we get home.

Instead, we spoke about the food, the decorations in the restaurant, and how we plan on packing our suitcases. Menial, fluffy topics.

Now that we're back at the hotel, in our bed, and the lights are turned off, I half expect Crew to strip me out of his borrowed shirt. The shirt he loves seeing me in.

But instead, my back is curled against his chest and he's holding me tightly.

A world of questions float around inside my head. A world of unease aches deep inside me.

What's he thinking?

Does he agree with Pops? Does he think our souls are connected?

Did Pops's letter freak him out?

Why is he so quiet?

Why isn't he kissing me right now like every other night?

Why isn't he teasing me, roaming his hands over me?

Is he pulling away?

The last question has tears pricking at my eyes, and before I can stop myself, I quietly ask, "Is everything okay?"

My voice breaks the silent night, and for a second, I wonder if he's sleeping since he doesn't answer right away, but then his arm grows tighter around my waist.

"Yeah. Are you okay?"

I have an opportunity to talk to him, to tell him how I feel. My worries and concerns. I consider Pops's letter and how he spoke about solidifying that connection, but as my mind races with the truth, my mouth can't seem to speak it.

My heart weighs too heavy and my answer comes out flat. "Yeah, I am."

"Good." He kisses my shoulder. "I did want to talk to you about something, and I don't know how to address it."

Oh God.

My heart twists in my chest from the unknown, from the thought of him telling me he's not interested, that he doesn't want to pursue this.

"What about?" I ask, trying to keep my voice neutral.

"When we get home, I was thinking, maybe . . . uh, maybe we do keep this secret for a little bit."

As if a tidal wave of sorrow roars over me, my heart plummets, and I can feel the first initial tug of him putting distance between us.

"I'm not ashamed of what we have or what we built here," he says quickly. "But I don't want there being any complications when we get there. I want the focus to be on family, on Pops, and on figuring out what's going to happen next. And I know if we go home showing us off, it's going to distract from all of that."

I nod, swallowing down my pain. "I understand."

"Do you? Because you sound upset."

I can't respond, not unless I want him to hear me cry, so I keep quiet. But Crew knows me too well at this point and he rolls me to my back, hovering over me. The tears I was trying to hold back fall down my cheeks. I attempt to wipe them away but more keep falling.

"This doesn't mean I don't want to be with you, Hazel." He helps me clear my face. "I just want to be able to figure everything out with a clear mind."

"I get it." I suck in a sharp breath and try to calm myself down.

"Hazel, talk to me. Please. I don't want you being upset."

My lip trembles, my heart races, and I try to come up with the words I need to say to him to help him understand my aching soul, but I can't find them. I don't know how to express the tumultuous feelings plaguing me.

Finally, I say, "I don't want to lose you."

"You won't."

"But I feel like I already am. We haven't spoken much tonight. I feel you pulling away. You didn't even kiss me goodnight. You might not think you're pulling away, but you are."

"A lot is on my mind, Hazel," he says, his tone of voice threaded with a hint of edge. "I'm not pulling away. I'm thinking."

"Okay," I answer, not wanting to get in a fight with him.

His eyes search mine. His hand reaches up to my face and his thumb gently strokes my cheek. There's something he wants to say, I can see it. It's resting on the tip of his tongue, but instead of saying it, he leans down, presses a gentle kiss on my mouth, and whispers, "Goodnight, Haze."

We don't have sex.

The next morning, we take separate showers.

On the way to the airport, he drives with both hands on the steering wheel.

On the flight back to New York, he sleeps and watches movies.

The entire time I mourn another crippling loss. First Pops, now Crew, and when we return, in the desperate, quiet solitude, possibly my home and livelihood. Because for someone like me, despite how much Pops has said he loved me as one of his own grandchildren, I'll be irrelevant.

Hidden.

Alone.

HAZEL: *Landed. Should be picked up by Crew's parents at the airport.*

Mia: *OMG you're home! I can't wait to hear all about your trip and meet Crew.*

Hazel: *About that. Please don't say anything about me and Crew.*

Mia: *What do you mean? Did something happen?*

Hazel: *I think so, but I'm not sure what. I don't think we'll be together after he leaves New York.*

Mia: *What? I thought . . .*

Hazel: *You and me both. We can talk about it later, but please don't bring it up. Okay?*

Mia: *Okay. Just know, I'm here for you. Anything you need.*

Hazel: *Thank you, Mia. Love you.*

Mia: *Love you, girl.*

Chapter Sixteen

CREW

We round a familiar set of trees, and my heart pounds harder and harder as we near the farm. My parents greeted us at the airport with signs and a blow-up picture of my face, along with obnoxious cheering. You'd think they were welcoming home someone from a year-long trip. I gave them hugs, held on to a smile, and then mindlessly chatted about German food for most of the drive to the farm, Hazel chiming in on the conversation.

But I didn't feel present.

I haven't been present since the castle.

My heart, my soul, is still attached to those stairs, processing Pops's letter.

His words, they dug deep under my skin.

And it has nothing to do with what he said about Hazel. He couldn't have been more correct about that. About our connection, about needing her in my life. It's what else he said that dug a hole in my brain and has been circulating over and over again.

What will make you happy in this life? What will bring you joy?

I know *who* makes me happy, that will never change. I've come to terms with that while in Germany. Hazel is my person, my girl. She's who makes me happy.

But *what* will make me happy—that's the question that's churning my gut and making me second-guess everything I thought about my future.

Growing up, Pops and I talked endlessly about playing football professionally, how if I put my mind to it, I'd go the distance.

In high school, I was named "Most Likely to Succeed."

I received a full-ride scholarship for football.

I was named All-American.

Going into my senior year, I had the best stats in our conference.

Everything was leading up to the combine, to me moving on to the next level.

I ticked off the checkboxes. I made the right choices. I put in the hours.

So why does it feel so empty?

"Here we are," Dad says, pulling the rental car into the long driveway. The farmhouse is lit up on the inside, and the porch lights, as well. Uncle Paul's car is in the driveway, as well as another car I don't recognize.

Dad parks, and Uncle Paul comes racing out of the house and stumbles down the porch stairs, biffing it into the grass.

Mom laughs at her brother while Dad says, "The man has never been graceful."

Uncle Paul stands proudly, brushes off his pants and shoulders, and then limps toward the car as Dad parks. He opens my door and greets me with a big hug. "Look at you, you handsome piece of meat."

"Don't call my son *meat*," Mom says.

"Hey, Uncle Paul. Are you okay?"

"Yes, just some old floorboard trying to make a fool out of me."

From the front, Mom says, "You make a fool of yourself just fine without the floorboard."

Uncle Paul snaps his attention to Mom. "The tension is already high, Marley. We don't need your jabs."

My brow furls. "Why is the tension high?"

"We haven't told them yet," Mom says in an annoyed tone.

"Told us what?" Hazel asks, looking concerned.

"Let's all get in the house and then we can talk," Dad says, exiting the vehicle and checking on Uncle Paul.

Just like me and Hazel, Dad and Uncle Paul were childhood friends, but neighbors. Dad was and still is best friends with Uncle Paul, and Mom had a crush on him—as Dad likes to say—for a very long time. But Mom will tell you differently. From the way Mom looks at Dad, I'm going to take Dad's word for it. They reunited on a road trip across Route 66—the Mother Road, to be exact. It was supposed to be one last road trip before Uncle Paul got married to Aunt Savannah, and Dad tagged along. They didn't get into the details, but what I do know is that Pops, Dad, and Uncle Paul did not make the trip easy for Mom, the only girl on the trip, and in the end, Mom and Dad ended up together, and they built Dad's soap brand into the multi-million-dollar business that it is now.

And that's one of the things I've wrestled with during the flight home. Hazel and I reunited on our road trip, but what can we do that invests *together* in our future?

Many years ago, we made a *romantic* pact to never fall in love with each other, and now I'm beginning to see why. Our lives no longer naturally converge. We're not neighbors. We don't have a fledgling business to build together. So, although it's easy to love Hazel, to want her forever, is it really possible? Or was that pact wise beyond our years?

Despite what Pops said we had.

Despite how my heart is now breaking.

Together, we make our way into the house, Uncle Dad and Paul helping with the luggage. When we reach the inside, there's a man sitting at the large, wooden dining room table with a folder in front of him.

I turn to Dad in confusion and he grips my shoulder. "Crew, Hazel, this is Mr. Earnshaw. He's Pops's lawyer."

Oh shit.

I glance at Hazel and her face pales. She immediately retreats inside herself, and her arms fold over her chest, as if to give herself a reassuring hug.

"Let's all have a seat," Mr. Earnshaw says.

Mom and Dad guide us to the table and I attempt to sit next to Hazel, but Uncle Paul takes that seat and I'm forced to sit across from her. I try to make eye contact with her, but she's avoiding me.

I don't blame her. I've been acting strange. I know I've been acting strange, but I can't seem to wake myself up from the daze I'm in.

"How was the trip?" Mr. Earnshaw asks while taking a seat. "Did you have a good time?"

"Yes, thank you," I answer. Hazel just nods.

I can practically feel her nerves from all the way over here.

"I'm glad to hear it. Your grandfather put great time into planning it. We were good friends, and I'm sad to have seen him pass. He was a great man."

"Thank you," Mom and Uncle Paul say together.

Mr. Earnshaw flips open his folder and says, "I appreciate you making the time for me. I apologize for having to bombard you like this, as I'm sure you two are jet-lagged, but I have family matter that's pulling me out of town tomorrow and I won't be back in time to take this meeting."

"Of course. It's not a problem," Mom says.

"I think we should get right down to business. Bernie left a letter for each Marley, Porter, and Paul." Mr. Earnshaw hands them out. "I'm unsure of the contents, but what I do know is that he wrote them to let you know how proud he is of all of you." Mr. Earnshaw pulls out another stack of letters and hands them to Uncle Paul. "These are for Savannah and the girls. Within the cards for your daughters, there is paperwork for savings accounts Bernie made in their names. It's not an influx of cash but something he thought they might want to use for college loans or building the next chapter in their lives."

"Thank you," Uncle Paul says, already tearing up.

"Now, I'm to read a note from Bernie. Please bear with me as my eyes are old." Mr. Earnshaw puts on a pair of round reading glasses and then picks up the folder. "'Hello, family—that includes you, Hazel.'"

I glance at Hazel but can't read her. Her head is turned down and her hands are in her lap. One look would tell me everything, but she's giving nothing away.

"'Thank you for being patient with my will. My intentions were to have it read to you right away to make the transition easy, but it mattered to me that Hazel and Crew went on their trip before the will was read. Now that they're back, we can get down to business. As you know, an investment group has been very interested in the farm. They've offered quite a hefty sum for the property and the land. But the decision to sell isn't on me.'"

I watch as Hazel visibly tenses. I want to reach out to her, hold her, let her know I'm there for her.

"'The decision is on you. The four of you all share twenty-five percent ownership of the land and the property.'"

My head snaps to Mr. Earnshaw. "What? Who's in the four?"

Mr. Earnshaw says, "Porter and Marley count as a single group since they're married. The four would be them, you, Paul, and Hazel."

"Me?" Hazel says, looking up. Her eyes are glazed over with tears, her face almost unrecognizable as she tries to comprehend what's happening.

"Yes, you, Hazel. Bernie not only saw you as a granddaughter, but as a business partner. He made a note of that in the files in case you questioned. You have done a lot for the farm and he wanted you to be recognized for it."

"As she should be," Mom says, offering a kind smile.

"You've always been part of the family, kiddo," Uncle Paul says, giving her a good shake and side hug, causing her welled-up tears to spill over her cheeks. She quickly wipes them away, though.

"Shall I continue?" Mr. Earnshaw asks. Dad nods. "'I'm giving you equal shares because this farm has meant something special to every one of you and I want to give you an opportunity to decide what to do with it together. If you decide to sell, the money should be split four ways. If you decide to keep the farm, you'll become a board of directors with Hazel as the CEO of operations. She knows the most about the farm at this point, and I've taught her everything she knows. She's the one who has helped grow this farm to the destination it is today, and I have confidence that she'd continue to grow it. The other jobs—well, that's up to you. All or nothing. But, if you can't come to an agreement by the fifteenth of February, then the farm will be sold to the investment firm, a stipulation I've already had drawn up.'"

"Wait." Dad stops Mr. Earnshaw. "I don't understand. If we don't agree on what, precisely? Are we supposed to move out here and help with the farm?"

"According to the stipulation, he wants at least two out of the five of you to be present on the farm in order for it not to sell."

Fuck.

Mom and Dad exchange glances. Uncle Paul's eyes widen, and more tears stream down Hazel's face.

Before I can ask her if she's okay, she pushes away from the table and says, "Excuse me." Then she walks away, out the front door.

"Is she okay?" Uncle Paul asks.

I shake my head. "Probably not."

"How much are the investors willing to pay?" Dad asks.

"Right now, the offers stands at 2.2 million dollars."

"Holy shit," Uncle Paul says. "What are we waiting for? We should sell."

"Paul," Mom chastises. "This is our home."

"I understand that, but he wants two people working the farm. Can you tell me which one of us plans on staying here? I can't move. Savannah was just promoted, and the twins are in high school. You two have to live in California for the business, and Crew is going to play professional football. Tell me how this is going to work."

"There's one more thing," Mr. Earnshaw says. My brain is already overwhelmed.

"Please continue," Dad says in an even tone.

"'If you don't decide to sell, the two or more people who decide to stay and run the farm gain a higher percentage of the farm, depending on how many people, so they hold the weight in stock, while the others split the rest of the shares. Mr. Earnshaw has the numbers, and he'll keep those private until a decision has been made. Until then, please give this great thought. If you decide to sell, know this won't hurt me. I saved this decision for you, because you're the ones who grew up here, and this is your home now. I love you all.'"

"Well, that makes the decision clear. We sell and all take equal parts of the investment," Uncle Paul says. "What about Dad's assets, like life insurance and savings?"

"That will come with the decision."

"And we have until the fifteenth of February to make a decision?"

Mr. Earnshaw nods and closes his folder. "I hate to drop

this on you and run, but I have to get home, as it's late. I left a few cards in the middle of the table. Please feel free to text, email, or call at any point if you have questions."

Dad stands and shakes Mr. Earnshaw's hand. "Thank you so much for talking with us. We appreciate you making the trip."

"Of course." Mr. Earnshaw pauses and looks at us. "Maybe the letters he left you will help. Or any letters you've received prior to tonight." Mr. Earnshaw makes eye contact with me and then takes off.

What the fuck, Pops?

"WANT TO TALK?" I ask Hazel, taking a seat next to her on the porch stairs.

Her head is buried in her arms, and she's shaking. "No." Her voice comes out all choked up.

"Haze—" I place my hand on her back and she scoots away.

"Don't. Okay? Just don't." She lifts her head and wipes at her eyes. "Please don't try to talk to me and tell me that it's all going to be okay. I've heard it, Crew. I've heard you tell me that over and over again for the past eight days. It's not going to be okay. Maybe for you, but not for me."

"Hazel, you don't know that. You didn't hear how much the farm is worth. 2.2 million dollars. That's a lot of money split four ways. That's a new start. You could go to college, find your passion—"

"You don't get it," she says, her voice rising. "This is the only comfort I've ever had. This land, this porch, these steps that I'm sitting on. You have a loving mom and dad to fall back on if you need them. You have a safety net. This farm has been my safety net ever since I can remember. This life I have, it's all built around this land, and I'm just supposed to give it up?"

"You're asking others to give up their lives, too, to move here," I say.

Her head jerks up and she turns toward me. "Wait, so they're actually really considering selling? It's not just a possibility? They're leaning toward it?"

"What do you expect my family to do? My parents have to be on the West Coast with their business. Uncle Paul can't move because he has a family to worry about."

"And you?" she asks.

"I . . . I don't know what I'm doing."

"I see." She lifts from the stairs and starts walking away, so I chase after her.

"What do you expect me to do, Hazel? Give up everything?"

"I don't expect you to do anything, Crew. Just like I didn't expect you to do anything about us."

"What's that supposed to mean?" I ask, getting in front of her so she can't walk away anymore. "I told you I was working on figuring out a solution."

"You were pulling away, and don't tell me you weren't. I felt it with every mile we traveled home. You realize the last time you kissed me was in Germany? You haven't held my hand. You've barely even looked at me since the castle."

I push my hand through my hair. "Because I've been trying—"

"If you say 'to figure things out,' I'm going to punch you in the face." She calls me out. "You can figure things out and still be affectionate, still show that you care about me."

"I do care about you, Hazel."

"You have a weird way of showing it."

Growing agitated, I say, "What do you want me to do? Waltz into the house with you and start making out with you in front of my family? Would that make you feel better?"

"Don't be a prick, Crew."

"Well, I don't know what you want. I'm trying here. I have a shit ton of things on my mind, and then this was just dropped on top of it all. I'm sorry if I'm not the perfect boyfriend at the moment."

"You were never my boyfriend," she says, looking away.

"What? Yes, I am. You're my girl, Hazel."

"I'm your vacation fling, Crew."

"The fuck you are. I told you, you're my girl. That I need—"

"If you needed me—truly needed me—then you'd be leaning on me right now rather than pushing me away. There's more to a relationship than just sticking your dick in someone, Crew." Her words ring sharp, branded with malice. "Relationships are about give and take, the good and the bad, and working out problems together, not pushing them further and further away and trying to do it on your own." She folds her arms.

"I don't know." I grip the back of my neck. My body is boiling with uncertainty, anger, irritation. Why did Pops have to make that stipulation? Why can't Hazel just run the farm on her own? "I thought . . . maybe we do long-distance for a bit, and then if I get drafted, we can figure out a visiting schedule or something, and when I'm not in season anymore, I can be with you."

"So, I would only see you a few months out of the year?"

"The football season isn't that long."

"It's long enough," she counters. "You're not going to want a part-time girlfriend. You're going to get tired of waiting around, and it's not as though I can just pick up—"

"You can," I say, hope blooming inside of me. "When the farm is sold, you can go wherever. You can come with me."

"So, I'm just supposed to follow you around?"

"You say that as if it's a bad thing."

"Crew, don't you think I should have a career too? Since I

was twelve, I've worked. I've built up a work ethic that I'm proud of. Am I just supposed to throw that away and follow you around?"

"Stop saying follow me around. You make it sound like a bad thing. You can still be your own person; you just refuse to be."

"Excuse me?" She rears back.

"Come on, Hazel. You've attached yourself to this farm—you've identified yourself as this farm. You don't even know who you are at this point."

"I have loyalty to this farm. There's a difference."

"We have loyalty, as well, but we also know who we are. We have separate lives. You've dabbled in woodworking, but why aren't you doing more with that? You're clearly talented."

"Because I don't have fucking time, Crew. You might not understand what it's like to work hard for a dollar because your parents have an endless amount of money, but I know what it's like to work. I know what it takes to keep my head above water. I don't have the opportunity to just *dabble in woodwork* for fun, because I'm working sixteen-hour days sometimes, and I'm too exhausted to even make myself dinner at night. I don't have options." She points to the farm. "That's my option, end of story."

"You have other options, Hazel," I say, my voice lowering. "You have me."

"You aren't reliable," she shoots back.

"Is that how you really feel, or are you saying that in anger? Because you've said some pretty shitty things tonight."

She tilts her chin up and she looks me in the eyes. "It's how I really feel."

"I see," I say. My voice sounds weak, even to my own ears.

"Tell me how I'm wrong. You went years without messaging me, and then as things start to get tough, you pull away."

"You're the one pulling away," I yell, flinging my arms out

wide. "You're the one who's trying to push me away right now. You have no fucking clue how much I'm dealing with."

"I've a pretty good idea."

"Do you?" I ask her, taking a step forward. "Do you really? Because I could guarantee you, you don't." I push both my hands through my hair and take a few steps back in frustration. "Do you know that while we were in Germany, I realized that I've been so fucking in love with you for as long as I can remember that it shook me to my core?" Her reaction remains stoic, unfazed. "And I've been wracking my brain to figure out how to make this happen. How to make us happen." I step forward and brush my hand over her face. "When I said I needed you, I fucking meant it. If I seemed as though I was pulling away, it's because I was trying my hardest to find a way to keep you in my life. You aren't in this world alone, Hazel, so stop acting as if you are. You have me, and I'm not going anywhere."

I reach for her but she steps away.

"That's where you're wrong. You are going. You're leaving."

"Did you not hear what I said? I love you, Hazel. I fucking love you."

She looks down, and my heart nearly tumbles out of my chest. It takes her a few seconds, but when she finally looks me in the eyes, she says, "Tell *your* family to do what they want with the farm." And then she pushes past me, leaving me in the dark by the big oak tree we used to spend countless humid summer days under.

I sink against the firm trunk and rest my elbows on my drawn-up knees.

"Fuck," I say, my voice choking up.

I told her I love her.

And she didn't even blink an eye.

What the hell am I supposed to do with that?

"ARE you sure you want to leave?" Dad asks, helping me with my suitcase.

"Yeah."

It's been two days since we've been here. New Year's Eve is tomorrow, and I just want to get back home. Get away from all of this, from all the memories, because being here is doing nothing for the progress I made while in Germany.

I haven't talked to Hazel since our conversation by the oak tree, and not by my doing. She's been moving around on the farm, getting chores done, and every time I try to speak with her, she brushes me off with work.

There's no point. She's done with me.

"I want to get home to train." Training—it's the only thing I can fall back on. It's what I know how to do.

"If that's what you want, we can do that." Dad looks over to the barn. "But you need to say goodbye to Hazel first."

"Was planning on it. It won't take long."

I jog to the barn, where I know Hazel is tending to the horses, and slip through the large door, shutting it quickly behind me to keep the cold out.

Hazel is brushing Midnight when she looks over her shoulder and spots me. She takes one glance and then returns to Midnight. With that one icy look, I know where I stand.

Hands stuffed in my jeans pockets, I say, "I'm, uh, I'm flying home today."

Her hand pauses for a second before it keeps brushing. "Okay."

"Are you going to say bye?"

She looks over her shoulder. "Bye, Crew."

"So, that's how you're going to leave it? I tell you I'm in love with you and you're just going to shut me out?"

Sighing, she turns toward me. "What do you want me to

say, Crew? It doesn't really matter because you're taking off anyway."

"I would stay."

"Until when? Until your next chapter in life?" She shrugs. "I'd rather you leave now."

"You could come with me," I say, trying one more time.

"Living in a big city, being the doting girlfriend at fundraisers? You know that's not me."

"That's a stereotype. You don't have to fall in line with the other wives and girlfriends of professional athletes. You can be who you want to be."

"And you out of anyone should know that this"—she gestures to the barn—"this is who I am. And I'm going to soak it up for as long as I can."

I bite down on the side of my cheek, trying not to lose my cool. "So, I guess this is goodbye, then."

"I guess so." Her eyes find mine, and for a second, I swear I see a touch of vulnerability, but then it's quickly shielded when she says, "Safe flight."

I slowly nod. Yup, that's the best I'm going to get out of her. "Thanks." I swallow back the pain that pushes forward like a freight truck. "Bye, Hazel."

I push past the barn door and jog back to the car, where Dad is waiting for me. I hop in the passenger seat and fasten my seatbelt.

"Ready to go?" Dad asks with trepidation.

"Yup," I answer, staring out the window toward the barn, where I know she is, with my heart in her hands.

"You okay?" Dad asks as we make our way down the country road toward town.

"Fine."

"You don't sound fine."

"Are you going to spend this entire ride badgering me?"

He chuckles. "Yeah, I am, so might as well start talking or else it's going to be a painful drive to the airport."

Sighing, I say, "I love her, Dad."

"You love Hazel?" Dad chuckles lightly, as If he's known all along.

"Yeah, I do. And I told her, and she didn't say it back. I don't even think she accepted my feelings." I lean my head against the headrest. "I think I've always loved her, but this trip with her, it solidified my feelings. I love her, and I don't know what to do about it."

"What do you mean you don't know what to do about it? If you love the girl, you be with her."

"She doesn't want to, Dad," I say, my voice cracking. "She doesn't want the life that I'm going to have. She was quite clear about that."

"And what kind of life do you want?"

"What do you mean? We've talked about this since I was young. To play football. Make something of myself."

"Is that what you want?" Dad asks, his voice full of concern.

"Of course," I answer without thinking about it. "There isn't another option for me."

"There are always other options. You just need to look for them. Sometimes they aren't right in front of you, waiting to be grabbed. Sometimes we have to be creative when it comes to carving out our own path in life. And with that comes sacrifices, as well."

"What are you saying? Do you not want me to go to the combine and become a professional football player?"

"I'm not going to tell you what you should do with your life. That decision is on you, and you alone. But I'll tell you this. When I reconnected with your mom, I realized that nothing made me happier than being with her. Nothing. Not my career, not my dreams, not my goals. Everything that mattered to me, that brought me true happiness, was with your mom. At the time, we were living on opposite sides of the country, and in order for me to be with her, I had to make some sacrifices. I moved to California to be with her. I left my comfort to be with her. And it was weird at first, I felt lost at times, but I could always come back to my initial decision. Being with your mom was the best decision I ever made, even if it meant giving up other things." He turns onto the highway and heads toward the airport. "If you learn anything from Pops's passing, it's that life is short and you have one chance at it, so make the most of it."

"So, what do I do? Give up everything I've worked toward as an athlete for someone who doesn't love me?"

"You really think she doesn't love you?" Dad asks with disbelief. "Come on, Crew, you're smarter than that. She's infatuated with you. We've known that for a long time, and then when we saw you two interacting in Germany on FaceTime, in the pictures—there was a spark in both your eyes. Your mom and I were surprised to see you two distance each other when you returned. We half expected you to tell us you were in a relationship."

I sarcastically laugh. "That was the plan."

"Really?" Dad asks in surprise. "What happened?"

"My head is what happened." I rub my hand over my brow. "Pops's last letter fucked with my head, and all I kept thinking about was what makes me happy. Hazel makes me happy, and I kept thinking of how it could all work, how we could make our relationship last. I wanted to give it good thought, to come up with a plan, and I felt like I was getting distracted. I kept getting swept up in, uh . . ." I bite my cheek, not sure how to say this.

"The physical?" Dad asks, and I feel my cheeks blush.

"Uh, yeah."

He chuckles next to me and pats me on the shoulder. "Happens to all of us. Trust me."

"Well, I thought I needed to distance myself in that respect so I could think of a way to solve our problem, and then I got lost in my head too much." I groan. "It's all fucked up. I felt like she wanted me to give her a definitive answer and I don't have one. And it doesn't seem as if she's willing to wait, either. I just . . . fuck, Dad, I just need a second to think."

"Then think. Take this time in California while you're training to think. Hazel isn't going anywhere. She loves you. Always has, always will. That won't change. But she does deserve an answer. If you're going to play football, then make that commitment and try to find a way to fit her into the plan. If you want to stay at the farm and take it over with her, then make that commitment."

"You think that's an option?" I ask. "What the hell would I do with the farm? I've no idea how to run a farm."

"You don't need to know how to run a farm. Your girl already knows how to do that. What you'd be is her partner."

"Why can't we just sell and she can take that money and come with me wherever I'm drafted? That seems like the easiest option."

"Is that what you think Hazel deserves? *Your* easiest option? Doesn't she deserve to thrive, to do what she's absolutely brilliant at? Something *she* has worked at for years and years as well?"

I sigh. God, that makes me sound like a total prick. *I'm not that person. I'm not.*

"Sometimes, easy isn't the option, because you realize it's the hard that will bring you joy and happiness." He pats me on the leg and then, as if to end the conversation, he turns up the radio and allows Journey to serenade us for the rest of the trip to the airport.

Chapter Seventeen

HAZEL

"Oh, Jesus, I didn't see you there," I say when I walk into the main part of the barn and find Marley standing next to Midnight, petting him.

"Sorry, I called out for you. I assumed you weren't in here."

I quickly wipe under my eyes, hoping she can't tell that I just spent the last half hour crying. "Sorry, was straightening up in the back." I swipe my hand under my nose and sniffle. *Pull it together, Hazel.*

Marley tilts her head to the side, studying me. "Are you okay, Hazel?"

Damn it.

Damn it all to hell.

Don't ever ask someone if they're upset when they clearly are, because all it's going to do is bring on the tears.

"Fine," I manage to squeak out before turning away. "Just,

uh, just need to clean up some more. Can you put Midnight in her stall?"

"Sorry, I can't."

I pause in my retreat.

"I've more important things to do, like talk to you." Marley steps up behind me and places her hand on my shoulder. "Talk with me, Hazel."

I can't hold them back, not when Marley is treating me like the mom I always wished I had. A sob escapes.

"Shit, I'm sorry." I wipe under my eyes again. "Just overwhelmed."

"With Crew leaving?"

"No." I shake my head, even though that's a lie. Of course I'm upset about him leaving. He . . . he loves me, and I've no idea what to do with that information, because I love him too, hopelessly and desperately, but at this point, I don't think it's enough.

"That's funny, because Porter called me on his way home from the airport and told me all about his conversation with Crew."

My stomach plummets as another wave of tears threatens to fall.

Marley turns me around so I'm facing her, and she lifts my chin ever so slightly to catch my watery eyes.

"Do you know what my husband said to me?" She talks with such calm reassurance that her voice soothes me, even if just temporarily. "He said that Crew loves you, and that he told you that."

My lip trembles, my hands shake, and I clasp them together to keep them from being too obvious.

"And Porter said he was confused because he thought that you loved Crew, as well. To my surprise, I said I could have sworn you felt the same way. Are we both wrong?"

A new batch of tears rolls down my cheeks.

"You don't need to answer. I can see it in your eyes. I feel it in your tears. You love him, but you don't know how to make that love work, right?"

I slowly nod.

"I can understand that. It took Porter and me some work to make things right between us, some sacrifices, but it was the best decision I ever made. Putting in the time, the energy, into our love, because I've lived such a wonderfully happy life so far." She cups my cheek. "I'm not going to give you a lesson on loving my son, because I'm sure he can't be an easy one to love, but I'll tell you this. He's grown into a beautifully loyal man, and if he says he's going to try to figure things out, please, trust him. Okay?"

There's something about the way Marley's talking to me, not just as a protective mother, but as a sincere confidant in my life who would give me solid advice, just like Pops would. The tone of her voice, her body language, her eye contact . . . it makes me believe what she's saying is true.

I find myself nodding. "Okay."

"It might take time, but you two will figure it out. I know you will. Do you know how I know?"

I shake my head, my voice lost.

Marley reaches into her back pocket and pulls out her phone. She flips through it a few times and then smiles. "I'm not sure you know this, but Crew was sending us pictures constantly throughout your trip. And this one—this one made my heart stop."

She turns her phone toward me and I catch a picture of me, sitting at dinner. I'm laughing, and Crew snapped a picture of it. The picture feels intimate, something a boyfriend would keep for himself. The way I'm looking at him, the way I'm leaning toward the camera . . . It's all there, my love for Crew captured in one photo.

"This picture says everything. The joy. The happiness. The love. It's all there in your eyes. And Crew looks at you the same way. I saw it on FaceTime, and I saw it in other pictures.

It'll work out, Hazel. Everything will work out, but you need to have an open heart. And if Crew contacts you, reaches out, please don't ignore him. I know it feels like the way to handle this tough time, but more than ever, you guys need each other." She pulls me into a hug and rubs my back. "We're here for you if you need anything. Do you understand? You're family to us."

When she pulls away, she grips my shoulders. "You okay?"

"No." I sob out a laugh.

She laughs, as well. "How about we go into the house? Paul made an apple pie and ran to the store for ice cream to go with it. I say we eat it before he gets home." Marley winks, and it makes me laugh and cry even more. Just like her son, she wraps her arm around my shoulders and guides me out of the barn. "Go ahead and rinse your face. I'll take care of Midnight and we'll have some pie."

"YOU KNOW, when we invited you over here for New Year's Eve, I thought you'd at least smile more than once," Mia says, sitting across from me on her couch.

"I'm sorry." I curl into the blanket she let me borrow. "I guess I'm not in a New Year's Eve kind of mood."

"Uh, yeah, you could say that. You started the night off with your depressing news about the farm, followed by Crew's admission of love to you, and topped it off with Marley's conversation. It's been a treat to have you over."

I chuckle. "Aren't you supposed to get everything off your chest before the New Year? I thought that's what this party was."

Party is a loose term. Mia and her husband, Johnny, who's currently quietly snoring in his recliner, invited me over to play cards and eat food, maybe dabble in some alcohol. I stayed away from the liquor. Given my current state of sadness, I didn't think it would be smart to dive this depression into a deeper, darker hole.

"No, it wasn't supposed to be that kind of party. We were supposed to have fun, and my husband wasn't supposed to pass out at ten-thirty."

I chuckle and rest my arms on my knees, which are pulled in tight. "At least you have him, despite his light snoring."

Mia looks over at her husband affectionately. "He's a good man. But so is Crew."

I groan. "I don't want to talk about that . . . anymore."

"The night is already a flop and we have a few minutes before the New Year. Might as well get anything you need off your chest right now."

"I have nothing else to say."

"Have you heard from him?"

I shake my head. "No. And I hate that I'm waiting on it, too. I wish Marley never said what she did, because every hour that goes by that I don't hear from him, I feel my heart breaking more and more."

"Not to be a dick or anything, but weren't you the one who turned him down? He told you he loved you, and you turned him away. I mean, I wouldn't be ripe and ready to contact you if I were him."

"Yeah, I know. I wouldn't even know what to say at this point if he did contact me."

The TV lights up even brighter, catching my attention, revealing thirty seconds until the New Year. When I was in Germany, I thought about New Year's Eve and how Crew and I would be together. I thought about how it would be the first time I'd kiss someone on New Year's. I thought about how I'd wake up the next morning, the new year, in the arms of Crew, holding me tightly. I never considered the alternate reality of being three thousand miles apart again and not talking.

I never thought I'd be fighting with my emotions every day about losing the farm.

I never thought love would be this hard.

I always considered it to be easy. Once you fall in love, things fall in place—but that's not the case here.

Everything fell out of place, actually.

"Ten, nine, eight. Johnny, wake up," Mia says, shoving her husband's arm.

"Huh, what?"

"The ball is dropping. Three, two, one." Mia raises her arms toward the ceiling. "Happy New Year's, you fools."

"Ah, Happy New Year, babe," Johnny says, getting up from his chair and placing a sweet kiss on Mia's lips. He then looks over at me and says, "Happy New Year, Hazel."

I smile, my eyes stinging. "Happy New Year, Johnny."

"I'm going to head to bed, babe. Come with me?" He holds his hand out to Mia.

She glances at me and I wave her on. "I'll be fine on the couch."

"Are you sure?"

I nod. "Yes, it wouldn't be the first time I sleep here. Go ahead. Have a good night, you guys, and Happy New Year."

Mia gives me a brief hug and then takes off with Johnny to their room. I put our glasses in the sink and then head to the half bath, where I get ready for bed. I have my own toothbrush in the medicine cabinet, because I stay here from time to time, and it's easier just to keep some items on hand.

After that, I take some sheets, a blanket, and a pillow out of the hall closet and head to the couch, where I set up my bed. Once situated, I lie on the couch and stare up at the ceiling, tears once again streaming down the sides of my face.

"I'm so lost," I whisper, as if Pops is sitting right next to me, listening.

Just then, my phone beeps with a text message. I wipe my tears and lift my phone to see a message from Crew.

My breath escapes me as my pulse picks up, thumping so

loud that I can barely hear the dull hum of the refrigerator in the kitchen.

He texted me.

He actually texted me.

Marley's words ring through my head, reminding me that I need to talk to him, even if it hurts.

With a deep breath, I open the text message.

Crew: *Happy New Year, Twigs. I know I'm three hours behind, but figured I'd say it anyway.*

More tears. After everything we said to each other, after what I didn't say, he still messaged me. Maybe he was telling the truth when he said he wasn't going anywhere.

Then again, a text message is just that—a text message. It could mean nothing.

It could also be a stepping stone.

I need to text him back, even if my mind isn't quite where it needs to be. I can't leave him hanging.

Hazel: *Thank you. Happy New Year (early).*

There, simple and to the point.

But then the little dots indicating he's writing back appear on the screen and I hold my breath, waiting for his response.

Crew: *I thought about New Year's while in Germany, thought we'd be spending it together. What happened, Hazel?*

I pick up the collar of my shirt and attempt to dry my eyes before texting back. I'm a complete mess.

Hazel: *We're both going down different paths in our lives.*

I press send and hiccup. The phone rings.

Shit. Why is he calling?

Do I answer? What kind of question is that? Of course I need to answer. If I don't, he'll know I'm blatantly ignoring him.

Trying to sound casual, I press the green button. "Hello?"

He's silent for a second and then says, "Thank you for answering." The rawness of his voice breaks any last wall I might have had erected.

I sniffle.

I try to suck in the sob that wants to escape, but I'm apparently not quiet enough. "Haze, are you crying?"

A sob wracks my chest. I hate this. I've never been one to cry so quickly or for so long. *Clearly, nothing my mother did ever hurt this bad. Never sliced through my heart.*

"Haze, please talk to me. Work this out with me."

"Work out what?" I'm able to say, catching my breath. "You left."

"To give you space. Isn't that what you wanted?"

"I don't know what I want," I admit.

"I thought you wanted me," he says, his voice trailing off, causing me to rev up with another wave of sorrow. When I don't answer, he says, "I see. I guess I was wrong about how you felt in Germany."

"I can't let myself have feelings for you, Crew."

"Why the hell not?"

"Because—"

"Because why?" he asks. He's irritated now.

"Because I'm trying to save the farm and you're trying to get rid of it."

He sighs. "Hazel, they're selling. There's nothing you can do."

"I can talk to the investors. I can try to convince them of the worth of the farm. I can fight for something that matters to me. Something that should matter to everyone else. It's not over, and I'll be damned if I don't try everything." I wipe at my eyes. "This was a bad idea. I never should have answered. I should go."

"No, please don't go," Crew says. "Please, let's talk out the options. If we do sell, you can come stay with me until we figure something out. The boys wouldn't mind if you spent the semester with me, and they're all pretty cool."

"You're not getting it, Crew. I'm not leaving the farm until someone pulls my body off it."

"And when they sell, then what? You're not going to be with me out of spite? You're going to have to go somewhere, Hazel. Why are you being stubborn?"

"If you think this is me being stubborn, then you don't know me at all. Goodnight, Crew." I hang up before he can say anything else, and I power off my phone before turning into my pillow and crying myself to sleep.

"THANK YOU, Miss Allen, for your well-thought-out presentation," Davie, one of the investors who's interested in the farm, says.

"Your passion for the farm is quite unique," Gary, the other investor, says.

I can feel a *but* coming. They're offering me praise, only to shoot me down.

"But"—See? There it is—"even though the farm is a lucrative business, quite profitable, to our surprise, the land is much more valuable to us," Davie says.

I try to stay calm. I knew going into this they would say that. I gave them the numbers, I laid out the business, now I need to bring the heart.

"This property, this farm, isn't just a source of income. It's home. It's home to many people. Visitors come from all around the state for our fall experience, to cut down their trees for Christmas, to go apple and blueberry picking in the summer. This is more than just a place of income; this is a place where families congregate. They build memories here, traditions. Babies' first pumpkins are found here, prom pictures are taken here, interest in the earth and agriculture—the backbone of this country—grows here. We offer the chance to drop technology for a day and just have good, unfiltered fun. This farm has hosted weddings, anniversaries, birthdays, family reunions, and baby showers. We aren't just in the business of making money, but creating memories, and this is truer than ever for me."

I flip to the last picture of my presentation. It's the picture of me, Pops, and Crew standing in front of the oak tree.

"This was my home for many years when I didn't have one. This was my safety net. This was the foundation where I grew into myself and became the woman I am today. Without this farm, without this man by my side, I don't know where I would be. I ask that you take more time to think about what you'd be stripping down. I ask you that you consider investing in the farm, rather than the strip mall and highway you have planned. I ask that you invest in families, in traditions, in this beautifully wonderful man who spent his entire life turning this farm into a place of solace and beauty."

Gary glances at Davie and they both let out a deep breath. Gary lays his palms on the table and says, "Miss Allen, I appreciate you taking the time to enlighten us, but I'm sorry. Our decision stands." He rises from the table with Davie, offers me an apologetic look, and then they walk out of the conference room.

The door clicks shut and I sink down into a chair.

A wave of despair and hopelessness washes over me as I drape my arms over the cold surface of the table in front of me.

It's done, Pops. I tried my best, but it's all gone, and I'll be sorry for the rest of my life that I couldn't keep your legacy alive.

CREW: *My mom said you had a meeting with the investors today. How did it go?*

Crew: *You can talk to me about it, Haze.*

Crew: *Please don't ignore me. I need to hear from you, make sure you're okay.*

Crew: *Please, Hazel.*

Hazel: *It went as well as you think it would.*

Crew: *I'm sorry. Want to talk about it?*

Hazel: *No. I'm going to take a bath.*

Crew: *Can I call you later?*

Hazel: *I don't think that's a good idea.*

Crew: *Okay . . . I love you, Hazel. In case you forgot. I love you so fucking much.*

Chapter Eighteen

CREW

"My suggestion to you is you need to slow down," Hutton says, helping me rack my weights. I sit up on the bench press and smooth my hand through my hair.

"I didn't ask for any suggestions."

"I'm giving them anyway. Dude, if you don't relax, take a day off, you're going to injure yourself, and you won't be able to compete at the combine if you're injured."

Hutton is back in town for a few days after winning the bowl with Brentwood. He came floating in on a high, only to be met by his best friend, who's in a shitty mood. To say I rained on his parade is an understatement. Even though he has little time here, he's spent at least an hour of every day working out with me.

"Maybe it's best if I injure myself. Then I won't have to deal with all the indecision racing through my head."

"Indecision? What the hell are you talking about?"

I blow out a heavy breath. "I don't know." I stand from the

bench and grab a towel to wipe down my face. "This doesn't feel right."

"What doesn't feel right?" Hutton picks up my water and hands it to me before picking up his own.

"All of this. Working out, training for something I'm not sure I want. Football. It doesn't feel right, not since my Pops passed."

"Are you thinking about quitting?" Hutton asks, shock in his voice. "Dude, you've spent your entire life working toward this goal."

"I know, and I feel as though it's been a giant waste of time." I gesture to the home gym my parents put together. "All of this—it's kept me going, moving forward. It's brought me to every next step in my life, and the responsible thing to do would be to show up at the combine, despite my losing record this past season, and give it my all to earn myself a spot as a top pick in the draft. But when I think about it, it holds no appeal. I don't get excited about competing. I'm not thrilled for the draft. I feel absolutely nothing."

Hutton pauses and gives it some thought. "You know, when I received Sir Charles No-Pants in the mail—"

"Who the hell is that?"

"Uh, the sweet, musical-playing cherub you sent me from Germany."

"Oh." I chuckle. It's light, but it's something.

"I named him, and he sits on my dresser except for the nights when I try to freak out the guys and stick him in other places around the house. Fucking great gift, man. But when I received him and pulled him out of the box, a large smile spreads across my face and I erupted in laughter, because I thought, 'Shit, Crew is back. He's fucking back. Before this past summer, he'd have sent me some weird pant-less-instrument-playing figurine because he thought it was weird.' It was an indication that the Germany trip really helped you clear your head, that you found happiness again.

But now I'm not sure. You almost seem more lost than before."

"That's how I feel. Lost." I drape the towel over the back of my neck and hang on to the ends. "I thought I knew what I wanted, but then I was thrown for a loop when Hazel stepped onto the plane. The letters, the time I spent with her—it's fucked with my head and made me think that I want more than what I've planned for myself."

"What do you mean?" Hutton steps one foot on the bench and then leans on his propped-up leg.

"I mean, what if . . . what if I didn't go pro?"

"I think people would be shocked. But then again, you don't owe anyone anything. Is football not making you happy?"

I shake my head. "I can't remember the last time it was fun. Even when we were winning last year, it felt hollow. It wasn't until I was in Germany with Hazel that I actually felt fulfilled."

Hutton slowly nods his head. "Remember this past summer when we were practicing out on the beach? Before your Pops passed away?"

I nod.

"You were throwing these bombs to me, and I was having the time of my life sprinting across the sand and catching them. I remember catching one with my fingertips and thinking, 'What a fucking thrill.' I wouldn't give up that feeling for anything. I looked back at you and you were pushing your foot through the sand, walking through the motions. There wasn't any joy in your eyes, more like you were just tossing the ball around because you had to, not because you wanted to. When was the last time you had fun playing football?"

I think about it, my mind whirling back to a specific day. "Summer, my junior year of high school. I was playing out back with Pops, my dad, my mom, my uncle Paul, and Hazel. We were a raggedy bunch. We dropped the ball, accidentally tackled each other when we shouldn't, and we had one of the best times I can ever remember. But there was no pressure to play, no pressure to perform. When things got serious, that's when the joy was taken out of it."

Hutton nods. "You don't want to do something you hate."

"I don't hate it. I just don't think I love it as much as I love other things."

"Other things, as in Hazel?"

I drag my hand over my cheek. "Yeah, football isn't even in the same stratosphere as Hazel."

"So, what are your options?" Hutton asks.

"Two," I say, looking him in the eyes. "Life with Hazel and life without her."

"I'm pretty sure I can guess which one you're leaning toward."

"More like jumping toward."

CREW: *Headed back to school today. You should come down and visit. Have you ever been to Georgia?*

Hazel: *Crew, after everything that's happened, I'm just not sure if we should be talking.*

Crew: *You don't have to talk to me if that's how you really feel. But I'm going to talk to you because I promised I'd never leave you again.*

Hazel: *It hurts too much hearing from you.*

Crew: *Then don't let it. I don't understand what's holding you back from being with me. It's simple, Hazel, just you and me.*

Hazel: *It's not that simple. Do you not have any regrets about the farm? No sentimental loyalty to the place you spent your summers? Or your parents, a place where they grew up? It's going to be demolished, Crew.*

Crew: *I do have regrets about it, but my regret of leaving without making sure we were good outweighs that. If Pops didn't want it sold, he wouldn't have set up the investors.*

Hazel: *I can't believe you'd say that.*
Crew: *Can we not argue, please?*
Hazel: *I really have nothing else to say to you at this point.*

"WHAT THE HELL am I supposed to do with this?" River asks, talking to me on Facetime while holding his figurine I sent him from Germany. Hollis called him to discuss my "present."

Keeping a straight face, I ask, "What do you mean?"

"I mean, where am I supposed to put this?"

"You got a tuba player," Hollis says, "I got a violinist."

"And what did you do with it?" River asks.

"Set it on my dresser." Hollis shrugs. "The heartfelt letter explained it all."

"My heartfelt letter said: 'This cherub's ass reminds me of yours,'" River deadpans, and I crack a smile. I forgot I wrote that.

"Ah, look, you got him to smile." Hollis points at me. "Finally."

River sets the figurine on the table next to him and then sits on his couch. Hollis takes a seat in the chair across from me, and I can feel both their eyes staring me down.

"What?" I ask, folding my arms across my chest.

River says, "I thought you were going to return in a better mood."

"I'm in a fine mood."

Hollis shakes his head. "False, man. The other guys are nervous to go near you."

"I really don't want to get into my issues right now. Can we talk about something else?" I hand the phone to Hollis, not wanting to stare River in the face, or either of them for that matter.

They fall silent, and then Hollis asks, "Did you try on any *lederhosen*?"

Sighing, I stand from the couch and head to the kitchen, where I grab myself a water bottle, and then head up the stairs to my bedroom. I hear Hollis shout, "I'm going to take that as a no."

Once in my room, I shut my door and lean against it. Bags for the combine are still unpacked, sitting in the middle of my room, reminding me that I haven't decided what the hell I'm going to do.

Dreams are a funny thing—you fixate on them for so long that they inevitably become a part of you. They mold into your being and become the driving force behind your actions, your attitude.

I'm going to go pro one day, Pops.

I declared it, put it out there in the universe.

And I trained. I missed three summers with Pops because of that training. I neglected the one person that matters the most to me because of football. And I lost time, time I can never, ever get back.

And for what? To say I became a professional football player? To play on the big stage, throw a ball for a living?

A dream for some. It was a dream for me, but I'm not so sure anymore.

I take a big gulp of my water and then go to my backpack. I unzip it and grab my laptop, and as I pull it out, a white envelope floats to the floor. I pause and stare at the familiar handwriting that says: "Crew – for emergencies."

Confused, I pick up the letter and take a seat on my bed. Setting my laptop to the side, I open the letter and steel myself as I find a new letter from Pops.

Dear Crew,

If you're reading this letter, it's because your parents have decided you need it. They see you going through a life moment and believe you need to hear these words.

First, I need you to know something, I love you. I know I said it every chance I got, but I wanted to say it one more time. I love you, kiddo. You remind me so much of your father that sometimes I almost found myself calling you Porter. And not just because you look just like him, but the way you chase your goals. How you set your mind to something, and you don't ease up until you have it.

But you also remind me a lot of your mom and her stubbornness. Which she gets from me, unfortunately. Why am I saying this? Because, if you combine your goal-driven self with stubbornness, you could possibly find yourself headed down the wrong path and too stubborn to admit to it.

I want you to remember this: don't mistake expectations for passion.

What you expect from yourself—that's not passion. That's your brain communicating to you to keep pushing. Passion is a deep-rooted feeling that you can't shake off. A strong, uncontrollable emotion you have for a particular thing or particular person.

You have a choice in life, this one life you get to live. You can follow expectations, check off the boxes, and accomplish what you or others believe is the path you need to choose.

Or you can follow your passion.

One choice will bring joy to others. The other choice will bring joy to you.

My advice: you have one life to live. Don't waste it on expectations when you can live joyfully through your passion.

I love you, kid.

Pops

"Fuck," I whisper, leaning back on my bed and pressing my fingers to my forehead. "Fucking hell."

Chapter Nineteen

HAZEL

"*Knock, knock.* Are you in a good mood or are you going to bite my head off?" Mia asks, holding a plate of cookies as she walks into the farmhouse.

"Too mentally exhausted to bite your head off tonight," I say, staring at the TV in front of me.

"Good. Saturday was touch-and-go with our friendship, and I thought I'd give it one more go before I divorce you."

Curled up on the couch, I give her a soft smile. "I'm sorry, Mia. I know you're trying to help. I'm not handling my emotions very well."

"Understandable, but remember, I'm your friend. I'm here for you, so please don't attempt to eat me with your lady fangs."

"I'll keep it together."

She hands me a cookie. "You don't have to keep it together. That's never fun. Please feel free to lose it. Just keep the abuse to a minimum."

I chuckle. "You're making me laugh. I don't want to laugh."

"That's evident from the permanent scowl you've been wearing. Word on the street is the pigs have been sending out S.O.S messages seeking help from the demon lady stomping around the farm."

"Anyone answer their call?"

"A rescue team is flying in tomorrow," she jokes.

"I'll prepare myself." I take a bite of the cookie, and I catch Mia looking at the TV just as the show I was watching comes back from commercials.

Raising a brow, she turns to me. "When have you ever watched ESPN?"

"Whenever Crew played," I admit. "I loved seeing him on the field, commanding the plays, directing his team. It always came so naturally to him."

"But he's not playing right now."

"The combine is tomorrow," I say with a sigh. "Wanted to see what they were saying about him."

"What were they saying?" Mia asks, grabbing another cookie.

"That if he has a good showing like they think he will, he'll probably be drafted within the first round despite his rocky season."

"That's really good news, right?"

I lean my chin against my knees, which are pulled up to my chest. "Yeah, it's good."

"So, why do you look so sad? You can't be sad when you're the one pushing him away. When you're the one punishing him for not giving up everything and coming to live on a farm with you. You could be with him, Hazel, but you're choosing not to be."

"This farm—"

"The farm isn't your life, or at least, it shouldn't be. You're holding on to memories rather than making new ones."

"I feel as though I'm giving up on him," I say, tears welling up in my eyes.

"Giving up on who?"

"Pops," I say, a tear streaming down my cheek. "He brought me into his life, offered me a place to make home, a job, a family, and then I'm supposed to just throw that all away? They're going to plow through this land, make it commercial. It'll be unrecognizable. How am I the only one who cares about that? Pops built this farm from the ground up. We're just supposed to neglect that and move on because he's no longer here? Where's the loyalty?"

"Why did Pops set up the investors, then? He knew what they planned on doing. If it mattered to him, why did he line that all up?"

"I don't know. Maybe because he wanted to take care of the family in case we couldn't take care of the farm." I grow irritated. "What I don't understand is why I can't just take care of the farm myself? Why does someone have to be here with me? Did he not trust me?"

Mia sighs and reaches into her back pocket, pulling out a letter. My eyes land on the handwriting and my heart seizes.

"Why do you have that?" I ask.

"Marley gave it to me before she left. She said to give this to you when I thought it was necessary. I think it's necessary."

She hands it to me and I quickly snatch it out of her hand but don't open it.

Sensing I need some privacy, Mia says, "I'll leave you with your cookies and letter, but I'm coming back tomorrow to check on you. Okay?"

I nod, still staring at the letter while she makes her way out of the house. When the front door clicks shut, I turn the envelope over and open it up.

I take a deep breath and read.

Dear Hazel Girl,

If you're reading this letter, it's probably because you're too caught up in your head. Am I right? I know I'm right. You're brilliant and hardworking, but your one downfall has been putting your blinders on. You tend to see black and white when you're like this. There's no gray for you.

I'm here to tell you, Hazel Girl, there's plenty of gray in this world. The choices you make in life can't always be clear-cut decisions. You're going to have to open your eyes to see all the colors in between when making a choice.

One of the things I always loved about working with you was your loyalty and dedication to the farm and to my family. But I noticed, when you got your mind set on something, you convinced yourself that was the only way to do it, and never sought out other options. You got fixated and, once again, those blinders went on and you didn't see the world around you.

You tend to crawl inside your mind and don't put yourself out there. I fear that you'll become so fixated on one thing, that you'll forget to look up occasionally. You won't remember to breathe in the fresh air. You won't remember to make connections. You won't find what's really important in life—love.

Work is just that—work.

Possessions are just that—possessions.

Both will bring you pain and joy, but they won't satisfy your heart.

Love is the only way to do that.

Please don't be so consumed with the black and white that you forget to learn to love in the gray.

I love you, Hazel girl.

Pops

I set the letter down and squeeze my eyes shut as I sink deeper into the couch.

HAZEL: *Good luck today. I know I probably haven't said it before, but I'm proud of you and everything you've accomplished.*

I stare down at the text I sent Crew, my heart aching from

his lack of response. But, then again, I don't blame him. I haven't been very warm lately.

"Hazel, are you in here?"

I pop out of the bathroom and find Mia walking into the farmhouse with a box of pastries.

"You can't keep bringing me food," I say, while pulling my hair up into a messy bun.

"If I didn't bring you food, you wouldn't eat." She pauses and studies my shirt. "Are you wearing Crew's shirt?"

I glance down at the Braxton College shirt he let me take while we were in Germany. I paired it with leggings today because it was the only thing that gave me comfort this morning.

"I am." Before she can question me, I say, "Can we talk?"

"Oh, boy. Am I in trouble?" She cautiously sets the pastry box on the dining room table.

I chuckle. "No, you're not in trouble." I walk over to the coffee pot in the kitchen and ask, "Do you want some coffee?"

"Sure," she says with trepidation. "Are you . . . okay? You seem surprisingly calm."

"Yeah, I'm fine." I bring over two cups of coffee and flip open the pastry lid, revealing cherry Danishes. I smile and say, "These look amazing. When we were in Germany, Crew and I became addicted to these pudding Danishes that were to die for. I was looking up recipes on how to make them just last night."

I hand her a Danish on a napkin and we both take a seat.

"Sooo, are we talking about Crew now?" She stares me down. "Frankly, I don't know how to approach your mood. I hate to be crude, but my ass is clenched, waiting for you to flip a switch."

I chuckle. "I'm not going to flip a switch."

"Um, okay. But can you understand why I'm skeptical? You've sulked around the farm for the last month, and then today, you're back to normal? What the hell was in that letter?" She leans forward and waves her hand in front of my face. "Are you drugged? You can tell me. Blink twice if it's a yes."

"I'm not drugged." I break off a piece of my Danish and say, "I just did some thinking last night and I wanted to talk to you about it."

"Okay. As long as you won't judge me for eating two Danishes, I'm here to listen."

"I would never judge you, because you know I'll eat two as well."

"Then I'm all ears. What's up?"

"I'm going to move."

"Uh, what?" Mia blinks.

"I read the letter you gave me yesterday. It took me a long time to decipher what Pops was saying, but I think I finally understood around two in the morning. I think I've been putting all my energy into a possession, like the farm, and it's given me tunnel vision. I've forgotten to look around and recognize that all my memories of this place are safely in my heart, and I don't need the physical place to help me remember. I don't need the farm to help remind me of home, because my home is in someone's arms."

"Wait." She sets her Danish down. "Are you saying you're going to move to wherever Crew goes?"

I slowly nod. "I think so."

"Oh my God, Hazel, that's . . . I mean, wow. Are you sure you're going to be okay with that?"

"I think it's going to take some time getting used to not having the farm, but this past month I've been miserable, and I don't think it's because of the investors looming over my head. It's the fact that I don't have Crew here with me. I knew it right away when I saw him on the airplane. My soul begs for him, my heart craves him. I can't stop that feeling, no matter how hard I try. The farm provides complacency and comfort, but I think it's time I venture out. Maybe find my way in this world."

"Well, I wasn't expecting you to say that when I came here." She picks up her coffee mug and brings it to her lips. "So, does this mean I'm losing my best friend?"

I sadly smile at her. "I'll come back and visit."

"Are you going to want to come back and visit, knowing what's happening to the farm?"

"I'll just avoid coming this way." I chuckle but it sounds hollow. I'm not sure I'd ever be able to come back here, knowing that everything will be knocked down. All the hard work, all the long days out in the sun, all of the memories . . .

It would hurt too much.

"You're really going to give all of this up?" Mia asks. There's no judgment in her voice, just concern.

"He loves me, Mia."

"And do you love him?"

I look out the dining room window toward the barn. "Yes, I love him. More than this farm, and he's something that I can't lose. I need to learn to love in the gray, like Pops said. Crew is in the gray. I can bear to lose this farm, but I can't bear to lose Crew. Not having him in my life has hurt more than anything."

"Well." She smiles brightly. "I think we need to celebrate." She lifts her Danish. "To new beginnings."

"To new beginnings," I say, tapping my pastry with hers.

We each take a bite and then she nods at my shirt. "So, go Braxton, huh?"

"Oh. I almost forgot." I get up from the dining room table and pick up the remote to the TV, flipping it on and to the correct channel. I motion for Mia to join me. "Come watch the combine with me."

"They televise that?" she asks.

"They televise everything when it comes to college football

and the draft. Grown men actually throw viewing parties for such events."

"That's insane to me, but then again, I've been known to watch florists make all sorts of centerpieces for hours on YouTube. To each their own, right?"

"Right." I turn up the volume and take a seat. Mia brings over my coffee and Danish for me, and together we watch. "One year, a man ran so fast, his penis fell out of his spandex shorts," I say.

Mia pauses, Danish halfway to her mouth. "Uh, excuse me?"

"Yeah, his spandex shorts couldn't contain the jostle of his junk, and it fell out the bottom. I watched the video a few times. Impressive is all I have to say."

She hunkers down on the couch. "Well, why didn't you tell me this was the X-rated version of *Magic Mike*? Let's go, combine! Show us the penis. Man, I wish I had some ones to throw at the TV."

"It happened one time." I chucklc, feeling lighter already.

"One time means it *can* happen." She motions to her eyes. "I'll be glued to this TV until I see some jiggling man bits."

"You have issues."

The announcers come back on the TV, and one with a beard holds his ear and says, "We're getting news from the field that one of the top picks of the season hasn't shown up." A graphic of Crew and his stats comes up on the screen, and everything in my body goes numb. "Crew Smith, All-American from Braxton College, is not in attendance."

"What?" I say, setting my coffee mug down. "Where . . . where is he?"

"Uh, was he supposed to report today?" Mia asks, just as confused as me.

"Yes, he was. Where's my phone?" I scramble for it and realize it's on the dining room table. I turn toward it just in time to see Crew walk through the door. Half-eaten Danish in hand, I stutter to a stop and grip my chest with my free hand. "Crew," I say breathlessly. "Wh-what are you doing here?"

"Hey, Hazel," he says gently.

"Crew is here?" Mia turns on the couch and gasps. "Holy shit, he's hotter in person."

Crew smirks, and his gaze immediately falls to the shirt I'm wearing. His eyes soften as he shuts the door behind him. Unable to move, I stand there, shocked, confused, excited.

Why is he here right now?

Why does he have that smirk on his lips?

Why is he walking toward me when I've done nothing but push him away?

Not breaking stride, he closes the space between us, his hand reaching for me. I hold my breath, thinking he's about to pull me into a hug. Instead, he takes my Danish and shoves the rest of it in his mouth.

Uhh . . .

"I was eating that," I exclaim lamely.

He chews and swallows. "Too slow, Twigs."

"Crew, I . . . I don't understand wh—"

"Oh God, his voice is sigh-worthy," Mia gushes next to me.

I love Mia, but I don't need an audience, not when I can barely formulate sentences.

"Mia, could we have some privacy?"

She shakes her head. "No, I'm good here. Thanks, though."

"I like her," Crew says with a laugh.

Irritated with my friend, I push Crew toward the kitchen to gain a modicum of privacy from prying ears.

Once out of sight from Mia, I cross my arms over my chest and quietly ask, "What are you doing here?"

He leans against the butcher block countertop, his broad shoulders pulling at the fabric of his long-sleeved T-shirt. His body language reads casual, a stark contrast to the nervous, fidgety appearance I'm giving.

"Why do you think I'm here?" he asks simply. "For you."

"But . . . but you have the combine today." I toe the ground, unable to look him in the eyes for more than a few seconds.

"And were you going to watch me compete in the combine?"

"Yes." I nibble on the inside of my cheek. "I sent you a text wishing you luck."

"Is that right?" he asks, so casual, as if we haven't been through a tumultuous ride when it comes to us. As if the last month hasn't consisted of me pushing him away every chance I've had.

"Yes." Nerves prick at the back of my neck and I twist my hands together, unsure what to do in this moment, other than blurt out what's been on my mind. I look up at him, his solid brown eyes connect with my mine, and I feel my stomach bottom out as I open my mouth and say, "I . . . I want to be with you."

His smirk turns into a full-on grin as he shifts and sticks his hands in his jean pockets. "Oh yeah?"

I nod. "I do. I would like to be with you. In a relationship capacity."

"And how did you come to that conclusion? Last I remember, you had nothing else to say to me."

Guilt washes over me.

That's exactly why I'm confused as to why he's here. "It was wrong to take my hopelessness out on you." I twist my hands together. When he doesn't say anything, I keep going. "It's taken some personal reflection to realize that I don't need a physical place to call home, but rather, I can find home in other places."

"Like where?"

"Like . . . your arms," I say, my stomach dropping as I

confess my feelings.

He slowly nods. “So, if I were to say, ‘I love you, Hazel,’ what would you say in response?”

My eyes connect with his, and for the first time since I made this decision, I can one hundred percent guarantee it was the right decision.

I take a step forward, closing the distance until there’s only a foot of space separating us, rather than the thousands of miles that I thought kept us apart only a few minutes ago.

“If you were to say you love me, right now”—I swallow hard, keeping my gaze on him—“I would say, ‘I love you, Crew. Very much. Always have. Always will.’” I take another step, and I cautiously take his hand in mine and link our fingers together. “And then I would tell you that if you’d still have me, I’d love spending my life following you around, wherever this crazy world might take you.”

His eyebrows slowly shoot up. “You’d give up the farm?”

I nod. “Easily. If it meant I got to be with you, then I’d step aside.” I take his other hand and love the feel of his strong thumbs running over the backs of my knuckles in a gesture of comfort. “This last month has been miserable without you, Crew. For a second, I associated my feelings of despair with losing the farm, but I realized that’s nothing compared to the pain I was feeling of not having you in my life again. A wise man once wrote me a letter and said not everything is black and white, and sometimes I need to love in the gray.” I squeeze his hand. “This won’t be easy, but I know life would be so much harder without you. I love you, Crew, with everything in me. You were meant to be my person, and I really hope you still want to be with me.”

I feel the hope pleading in my eyes as I stare up at him.

And when he smiles, the unease in my chest starts to fade away.

When his hand releases mine and cups my cheek instead, my heart beats faster.

When he pulls me in closer and dips his mouth to mine, my soul feels at peace.

Slowly, his lips caress mine, a gentle kiss, a reminder of the connection we share. His hand slides behind my neck, cupping me gently, tenderly, as if he holds me too hard, I might vanish. Little does he know, he's branding me, making me his. No one will ever replace this man in my life, no one has ever come close, and I'm going to spend my life making sure I show him just how much he means to me. How much I love him. How much I need him, and only him, to be happy. Nothing else.

He smiles against my lips and pulls away softly. Foreheads connected, he says, "I love you so fucking much, Haze."

"I love you, Crew."

He pulls me into a hug and I rest my cheek on his chest, holding on tightly, not wanting this moment to—wait. I pull away just enough to look up at him.

"Why aren't you at the combine?"

He chuckles. "That's what I came here to tell you, but then you started talking and were on a roll, so I let you go first." He tips my chin up and says, "I contacted Mr. Earnshaw yesterday after talking with my parents and Uncle Paul. I'm staying here, on the farm."

"What?" I ask, my pulse skyrocketing as I take a step back. "You're . . . you're staying?"

He nods. "It took me a hot minute to figure it out, but I also received some words of wisdom in the form of a letter and realized that I was living out expectations, I wasn't living out my passion." He reaches out and cups my cheek. "Football was expected of me, but you, Haze, you're my fucking passion, and I would do anything to hold on to that."

"Are you saying what I think you're saying?"

His smile is from ear to ear. "Are you comfortable being business partners with me? Running this farm? Dating? Possibly living out a happily ever after under the oak tree?"

My hands go to my mouth in shock. "Crew, you can't be —" My voice cracks as tears spring to my eyes. "You can't be serious."

"I've never been more serious about anything in my life." He takes my hands in his again and brings me in close. "You make me happy. This farm makes me happy. This life we could create—the thought of it brings me joy. I like football, always have, always will, but my love for you, for this land, for these memories, it eclipses that any day. I want this, you and me. This farm. Pops watching over us. I couldn't be surer about a decision."

"Crew, I don't . . . I don't know what to say."

"Tell me you're ready to go into business with your boyfriend."

I chuckle, and I'm a snotty, wet mess as I nod. "I couldn't want anything else."

I stand on my toes and wrap my hand around the back of Crew's neck, pulling him down to me. With a wet of my lips, I lift my mouth to his—

"Hey, uh, sorry to interrupt," Mia says from behind us. "But I have Marley and Porter on FaceTime over here, and they're dying to know what's going on."

Mia holds up her phone, and Porter and Marley wave at us.

"Look, they're holding each other. I think that's a good sign," Marley says.

"Oh, you should have heard what they said to each other." Mia clutches her heart. "What a romantic spectacle."

"So . . ." Porter says. "Are you two officially together?"

Chuckling, I look to Crew, who nods. "We're together." He leans down and places a kiss on my lips as Marley, Porter, and Mia cheer. "Consider me a resident of New York in a few short months once I graduate."

"You're really going to live here," I say in awe.

"I'm really going to live here, Haze . . . with you."

Epilogue

CREW

"I'm nervous."

"Why are you nervous?" I ask Uncle Paul as he hops up and down in place.

He adjusts the collar of the red Santa suit he's wearing. "I've never been Santa before. This is a big task, one you know I don't take lightly. I've been practicing my *ho ho hos* ever since July, when you asked me. I still don't think I nailed the baritone that is the epitome of jolly. How can I go out there and convince kids I'm the man with the plan in the red sled when I can't *ho ho ho* correctly?"

"I heard you practicing this morning," I say, trying not to laugh at the white beard that he spent an hour coloring this morning. "I thought Santa was in the other room."

"You're just saying that to make me feel better."

"He isn't," Hazel says, walking up to me and wrapping her arm around my waist. I kiss the top of my fiancée's head and hold her tight. "This morning, Crew was bragging about your Santa impression to his friend Hutton on the phone."

"Were you?" Uncle Paul perks up. "What did you say? You know I hold Hutton's opinion in high regard."

"I sent him an audio clip of you, and his exact words were, 'damn.'"

Excited and now prancing in place, Uncle Paul says, "Oh yes, oh yes, that's the feedback I want." He picks up his Santa hat and says, "Thank you, this was exactly what I needed." He lets out a deep breath. "I'm going to go get into character and eat some cookies. Let me know when the crowd is ready for me."

Uncle Paul pats me on the back and then heads downstairs, leaving me alone with a very clever Hazel.

After Hazel and I made up, she came back to Braxton with me for a few months since there wasn't much to do on the farm tourism-wise once the Christmas season is over. She had a few of the employees watch over the animals, and she spent some time with me in the frat house. If anything can make a relationship stronger—or break it—that's where it would happen. But I'm glad she was there, because the fallout of me not going to the combine wasn't great.

I took significant heat from fans and students around campus, but it wore off, and I was able to settle into a routine for my last semester, taking Hazel with me to classes, and then studying with her at night. We worked on plans for the farm, how we were going to expand and try to capitalize on every season. Thanks to my marketing degree, we've come up with some great ideas and have formed a five- year plan on how to accomplish our goals. *Our* goals. Not Pops's. Not my parents'. *Ours.*

I wasn't really sure how much fun I'd have with the farm, but working with Hazel, planning everything out, I quickly realized just how right my choice was.

After I graduated, I moved out of the frat house and

straight into the farmhouse. Mom and Dad joined us for the summer and Uncle Paul visited so we could go over the plans. Since they have a stake in the farm still, they couldn't be more thrilled about our plans. We also found out Pops wasn't necessarily truthful in his will. There was a little addendum that Mr. Earnshaw was told to hold off on reading, and that was, if everyone agreed, Hazel could have taken the farm on her own, but being the meddler that he was, Pops wanted to try to get us to open our eyes before that was an option.

I'm glad he did, because this past year has been the best of my life.

At Thanksgiving, I proposed to Hazel.

She said yes, and we're slated to get married under the oak tree next summer. According to Dad, there's a honeymoon trip Pops planned out, you know . . . just in case. We plan on taking it. I can't wait to hear him say, "I told you so."

"Are you ready for tonight?" Hazel asks, her hand traveling up my chest, the glint of her ring shining in the light. Mom gave me her mom's ring to propose with, and I don't think I've ever seen anything more beautiful. Generations of love all surrounded by one ring.

"I think I am. Are you?"

"I believe so. I have a stock of tissues on hand." She chuckles. "Why did we decide to share the recording of Pops reading *'Twas The Night Before Christmas* with everyone?"

"Because we're not the only ones who miss him this time of the year."

This year's Christmas festivities have led to tonight, Christmas Eve.

We're calling tonight the Festivity of Family and Friends. The tickets are sold out, have been for weeks. It will be a dimly lit night of cheerfulness, with a hint of magic in the air. We'll light up the farm with twinkle lights, sing Christmas carols, play Christmas Eve games, have an appearance from Santa, and of course, indulge in some Lebkuchen—homemade from our kitchen. Hazel and I spent months perfecting the recipe and have been selling it all winter. It's been a huge moneymaker for us, along with the Schneeballen we decided to make as well.

The night will end with everyone hovering around a bonfire while Pops reads to us. A grand finale I'm sure no one will be expecting, not even my parents.

"I can't wait."

She stands on her toes and presses a kiss to my jaw. "I love you, Crew."

"I love you, Twigs." I smooth my hand over her hair. "This time next year, we'll be married."

"According to your uncle Paul, he's hoping to have grand nieces andnephews soon from us."

I snort. "He has some time before that happens."

Hazel raises a brow. "So, if I were to tell you that I was pregnant right now, you wouldn't be happy?"

My heart stutters in my chest as my eyes widen. "You're . . . you're what?"

She laughs and shakes her head. "Just kidding, but glad to know where you stand."

I let out a sigh of relief. "Hazel, you know I fucking love you, but I want to enjoy my twenties for a little while longer before we bring children into the picture."

"Me too. It's why I'm religious about taking my birth control. The way you're always pawing at me, I use extreme caution."

I chuckle and lower my mouth to her neck, kissing along its column. "Do you blame me? You're fucking beautiful and you're all mine. Which means, I want you every moment I can have you . . . like right now."

Her hand connects with my chest and she pushes me away, giving me a stern look. "I told you to keep it in your pants until later, Smith." She points her cute little finger at me. "I have a very nice Christmas present planned for you later.

Don't make me take it away." Leaning forward, she whispers, "It involves your penis in my mouth."

I laugh and hold my hands up. Fuck. *And I'm not meant to visualize that for the rest of the night?*

"Can't jeopardize that. I'll keep it in my pants until then." I pull her in for one more kiss and then link my hand with hers. "Okay, you ready for this?"

"Ready."

Together, we walk downstairs, where we find Uncle Paul hovering over the cookies, Mom and Dad next to him sharing a Schneeballen, and I can feel Pops's presence. He's here, with us, because he brought this all together. He brought us joy. He brought us romance. And he brought us a lifetime of happily ever afters.

Made in the USA
Middletown, DE
20 March 2021

35914171R00186